Born in Detroit, Dinah Lee Küng
of California (Santa Cruz and Berkeley) and worked for twenty
years as a reporter in the Far East for *The Economist*, *Business-
Week*, *The Washington Post* and *International Herald Tribune*. She
won the Overseas Press Club's 1991 award for Best Reporting
on Human Rights from Abroad. She now lives in Switzerland
with her husband, a veteran of the International Committee of
the Red Cross, and their three children.

Her previous novel, *A Visit from Voltaire*, was longlisted for
the Orange Prize for Fiction 2004.

UNDER THEIR SKIN

UNDER THEIR SKIN

Dinah Lee Küng

HALBAN
LONDON

First Published in Great Britain by
Halban Publishers Ltd
22 Golden Square
London W1F 9JW
2006

www.halbanpublishers.com

A catalogue record for this book is available from the British Library.

ISBN 1870015 96 7

The publishers gratefully acknowledge
The Japanese Tattoo: by Sandi Fellman, Abbeville Press Publishers,
New York, for part of the cover illustration.

Typeset by
Computape Typesetting, Scarborough, North Yorkshire
Printed in Great Britain
by MPG Books Ltd, Bodmin, Cornwall

For my three favourite musicians
(in order of appearance)
Alexander Joseph, Theodor Bernard and Eva-Marie

Chantal Villard leapt off the number twelve tram into a warm September rain washing across the rue du Marché. She tossed the morning's *Le Temps* on top of the soggy debris spilling out of a roadside bin. A Monday morning was too busy, too *surchargé*, to finish the paper. In her rush to set up the clinic before Dr Micheli arrived, the harried brunette had overlooked four small items scattered through the Geneva daily's sober layout:

An editorial about the World Health Organization promising three million HIV-AIDS patients in developing countries anti-retroviral therapy by 2005. The paper asked, "Any time the global health body undertakes something new, it cuts back somewhere else. So who will suffer?"

An ad selling tickets to hear the finalists in the annual Sion Violin Competition conducted by Maestro Shlomo Mintz.

Three lines from Agence France-Presse in the margin of the international news page reporting the assassination of Japan's second most powerful mobster, the *yakuza* Hirano Onishi.

A listing for empty office space on rue Versonnex, lake view, fittings suitable for a medical clinic.

Chantal had read the morning's news, but missed the entire story.

Part I

Nature permits us indeed to mar, but seldom to mend, and like a jealous patentee, on no account to make.

Nathaniel Hawthorne, *The Birthmark*

I

The dragon flared its nostrils over its bristling snout. It unfurled its emerald scales with each muscle shift. Crenellated horns curved downwards over its ears. Unfortunately, its bloodshot expression was slightly cross-eyed so it resembled a demonic ram in need of glasses. Myopic or not, how ferociously would the tattooed monster resist his imminent extinction?

"*Eh, bien*, Monsieur Shino. I confess I do love a professional challenge."

No question − the consultation of this stubby Japanese businessman at Dr Roman Micheli's dermatology clinic was the most colourful point of what had been an otherwise drab Monday. The doctor refocused his camera on the hair-thin silver rings threaded through each of the patient's nipples and snapped a wide-angle shot.

Overeager to please, the Japanese grinned from his perch on the examination table at Chantal. He flexed his shoulders forward and back to better display his dragon's menacing fangs with a shy, almost endearing pride. The nursing assistant suppressed a giggle.

Roman arrested Shino's calisthenics with a firm palm. "That's not necessary, just relax. Now, please, lie down on your back and breathe deeply."

The thick-set man shifted his weight, crumpling the white paper covering the table. His clumsiness sent the hard little pillow tumbling on to the floor.

"So sorry."

"Not at all, Monsieur." Roman rescued the pillow and

wedged it back under Shino's head. He angled the man's torso a few degrees better to face the camera. The dragon's flaming breath spreading across Shino's chest felt cool to the doctor's touch. "Exhale, please. Good. Now please lie on your stomach."

What was this? Roman stepped back for a panoramic survey of Shino's shoulder blades. This tattoo resembled a geisha in a kimono embroidered with golden chrysanthemums and peonies. But if it was a geisha, why did one of the silken sleeves reveal a man's rippling biceps? Was this person – coral lips snarling downward at both ends, tangles of black hair tumbling to the waist, hairpins flying – a hermaphrodite or a transvestite? Its left hand gripped a thin, curving sword, poised to slash across the neck of a dwarfish devil cowering about ten centimetres above Monsieur Shino's waist.

The doctor adjusted the overhead lamp to deflect shine bouncing off the colourful skin. The half-man half-woman's eyes darted in Chantal's direction, seemingly suspicious of the nurse preparing photograph labels with professional discretion.

"*Merci*. We're almost finished." Roman ran off a last sequence of photos.

The patient mumbled up from the pillow, " . . . that is Benten Kozo, famous thief disguised in woman's clothes, caught stealing – "

Frankly, Roman wasn't interested one jot in Benten Kozo's criminal record. More interesting was the vivid turmeric yellow of the kimono. He pressed down on the patient's dorsal muscles to estimate dye penetration and commented, "The colour shading is most impressive."

Shino looked surprised. "First time you see work of Horijin? He is very famous Tokyo tattoo artist." Awkwardly gesticulating backwards at his own spine, he said, "*Hai*! This tattoo of Benten Kozo was copied from *ukiyo-e* print – "

"You can sit up, now, *s'il vous plaît*."

The Japanese heaved himself into a sitting position with a grunt and continued: " – Master Horijin makes tattoo with

4

sixty needles, bamboo handles tied with silk – all different – like a painter. He makes the skin come alive." Smiling at Chantal, Shino rotated his left arm and concentric clouds pricked around the grimacing Benten Kozo began to swirl. Only then did Roman and Chantal see that the Japanese sheltered an intricate spider's web etched under each wiry armpit tuft.

Roman noticed his assistant struggling with another outburst of titters. "Pack up the camera, Chantal." One must be firm with the staff, even with a pretty face. No patient in his clinic was laughed at, just as no medical challenge was spurned. People from all over the world brought their dermatological problems to Geneva for Dr Roman Micheli's cool and professional attention. As a doctor, Roman was implacable, impartial and impeccable – three qualities that any patient could count on – even a Japanese shedding his innocuous grey jacket to reveal a Technicolor blockbuster of Asian icons.

Already Roman's trained eye was working like a prism to break the images into a range of hues – coal black, Indian red, persimmon, many blues, but fewer troublesome greenish tones. Too much cadmium in the reds to be healthy, he thought, although that very mix might be the Tokyo master's recipe for a tin-white iridescence that was interfering with Roman's photography.

"High winds are a symbol of destructive path of Benten Kozo's life." The Japanese had stopped animating his frame to take a contemplative breath. He nodded at the window where rain gusts obscured the clinic's view of Lac Léman two blocks beyond.

"The use of colour is *extraordinaire*. Your master is to be felicitated."

Shino demurred, "No, no. My tattoos are very unimportant. Much better Horijin skins become gifts to museums. Hundred dead skins already in Tokyo University."

Roman froze, pen poised over his entry into Shino's new dossier. "Preserved human body tattoos?"

The affable Shino nodded.

Roman refrained from asking whether Tokyo tattoo curators favoured drying or pickling and concentrated on the medical task in front of him. He imagined the lurid art of Shino's body divided into a grid of square centimetres and mentally catalogued their appropriate pigment-specific laser rays to calculate, very roughly, the months or even years, it might take to remove Shino's tattoos.

Apart from Benten Kozo's smoky-grey mane, there was the bizarre *objet*, plain and symmetrical – something like a cooking pot? – sitting equidistant just below Shino's collarbone. Below the pot lay the coiling dragon accompanied by a golden carp, ridden in turn by a cherub as gleeful as a child straddling a rocking horse.

A *trompe l'œil* apron of exquisite pleats draped the man's hindquarters, while the turquoise, carmine and pus-yellow of a small cobra nestled in the crook of his back overlooked by some sort of horned demon clutching a bolt of lightning in his paw – all this no less startling than the very real lightning that danced across the lake's surface outside the clinic.

Roman thought he had photographed it all, until he noticed the regular pattern of charcoal serpentine scales – an easy colour for the laser to disperse – decorating the man's upper thighs and disappearing right up under the short hem of his gown.

"There is more? Please lift the robe for a moment, *s'il vous plaît*? Ah, ha, I see. Well, uh, *merci*."

At the sight of Shino's genitals, Roman struggled to balance professional detachment with the necessary artistic appreciation.

"*Eh, bien.* That is a first for me, Monsieur Shino, in over fifteen years of laser work. There may be complications when we come to that sensitive area."

Shino burst out, "*Hai!* Pain!"

"*Oui, Monsieur.*" Roman rested one weary foot against the bottom rungs of the examination stool. "You are my first patient asking for such extensive removal."

"Tattoo bad for health, yes." Shino wagged his head. "*Ire-zumi* legend say tattoo make life good. Life is shorter, *hai*, but more better. No woman can resist *irezumi*."

"*Irezumi* — ?"

"*Ire-zumi*, Japanese for 'put ink into skin.' *Irezumi* is the brotherhood of tattooed."

"How exciting. But despite these, uh, attractions of life in your brotherhood, you're sure you want the tattoos removed?" Shino nodded, and Roman continued, "And you don't even inquire about discomfort?" He indicated the length and breadth of Shino's vivid body. "It is *évident, non?*"

The Japanese jerked his square head like a mallet hitting wood. "Pain noooo worry."

"Well, we'll see. Please dress, then take a seat in my office next door."

Roman switched off the overhead lamp and washed his hands for the thirteenth time that day. The mirror hanging over the chrome sink reflected dark stubble gaining on the hours.

Shino made the usual sounds from behind the changing curtain — the zipping of trousers, the jangle of belt buckle — but was hardly a usual customer; the seasons brought their shoulder butterflies, buttock roses, motorcycle insignia and Sanskrit scribbles circling the forearms. By the time such tattoos reached Roman's clinic, they were always regretted. Tattoo removals were the least challenging side of the Micheli practice, but undeniably each image came with a story, usually banal, and brought unmistakable gratitude when its tale had been laid to rest by Roman's laser wand.

Mon Dieu! Here was no mere story, but an entire, ambulatory *bande dessinée!* The stabbing torture this exotic foreigner must have endured to turn himself into a rainbow storyboard! How long had these tattoos taken to execute — three, four years? — long enough for any novelty or social caché in Monsieur Shino's alien world to wear off before even his sexual organ was transformed?

7

Why had he come to Geneva? And hadn't Roman detected some fleeting regret, some glimmer of hesitation crossing that nondescript face? Roman cut short his wonderings. He was as keen as ever not to let appointments pile up outside. He wasn't in the habit of examining patients' hidden psychology overly much; he was trained to cure their skin anomalies, irregularities and eruptions; they betrayed more than enough inner psychology for Roman's purposes.

The homely Asian sat waiting in the office. In his shapeless suit and long-sleeved shirt, knees and feet pressed together, hands clenching his leather portfolio, Shino looked as hapless as a tourist accidentally separated from his package group. Roman clicked his ballpoint and perused the registration form.

"You first sought treatment in Japan?"

"Not so," Shino nodded. "Company transferred me to Geneva. I learned French in Paris three, almost four years ago. Now I work here."

Roman decoded Shino's block printing. "In publishing?"

Shino smiled with an air of satisfaction. "Newsletters about Japanese banks and companies in Europe. Very profitable, subscription fees very high, though circulation very modest."

"I see. Well, it's your blood circulation that concerns me. Let me explain. By emitting different wave-lengths, the laser pulses of different colours target different cells, or in your case, lock on to other pigment colours, and leave the healthy cells untouched. Rather like smart bombs, *non*? The pulse emits units of light at a density high enough to shatter the inks into microscopic fragments."

The Japanese man stared and nodded once.

Roman persevered. "Your immune system then engulfs and digests these broken fragments, transporting them to the blood and lymphatic systems that remove debris from the body. You follow?"

Shino shook his head, and said, "*Hai.*" Roman took this to mean assent.

"Each area needs about six weeks between treatments to

flush away the dye particles, so we see what's left and pass over the area again. That means that even if we rotate around your body quite strategically, your case will require over a year. Also, given the natural tones of Japanese skin, you risk some loss of normal pigmentation if we laser too aggressively. And I must add, finally, that the more professional the tattoo, like yours, the harder to avoid scarring. Between twenty to forty per cent of patients with densely placed organometallic dye pigments that deep see only incomplete removal."

Shino's eyebrows drew together like two bristling caterpillars meeting in the centre of a lacquered plate. "Must be complete. Also, must be faster, please?"

"I can only do my best." Roman glanced at his watch. Priority went to more urgent, medical cases. However, to speed things up they could start with an intense and broad band of laser light useful for various colours at once. "You forgot to enter your insurer, here." Roman indicated an empty blank on Shino's form.

"*Hai?*"

"Insurance, Monsieur. After I review the photos, I will send you the estimate by post."

"Hawwww," Shino's mouth exhaled in a whoosh. "No, no insurance company. I pay cash." He rose to present his calling card in cupped palms across Roman's desk.

"Between fifteen and twenty thousand francs, Monsieur? Reimbursement is not impossible. Your epidermis is full of too much cadmium to breathe properly – "

Chantal rapped at the door. The last patient of the evening, an African diplomat whose tribal keloid scarring had got infected was restless.

"Well then, arrange cash payments as you wish with Chantal outside."

The squat man bowed low in front of Roman's desk: a person even shorter than Roman himself, an unprepossessing male who alleged that panting hordes of Tokyo females had lost all their allure. He was indeed a curiosity. "Dr Micheli, if you remove tattoo, cash cannot pay you back. I will owe you my life."

Roman chuckled with the innate good humour that occasionally broke through his contained Swiss demeanour. He shook the man's chubby hand and escorted him back to reception. "*Eh, bien*, Monsieur Shino, I don't want your life. I assure you mere cash will do. As would Swiss francs, credit cards, pieces of eight, shares in Sony – it matters not – because if I have the medical satisfaction of successfully removing your tattoos despite all the odds I've carefully described, that would be more than enough professional satisfaction."

"*Arigato, arigato.*" The Japanese worked his steps backwards, bowing slightly, and then more deeply, until he smacked into Chantal advancing through the doorway with her bulging appointments book, urging him, "The next patient, Doctor . . . ?"

Roman dropped Monsieur Shino from his thoughts as fast as Chantal plopped the African's file next to Isabel's framed photo. How was his doctor wife getting on in India? He was so proud of her dedication, he happily accommodated her long missions for the World Health Organization.

After all, Isabel's frequent absences freed Roman to focus on being the best laser dermatologist in Switzerland – and of course, the best in Switzerland had to be the best in the world. He glanced through the Honourable Elangu Wanga's records. There was always one more patient. Even the most extraordinary story must give way to the next on time.

2

Isabel wasn't wondering about Roman's day. In fact, she hadn't given her husband a glancing thought for more than twenty-four hours. Leprosy, not love, was her life's passion. It was also the nemesis of her every waking minute.

Jouncing across the plains in a rented four-wheel drive, Isabel could feel nothing now but dread at confronting the inestimable leprosy missionary, Father Ashok Shardar. When her old medical acquaintance boycotted last month's policy meeting among India's leprosy elite, it wasn't because he had a migraine under that bushy mane. The wily Jesuit doctor knew very well that the WHO had made a global decision to redirect leprosy patients away from small specialized clinics like his own New Hope Leprosy Mission. Geneva was dead set that from now on, leprosy would be viewed as just another garden-variety disease to be treated in state health clinics across each country.

Unfortunately for Isabel, the priest was proving hard to dislodge from his venerable lair. Armed with the authority of his years and loyal following, the proud old fox had dug in for a turf war against the WHO's policy of redistributing leprosy resources. His humble touches – those roughshod *chapplis* strapped around his bony ankles and the stinky local cigarettes – none of these homespun props fooled Isabel; if he persisted, Shardar would prove a formidable obstacle to the success of her regional assignment.

If only he'd accepted her invitation to come to Geneva – all expenses bloody-well paid, Isabel fumed. She would have seated him next to her at the bottom of a conference table to listen for hours as the serried ranks of The Leprosy Advisory Group bickered away. He wouldn't be so bolshie then, would he?

Sitting inside Shardar's office now, a mosquito coil burning at her feet, the cement-block walls shedding curls of yellow paint like dead skin, Isabel squirmed at her clear disadvantage. How feeble all her well-rehearsed arguments looked here on the old man's patch: a domain reached only after a four-hour jolting drive north for fifty kilometres to reach the first town with a guest house that even warranted a guidebook listing – not to mention the three-hour flight from the MTV glamour and cellphone buzz of the Oberoi's air-conditioned grandeur down in Delhi.

Despite the heavy air, the mission seemed to float in dust that scratched each time she blinked. Cicadas hummed in the trees shading the low-slung twenty-bed clinic on the opposite side of the courtyard, but Isabel shrugged off their lullaby with all the backbone a Hanford upbringing could muster. She longed for a bath and early bed, but this meeting with the priest came first.

˙ Her khaki linen, fresh and crisp in Delhi, now drooped around her thighs like a Hindu holyman's dhoti. She'd entrusted the dress to Father Shardar's former leprosy patients working as dhobis in the "laundry," an open shack equipped with bins of brackish water at the back of the guest house. To do otherwise would have been an insult to their rehabilitation, so the garment had come back, soaked, pounded, wrung, line-dried and expertly pressed – without any starch.

Her spirits drooped as well. Her syrupy tea steeped with cardamom and cinnamon hosted a fly on the skin of milk coagulating across the surface. The Indian missionary sat her out, reckoning that heat and frustration would wage his battle for him. How could she recover the grizzled veteran's good-will, whittled down by her unwelcome arrival, her official announcement, her own implacable stance? She listened to his predictable tirade:

"I am sorry to see you waste your valuable time, Doctor Hanford. Why should an old priest drag himself to Delhi like a schoolboy or idiot babu to watch you dismantle his life's work? So instead you bring the meeting to me!"

"I'm sure I'm not wasting my time," she said, in her heart not sure at all. She tried a conciliatory tack, "Leprosy has been your life's work and I can't think of anyone who's answered the call better than you. But there's a saying, isn't there, Father Shardar, that the best can be the enemy of the good? No one questions you're the best doctor, provided the victims reach your door. But India's lagging behind the global targets. This country's got too many pockets of disease that nobody's treating."

"Targets! Five hundred and fifty-one patients from all over the valley trust and respect me. They won't go to another doctor." He wagged his head with pity for Isabel.

"They don't need a specialist with your qualifications. Tell them that. Let them go."

"They won't budge," Shardar snorted.

"You know the new priorities: training public health workers. Getting at the uncovered regions through state clinics." Isabel heard her voice growing shrill, so she paused. "If you had objections, you should have voiced them last month in Delhi." She swatted at a fly with a studied carelessness. She missed.

Father Shardar sat behind his wooden consulting desk, barricaded by a sturdy black rotary telephone and a tower of files. His frayed white coat bulged with sweets for children and tissues for ladies. Patients travelled to New Hope for days by bus, ox-wagon, bicycle, even on bandaged feet to swallow their medicine under his paternal gaze. Terrified spouses, mute children, stoic grandparents uncloaked their lesions for his verdict. Some of them, ostracized by contagion, never returned to their villages. Instead, they joined Father Shardar's unofficial tribe of the beholden, a colony of the prayerful cured and converted.

The elderly man stroked his beard with a sinewy hand. "Hah! You think just anybody could do what I have done for the last forty years, young woman? Go ahead. Please. I will carry on without your international say-so."

He called her a young woman. How touching – and suspicious. Her eyes narrowed. "How will you carry on?"

"Lion's Club of Mumbai," he said with bravado. "The Christian youth groups. Delhi Rotary. Loyal friends won't desert me. And things are looking up in Rome. We might see possible beatification of one of our nuns. One new saint can bring in more money than your entire measly budget. And these so-called NGOs know what we need on the ground, unlike your Geneva poobahs. You'll see. We Indians know what independence means."

Isabel felt her gorge rise. "We can't bicker like this over who owns this disease. You're not the only leprosy missionary being asked to hand over the keys of his kingdom."

Shardar went on, defiant: "Maybe I'll try those Stanford and Berkeley software chaps buying garden villas in Bangalore and Poona. It's time they gave something back to Mother India."

He paced out of the front door on to a rickety porch lined with wicker chairs, his "waiting room", and gazed across the sloping valley of one-storey wooden shacks with their door-steps settling into dried mud cracks surrounded by scraggly terraces of onions and chillies parching in the sun. Thanks to evils more modern than leprosy, the New Hope Mission found itself dangerously close to the Line of Control, the dangerous border dividing disputed Kashmir. The evening's dusky light glinted off barbed-wire fencing running along the perimeter of the high hills sloping up to the deadly northeastern zones.

Curfew would be falling soon. Isabel stood in the doorway, behind the old man, to offer her silent companionship as a sop to his futile protest. Below the porch, a thread of water meandered through an irrigation ditch in the *doob* grass under the veranda posts. The precious liquid seeped downhill to its desperate duty under the fading orange sun.

In the crook of the narrow valley below, a group of village women repaired a tenuous section of the life-giving canal. They flicked oiled ropes of braided hair out of their way and tossed lengths of cotton gauze back over their shoulders. Wizened crows in rags, they stopped slinging their baskets of wet earth from one pair of hands to another to point at a weak angle in the feeder stream uphill.

The elderly housekeeper Chitra shuffled into the office. Her clubs of feet were shod in trainers stuffed with newspaper to fill the empty toe spaces. She saw Father Shardar had offered no second cup of tea to his guest, so with deft manipulation of her fingerless paws, Chitra placed the mugs on a tea tray and headed back to the open-air kitchen.

So Isabel was expected to step back, to play the enlightened colonial granddaughter showing respect for the revered native. She shouldn't bully a local saint who pressed a Bible into the hand of each patient along with his medicines, should she? For that's what he prescribed: a blisterpack of ROM pills containing 600 mg. of rifampicin, 400 mg. of ofloxacin, 100 mg. of minocycline and a walloping dose of Divinity.

Well, if the priest played on her guilt, Isabel would ignore her upbringing, trespass on the sanctity of the clergy and exploit his hospitality. He'd never actually evict a WHO administrator (poised for a promotion to management level P6) who'd come all the way from Geneva, would he? Her mother Marjorie had grown up with Indians like Father Shardar and always taught her daughter, "Gracious, but firm. Always firm."

Isabel sighed. She'd been tactless to quote Geneva authority as if it carried any weight out here with Shardar. She could imagine what field workers thought of desk-bound bureaucrats barking orders from Switzerland. Isabel suspected that in Shardar's eyes, she and her colleagues at WHO headquarters were faceless white-collar menials who changed jobs, relocated, uprooted, upgraded, moved on. Theirs was only a temporal power.

The Father Shardars looked heavenward for their reward; they were a stoic elite, an ancient brotherhood. They traced their spiritual lineage to the grim Hadean hostels run by Templar knights carrying their leprous brothers back from the Crusades. They invoked their mission martyrs, who stared the ugliest of afflictions in the face and managed the nightmare without cure. Until the end of the twentieth century, only the Father Damiens, Wellesley Baileys, Dr Cochranes, Dr Brownes – the medical heroes and saints – were willing to tackle leprosy and sacrifice their futures to scrub away the sins of the world. Nations changed names, governments changed hands, but the dark dominion of leprosy held sway for a millennium. As long as a simple diagnosis had been an absolute death sentence, the leprologists reigned unquestioned over the living dead with a benevolent nobility. Nobody ever forgot to starch Shardar's white coat.

"It's over, Father. The isolation, the specialization, it's all changed. Now that the treatment is so simple and free – "

The stiff silhouette in the waning shadows didn't budge. "Do not lecture me. This is not about treatment, this is about shoving leprosy off the table as soon as possible – "

Isabel fiddled with her limp sleeve cuff. "The competition from malaria and HIV's getting worse. Polio needs an eleventh-hour mop-up. We have a deadline – "

"Your deadline, not mine!" Shardar waved a finger in her face. "Speak up at those meetings! Here! Take more photos! Take more case histories!" He shot inside to his flimsy tin cabinet spilling over with files typed by Mrs Basu on a battered Smith-Corona manual.

"The stigma sticks," he shouted.

"Exactly! Don't you see the problem? The old-fashioned fuss you make has become a bad habit – "

"My treatments are a bad habit?" Father Shardar's eyes bulged.

" – holding us back. People are scared off by these photos! They're hiding from screening. These damn burkas they're forcing on the little girls up in the hills only make detection harder. Stop making your patients trek in. Let the outlying districts treat themselves. Let them use the Accompanied Multi-Drug Packs."

Shardar pounded his rickety desk. "Self-medication? Amateur Medicine!"

Their argument froze at a polite knock on the door. New Hope's mild-faced surgical assistant, Dr Singh, entered the room. He looked embarrassed at overhearing two professionals shouting. He ushered in a patient, a weathered man powerfully built across the chest and shoulders with both hands swathed in spotless bandages.

The two Indian doctors unwrapped the gauze to test the muscles' mobility restored by Dr Singh's surgery. Isabel observed Father Shardar's cheery salutation to the man – some kind of driver? Bicycle delivery man? A kitchen *khamsana*? There was no mistaking the vulnerability in his face, the absolute rock-hard peasant faith in the two doctors bending his fingers, stretching his palms and pulling at both thumbs. Leprosy, fear, restoration, gratitude – universals that ignored the more modern plagues of warring religion, dialect, caste, the "us" versus "them".

Isabel resisted guilt welling up inside her as Dr Singh left with his patient. Shardar must relinquish his practice to the general hospital. Surgeons like Singh might be lost to the wards tending earthquake casualties and landmine victims coming down the northern roads, but in the long run more patients would come forward, more surgeons would be trained.

Shardar didn't miss his opening. "You would hand a blister pack to that terrified boy and send him back to the shanties to treat himself? With no running water, only a sewage gutter in front of his door? Oh, I know how in London you treat AIDS! Educated people gulping cocktails of pills for breakfast, lunch, and dinner."

The priest wagged his head with derision. "You think my leprosy patients up in the hills could manage that? Without so much as a wristwatch or calendar?"

"With follow-up, in case of complications."

Shardar moved in so close Isabel smelled whiffs of Imperial Leather soap. "I see the English passion for do-it-yourself now extends to leprosy treatment!"

"Really, Father!"

"You want to replace my decades of experience with new diagnostics that you yourself admitted only last year aren't yet ready. To some whippersnapper trained in vaccinations and snake bites?"

"It's all in the works." She gathered up her papers.

"In the works! In the wooorrks!" he sang in mockery after her. "What's next? Take two aspirin and call me in the morning?"

"If you'd come to Delhi, you'd have heard your own name put up for the new national task force. You'd be in charge of monitoring drug flows, cutting back theft, setting training standards."

"I am no paper pusher. I am no policeman. I am a doctor and I belong here with my patients."

Father Shardar folded his arms rigid, defending the centre of his tiny realm festooned with yellowing posters of lesions and "lion's mouth" and finger stubs and foot stumps curling off the crumbling walls.

"We'll go over the details tomorrow," she murmured and collected her satchel. Crossing the porch, she saw that the trickle of precious water had escaped the village crones yet again. They laid their baskets down for the night. Laughing children danced down the pebbly path below the clinic, pointing at the rebellious stream now tumbling past the shacks. Their doors would soon be bolted against the terror carried closer by fanatics moving under cover of night.

Shardar snapped at her departing back, "And to think I took you for one of us." He slammed his own door.

Isabel heard his cutting dismissal. She slipped on the last of the crumbling cement steps.

She righted herself and looked up to see a graceful child in a faded woman's paisley blouse, cut down to size. Isabel took the dusty hand outstretched in rescue. Noisy diesel tractors clogged their progress back to the guest house. They reached the general store with its mix of Indian and Chinese teas, tin basins, mosquito nets, fly swats, spices and garish soaps. From the murky reaches of the back room, an Indian beauty warbled on a small television.

The child showed the western lady doctor down a short-cut through alleys of corrugated sheet iron, cinder blocks and wooden hoardings to reach the faded elegance of the colonial-era bungalow. In thanks, Isabel reached into her satchel and offered her tiny Bodhisatva a bright green stuffed Beanie Baby frog, a duty-free talisman kept on hand for just such a spontaneous moment. The most innocent of smiles at the floppy amphibian gift erased all the sour after-taste of Isabel's interview with Shardar.

She would arrive in New York in three days. Swabbing the grime off her face in the evening shade, Isabel still hardly thought of Roman. Isabel dwelt instead on her embattled boss, Frank Norton, fielding the inter-agency squabbles weakening the leprosy campaign back in Geneva. For the sake of the patients, Isabel had to win over the Shardars of the entire teeming South Asian sub-continent. For the survival of her childless soul, she pulled Beanie Babies out of her battered bag, one by one.

3

No sun penetrated the dawn fog unrolling across Lac Léman like a thick carpet, its wisps caressing the base of the *Jet d'Eau*'s mammoth spigot. Eight tons of sparkling silver that shot five hundred feet in the air at one hundred and twenty miles per hour all summer now lay stoppered by the early winter's hush.

Small jetties dotted the lakeshore where anchored sailing boats slept off the excesses of their July regattas under royal-blue canvas cocoons. Empty rigging clanked through white vapour encircling the masts. Clusters of gulls swayed forward and back on the crossmasts, riding the currents of the descending Rhône. Through much of the winter, this cloud cover muffled Geneva, drawing the small city in on itself.

On the hill overlooking the lake, where once only the closed ranks of Geneva's high-born *citoyens* resided, Roman opened his eyes to the ring of his bedside phone. He reached across Isabel's unused pillow.

"Micheli."

A familiar German bark hit his sleepy ear. "I call once again about your cat, Doctor. Do I have to remind you that it is six in the morning? It is your cat miaowing outside that wakes us up."

"*Désolé, Monsieur.*"

Naked but for his briefs, Roman padded down the parquet corridor to unlatch the noisy frame of the old kitchen window. The German investment banker downstairs had complained before – about the cat, the window, *n'importe quoi*. Roman swung the window back and forth twice more to make sure the creak of many centuries remained in good working order.

Spaghetti settled at his usual spot below the hissing red espresso machine and readied himself for Roman's latest theological musings.

Most weeks Roman had more frequent conversations with the sleek Siamese than with his distracted wife. Dark circles under her eyes, irritable with time changes, his *amore* travelled eighty per cent of the time when she wasn't spending all her weekdays and many evenings drafting fund-raising appeals at WHO headquarters across the river.

Anyway, Spaghetti was more interested than Isabel in Roman's morning monologues (and perhaps understood Roman's French mutterings better). At sunrise, the faithful – surely not just hungry? – cat trotted surefooted across the precipitous shingles of the close-packed Vieille Ville townhouses. He laid his paws on the Michelis' kitchen window four storeys above the cobbled courtyard and peered through the darkness at the chrome high-tech appliances. Finally the dark-haired owner smelling of after-shave padded on two paws into view.

"... I am thinking just now that you and I – cat and man – are a parallel for my human relationship to God. *Alors –* "

With an arabesque of the hind leg twisted behind his chocolate-tipped ear, Spaghetti scratched under his flea collar.

"... No doubt it is as frustrating for God to communicate with me as it is for me to talk with you, *non*? Our only shared vocabulary is scratching, window-opening, and this can of *boulettes d'agneau*. Imagine God right now, trying to convey to his human, *moi*, some enormous idea through the tiny funnel of three-dimensional physics. What do I understand? The message of His Eternal Voice? *Non*, no more than you understand my words right now."

What Spaghetti did understand was that the owner would soon open the refrigerator door, illuminating the dark kitchen with an inexplicable biblical glow. From this burning bush of modernity, the hairy-chested god would bring forth a harvest of milk before the blessed light went out.

"Reflect, *mon pauvre*, on your incapacity to understand the electricity that powers this light or the factory that made this can. Then imagine I walk six blocks to treat people you'll never see, speak languages you've never heard, use machines you would find miraculous – well," Roman chuckled, "I admit, so do most of my patients. Now, if you were an atheist cat –" Spaghetti rubbed his promiscuous hips against Roman's bare ankles, "– you would say, 'I have never seen these things! Life beyond the rue du Perron? All the cats I know meow. The world exists only as far as I can measure it, whisker by whisker.' And to be honest, don't we humans say the same thing?"

An aroma of lamb gristle drifted towards the cat's sniffing muzzle.

The bowl took too long in descending from countertop to floor for the cat, who protested his deity's fickle distraction.

"Be patient, you mongrel," Roman sealed the half-empty can with a neat square of tin foil. "The universe probably has twenty, thirty dimensions that elude me. If your animal ignorance does not annul my wider world, then my own deafness certainly cannot disprove His Presence. My blindness does not eliminate God, but it must frustrate Him enormously. Don't we display enormous hubris in our limited senses *mon chat*, not to give the benefit of the doubt to God's existence!"

Roman rummaged around in the drawer, frustrated most at this moment by his wife's lack of domestic discipline. Isabel's less than delicious effort at fisherman's pie before her India mission had disturbed Roman's ideal arrangement of utensils. He glanced out of the window at the curtain of freezing mist obscuring the domes and rooftops, mumbling his private prayer, "Show me proof of this greater world I cannot see! If not proof, then give me faith."

Twelve hours later, Roman pulled the last manila folder off Chantal's counter and ran his eye down lines of cramped handwriting. Insurance company but no medical history. *Mon*

Dieu, could no one complete a one-page questionnaire these days? His scientific training, not to mention his Swiss soul, wearied of these imprecise foreigners – everyone and everything passed through Geneva these days. Compared with his youth, Switzerland was one big transit lounge ...

He would treat himself to gorgonzola sauce tonight. Isabel complained it went straight to her hips, so why not profit from her absence? He passed his palm across his stubble. Last appointment, then gorgonzola.

"Please come in, Monsieur."

A heavy-footed American in olive uniform waited in the padded chair next to Chantal's aquarium. He rose to an imposing height and lumbered towards Roman's private office.

"Sorry about the full uniform, Doctor," he pointed with mock modesty at a battery of ribbons and medals pinned to the hard-edged gabardine of his jacket. "I'm running a little late for a reception." White letters embroidered on his breast pocket read, "Sullivan".

"Then, as your brave countryman so famously said, 'Let us roll'." Roman settled his aching back into his swivel chair and surveyed the healthy epidermis of the thick, bland features of the man opposite. "How can I help you, uh, is it Colonel?"

Might he have an eagle tattoo – or perhaps a badly-scarred wound underneath that imperial garb? Roman waited.

"Well, Doctor, I'm seeing you about my daughter on the recommendation of Doctor Jonathan Burden."

Burden. After twenty years. *Bizarre*. *Oui*, one of God's little jokes.

"Ah, yes, the New York dermatologist – "

"Yup. My little girl has a rather serious birthmark on her face – "

"I see. The type of mark?"

"Well, what they call a port-wine stain."

Routine, after all.

"Her Romanian birth parents took one look and dumped

23

her. My wife and I adopted her while I was stationed in Rome some years ago."

The gorgonzola sang its siren call to Roman's rumbling stomach. "*Bien*, shall we make an appointment for me to examine her? As you said, it's getting late."

The Colonel shifted his feet. He patted the flat green cap folded across his muscular thigh. "Well, now there. You've just put your finger on the exact problem, Doctor. My wife and I planned to have Mira's mark removed as a matter of course, especially when we heard that lasers were getting more sophisticated every day. We were just waiting until we had some time back in the States – "

"Where you consulted Doctor Burden?"

"That's affirmative, Sir. We saw a GP in Connecticut, and he referred us to one of Doctor Burden's clinics – "

"Of which there are so many," Roman commented dryly. "And?" He glanced at a tiny clock in front of Isabel's framed portrait, hidden from the patient's view.

"Well, that's when the problem kind of crept up on us."

Roman waited.

"You see, just before starting the treatment, Mira suddenly changed her mind. That was when she was around fourteen."

"Did Doctor Burden suggest counselling?"

Clearly, the Colonel was approaching the heart of his strategic briefing. He spread his knees wide apart and planted one shiny black shoe half a yard away from the other.

"Yessir. We were set to go with that, but then I was made assistant military attaché in Beijing and that pretty much postponed therapy. Then my wife, she came down with cancer – "

"I'm sorry," Roman said. It sounded too automatic. At the end of a long day of morning treatments and afternoon consultations, the sympathetic chords strummed less reliably.

"Anyway, that's when Mira really plunged into her violin-playing. I mean she'd done six years of Suzuki Method back in Connecticut like a lot of other kids, but there was this teacher in Beijing who was a real fireball. Mira just took to her like, well, I don't know what. I mean, she was always good at practising, but in China it got like she didn't want to do anything else. Now she might go professional."

The American ran his hands through his brush of greying hair. His story seemed harder to get out than he'd figured.

"Nothing's been more important than her violin, especially after Lorraine's death. And," the American's hands flew into the air in frustration, "don't get me wrong, Doctor Micheli. Mira's always been a real good sport, so talented that everybody just can't help but love her. I couldn't look you in the eye and say that the birthmark has made a real big difference to her life so far, but I always warn her, things could change. It's for her own good that she get this thing removed. So I looked up Doctor Burden's card and he referred me to you."

"The child is how old?"

"Almost twenty-two now."

"Twenty-two!"

"Yessir. We were posted to Rome in the late eighties and my wife found Mira at an orphanage outside Bucharest a year after we arrived. All the other foreign couples were asking for newborns. Mira was already five and so rejected because of her face, she would hardly talk."

"Shall I recommend an English-speaking therapist here in Geneva?"

"Mira just won't let me make any appointments."

"Monsieur, I beg you, it is late in the day. I do not wish to be impolite, but I cannot treat *une invisible*."

The inky sheen of those heavy-soled shoes mirrored the Colonel's deliberate shift in weight toward Roman's desk.

"I had this idea of getting the two of you together, kind of unofficially."

Roman heard Chantal dropping instruments into a metal sterilizing bath; their clanking signalled the end of another long day. "And you propose?"

"I took the liberty of bringing these two tickets to a concert here in Geneva. I'll invite you backstage."

With hesitation Roman studied the meaty hand holding forth the white envelope. The gesture seemed inexplicably portentous. Roman's instincts told him to refuse.

"Colonel Sullivan, I appreciate your determination. I have not seen your daughter's case, but I should tell you I have known of some instances where it was no tragedy to have such a mark on the face. Provided it is not too disfiguring, even pride in its unique appearance is not unheard of. As a doctor, I can predict that the birthmark may suffer some deterioration with age, some thickening of the dermis. In the meantime, I suppose a twenty-two-year-old knows her own mind. She accepts God's design. Leave well enough alone."

"Please, Doctor." The man's outstretched arm pushed Roman into a corner of awkward impatience. The envelope's emblazoned US Mission seal exuded an unwelcome officiousness. With undeniable dignity, the Colonel laid the tickets on the desk.

" I'll check my schedule," Roman relented. "It is unorthodox – "

"Thank you, Doctor." The Colonel stood and placed his cap on his head, nearly scraping the ceiling's insulation panels with its brim. A final handshake and Roman was alone at last.

The treatment rooms stood dark. The eerie green light of Chantal's aquarium bathed the row of empty chairs in the waiting area.

Curieux, a Jonathan Burden referral. After all these years.

He washed his hands in the bathroom off the reception room and gave them a dollop of moisturizer, a soothing punctuation mark at the end of every day. Over and out, he smiled to himself. He slipped out of his white cotton jacket and reached to the back of the cupboard for the soft Italian lambskin of his coat. He distractedly transferred the American's envelope to an inside pocket.

Thousands of working days ran into each other. Roman took few holidays. Isabel journeyed all the time. He must try to call her as soon as he got home, but to tell her what? Of

M Siegler's second rhinophyma session before eight? Mlle Barre's driving her itching eczema all the way from Neuchâtel, her hair still wet with an orange-scented shampoo? Three cases of excessive hair growth – the Iranian pharmaceutical student was simple enough for Chantal and Lise while he lunched on an avocado-and-crab salad at his desk.

Chantal had left time for a long consultation right after lunch; the case of Ayad Salim, an Iraqi boy covered with pinpoint scars from an American cluster bomb set off by the family cow in a village south of Baghdad. The boy's whitened right eye, blinded by the explosive shower, could be corrected by a cornea transplant. Roman's contribution was to laser away literally hundreds of blue freckles disfiguring the thirteen-year-old's face and arms.

Roman had waived all fees, of course, but after a lengthy preliminary to set-up timings and coordinates with the boy's Geneva sponsors, Chantal and Roman had lost even more valuable time wrestling the self-conscious child's over-sized sunglasses off him. Only Roman's inspired offer to let Ayad try on his impressive laser goggles if he relinquished his scratched black shades won the doctor a few minutes to examine the discoloured eyelids blinking warily. Watching the minutes tick away, Chantal's manner had crispened for the remainder of the day.

Oui, the schedule had slipped. They had seen two referrals of possible pre-cancerous photo-ageing – upper backs and noses, then the skate-boarder from Rolle with cherry angiomas on his chest. Mme Piguet had been upset when he did an immediate scrape of the suspicious lesion on her temple for a lab test. Tomorrow he'd start on the Japanese. Those rust-reds presented a risk; the pigment's ferric oxide might convert to ferrous oxide, leaving an unsightly black nearly impossible to eradicate.

The most medically challenging cases were usually the dramatic disfigurements doled out by God – or Nature – as one wished. Roman was too wise a doctor to make science his

God. Nature, not man, constantly surprised him. Still, how unexpected to remove a true work of art, for once man-made!

He put the lasers, million dollar miracleworkers, to bed one by one. What would that Tokyo master with his bamboo-handled needles say if he could see Roman's behemoth tattoo removers? He left the door ajar for the cleaners finishing just across the foyer and punched the button to call up the mirrored lift.

The ground floor arcade linked to Geneva's main department store echoed to his footsteps. All lingering shoppers had been shooed away over an hour ago. Through the locked glass doors Roman could see a battery of lipsticks ranked on a sort of dashboard of beauty as symmetrical as a control panel on a female war machine. The rows of make-up and perfume sprays waited at alert. Beauty! Now that would be a rare bonus in a medical case seeking out Dr R. Micheli's portals. Had he ever seen truly perfect beauty? Certainly never passing the Guerlain counter, he reflected.

He strode up the shopping boulevard. Then using a series of paths and shortcuts, headed sharply uphill towards his apartment in the Old Town. He recognized a slight acquaintance and dodged other homeward-bound strangers. He admired the picturesque old carousel circling its coloured roof lights against the autumnal dusk and as he did every evening, he nodded to the organ grinder with his Persian cat – all fellow fixtures of Geneva life.

Gorgonzola and pears – *oui*, pears were good this time of year. He bought a pair of Bonnes Louises from the metal baskets hanging on the stone doorframe of the Épicerie Pizzo, then entered the passage des Degrés-de-Poules, a dark tunnel opening to the left of the shop – an all but secret set of steep steps that propelled this native upwards until he emerged breathless to overlook the entire city from the neglected rear of St Pierre. He would stir a bit of tonight's pasta water into the cheese sauce the way his father taught him.

How lovely Geneva was – tucking itself in for the night – an international city on the human scale of a large town, only one hundred and seventy-five thousand souls, (once all those commuters rode home to Carouge, Lancy, Meyrin.) Wide open to the world and all its agencies, yet somehow a man felt safe here. Change came to Geneva, but in controlled Swiss measures, like prescribed vitamin doses. Two hundred years ago, Roman's father would have been a scorned immigrant serf – officially registered as a mere *inhabitant*. His son could only have qualified one category higher, as a *natif*, still denied the privileges of the listed *bourgeois* or higher. Only *bourgeois* enjoyed the unattainable rights of the founding Calvinist oligarchs and they included his mother's forebears, *les citoyens*.

Time had worn down the *citoyens'* power. Imagine, there were now more Catholics in Calvin's "Protestant Rome" than Protestants, but the shift was discreet, never *vulgaire*. When had Roman last attended Mass? Frankly, no one stayed terribly religious once they settled down to the sober pleasures and duties of being a successful Genevan.

As Roman pondered how the twenty-first century had managed to lend religious fervour such a bad odour, a shopgirl loped downhill and took in the doctor with a glance – a man slightly shorter than average, wearing an expensive three-quarter-length coat, pressed dark trousers and a wide gold wedding band. The girl favoured Roman with a smile, giving every sign of liking the look of a healthy, handsome man at the peak of his mature attractions. In short, that evening Roman was, no more or less, a comfortable professional whose existence stood in moderated Swiss order.

The leaves shifting across the cobblestones lining the place de Bourg-de-Four collected on Roman's doorstep in crackling layers of flame and gold. The Michelis' apartment had once belonged to Roman's inestimable maternal great-grandparents. No one could remember it ever going on the market. When he unlocked his front door at the top of the pock-marked granite stairs, he earned only a sleepy Siamese nod.

"Poor Spaghetti, my day's work is done, but you must ready

yourself for another night of marking territory. Yes, caterwaul for food, the way my mother said her nightly rosary. And I will bestow as usual. I do exist, so much exists above and around you unseen, yet you understand nothing of it."

Roman changed out of his work clothes and muttered, "For that matter, neither do I."

4

Surprising, Isabel thought, that today's impromptu lunch in mid-town Manhattan with her ex-boyfriend Jonathan Burden was her husband's suggestion – once the Micheli couple had managed to catch each other by mobile, and after Roman had told Isabel of some funny tattooed patient with a piece of jewellery round the tip of his willy.

Odd, it was Roman who realized her old beau might cough up some promising donor names. She needed to find money that wasn't tied to the old leprosy school, money that would bolster her "secular" policy. Until then, the WHO was virtually hostage to the traditional leprosy players and their steady river of cash. She wouldn't have had the courage to dial Jonathan's clinic without Roman cheering her on, boosting her morale.

Phone calls between the Michelis were always upbeat, economical, and to Isabel, although not quite a – oh, dear, what was that glancing feeling again? Something about her perfect marriage that niggled? An ideal alternative in the back of her mind? A parallel romance waiting for the two of them once they'd finished being medical school mates counting their twentieth anniversary of connubial companionship?

The mobile phones got smaller, smarter, cheaper, but thank God, the Michelis' lovely understanding never shrank. What would their conversations be like if they weren't true friends? Spats? Scenes? Never. Their marriage simply had no time to be less than perfect. They enjoyed no margin for mucking up a relationship that had already survived gruelling forty-eight-hour shifts as residents in Columbia Hospital's dermatology department. Theirs was a collegiality indelibly forged in the daze of night-shift sleep deprivation.

What if they'd had children? Isabel shuddered at the prospect of nanny headaches, exam results, parents' evenings, GCSEs – the English Mum's lot. Her career in tropical disease administration would have been – well, wouldn't have been. How could she commute from Geneva to India to Manhattan and back if she had to fret over summer childcare? There wasn't a single mother assigned to the Task Advisory Group or sitting on the WHO Expert Committee on Leprosy. With her travel load, imagine! Remember what happened to Margaret What's-her-name when she applied for compassionate leave a few years ago? Actually, what did happen? No one had heard from Margaret for ages.

The taxi ride down Fifth Avenue to Jonathan's chosen restaurant was a surprising pleasure. The Punjabi driver's family had resettled post-Partition not far from where Great-Uncle Colin had served as district officer. Chatting to the back of his head had eased Isabel's nerves – so silly after all these years to worry what Jonathan might make of her now that twenty years had passed.

She hated the suit she was wearing, the only thing not dusty and crumpled by India. Jonathan's chosen restaurant was bound to be chock-a-block with fashionistas. Social X-rays filed into the dining room and looked right through Isabel. She knew she looked dowdy and alone on the banquette against the mirrored wall. She should have worn black. Trendies in New York dressed like Genevan Calvinists, Isabel marvelled, as if they were fitted out for predestination on heaven's catwalk. Blushing at her gauche punctuality, Isabel fingered the stem of her water glass. To the tinkling of an arctic Perrier, she pretended indifference as she mentally reviewed her disastrous morning.

The ten a.m. meeting with the Weltworth Foundation had gone disastrously. This time the entire board had turned up to listen to Isabel's appeal, which was in itself weirdly unsettling –

their forces massing against her. She had laid out her points – wasn't it redundant of Americans always to say "talking points," like the way they said "real time," and "actual fact". Oh, dear, she was cranky today. Jet lag muddled her irritable thoughts.

Anyway, she'd stressed her points so often during three hectic days of New York meetings that her bid for matching funds felt like a circus routine a trained seal could perform backwards to better effect: all the WHO sought was more support for shifting leprosy care from its traditional private operators to public health systems –

"And we'd like to see less dissent between you people in Geneva and the leprosy NGOs," a bat-eyed epidemiologist had chirped from the far end of this morning's boardroom table. "You've got a war on your hands, Doctor Hanford. We'd like to see all the leprosy actors get on the same page, something your WHO leadership hasn't managed so far."

And exactly what did "get on the same page" mean? Before Isabel could stop herself, this frosty challenge was out of her mouth. Now sitting alone at the small white restaurant table, she cringed at the memory of her retort icing up the Weltworth Foundation's mahogany playing field. Clearly, one of the leprosy NGOs had been whispering in the ear of this google-eyed medical adviser. She'd attacked Isabel: "Some experts say the WHO should stop pushing this deadline so hard. Claiming you can shorten treatment to a year with your home kits, saying you're just mopping up the last six countries!" The Weltworth's wizened Dr Magoo had persisted, "The NGOs tell us you're raising false hopes. They say the governments will cut back their contributions on the excuse of your WHO deadline."

There were nods and grumbles up and down the long table in support of Dr Magoo.

Isabel rallied: "Well, we're quite confident that free medicines will continue after our deadline has been met. Social rehabilitation will continue. But, indeed, I'm sure some of your sources are feeling a little threatened," Isabel demurred. "Keep in mind that when leprosy is no longer endemic, certain interests may find themselves out of a job."

The Weltworth directors hadn't reacted well to Isabel's insinuation about vested interests. Perhaps she'd even been too cold. Yes, it was her inflection, the condescension that queered her pitch. Her father's pukka cadence escaping her lips.

Isabel glanced around the bustling restaurant. Two women entered in teetering heels and chatted simultaneously on separate mobiles on their way to a corner booth. A quintet of businessmen claimed the circular table centre stage and ordered without menus. A lanky balding man, glasses hanging from a gold chain, crossed her eye line on the hunt for his table. He doubled back, leaned over and kissed her.

"You look marvellous, Izzie."

"Oh! My goodness! Oh, gosh! Jonathan! You look almost acceptable yourself."

Ambushed by this double-cheek-kissing, Aramis-dripping stranger, she flushed under her freckles. This man had Jonathan's voice, but was missing half of Jonathan's hair and all his acne. Of course, he wouldn't be wearing his night-shift trainers or his rumpled resident's coat to lunch – what had she been thinking?

"Good afternoon, my name is Harold and I'll be your waiter today – "

"Harold, you're always my waiter." Jonathan laughed with undisguised complicity at Isabel, all the while raking in the view of every face, smooth or pitted, in the room mirrored behind her head.

"Yes, Doctor Burden." The waiter bestowed a strained smile on Isabel. "The specialities today are halibut in fig sauce with garlic mashed potatoes or turbot in Banyuls sauce with sautéed snow peas. Or perhaps our miso-marinated mahimahi with orange soba noodles or grilled tuna with papaya salsa? For dessert, we have blackberry custard torte, macadamia coconut cake and a selection of artisanal sorbets ... "

This was Jonathan? With a sailing boat tan, in cashmere? The stranger focused on the specials of the day over half-moon horn rims. Isabel gazed at his polished dome and tried to imagine him back into the benzedrine-downing, long-haired all-night rock man of her med school romance.

"Izzie?"

"Oh, the fish'll be lovely, thanks, with butter, please."

Both men stared at her.

"Uh, the first one? I think it was halibut?"

"I'll have the usual trout, Harold. Half-portion. No butter. Potatoes steamed, not sautéed. Vegetables *al dente*. A little wine to celebrate this reunion?"

"Oh, I know this is an occasion, but with jet lag – no sooner does it start to fade than I'm back in the plane. I was in Delhi on Tuesday and I'm leaving for London tomorrow."

"No wine, then." Harold whisked away the over-sized menus like collapsing jib sails.

"Soooo. How many years has it been?" Hell, Jonathan was examining her crow's feet.

"Well, not since that Paris conference in '85? Roman brought me along? When he bought his first machine?"

"And how is Roman?" Jonathan snapped a minuscule carrot in two.

"Hasn't changed a hair!" She died a moment's shame "– quite dedicated ... well, you'd expect that ... terribly busy ... well, aren't we all? My travelling gets quite frantic sometimes, but we both absolutely love it. Geneva's super, you know, not as large as New York or London, but quite international as small cities go. He sends you his best – "

"I sent him a referral just the other day. First time."

"Quite. Roman was surprised – and of course, pleased." Jonathan scrutinized the lines running down the sides of her mouth.

"I read Roman's book *Limits of Laser*. You know, I've always admired Roman, and not just because of you, Izzie – "

"Oh, I hope I'm not that vain – "

"You were quite a catch for him. Well, I wasn't surprised, once my pride recovered. Roman's a man of real character. That's not always true in our line of work."

"Really, Jonathan, I hear nothing about you but success after – "

"Publicists are paid, Izzie."

Isabel tried to imagine Roman hiring a publicist.

"To stand out, you need plugs in *Vogue*, demos on the *Today* show, subway ads. Otherwise how do you set yourself apart? Remember that joke? What do you call a guy who graduates last in med school?"

Isabel drew a blank.

"Doctor! Right?" Jonathan leaned across the table, glasses dangling, to avoid the eavesdropping of two taut-faced scarecrows lunching inches away from his elbow. "You heard my marriage to Andrea broke up – ?"

The fish specials took a surprisingly long time. Isabel glanced at Jonathan's photos of the original Brooklyn clinic and his Long Island summer cottage. He joked they were his personal before and after shots. The more she learned of bicoastal Burden, commuting between his show palaces and various clinics, the more genuine tenderness edged aside her self-conscious anxiety. Jonathan seemed out to prove he was different now, up front, capable of saying things, getting it all out on the table. His celebrity divorce – what would *he* call it – the five-hundred-pound gorilla? – had been acknowledged, so now everybody could tuck into their sauce-free fifty-dollar halibut and three underdone potatoes. Watching the top of his sun-kissed forehead bowed over his plate, Isabel suspected some expensive time spent on the couch.

"Children?" she asked.

"Oh, sure." He extricated his puritan fish from the bone.

"Lucky for you. Roman and I finally gave up. Actually, we never started."

Had she caught Jonathan's confessional contagion? She switched subject, complaining that leprosy was a success on its way to backfiring. "Now the leprologists are too proud to hand treatment over to general health workers."

Jonathan turned theatrically grave. "Oh, man, can I relate? Professional jealousy really cuts into doing worthwhile work, doesn't it?" His gaze drifted back to the mirrored room.

Isabel speared a baby potato. "Imagine, Jonathan, all the serious money's being drained away – sucked off by HIV, malaria, avian flu. What we did have was denominated in dollars; now we'd be better off with rupees."

"Mrs Lear's resolved well …" Jonathan murmured and turned back to Isabel. "'S'like ol' times, you know. Remember how your heartfelt tirades about pesticides contaminating the Common Market used to give me such a boner?"

"Really, Jonathan!" she blushed.

"Sorry, it just took me back –"

"A world without leprosy. We could do it with a boost of funding out of New York."

Jonathan shrugged. "I guess leprosy's just not Disease of the Month."

Isabel persisted. "The problem is that the leprosy NGOs can't bear the idea of being cured out of business. They raised seventy million dollars last year just by putting up scary posters. They just adore the negative message." Isabel wiggled her fingers in the air. "Then they flout our policy directives. Now everybody knows we're at war with them."

"Gave you the finger, huh?" Jonathan giggled despite himself. "Here, try these people. Lotta their clients have tax headaches." He scribbled down a legal firm on the back of a brochure for one of his spas. His voice softened with affection: "Izzie, I suspect you're contemplating mischief."

"I am. How many leprosy patients are in New York?"

"I don't know." He smoothed away non-existent frown lines with well-manicured fingers.

"Five hundred outpatients at Bellevue Hospital. At least one in New Jersey State Prison."

The fashionable skeletons at the next table froze, forks mid-air over their low-cal lobster salads.

"For Chrissake, lower your voice, Izzie," Jonathan shot a panicked glance around the room. "Are they allowed to work in New York kitchens – ?"

Isabel ignored Jonathan's anxieties and mused, "Maybe I'll warn the Maxwell people this afternoon of the dangers of drug-resistant leprosy cropping up, like we've seen with TB – "

"Drug resistance – ?"

"I exaggerate," she sighed. "More than twelve million patients in our programme have shown no antibiotic resistance. And in fact, the incidence of leprosy in the US is dropping. Only one hundred new cases last year."

Jonathan exhaled the very oxygen he shared with the lepers of the five boroughs. "Whew, that's a relief. I mean, that's good news, isn't it?"

Isabel rolled her eyes. "No, Jonathan. That's bad news. The only thing that pulls in money is a big scare, so I'm here. We don't have leprosy in London, not to mention Geneva."

"Poor you."

"For fund-raising, it's dire."

"Dessert for us?" a voice above them chirped.

"No, Harold, dessert for us." They ordered fruit for two.

"How 'bout germ warfare?" Jonathan assumed a comic baritone. "Coming up at eleven, leprosy terrorists on the Staten Island Ferry. Stay tuned. Ooooo, I'm creeping myself out."

A disconsolate Isabel explained, "*Mycobacterium leprae* takes three to four years, low immunity and genetic disposition to surface. If Al Qaeda dumped a vial of it on the subway, the bacteria would just commute to Queens and back for years."

"God, Izzie, you sound disappointed!"

"Well, I'll allude to TB resistance this afternoon – it's a cousin bacteria. Perhaps the spectre of cripples in ragged shrouds clanging bells in front of FAO Schwartz will do it?"

Jonathan shook his head. "You know the saying, hate the sin, love the sinner? There's such a thing as being too good for your own good. I say, love the virtue, pity the virtuous. Why do you care so much? You're killing yourself."

Isabel left faraway sorrows unspoken. "It's personal. Let's just say I'd go to the ends of the earth for my leprosy patients." My patients. She'd cringed at Father Shardar using the same words only days ago.

"You never stop working. Even over lunch with an old friend."

"Oh, I'm not such a saint. I'm hoping to make P6 next year."

Jonathan nodded politely. "P6? Big pay raise, huh?"

"Not much more money. But a higher rank. I've been trying to crack the glass ceiling for donkey's years."

"Well, as long as they don't make an ass of you," he joked, bewildered by anyone powercrazed for leprosy administration. They sipped coffee in embarrassed silence, until Jonathan dredged up an anecdote about a Botox shot gone haywire. His lawyers had it sewn up. A malpractice suit was practically a coming-of-age rite in Manhattan.

"Golly, Roman's never been sued. Geneva doctors are rather regarded as unquestioned gods."

But Jonathan had swivelled around to air-kiss a former patient. He turned back to Isabel. "Over here we're just paid like gods. I have to plough it all back into premiums and lawyers, so it equals out."

He signed the bill with a flourish, then with sudden energy, asked, "Izzie, would Roman be interested in a partnership? Expanding his Geneva practice?" Jonathan's cheeks gleamed with eagerness – or moisturizer.

She blustered, "Oh, I'm afraid Roman lags behind the times. He still laughs at French doctors who set up Botox parties at the Intercontinental – "

"Well, it'd be great, really great, to have a Swiss outlet. If Roman's not even Botoxing, he's way behind the curve. I want to get into Dysport – it's all over France and Germany – but it hasn't got FDA approval yet – "

"Dysport?"

" – botulinum type A with a higher protein load, lasts longer – "

"Well, you know Roman hasn't changed – "

"Plus sales of my cosmetics, lotions, tanners, and even building name recognition on into Eastern Europe – with a cut for Roman, of course. I just need a licensed practitioner at your end. He's laid a good base, right? I'd inject some glamour, new machines, training. Market to the metrosexuals – "

"I don't think, really – "

"People these days want a familiar name when they travel. I'm branded. It isn't just lasers, Iz." Like an Indian guru, Jonathan chanted, "Rejuvenation, relaxation, restoration – preventive medicine."

"Really! What I need is funds, not a partnership for Roman."

Jonathan backed off. "You know me, Isabel. I'm not really into disease. I only went to med school to please my mother, but I've made it work for me. Remember my joke that laser stood for 'latest advanced source of extra remuneration'? I could beef up the action in Roman's corner. He'd better consider my offer, 'cause there's a Botox backlash here in Manhattan and coming soon in London and Paris. I hear Geneva's middle class is still pretty much Terra UnBotoxa. The Yanks are coming, whether Roman likes it or not. I could fly to Geneva – "

Isabel laughed uneasily, "Jonathan, don't sound so threatening – "

"You know, Izzie, I could work wonders on those glabellars between your eyebrows . . ."

Isabel managed a smile riddled with the unfashionable furrows of irritated middle-age. She took in Jonathan's smooth patter and guileless offer of a free Botox trial the next time she "blew" through Manhattan, but all the while, she was thinking it was a jolly lucky thing Jonathan had slept behind her back with that pharmacist in time for her to flush his cut-price engagement ring down the waste disposal system on the pediatrics floor.

And suddenly, that long ago Wednesday afternoon of tearful betrayal came flooding back. An indignant, swollen-eyed Isabel had accepted a coffee and bagel from the shy Roman Micheli in the hospital canteen. A week later they shared croissants in her apartment while her room-mate worked her shift.

Within six weeks, Roman had let his lease on a rat hole on West 116th St expire and when he wasn't working on the development of a revolutionary new laser machine up in Boston, was to be found at Resident Dr Isabel Hanford's tiny apartment on East 92nd.

She'd been lucky. And besides, for all his flash, when had Dr Jonathan Burden ever encountered a glistening ring encircling the glans of a penis tattooed to resemble a cobra?

5

Roman peered through a magnifying glass at Mme Olivier's perioral area. Her crevasses resembled Alpine valleys smudged with glacial crusts of waxy lipstick running northwards from the upper lip to the nostrils. Where his laser had just passed, the dermis was starting to swell, puffing her naturally harsh expression into a lop-sided sneer.

Chantal knocked on the treatment room door and thrust a message into the doctor's free hand. It read: "Concert? Colonel Jack Sullivan."

Mon Dieu, the busy days had wiped out any memory of the American's suggestion of an unorthodox diagnosis by footlights. The "case of the reluctant case", that was the invisible Mlle Sullivan. Roman smiled to himself and resumed zapping Mme Olivier. Whenever he thought up a pun or witticism in his wife's mother tongue, he stored it up to present like an old-fashioned corsage kept fresh in the refrigerator until her return from the latest business trip.

Straightening up with a sigh, he slid his purple goggles up on his perspiring forehead. Was the building's heating system playing havoc in the changing autumn weather? He felt like crossing himself, saying an *Ave Maria*, anything to avoid a bout of flu.

"In about ten days, Madame, the swelling will subside and the wrinkles will be reduced."

"Mmm," nodded Mme Olivier. "Do more," she managed to mumble through the compress protecting her tooth enamel from the laser's beam. "Do the lip."

"I stop short of the lip tissue to avoid removing the pigment of your natural lip line."

"*Encore, encore!*" she insisted.

"That will suffice for today, Madame."

The Olivier woman exhaled Marlboros and mint. Roman could do little for her prematurely deep nasolabial folds, even less to correct the sallowness of her upper lip area or pebbly skin texture. At least the lines would flatten out somewhat. The aggressive whiff of *Eau Orange Verte*, the metallic shine of her jacket, the Vesuvian eruption of a Prada leather bag – all screamed expense and stress. What did she do again at that office of hers? He'd treated many like her and knew his optimal result might still disappoint. They always thought that if one laser pulse worked a little, ten would do a lot. Medical patients far homelier than this woman were grateful for modest corrections. Sun-blotched pool-loungers fading into the dusk of their allure couldn't conceal their crestfallen realization that the doctor erased only wrinkles, not their cause – those disappointing children, that contested divorce.

Why did so many people think only in absolutes of black and white?

"Chantal will give you my prescription for a mild painkiller." He patted Mme Olivier's shoulder. A fleeting glance said here was yet another woman in need of passionate caresses, not professional condolences. Roman could laser away lines, not loneliness.

The backlog was mercifully slight this morning: Mlle Rosacea murmuring into her mobile next to the aquarium and a spider angioma case – Chantal must stop calling that one Spiderwoman – idling through last month's *Edelweiss*. Not good, not *chic*. Who'd stolen September's Paris *Vogue*, hefty as a telephone directory? Chantal had forgotten to restart the DVD player that hung from the ceiling in the upper corner of the waiting room so that patients could view coming attractions in laser technology. Roman sauntered over to push *play*, then crossed to the lobby closet. At the sight of her doctor rifling though the inside pockets of his coat, Rosacea made a theatrical show of checking her watch. Roman ignored her.

Yes, the envelope was still there after weeks of neglect, squashed into the curve of his chest under the silky lining. He extracted two tickets of bent blue cardboard. Fifth row at Victoria Hall. Tonight.

Shouldn't Chantal call the poor man with some excuse? He could stage an emergency – though dermatology offered precariously thin cover. He heard the echo of Isabel's mocking laughter as she smoothed her freckles over with powder, insisting he attend a medical colleague's painting exhibition: "Oh, change your clothes. What emergency would convince a heart surgeon that you couldn't make his precious gallery debut? Killer warts?"

Surely he could think up something. He swabbed off Mme Olivier's anaesthetic gel. Chantal interrupted Rosacea's mobile-phone chatter to prep her.

The truth was Roman and Isabel were stick-in-the-muds of routine. Isabel required a good rest after each business trip. She spent more time in hilltop Himalayan missions and humid clinics than in a small city buttressed by money that she dismissed as "too old to come out of its musty villas or too new to have the good sense to call it a night".

For Roman, it meant, simply, going to his clinic and going home. In a country that prided itself on "extreme" winter sports, Roman could have captured gold for extreme hibernation.

He wasn't staid or stodgy, *non, non*, nor shy or *timide*. He simply liked the comfortable predictability of his schedule. The demands of providing discreet medical care for his groaning roster of patients satisfied him. After all, he saw enough of the human Geneva lying on its collective back all day. By nightfall he relished a delicious pasta, a good book, and the undemanding affection of someone who was out of town three-quarters of the time and left him in peace; someone whose true passion was thundering up dusty footpaths on a motorbike, to ensure no one was pilfering her patients' rifampicin to treat gonorrhea instead. Someone whose idea of a lovely day was tramping in disposable booties through some dicey pharmaceutical factory on the Indian plains. For some reason, the vestigial colonial in Isabel Hanford needed her farflung missions as much as she needed Roman and in many ways, that suited Roman just fine.

The Michelis took two vacations a year. In August they soaked together in the mineral whirlpools of an Italian spa and ate rich meals set off by musky red wine that smelled of earth and autumn harvest in the sun.

"For their sins," Isabel joked, they clocked in every Easter for ten wet days with her slightly gaga mother, Marjorie Westcott Hanford. The once redoubtable aged parent was now much reduced in form and fire: she could do no harm. The accommodating Roman acknowledged his exotic cast in Marjorie's eyes and tolerated her arch references to "our Italianate son-in-law". Wearing borrowed Wellingtons a size too large, he slogged behind her crooked figure across Suffolk sugar beet fields. He showed genuine pleasure in an equally soggy tea in her under-scrubbed kitchen. He would explain the laser business every year to this hardy antique rubbing Boots lotion on her mottled hands. He would amuse them both by topping her up behind Isabel's back with the Beefeaters hidden in the unused bread machine. Had Marjorie lived in Geneva, perhaps he might have taken her to Victoria Hall tonight. Isabel preferred the ballet, admitting she could claim disability compensation on the strength of her tone-deafness; they rarely went to concerts together.

Alone, never.

Ah, these tickets ... who could use them? Roman switched on the pulsed-dye laser and looked up the patient's depth measurements while the machine warmed up. Her last appointment had been over three weeks ago and the dermis was misbehaving; both her cheeks had sprouted new vessels.

"Have you been naughty? You are staying away from spicy foods?"

"*Oui, Docteur.*"

"Then what are you using on your skin? Nothing containing Retin-A, I hope?"

"A cream, Renova."

"Stop it *immédiatement*. It stimulates new vessel growth."

Anyway, taking appointments at six in the morning ruled out midnight bedtimes. The Rosacea lay a chastened, wide-eyed bug under her protective goggles. Roman aimed the wand's spurt of numbing cold water followed by rapid flashes of light along the red threads. Mlle Rosacea's skin was of the Scandinavian type. The beam provoked instantaneous eggplant discolorations, all perfectly normal. In twenty minutes, she would resemble a clown daubed in purple polka dots.

To Roman's delight, his last WHO opera "duty" as Isabel's escort had turned out to be hilarious – an avant-garde *Tales of Hoffman*, all nude. In this production, Offenbach's bordello featured severed pigs' heads, *ménages à trois*, and full-frontal simulated sex – an evening that had turned staid Geneva on its head. The show was a busman's holiday for Roman – all that skin! – but his Italian blood rejoiced at the soaring voices. *Ah oui*, that performance had made leaving the apartment worthwhile.

Eh bien, why not surprise Isabel when she called him from New York? This sudden whim startled Roman. Mopping his damp brow, he broke his goggled concentration long enough to tell Chantal to call the US Delegation to the UN. Roman would go to this concert, alone. It was delightful after all, not to be stodgy. With a wave of the next file, he returned to Spiderwoman in Room Two.

By day's end, lightheadedness and a recurrent flush had joined forces with a sore throat. Doctors did get sick, but were the last to admit it, even when the signals of incipient infection were obvious; a Genevan native like Roman prided himself on his unfailing radar for kerbside parking, but this evening, he was not himself. Defeated by the clock and throbbing temples, he swallowed his pride and descended to the underground

Parking Dufour. He dashed weakly past Radio Suisse Romande technicians sheltering impatiently inside their sound truck from drizzling skies. He raced towards rue Bovy-Lysberg on the heels of another late arrival. With only one more block to navigate, but it seemed a very long stretch for his aching muscles to reach Victoria Hall. He passed with some relief below the languid stone nude leaning on her carved harp above the heavy double doors of the grandiose facade. Her posture – loitering between the engraved names *Handel, Bach, Mendelssohn, Mozart, Wagner, Liszt, Beethoven* flanking the double marble columns – advertised, "What is your hurry? I have heard it all and I am in no rush."

He entered the lobby to the wet swish of snapping umbrellas and the chatter of music-lovers still queuing for seats. Who else wanted last-minute tickets to see no-name violin finalists on a soaking Monday night?

His stomach rumbled. He'd skipped lunch to treat that emergency Quincke Oedema – lips swollen with histamine to monstrous dimensions by a urticaria attack – an old-fashioned dermatological dilemma. Now he regretted his professional compassion. The snack bar had just closed.

The Colonel was nowhere to be seen among the chatting clusters. Roman nonetheless recognized a few faces who returned his polite nod. *Ah oui*, nothing had changed in all these years: the sparkling chandeliers, the cognac velvet banquettes lining the bar and the oil portrait of the shy young Queen Victoria smiling down upon the gathering. He'd been to the opera with Isabel on and off these last years, but he could no longer count the years since he'd come to this old concert hall.

Roman and his wife were not considered part of "true" Genevan society. That hermetic group excluded the Michelis on many counts – his Catholic immigrant father as well as his marriage to the English Isabel and her working life in what *genuine* Genevans dismissed as "the international community", that transient city-outside-a-city on the other side of the

Rhône. Taking in the furrowed faces dotting the seats along the wall of the bar, Roman felt as if the old world of his childhood had been waiting for him here, night after night, in case he chose to look in on them again. He recognized a prominent private banker, the old Rombard, adjudicator of Genevan society. It pained Roman to watch the bent-over figure fumbling on two canes to escape the pushing around the coat check.

From the other side of the foyer, an elderly friend of his aunt's – long ago retired from the Hospital committee – tossed a hopeful wave in his direction. Roman had thought her dead. Two dowagers in worn Chanel bouclés and faded Hermès scarves smiled sagely to each other and sipped their Kir Royales. They'd gone to school with Roman's Huguenot mother, the rebellious Clarisse, until she'd eloped with a handsome Italian refugee medical officer. Micheli senior had fled Milan in '44 still in uniform, *distingué* but penniless. *Hélas*, didn't Clarisse's younger boy look pale tonight?

Finding his assigned seat in a loge box on the left side of the great hall, Roman fought off a wave of regret at Isabel's empty chair beside him at the rail. He'd turned off his mobile for the concert. Perhaps she'd tried to call? *Voici* Col Sullivan, emerging from behind the crimson hangings on the left side of the small stage. *Mais oui*, he would have been downstairs with his prodigy. Roman observed the heavy-set American in an ill-fitting civilian suit look up to admire the rococo gilt hall. It was a narrow, elongated horseshoe – certainly not the type of sleek, clam-shaped auditorium the Colonel would have known back in the United States. Two rows of balconies reaching high above and opposite Roman's section were empty. It was hardly a sell-out.

Col Sullivan's spaniel eyes ran down the low boxes lining both sides of the central floor all the way back to the distant upper balcony, but he somehow missed Roman's receptive gaze.

The giant surrendered at last into a seat in the right-hand

corner loge. A hush fell over the audience as the Prague Philharmonia emerged from backstage, the female musicians rustling forward in bright multi-coloured skirts of raw silk. They tuned and there it was again, washing over the sea of heads that included Roman, that humble but classic chord, that immutable hum of mi, la, re and soh, blowing its whiff of eternity through the old building. A pregnant hesitation followed, then Roman saw the bear-like arrival at the podium of the celebrated Shlomo Mintz, the conductor's gold hair shining under the lights.

Mild applause warmed the hall, with its thin wooden boards underfoot, its rickety loge chairs, and the heavy velvet hangings. Roman searched out the first seat in the second row and with that, he remembered the smell of his diminutive mother's neroli scent, the warmth of her whispering an explanation of the orchestra sections as she undid her hat pins and lifted a decorative concoction from her tight dark curls, removed her gloves, then the flutter of the programme . . .

A pear-shaped young Hungarian in black tails strode downstage and took a firm stance at the footlights. The Mintz baton went up and the third-prize soloist opened with bravado, if not complete confidence. Roman relaxed into the music; a strange comfort soothed his weakened spirits as he listened to the opening strains of Max Bruch's "Scottish" Fantasy. The contestant was only twenty-three, but there was no doubting the out-dated sweetness of his touch. He played with mannerisms that conjured up the grandeur of nineteenth-century soloists doing the Grand Tour by carriage; there was a bit too much sleeve-adjusting and wiping off the violin between passages. Roman forgave him his unfortunate build and archaic posing for the singing resonance of his instrument, even though Bruch's thrumming theme with its hint of heather and bagpipes was taking on an overly saccharine flavour. The soloist finished phrase after phrase with a formalized arc of the bow, as if by trying hard and often, he might at last levitate his heavy bottom above the hardworn stage.

49

The finale was marred by the impression that despite his virtuosity, the gallant Czechs had to tow the boy along in their wake like a flat-bottomed dinghy. At long last, his determined trills signalled Bruch nearing the shift in key and with rising arpeggios and leaping octaves, the ensemble signed off with one clean finish together.

Roman took a deep breath and glanced at his watch. The Hungarian nodded thanks for his single curtain call, received a double-handed shake of consolation from Mintz and waddled offstage.

A mounting fever left Roman moist and chilled, both hungry and seasick. The folly of this evening had become obvious; yes, he must get out of here. He braced himself to sit out the runner-up, a Finn playing Brahms. If the Budapest contender struck him as a a throw-back to the heyday of Schumann and Berlioz, the northerner, with his shaved head bent over a charcoal high-collared shirt, resembled a technician straight from Nokia. In his youth Roman had heard the central melody of the adagio as a soaring love song, but perhaps the Finn's generation made love to computers, for the cerebral young man executed Brahms with the precision of a software programmer.

The audience applauded the man's explosive display – velocity, memory, and stamina were hard to ignore – but the boy clasped his instrument like a shield to his chest, and received his due share of applause without joy.

The purpose of the evening had eluded Roman and even the music, which was so familiar, had offered less succour than expected. Everything seemed out of kilter. He was too unwell to appreciate these earnest performers. He would flee un-detected during the interval and send his excuses to Sullivan tomorrow. The weary doctor rallied his energies and thought longingly of bed. His impromptu outing had turned out flat and misguided and for that he felt genuine regret. It was not nostalgia he experienced, *non*, it was a sense of real sadness. The concert had left the aftertaste of a stale museum visit, of view-ing dead art –

"Found you! Thanks for coming, doctor." The Colonel's grip was dry and hard. "What'ya think so far? Mira's all ready backstage. Pretty relaxed now the pressure's off. I think she's finally realizing she won. Maestro Mintz is being so nice to all three of them. Well, I guess they've earned it, starting out in a pack of seventy. Unbelievable, but my little girl pulled it off."

Despite his bonhomie, the anxious father looked pinched, the reddened turkey folds of his neck chafing under his white collar.

"Drink, doctor? How 'bout a champagne or brandy?" Roman started to beg off. "Let's blow some of that prize money, right? The dress you're going to see cost me a helluva lot. Lorraine used to sew them herself, but I'm not so lucky now." The man looked in danger of succumbing to tears of relief or regret.

"Water, *merci*. With pleasure."

This courtesy would give nauseous Roman the chance to explain his imminent faint-headed exit. A mineral water would allay his thirst. Unfortunately, his *merci* must've been misheard by the Colonel as "whisky" because the American had turned his back on the champagne stand in one corner and was instead easing his bulk through the throng of shorter men pushing, money in hand, at the main bar. Within a minute or so, he'd handed Roman – not a restorative San Pellegrino – but a fat glass of amber-hued whisky and soda.

An envious Roman gazed up to see the American gullet dispatch an iced Coca-Cola. Roman managed one polite sip of his liquor. A finger's grip of tension eased off his queasy brow and he delayed his excuses for a moment. His subdued manner escaped the attention of his host: the Colonel had quickly embarked on small talk to fill the break: "Call me a cultural gorilla, but I'm amazed by that Finnish guy's lack of rapport with the strings. He plays for himself and nobody else. That's my impression. He won for interpretation of the imposed piece, but he left the special school kids' jury cold. And anybody can see why."

Bewildered, Roman nodded upwards at the Colonel's jutting chin wagging its uninterrupted discourse on the subject of double-stops, tonality, and nuance. "... the Hungarian's colourations were interesting, but I'd say the variations came out too kitschy, wouldn't you?"

People around them jostled and heaved, lapping in waves against the bar. The American's unexpected fluidity on the subject of string playing mesmerized the perspiring doctor. Roman could only listen, gripping his anchor of a whisky with both hands.

"At this level, they're all hot, you know what I mean, they're all terrific musicians. So it depends on how they handle the pressure, who's on top of his game on the night. There was a fantastic guy from Yerevan in the semi-finals ..." Col Sullivan then stared across the heads of the crowd and sighed to himself, leaving the Armenian's tragic fate hanging unnamed in mid-air. Roman's imagination flashed with car accidents, instrument theft, finger bashing or torn shoulder muscles.

"What happened?"

The huge shoulders shrugged. "Ah, man, the poor kid's bow hairs started stripping right off during his finale cadenzas. By the time he got to the allegro vivacissimo, he was plucking them off between solo passages like some Kentucky chicken farmer ... Oh, but that was nothing compared to the French girl. Wadda meltdown ..." The Colonel rambled on, citing the honourable fallen of the musical battlefield while Roman sipped and nodded, nodded and sipped. The incongruity of this combat expert scrutinizing violin competition as a tennis teenager's father might rate forehands and footwork was hypnotizing. Before Roman could stop himself, he'd relieved his parched throat with the dregs of the unwanted whisky.

He attempted to manoeuvre around his towering companion to slide his empty glass on to the bar. The Colonel's generous paw snatched it up. "'N'other whisky? –" The man's hospitality was smothering.

"No, thank you. In fact –"

Victoria Hall's chimes sounded the closing of Roman's escape hatch as the proud father threw his enormous biceps over the Swiss doctor's shaky shoulder. "OK. Let's watch my little girl do her thing. Boy, are you in for a treat."

6

The whisky fumes and jabbering crowd suffocated Roman. With difficulty, he scaled the stairs back to his box. A hard-edged blonde occupied Isabel's seat for the second half of the programme, sending her piercing anehyldic perfume wafting under Roman's nose. She'd stashed her lambskin tote under his seat. Reaching with murmured *"pardons"* to shift it back, they knocked heads with a force that robbed Roman of a moment's focus. He gripped the railing to steady himself. This evening was not a success, to say the least.

Mintz returned to the footlights in a fresh shirt, his gold-red thatch catching the spotlight, forehead shining with anticipation. He bowed to the applause and settled his Czechs for the final lap. They looked tired now, another night shift nearly finished, their own prize-winning solos fading into memory. Their knowing asides betrayed no envy – only sympathy and solidarity with the catgut gladiators braving centre stage.

Roman heard the gentle rustle of taffeta as a small figure swept through the ranks of the strings to land, violin aloft, at the conductor's podium. She shook hands with the leader of the first violins; then she bowed slightly to Mintz and carefully laid a folded white handkerchief on the podium a mere step away from his gleaming shoes. She turned her bare shoulder and tuned her instrument, one ear cocked to a cue from the string section. She rotated to face the audience.

This, unbelievably, was Col Sullivan's "little girl".

Dark tumbling curls were fastened loosely to the back of her fine-boned head. Her nose, too long and narrow to be conventionally pretty, balanced between large black-lashed eyes ringed with eyeliner. She wore a strapless corset of bordeaux satin over a stiff skirt embroidered in gold threads that dropped in a wide A-line to the floor. Her figure poured voluptuously over the boned bodice, but her thin arms were taut, her hands like delicate hummingbirds poised mid-flight.

Roman strained to examine her face, but she was swaying away from his box into the embrace of the orchestra, eyes focused inward to the opening strains of Tchaikovsky's Concerto in D major. Her torso moved just enough to follow the allegro moderato introduction. Then, eyes closing completely, she raised the polished instrument to her cheek and with her right arm circling towards her listeners, she poised the bow across the strings.

Despite the heavy paste of stage foundation, Roman had seen it. Even without theatre binoculars, his expert eye had traced the outline of a port-wine stain of purple to pinkish colour, probably of moderate depth, extending from under her left ear across the line of her jaw and a few inches down the side of her neck to make a half-circle cutting into her cheek and ending below the left ear. Trust the Colonel to omit mentioning a coincidence bound to frustrate Roman's examination; the birthmark mapped almost exactly the area where the violin rested under her cheek. Her mark and the press of the violin mirrored each other, one masking the other with beauty and sound.

Her violin took up the announcement of the orchestra with a flirtatious hesitation in the introductory bars of the Russian's opening song, until soaring cadenzas erupted from her white shoulder, then subsided into a second theme. Within minutes, her slight body had relaxed but instead of retreating again into herself, she seemed to expand, as if she were questioning Roman himself, moving towards his seat.

Behind her wine-coloured figure, the cello players swayed from side to side like trees in the wind. A clarinet broke through the leaves. The girl played a little ahead of Mintz's beat, a dancing figure signalling three upward notes to the ensemble and answered by three downbeats of Mintz's baton. Roman felt the ensemble mount the music with Mira Sullivan's elbow circling madly, leaving them to return in full marching step to Tchaikovsky's peasant-like theme. Trumpets sounded, the girl rested, sweat drops breaking out on her hairline. She absorbed the orchestra's energy, moving along the currents together.

Now, she returned to the pastoral song again, rippling a spiccato variation off her fingertips. She was so alive! Almost greedy to sheer off layer after layer of the chords, digging at something obstructing her way, then rounding back again like a three-year-old playing in the wind with a stick of willow.

Roman was no longer a prosperous dermatologist watching a student prizewinner, no longer marvelling at the *justesse* of her highest notes or her delicate harmonics; a communal energy had seized the whole audience of which he was a grateful part. Was it so obvious, after all, to know what Tchaikovsky was thinking? So simple, so grand? Some of the violinists smiled as they laid their instruments on their knees to watch the young woman dive into a dazzling solo passage. Her left hand located a sweet high note, then slid down and up once more to repeat the tremolo hanging in the almost silent air. The she slid in a glissando ending in a trill, to evoke a faint voice remembering – no longer a march – but a third version of the theme, calling to all of them from a solitary, perfect place.

Roman's thoughts wandered off. The music evoked a glimpse of the impressionable boy Roman Micheli nestling down in that other seat a few rows away – and a second impression of a child – not himself exactly – watching Mira Sullivan up on the stage. A being like Roman, but not Roman at all, an essence of all the youthful energy flying past their heads as the strings answered any question Tchaikovsky dared throw at them.

And just when Roman was sure Mira Sullivan's hand was going to fly off into the tuning pegs, out of control, her bow flew around like an extended wing lifting all of them skywards. The chestnut cloud of hair flew loose around her shoulders and the silk of her skirt shifted from purple to burgundy to maroon with her hips' swinging movements.

When the first movement ended, an enthusiast near Roman broke tradition to applaud, but Mintz signalled the audience to hold back, as the panting girl reached for the handkerchief to pat the perspiration from her brow. Then the conductor nodded to the horns, who took up the second movement, Tchaikovsky's famous Canzonetta. The Sullivan girl's stage make-up no longer hid the reddening cheek, but her exertions suffused her entire face, engulfing the birthmark in a general flush. Her perfect bosom, so full on someone so slight, rose and fell with a passion that somehow embarrassed Roman.

The girl took up the soothing andante, woodwinds crooning behind her. The composer had been generous to the brother-hood of flutes and oboes. Roman closed his eyes. His brow burned with fever. His head throbbed, with – what was that? His paternal grandmother singing to him in Italian on a still summer evening when he couldn't sleep, not when the sun lingered in the sky and the smell of oregano in the garden perfumed the daybed in her dining room. Suddenly, Mintz lost patience; with a downward thrust of his baton, he crashed into the dithering winds' indulgence. Conspiratorially, Mira took over without pausing to signal – already, the finale!

With a powerful stroking of the strings, Mira Sullivan dived into a rapid-fire scherzo outlining the strongly folkloric Canzo-netta theme. Then she laid it out slowly for them all, musicians and audience alike, as if to say, here is our song, here is our common anthem to our frail but gallant humanity. Gathering force, she rounded them up, her fingers leaping up and back down her strings. Dozens of arms flew in a semi-circle around her, a single soul she'd forged out of them all, playing out its collective breath. The delighted Mintz bounced on his toes, galvanizing the entire ensemble to mimic Mira Sullivan's accelerations in a frenzy of notes and emotions.

The third violins, no longer merely finishing the night shift, galloped along the windswept steppes of Tchaikovsky's imagination. The woodwinds claimed their solos. The oboes called back to the violins. The dynamic girl at the footlights sheltered them under her wing. Whirling Cossacks filled the air of Victoria Hall, horses' hooves beat across the grass between the dowager building's narrow aisles and heavy drapes until the bass violas took charge and ordered Mira, bolder than ever, to restate the theme.

Her low resonant notes seemed stolen from the viola section, but the girl couldn't contain herself to their range for long. She cantered off to Tchaikovsky's Slavic beat into the upper register of her finger board. The playful woodwinds tossed the song among themselves in droll fashion, oboe to flute, clarinet and finally back to Mira Sullivan who chastened their frolic. The clarinets followed obediently, then the oboes, and all settled down when suddenly, the irrepressible soloist took off again and coquettishly summoned them into a swirling dance. Roman's heart squeezed with excitement, watching five white fingertips speeding up and down the neck of the violin, elbow circling madly ahead of the dozens of others to reach a final chord that lifted the exultant Mintz into a leap on the podium in sheer joy.

The audience erupted to its feet.

Chairs scraping, seats snapping, Roman rose on unsteady legs, clapping his arms above his dizzy head. The osteoporific rows of stolid Genevans were losing control, applauding until no single clap of hands could be distinguished from the thunder of this surrender. An unfamiliar sound rushed towards Roman from the back of the hall; the rumble of shaking wood rolling right under his feet as the audience stomped its feet on the worn planks. He had never witnessed such a frenzy between these walls.

Mintz stepped off his wooden box and took the young woman's hand and pulled her to him with a gentle kiss on the purple stain, now cruelly exposed by heat and wear, gleaming from ear to cheek to throat under the harsh lights. Hand in hand, they acknowledged the audience's accolade. Then the proud conductor turned to recognize his triumphant Czech troops and the tired, grinning old pros stood up, still tapping their bows against their music stands. They bowed again to shouts of *bravo, bravissima,* as the young American disappeared behind an enormous bouquet thrust into her arms.

How long had Roman shouted with them all, through his raw throat, his pounding brow? The blonde was already nudging him clear of his box. He drifted with the current up the aisle and down the stairs in a river of satisfied music lovers heading for their coats, the umbrella stand, a good night's sleep. Roman floated along the reverberations of sound towards the heavy street doors, clutching his programme –

"Doctor, where're you going?" A hand pulled his upper arm against the human undertow towards the door.

"Of course," Roman stammered. "Of course, Colonel. I'm sorry, I didn't forget, *non, non –* "

"Well, you're certainly headed the wrong way. You can't be running off because you didn't like her performance?" The larger man chuckled at this preposterous idea. The hesitant stranger who'd consulted Roman in the clinic now overflowed with the confidence of someone who'd watched a child's genius take root and flourish year by year. Where his daughter's virtuosity was concerned, the gauche soldier stood on solid ground. He ushered Roman back up the stairs and down the aisle of the emptied theatre, on to the stage to pass through the red velvet barrier and descend a tunnel of dark stairs.

A child of Geneva and yet Roman had never before seen backstage at Victoria Hall. Like any non-performer, he started at the grubbiness of the unadorned space furnished with the mechanics of stage magic. The plain room was jammed with perspiring musicians, their ties pulled loose, cigarettes lit. Impervious stagehands marched through the hubbub carrying stacks of orchestra chairs. Roman suffered the press of sweaty bodies in black jackets and creased silk wreathed in tobacco smoke. Through the swarm, he made out three dressing-room doors facing the bare linoleum foyer.

Just inside the first door, the celebrated Mintz himself was pulling off his collar studs and making his practised farewell gestures to well-wishers. He looked exactly the way Roman felt when he pulled off a stained white coat in anticipation of a seamless recovery for the patient and a well-earned meal for himself. The two male contestants stood in their shared dressing room off the centre of the foyer, each greeting his fawning constituency with his back turned to his rival's friends and family.

The electric bulbs of the farthest-most dressing room cast a golden rectangle on the yammering throng engulfing Roman and his ruddy-faced Homer. The Colonel's large feet proved surprisingly deft at cutting through the mob and avoiding the cello rests, resin chips, moleskin wipes, jackets, cigarette packets, sweet wrappings and yoghurt pots while Roman, a graceful man in ordinary situations, stumbled over this alien terrain of litter and music stands.

A queue trailed out of the dressing-room doorway. Half a dozen bobbing heads blocked Roman's view of Mira, some-where in the recess. Admirers clustered towards her, some flapping programmes to cool their brows, like a flock of over-excited geese. Others chatted to each other, waiting for their chance at the victorious star. Every few seconds, it seemed, Mira kissed or greeted or hugged yet another fan.

This backstage hysteria was foreign to Roman, whose office, like his life, was a study in discretion and discipline. What a ridiculous way to meet a potential patient! In the calm of his clinic, he could extend his hand, direct her to a seat, ready himself to take notes, assess, and treat. The start of any new case was just that – a medical introduction to a situation in controlled isolation. He turned back, ambivalent and unseen in Col Sullivan's shadow. Nothing could be expected of a doctor in such a public setting. In fact, there probably wouldn't even be a chance to –

The Colonel's baritone again cut off Roman's retreat. "Mira, honey, meet Doctor Micheli."

Roman felt himself rudely pulled past the line-up into the inner chamber. He blinked against the glare of make-up lamps as he was pushed, wavering and confused, into the presence of the fiery goddess of the stage. But the goddess had vanished. As the reluctant gaggle around her parted for the Colonel and his guest, Roman saw only a freshly-showered college girl in an unflattering spangled stretch top and tight white jeans. Her left cheek, now unmasked by soap and water, shone raw purple under a polite expression.

At least the hand extended into his was as it appeared on stage – something that should be sculpted, the Italian in him whispered. He took it with care, and bowing, kissed it gently. "*Enchanté.*" The face was that of a potential patient, but the hand was that of a prodigious talent. And after all, he'd been offered only the hand so far.

Mira giggled and shot a look at her father, entirely the little girl that Col Sullivan protected and adored.

"I hope you enjoyed the concert, Doctor."

"Absolute joy, Mademoiselle. You seem to have captured the composer's happiness in its entirety, just to give to us as a gift."

Mira squinted at him, slightly challenging. "Did you know Tchaikovsky wrote that piece just after attempting suicide?"

"You surprise me."

"Yes. His marriage had just collapsed." A look of mischief crossed her face.

"You played it wonderfully. The concerto is a beautiful work of art. You did it more than justice."

"Funny, when you think that critics in Tchaikovsky's day said it stinks. They called it long and pretentious." She had a provocative streak, but Roman felt too queasy to joust.

"All the more to your credit, Mademoiselle. Now we all know the critics were wrong. My congratulations on your prize."

She shook her head, the birthmark catching the merciless glare of her dressing table's halo of halogen. "But you never know at the time, do you? Sometimes you get things wrong the first time and only understand them better later – " Someone was waving his programme over Roman's shoulder, trying to butt into their conversation, but Mira glanced at Roman as she reached across and signed it with an efficient flourish. "My father warned me you were coming. He's got some idea – " she broke away from Roman to wave off friends, "Oh, thank you, yes, I'll call, – sorry – "

Roman responded, "I don't know why seeing me backstage would make any difference to your medical considerations, but seeing you perform was a pleasure in itself – " A tall young man pushed Roman aside with minimum apology. He handed Mira a handful of stapled documents, saying, " – I do wish you luck with this, Mira. If there's anything I can do – "

"Thank you, Charles. I'm so grateful for your help. I'll call you after I've heard from them."

Roman tried to slip away under cover of the skinny Englishman's business, but his trouser leg was pinned down by the unseen foot of the Colonel himself.

"Hold on, there. This doctor's standing right here in front of you, Mira. Now you can't refuse at least to make an appointment. Not to his face."

Mira's glance mixed forbearance and impatience. Roman winced at such an unfortunate choice of words! His fever and dizziness grew worse. Cigarette and perfume choked him. He thought of tomorrow morning's five-thirty alarm with dread. A final admission that he was undeniably, ridiculously, inconveniently sick engulfed him. Given the heights of artistic subtlety he'd just witnessed on stage, wasn't there a way to bring the evening to a quick and civilized conclusion?

The Colonel blustered on, "Don't you want to be – ?"

"Oh, spit it out, Dad – "

"Well, normal?" The Colonel blurted out his repressed exasperation, the very picture of a soldier whose strategic planning faced capitulation. Roman groaned. The word "normal" scandalized his ears; ill-chosen, offensive, and from every psychological standpoint, counterproductive. All his medical culture reared back at this tactless misfire. He suspected that as long as the devoted Mrs Sullivan had lived, the Colonel's wishes had been muted by maternal protection and bolstering.

For the first time, Mira stopped half-nodding to the clamour on all sides to give her father and Roman her full attention.

"Doctor Micheli. I know what my father is trying to do for me. I appreciate your coming here at his insistence. You may not hear this very often in your line of work, but for me to become what you and my father probably think of as normal, well, I'm sorry, that would be my idea of Hell."

Roman bristled. The girl's manners were as confusing as her father's. The whole scene had turned distasteful and the magic of the evening was shattered. "Do not mistake me for someone who would make you *average*, Mademoiselle. *Au contraire*. That is an option I leave to you."

The Colonel fumbled, "She didn't mean it like that, Doctor. Please, wait, wait."

Roman nodded to the open-mouthed father and took a lingering, uncompromising look at Mira's cheek. He ignored the challenge in her eyes and the graceful arms folded against her chest. Without another word, he filed out between the lingerers and took the Artists' Exit to find the relief of the cool night breeze in the empty alley outside. For the first time in seven − or was it eight years? − he'd call in sick tomorrow morning.

Even though he was a doctor himself, he was suffering more than he realized.

7

Isabel unlocked the apartment front door to discover Roman waging the fourth day of his solitary battle with a virus. She took charge of his damp sheets, the overworked toilet, the bed tray and thermometer; but it became obvious that this same spouse who cured whole nations of a biblical plague was rather impatient playing bedside nurse to one shivering flu victim.

"Really, after three years, the least Mrs Siskovitch could've done after she finished vacuuming was to make you tea and toast. Even come in an extra day."

"*Cara*, she offered but I didn't want anybody."

Isabel turned to Spaghetti in amused resignation. "Typical doctor, totally denies he's sick."

"*Non, non*, I am sick. *Ça, c'est évident.* I don't want to trouble you, that's all."

"I have to go to the office to catch up." She gazed at his pallid face for a moment and concluded, "You do look frightful." She jumped off the edge of the bed and with a brisk flick of her wrist tossed her travel clothes with his fetid pyjamas in the laundry bin.

Isabel's bustling dispatch wearied the invalid. "I just need a shave."

"You'll need a lawn mower."

He sensed he was over the worst when the clinic's growing backlog weighed more on his mind than the daunting challenge of a half day's routine with semi-strangers. Chantal phoned to reassure him that Lise and she were handling the minor cases quite well, but it was time to get out of bed.

At last, bolstered by an exceptionally strong espresso, a thinner Roman set down the hill from the Vieille Ville at dawn. With weakened step, he navigated down his familiar shortcut to the clinic. During his bout with flu, Geneva's weather had turned a sharp corner – the lake had lost its midday sparkle. Chantal greeted him from behind a horrific pile of manila files; she'd readied the first rescheduled appointment. The Japanese waited for his laser session in the treatment room overlooking the rue du Rhône and the flat grey lake beyond.

"*Bien*! And where shall we start, Monsieur Shino?" Roman sighed.

"*Hai*!" The enthusiastic Shino bobbed a few times from his perch on the narrow treatment bed. The serpentine scales covering his pudgy knees protruded below the starched medical gown. Roman handed him the protective goggles and pulled his own purple headset over his eyes. In the mirror, he looked like a scrawny Dr Frankenstein wielding a superhero laser gun. *Mon Dieu*, he must've lost four kilos in a week.

"Now. Let us test two different settings for the reds and yellows. After a few weeks' healing, you should see only a white rectangle here."

Shino glanced with regret at his snaky kneecaps.

Roman paused, laser poised mid-air. "Monsieur, have you given this enough thought? You want all this removed?"

Shino hesitated, then shook his head "no", but gestured "yes".

"Yes? No? Yes. Good. Perhaps the outer hip is a better place to test. Please turn just a little . . . *merci*."

Roman placed a steadying hand on the left thigh. A tattooed *trompe l'œil* skirt of jonquil-yellow rope and red tassels covered the hips. The buttocks sported a tattooed modesty cloth hanging from a belt.

Shino mumbled: "Traditional wrestler apron – "

Thwack, thwack, thwack, thwack. The laser's pulse caught Shino mid-sentence. Roman concentrated the shots half a centimetre

apart in careful rows, the geometric symmetry of his progression across the goose-bumped hip obliterating the sinewy
rope design. *Thwack, thwack, thwack, thwack . . .*

". . . symbol of sumo strength in the ring . . ." Shino stammered.

The area reddened up instantly, swelling and radiating
through the tattoo and outwards from each laser point. Chantal
had booked the Japanese a double session totalling an hour.
There would even be time to test the persimmon of Benten
Kozo's kimono hem, fluttering on to the left buttock.

Thwack, thwack, thwack, thwack, thwack, thwack.

"Please, no smoking during treatment, Monsieur Shino. Did
Chantal offer you a numbing gel? No need?"

"OK. Good, good."

Thwack, thwack, thwack, thwack.

Shino dug his chin into the crisp paper pillowcase. The laser
felt like a vicious rubber band snapping and crawling across his
hip. It spurted chilled water a millisecond before the brief
burning zap, over and over and over.

The Japanese exaggerated his breathing in order to relax. He
imagined himself no longer in a Swiss dermatologist's office,
but far away. He was the main character in one of his favourite
fantasies, *hai!* riding his motorcycle with the other *bosozuku*
"speed boys" like back in the old days, only in Shino's fantasy
today, defending Tokyo under threat from a cohort of invading
space aliens.

Thwack, thwack, thwack.

Hai, the man lying pinned down, eyes closed, was no longer
Shino Watanatra, a sorry, if well-meaning character whose
sense of honourable obedience, of *giri*, had led to this: the tragic
removal of years' worth of painstaking artistry and his very
excision from the close-knit ranks of the *irezumi* brotherhood.
Ie, no, no, *thwack, thwack, thwack*, he could play the heroic
sumo Space Rider, his thick black hair fastened into a bobbed
tail on the crown of his head in a rakish knot flopping forwards.
His cartoon-eyes widened with determination as he warned the

sleeping city of extra-planetary aggressors. His massive bike wheels screeched down the narrow alleys of old Tokyo. Two hundred pounds of dense lard and muscle garbed only in a wrestler's skirt, he thwarted the evildoers from – *thwack, thwack, thwack.* The maddened aliens attacked Space Rider Shino, their laser gun rays snapping off the sumo hero's invincible thighs like tiny firecrackers. Over the engines' roar, he bellowed to his gang behind, warning the panicked population to burrow to safety.

And if his enemies should catch him, locate him before he'd disappeared into the anonymous sea of faces forever? Could he still imagine himself a hero in the face of their revenge? Yes, the humble Shino, "newsletter publisher", secretly knew he was already an unsung hero back in Tokyo.

"Please turn slightly this way . . . *oui, merci, Monsieur.*" Wasn't it true of any man, not just the powerful Boss Tanaka and his dreaded enemy Onishi? Perhaps even this unlikely foreigner, this wan westerner with a hairy hand positioning Shino's hip under his merciless beam? Of course, heroes should be hairless. Only villains were covered with pelts as thick as his laser specialist's, but perhaps once or twice the doctor also had imagined himself a secret hero?

Shino smiled to himself as the unlikely vision of the goggled Micheli-*san* joined the *manga* fantasy. Although in Micheli's case, it should be one of those hardcover cartoon books, a French *bande dessinée*. On a working stint in Paris, applying the *sokaiya's* unsavoury extortions on a Japanese bank or two, Shino had already discovered wonderful tales of hard-eyed women spies and gangsterish action heroes. The sophisticated illustrations fascinated the Japanese, bored by his dog-eared *mangas*. Now at least once a week the nondescript Japanese "businessman" strolled into a Geneva book shop and indulged his passion for the art of the "*BD*".

"Monsieur Shino, you seem to be enjoying yourself. Is this not a little painful?"

Shino grunted off the doctor's solicitation. The shrug of his shoulders made the thief Benten Kozo lift his persimmon robe in salute.

Late November passed in blessed quiet, with the curiously cheerful Shino's name decorating many pages of Chantal's well-thumbed appointment book. Isabel stayed in Geneva long enough to reassure herself that Roman had recovered his strength, thanks to shoving him into an early bedtime after each supper of clumsy stew or lasagne tasting of too much tomato purée.

Finally, one early evening Roman waved his wife off to a conference in Santo Domingo on "Contagious Disease and the Media" with a soupçon of relief. He relegated the leftovers of her Delia Smith bangers and mash into Spaghetti's bowl, and serenely soaked dried porcini mushrooms in warm water for a solitary risotto and glass of Barolo. Roman didn't blame Isabel for spending so much time in the field. Sometimes they shared only a single weekend a month together, but on days like these, when Geneva huddled under a sheet of rain, who could blame her heading for the sun? Why shouldn't Isabel pursue her dreams of saving the Third World from a millennial scourge, especially if the Third World offered better weather?

During a brief lunch break, he wandered out on to the main shopping boulevard. The streets sported garlands of electric fairy lights, but this meagre illumination in the drizzle gave the impression the conscientious town fathers were anxious to get the whole Christmas affair over with. A large truck was double-parked in the wet mist so an anorak-clad team could unload a portable ice rink for the coming shopping season.

Roman idly bought a bottle of Parure *eau de parfum* as a Christmas stocking back-up. He wandered farther to H&M full of thumping rock music and racks erupting with garments. He was looking for something un-doctorish – although he didn't exactly say to himself "un-Isabel-ish". He imagined her russet hair over the peacock blue of this silk blouse or her childless hips squeezed into these burgundy velvet jeans. No, not burgundy, why did that colour make him uncomfortable? Could she fit into these hip-huggers in forest green? Nothing seemed quite right. After more than a precious half hour of his allotted sixty minutes, Roman acknowledged his suspicion; these trendy garments were all wrong for his middle-aged wife.

He laid out his bundle on a display table. He knew from seeing his younger female patients that the ruched silk blouse was *à la mode*, but surely Isabel wouldn't allow her midriff to hang out below. He now realized that the apricot sweater was also too short and the green jeans would sit somewhere just above her pubic hair. The colours were perfect for her, yet as he floundered up and down the collections, he saw the clothes were simply too young.

He gobbled down a ham baguette out on the street, and now he had fifteen minutes – not long enough to try a third store. There was Escada two blocks down, but Isabel scoffed at their overblown styling: "Big shoulders, big hair, big Germans." Bon Génie carried designer clothes, but that meant a purchase of *importance*, something she'd no doubt return.

When did a couple in the course of their endless honeymoon – uninterrupted by kids marking the passing years – discover that they were irretrievably middle-aged? Mid-forties? Later? Parents could measure their incipient decrepitude using those home-made height charts pinned to doorways. You've grown, I've shrunk. Who needed to look in the mirror to guess at the crumbling of your own bones when the Mastercard charges from Lego bricks to mopeds read like a family saga?

Roman halted under his umbrella behind a cluster of pedestrians listening to a whiskered fiftyish emigré from Hungary, Poland? The beggar played a battered violin outside the wide front doors of C&A. His hand-lettered sign propped on the greasy velvet of his hardshell case read, "Lost orchestra job", in badly spelt French and English. The musician played a dispirited rendition of Vivaldi's "Winter", his gaze wandering to Roman. The doctor tossed a five-franc coin into the case. The man managed a crushed smile over the edge of the violin and nodded.

"All that vibrato is too romantic for Baroque," he overheard a girl say behind his umbrella dome. Roman edged away from the group, but the voice followed him. "Hello, Doctor Micheli. I was just on my way to your clinic to ask for an appointment – to apologize to you. It's over there, above the department store, isn't it?"

Mira Sullivan smiled up at him through the rain, one hand sheltering her eyes from his umbrella spines. She wore a white plastic raincoat and hat. Her throat and half her face sheltered under a mulberry scarf.

Roman shook her hand. "I don't charge fees for apologies."

"I could see from your expression the other night that I offended you. I wanted to say sorry."

"Your father's suggestion?"

"Oh, no. He'd only get his hopes up."

"Well, I have ten minutes before my next appointment. You give me your apology over a coffee." Roman felt avuncular; the shadow of the caring, pushing Sullivan senior worried him.

He led the way up an escalator to the old Radar Brasserie smelling of choucroute and stale pastries. The lunch shift was scraping up the last of the crème brûlées and Roman and Mira waited in the press of woollen coats and sweating waiters for a table against the plate glass window one floor above the street. Roman ordered a *ristretto* for himself and a cappuccino thick with whipped cream for Mira.

Roman searched her open features beyond the girlish macintosh and rain-frizzled hair for a glimpse of the luminous artist with the pulsing décolleté. Mira rubbed her cheeks to warm them and immediately, her birthmark flushed dark fuschia-blue. A child in nappies leaned over the banquette behind Roman's shoulder to stare at Mira's face.

"It didn't come out the way I meant," she resumed without further ado. "When I got home, I realized that probably everybody you meet aims at one thing – to remove marks like mine."

Roman reflected a second too long. Had he ever met a patient who *didn't* want treatment? He'd read of such cases, but Mira Sullivan was his first live refusal. He fingered the chocolate square on his saucer. "Well, *c'est évident*. Anyone who likes their birthmark isn't likely to seek me out."

"So you admit there are others like me – "

"*Mais oui*."

She lifted a spoonful of whipped cream to her lips and licked it unselfconsciously. "You've just never met them, that's all."

He chuckled, "I'm busy enough, Mademoiselle."

"You don't understand."

"One can make a fetish of the wrong things. Confuse an accident of nature with proof of individuality."

"Hmm." She looked away for a moment, then asked, "Are you very famous? My father was so excited you'd accepted the tickets."

"I helped develop the pulsed dye laser after graduating from medical school in the eighties, in the States."

Mira said in a distant voice, "Yes. I've read about those machines."

"Our research improved the pulsation and ensured that the skin had breathing time between emissions. Less risk of burning and scarring. Then I worked on the Q-switched laser – "

She listened, toying with her spoon.

" – but that was a long time ago." Roman flashed on those early days of night shift. Crazy Jonathan had made his fellow students laugh over their pizza cartons until they were holding their stomachs, falling right off their folding chairs with the hilarity of his idea for a chain of beauty clinics featuring lasers. Isabel had mused out loud whether lasers might eliminate leprosy lesions. Those had been days of so much promise. Most of the promises had been fulfilled.

"You're not interested in technicalities. Your father imagined I was a hypnotist, perhaps? Well, we both let him down a little. Perhaps he hoped I would cast some superhuman psychological spell over you which would change your mind at the touch of my hand." Roman waved his wrist.

Mira laughed. "He's a wonderful dad, but he's not a musician. He sees the business side clearly enough. He thinks the big agencies would slobber over me if my face was fixed. That's his word. 'Fixed'. When he goes into a CD shop, he doesn't hear the music, he just sees all the posters of Anne-Sophie Mutter and Hilary Hahn, and asks himself, 'Why not my Mira?'"

Roman tossed back the rest of his coffee and adjusted his coat. His next patient had been waiting five minutes. "And why not his Mira? You're afraid?"

Mira reacted with indignation. "Afraid? Me? Tell me, do this many people usually notice you in a coffee shop?"

"I don't frequent this restaurant –"

"You know they're staring at us? Don't you think it takes courage to leave the apartment each morning looking like a freak who spilled cranberry juice down her cheek?"

The pouting, the bravado, this was more in line with Roman's training. "On the stage I witnessed an artist. Now I hear an adolescent."

"I knew you wouldn't get it."

"I beg your pardon, Mademoiselle. Again, you insult in your American way. I flatter myself there may be a little artistry in what I do."

He paid the bill and prepared to leave. It was the second time this girl had led him around by the nose only to offend him.

"All right, then. You're not a musician."

"I see. You fear losing your gift, somehow?" He had seen the way the violin settled like a missing puzzle piece against the stained cheek. With relief Roman thought he now understood. He surveyed her mark again, assessing the depth of the vascular deformation by the shade of purple, so blue outdoors, glowing pinker in the restaurant's indoor heating.

"Not like I'm some kind of, of magical thinker. It's not that, exactly. Of course at first it was comforting that the violin hid the mark. Then the music became a way of talking without people watching my cheek, or what's worse, trying not to watch my cheek, sort of looking away to the good side, you know?"

Roman nodded.

"And then I realized that without the birthmark, I never would have discovered what the music could do. Maybe it's superstitious, or religious . . ."

"Religious?"

"Do you know how lucky I am? Have you ever seen photos of Ceaucescu's orphanages – the iron beds with four kids to a mattress? The filthy sheets? My Mom saved me, gave me everything. She bought me a tiny violin, a one-eighth, no bigger than a cigar box – " Mira thrust those graceful hands in front of Roman – "and I couldn't let go. Then we met Madame Chu – "

"The teacher in China?"

" – Moscow-trained. She played professionally before the Cultural Revolution, then wasted years playing *The White-Haired Girl* ballet over and over. She never stopped practising western music in secret. Somebody turned her in. They exiled her to the countryside as punishment."

Roman forgot his waiting patient as he watched those graceful hands moving back and forth. Mira chattered, almost as if she were playing an invisible accompaniment to her own story on a finger-board in the air. They were such agile hands, the nails trimmed down and polished, the wrist dancing with unbelievable flexibility.

". . . Of course some musicians had lost their skill, or even their minds, but Madame Chu said that getting the music back without fear of punishment was like going to heaven . . ."

Mira stared straight into Roman's eyes.

"You're not really following all this Chinese stuff, are you?"

"*Oui, bien sûr.*"

"Do you know what we had in common, Madame Chu and me?"

He thought of Seigler's third and final rhinophyma, all the layers of blood-rich and encrusted excess growth removed with

73

the CO_2 laser, the nose reshaped to its former smoothness. That would be less confusing than this.

"If I'd been left in that rusting crib, I'd have starved by now, or been mentally retarded, stuck on some lousy farm. I'm as grateful as Madame Chu when they let her play her violin after ten years of shovelling pig shit. It was my birthmark that caught my mother's eye, that saved me, that God used to protect my talent."

Talent seemed a feeble word to Roman, recalling her soaring performance. He'd applauded her with frenzy. How could two people occupy the same troubled body – that breathtaking dynamo of whirling fingers and moist bosom – and this fey girl with the philosophy of a college freshman?

"Mademoiselle, in a single week I see hundreds of patients. I doubt any of them keep a Faustian pact as part of their condition. I'm sorry, I must go now. If you change your mind, call Chantal for a consultation."

He shook the raindrops off his umbrella and slid out from the banquette.

Mira grabbed his coat sleeve fast. "Doctor Micheli, isn't there something in your life, something you really want, but you say to yourself, 'If I had that, on top of everything else, I might be tempting fate?'"

"No, no," he demurred.

Winter's weak sunlight stroked the pebbly texture of her throat. Roman saw the beauty laser could restore – virginal and yet womanly in the dark Gypsy style, ready for what life offered the lucky few.

"You think I'm crazy, don't you, Doctor?"

He extracted his coat from her grasp. "Perhaps your violin says you are not, Mademoiselle. I'm a man of science, not a priest."

"You're not a Swiss Aylmer?" She knotted up her mulberry scarf and followed him to the arcade escalator.

"Who?"

"Probably too American for you. Nathaniel Hawthorne's

short story, *The Birthmark*? We read it in high school. The husband Aylmer is a man of science like you. He loves his bride, but detests her birthmark. That was Hawthorne's symbol of Mrs Aylmer's human imperfection, the uncontrollability of her fertility. It was Nature's challenge to Aylmer's delusion that man could conquer anything. The birthmark obsesses Aylmer. He locks himself in his lab and finally emerges with a potion to remove it. His poor wife loves him so much, she drinks it up," Mira's hand waved in the air, "and abracadabra, the mark disappears!"

They had reached the bustle of the street.

"This story clearly made an impression on you."

"For sure. You see, Aylmer loses the gamble. A minute after the birthmark fades, the potion murders his wife." She punctuated her sinister tale with an insouciant wave of farewell.

Roman had lied. He hurried back to his appointments in a fit of indignation. A stranger like Mira Sullivan had no right to his uneasy secret. There was indeed something God had denied him. Witnessing as he did the parade of misshapen and malcontented in his clinic, he didn't complain. Isabel was a loving, hard-working partner. Laser research had moved beyond his pioneer efforts so that now his practice was thriving and his lasting contribution to his profession was secure.

On summer Sundays, he crewed on his brother-in-law Fede's sailing boat, skimming across the lapping little waves, then lunching on a dockside terrace on fresh perch in lemon sauce and sipping a vintage grown on the nearby slopes of Mont-sur-Rolle. In winter, he and Isabel skiied in strong, sure strokes across the dazzling snow of La Givrine plateau. There were occasional weekends of Alpine skiing in Chamonix with an ophthalmologist who used lasers on astigmatism, his best friend Dr Rudolf Kessler, and wife. Or quiet dinners *à deux* in restaurants dotting the Old Town.

"Contented, darling?" Isabel would ask at the end of a relaxing evening, scraping up the last of her chocolate mousse.

"*Si, cara.*"

Of course he was not contented. His secret desire had crept up on him only two or three seasons back, once his life had moved from challenge to routine to pleasant stagnation. Couldn't he kill this nagging ache that there was something or someone waiting almost fully formed, yet with indistinct features?

Dr Roman Micheli craved a son. He didn't want "children", "kids", "*des gosses*", "*les mômes*", or "a baby". He didn't even want a daughter. His dream of *un fils* embarrassed him as too specific, too *égoïste* and so remained unspoken.

The Micheli apartment legacy had been the young couple's only lucky break; but once they had cleared away early debts for Roman's first machines and managed the crippling insurance premiums during the sceptical days of laser treatments, Roman had urged his wife to consider getting pregnant.

"It's a bit late, but I suppose it would be healthy to go off the pill for a while," Isabel had prevaricated. "It's not as though my measly salary in the Tropical Diseases Department is such great shakes. I wonder . . ."

Roman had been too respectful of her embryonic career at the WHO to request a fertilized embryo. Around the time of her first promotion, the pill packet disappeared from the bathroom shelf and his hopes rose. Only when making love did Roman learn from the tell-tale tickle of a plastic thread that Isabel had switched to an IUD. She boasted she had lost a bit of weight in the bargain.

Their savings grew, but Isabel set off on yet more missions abroad while Roman's caseload overflowed. Leisure time shrank to a pinpoint. The changing seasons brought the autumn launch of his book or the sad spring that laid to rest the uncomplaining Edward Hanford, that paternal shadow in his Marks and Spencer's cardie and slippers. But they brought forth no issue.

Then only last year, Isabel started cheating on Roman.

One spring evening, she returned from the airport, exhausted as usual. Was that the tour she'd taken with that Dr Carlos

Campagna to Brazil? Roman remembered references to crazy Carlos, *azulejos* and *viño verde*, Portuguese punctuating her chatter. Of the six countries in the world still struggling with leprosy, it seemed Portugal and its ex-colonies had walked home with the dubious top prize.

"Only because we didn't have anyone to speak the language," Isabel said. "That's all changing, thanks to Carlos."

"He sounds like an excellent addition to your department," Roman commented.

"He's a bit of a wild card, makes me laugh, but God, he works hard," Isabel conceded. "Divorced, a litter of kids to support. I feel rather sorry for him."

She regaled Roman with tales of at least half a dozen small clinics and hundreds of cases, all children. Roman had prodded Isabel like a spy penetrating his counterpart's cover, over dinner, during her bath. Like a tortured lover, he parsed her offhand replies for evidence against her. She glossed over details of delivering the blister pack shipments and upgrading the standards of the Brazilian researchers to match the Delhi labs.

"Look, darling, you have to see these." Still wet from her bath, Isabel hastily tied up her dressing gown and emptied her briefcase on to the bed. She fanned out photos of infant and toddler cases Carlos and she had caught early. Nameless children grinned up at Roman from all over the marital bedspread as Isabel rabbited on about harvesting more youngsters with only a single lesion, assuring cures, relieving parents.

Dirtied by surging resentment, Roman continued his discreet, obsessive grilling over the subsequent months. She'd fallen in love without him. He would have preferred her colleague Carlos, her boss Dr Norton − any rival adult male. Even a specific child could have been discussed, but instead Isabel had fallen for dozens, hundreds of little patients. She was smitten by their appalling living conditions and the tongue-twisting nicknames bestowed on their pathetic pets − a gecko, a mouse, or garden snake pampered in some battered shoe box. One day Roman cancelled two appointments just to drive

Isabel to Cointrin Airport as a treat – only to surprise her buying Beanie Babies as gifts for her clandestine kiddies while she assumed he was parking the car.

"I think we should adopt," he said at last. As soon as the words were out, he knew adoption was not for him but he was desperate. "After all, you love these children so much, perhaps one of them is very special to you? Needs a home?"

"Oh, I'm far too busy. Once I make P6 in a couple of years . . ."

There remained no more than two years to her goal – the deadline of the leprosy campaign. Down to the magic, if arbitrary figure of one leprosy sufferer out of ten thousand clean. The Michelis would buy a country house in Umbria not far from Roman's ancestral roots. Or maybe get their own sailing boat. Isabel even mentioned a trip to India to retrace the Hanford footsteps forgotten in the colonial dust.

Now she'd added an adopted child to the very bottom of this fantasy list. It was obvious why. She didn't need to house a single child in an apartment where she spent only a quarter of her nights and even fewer of her days. She had hundreds of children already all over the world.

All Roman wanted was one.

8

"Oh, I forgot. Something terribly funny happened with Jonathan in New York. It completely slipped my mind."

Roman was pounding veal cutlets for egging and breading with grated parmesan and breadcrumbs. All he'd heard so far was that Jonathan was balder, prosperous, superficially more sincere, and not a jot smarter than when Isabel and he had left the States.

"Did he come up with any references?"

"Oh, yes. He e-mailed a jolly long list of prospects – American pharmaceuticals panting after a do-gooder profile. Two have partners in Basle, so that's quite helpful. And some big noise in Botox processing. I bet he hinted to them that a donation to the WHO might offset some publicity about side-effects. And those frightful Maxwell people promised me one more meeting. I think my lepers-on-your-block approach might've spooked them over to our side." She bit into a chunk of cheese. "I'm a wicked girl, aren't I?"

"I would report you, if I only knew where . . . " He tossed a knob of butter to sizzle in the pan and rubbed his hands on a fresh tea towel hooked into his belt. His insistence on a pile of white cloths, sharpened knives, alphabetically-ordered spice jars and carefully-stacked and seasoned pans lined with paper towelling had long ago forced Isabel's retreat from the stove.

"So, you forgot to tell me . . . ?"

"Oh, right. Now, don't laugh, Roman. Or do laugh, actually. I certainly did."

Roman tossed chopped parsley into the pan and squeezed

79

lemon juice over the sizzling meat. A dash of white wine, a pinch of paprika –

"Jonathan suggested you as a partner in a Beverly Hills Beam here – "

"*Quelle horreur!*"

"Well, my response was a trifle more measured, but exactly. He's aiming his sights eastwards. With Botox tea parties and private-label cosmetics, green tea shampoos, Arizona stone massage, ginseng soap, eye of newt and toe of frog . . . "

"I would swallow hemlock first."

Isabel stroked Spaghetti's chocolate paw. "I knew you'd say something like that. What's the Latin name for hemlock?" She was first and last a doctor.

"Did he propose alternate allies for his invasion?" Roman ran down a mental list of the few laser and cosmetic dermatologists in Zurich and Lausanne. He was the only suitable private laser practitioner in Geneva.

"Didn't mention anyone. Hmm, that smells delicious."

They ate their veal in compatible silence. The stone walls of their solid eighteenth-century building fought off brisk November winds rising from the lake below. Their nest, decorated in jade greens and burgundies glowed with Renaissance warmth.

Isabel drank a second glass of Marchese Antinori. Roman recognized the signals she sent him across their small table by the fire, a white damask island of peace and understanding with his grandmother's worn silverware dully reflecting the flames . . .

Later, as he held her familiar white softness in his arms, stroking the soft red down that ran between her navel and her thighs, he heard her murmur, "Darling, what do you want for Christmas?"

Roman wondered what might already be tucked out of sight: some men's cologne wrapped in rough recycled paper carrying the sandalwood smell of a Third World duty free shop, or an extravaganza treat, like his coat from Milan.

He kissed her eyebrow and rose from the warm sheets and heavy sweetness of her body to trudge to the bathroom. He caught the reflected sight of his thick black hair hanging loosely into his eyes, the flush of bedding Isabel subsiding through his chest hair, his penis lubricated with her familiar juices. For a moment the sight of his wide eyes in the overhead lamps and his long hair tossed out of control reminded him of something – yes! – his Japanese patient's tattoo of "Superboy Kintaro", that laughing rosy cherub with the wild hair clinging in flight to a giant carp covered in turquoise, black and silver scales and known to Shino as the "King of the River". The laughing Kintaro boy was positioned midway down a slippery descent of the left outer thigh. Roman sluiced his own thighs down in the shower.

"Christmas? Oh, you know me, *cara*, anything'll do. A summer home in Como. A Maserati. Don't go to any trouble."

Isabel laughed, "And to think I booked the entire orchestra at Victoria Hall to serenade you for New Year's Eve! With soloist!"

A disconcerted Roman turned around and stared out of the bathroom into the blackness of the bedroom beyond. Isabel had already drifted off into contented sleep.

"What is this, Chantal?"

"It is a surprise, *non*? Two letters came this morning."

Roman's black eyebrows shot up with an incredulous retort: "Bouvier again. But he never sent two in one week."

"I could place a call for you between the Japanese and the Cordobas boy at ten."

"I can't accept this. First, bring me the other letters. With a coffee. *Merci*. Then bring me Geneva Cantonal's number."

Roman heard the usual symphony of impatient shuffles and coughs coming from the waiting room. He steeled himself and put on his heavy-rimmed reading glasses.

He spread out six letters from Albion Insurance refusing coverage of laser treatment for over half a dozen cases. He added the two new ones: an Algerian-born student just eighteen, whose facial port-wine stain was considered "only a cosmetic case". He was just three weeks over the age limit under which Albion had to absorb his fees. The treatment was only delayed by exams, summer holidays, and then an unexpected family funeral. But Albion's medical adjudicator, the petty, despicable Dr Ferdinand-Emmanuel Bouvier jumped at the excuse to rescind compensation.

The second refusal infuriated Micheli even more. An agriculturalist who had spent her life on distant assignments had never sought treatment for a birthmark that discoloured her entire left leg from heel to buttocks. The affected thigh now showed purpurations of blood blisters spreading upward from the knee. This degradation was medically predictable and Micheli could laser away the blisters, lightening the mark in the process. He could hold the damage at bay.

But Albion denied treatment for her leg as it "wasn't gangrenous or cancerous". Roman protested. Bouvier stalled and demanded more tests – blood circulation trials, two separate days of magnetic imaging in a clanking MRI tunnel, then a consultation before a dozen doctors convened by the conservative Dr Petitpierre at Geneva Cantonal. This morning's mail brought Petitpierre's compromise; that Roman treat only the blisters, leaving a checkerboard leg of purple and white squares.

"Patients are waiting, Doctor." Chantal busied herself at the filing cabinet a few feet from his desk. Roman placed a call to Petitpierre who laconically waffled about precedents set and savings involved.

"I do not do patchwork quilting," Roman spat down the line so fiercely before slamming down the receiver that Chantal backed away from the cabinet and left his office door ajar.

Bouvier again. Always Bouvier who denied coverage. The cases might vary, but the refusals were the same.

The jealous Bouvier had poo-poohed the arrival of lasers as newfangled inventions for profit, not real medicine. Bouvier hadn't weathered the heartbreak of pioneer results, consulted with engineers for years to upgrade the speed, the spiral or spectrum of each improved model. He'd railed at Dr Roman Micheli's rates, the machine overheads, the "outlandish" applications. Bouvier whispered around the corridors and coffee breaks of the cantonal corridors, why should we pay for Micheli's toys?

Dr Bouvier himself was nothing more than a dermatologist with a traditional practice – with his cortisone creams and liquid nitrogen and old electro-desiccation rods – in a stuffy building next to the Natural History Museum.

"He should be in the Museum with the dinosaurs, instead of next to it," Roman spat. Not for the first time, he reflected on a bit of conference gossip from his friend, Ruedi Kessler.

"It's always Albion giving you a hard time, *ja*?"

Roman nodded, surprised the discreet Swiss-German should raise the subject in the middle of a machine demonstration.

"We always lose on the references sent to Bouvier," he whispered back.

"Ah, *ja*, Bouvier's a *schlitz*. His uncle sits on the board and the family trust holds a large block of shares, you know, *actions*."

Roman had turned to stare disbelieving at his friend's knowing wink. "*Non. Insupportable.* Denying patient care – ?"

The cynical Kessler nodded, " – to raise the family's quarterly returns. Albion shares are well up on Familias and Medisure."

"I don't follow the market." Roman pondered his minor role in a ramping up of Albion profits. "Why hasn't anyone complained?"

"You're a Genevan. Petitpierre always backs Bouvier up?"

Roman thought of the mealy-mouthed hospital team parcelling out scraps from Bouvier's assessments time and again.

Kessler's green eyes stayed riveted on the newest invention beeping away for their edification. "Who would challenge one of Geneva's oldest medical dynasties?"

The Zuricher was right. Roman knew he didn't have a chance raising a protest against the Bouvier clan. Squalid allegations over Bouvier's conflict of interest would rain down retribution on Roman's head. Doctors were a professional brotherhood. They couldn't air their squabbles like mafia dons or American divorce lawyers. Deflated but enlightened by Kessler's insinuations, Roman had kept his counsel. He too was Genevan.

Now this morning brought two more terse Bouvier letters as tangible rewards for his inertia and cowardice. He derived small comfort from his mother-in-law Marjorie's old Hindu saying: "Sit on the banks of the river long enough, Roman, and the bodies of your enemies drift by."

Sooner or later, would someone send the bloated Bouvier floating away?

Threads of forbidden nicotine drifted over Roman's desk. He spotted M Shino waiting in the treatment room across the corridor. The Japanese man's buttocks were a raw pink and ochre, his treated skin positioned below a row of chrysanthemums at the base of the hermaphroditic Benten Kozo's dishevelled kimono. Shivering in the air-conditioned cell, the Japanese had tried warming himself with a forbidden cigarette. He was watching the doctor's private drama with an air of innocence. Had he eavesdropped on Roman's outburst to Chantal? On the angry exchange with Petitpierre?

Roman abandoned his Bouvier paperwork. The Japanese stubbed out his cigarette and bowed in sheepish defence. "Today very long session."

"And how is business publishing these days?" Roman pulled on his gloves with an expert snap. He spread Shino's treated flesh and pressed at the discolourations of dispersing dyes. One patch had scabbed over. He applied an antiseptic cream.

"Good. Japanese companies in Switzerland and France like good publicity. Sometimes pay us more not to publish." He giggled strangely.

Roman handed Shino the violet goggles. "*Eh bien, Monsieur.* Shall we let your lower regions rest? These monochromes on your chest will go *rapidement*. What is this symbol?"

In contrast to the other tattoos, the black and white vessel etched on Shino's sternum was primitive, almost modernist. The round medallion sat between his ringed nipples.

"Rice pot symbol," Shino struggled to find his words. "*Sooo*. Meaning very simple. A rice pot. *Hai*. He who eats from same pot is my brother. All *irezumi* with this tattoo are part of my *nakama*."

"A sort of men's club, *non*?"

The Japanese nodded, "*Hai*."

"You're sure you want it to go too?" Roman pointed his laser gun at the ceiling, holding fire.

Shino shook his head, meaning yes, Roman realized, "Yes, must go."

Roman set the machine depth and the laser beam set off along effortless mental grids made automatic by years of practice. *Thwack, thwack, thwack, thwack, thwack,* the flash of light and spurt of ice water plodded back and forth across Shino's rubbery breast bone.

The patient heaved a sigh of resignation. The man's muscles relaxed. They had to spend a full hour together.

"You have a family, Monsieur?"

"Mother. In Kyoto, now eighty. Her hearing is not so . . . "

Half-listening, Roman scrutinized the rice pot. Tattoos were as alive as their owners and the ink in the sub-dermis shifted with the years. The division and redivision of cells carried pigment from daughter cell to daughter cell, bleeding and blurring the colour. The once-fine lines of this perfect oval were fuzzier than Shino's more recent tattoos.

"This must be your oldest tattoo, I think, Monsieur?"

"*Hai*. Eighteen years old. *Kobun* ceremony. Drink saké at Shinto altar."

"*Kobun*?" Roman worked his ruby laser around the ancient shape. He stretched the Japanese's pectoral skin taut with his left hand, his right hand blasting the ageing symbol into tiny fragments.

"The *kobun* swears loyalty and service for life to the *oyabun*, his employer."

85

"Ah. Some sort of fraternity rite."

Roman wasn't terribly interested in Japan. Meeting Shino jarred some vague impression that the average Japanese joined his company for life and spent his vacations with fellow workers on sex holidays like a school of spawning fish.

That reminded him, Isabel was buying *sushi* for dinner more often – she worried about her cholesterol. Roman worried about farmed salmon full of dioxin and tuna drenched in mercury. He had to raise an eyebrow at any shrimp that made it all the way to the delicatessen counter of a landlocked Alpine country. Was it also true of exotic human imports landing on his treatment bed? An amusing idea ... *Thwack, thwack, thwack.*

Shino tried meditating the way Boss Takahana did before meeting other bosses, but the laser's rubber-band slap reminded him instead of naked male muscles hitting the floor, of wrestling with *oyabun* Takahana after a long day of chauffeuring the old man to shareholders' meetings and *sokaiya* shakedowns. He saw a *tatami*ed room with three low dining tables arranged in a horseshoe, the place settings scattered with cigarette ash and whisky bottles, strands of cooked noodle and crumpled paper napkins.

Shino's arms pushed back Takahana's sinewy forearms and flipped the old man right over. The party rallied and hooted. He could have hurt the Boss right there and then, even employed his uglier skills and strangled the old man in cold blood like a chicken. A few seconds away from triumph, Shino looked down at the ageing racketeer's heaving chest. The room exploded with the revellers' countdown. Shino was seconds away from besting the legendary Takahana.

At that instant, the white-faced gangster reeking of Suntory and sweat read the *giri*, or sense of obligation crossing the face of his *kobun*. The quick-witted old man absorbed Shino's force and with a lightning twist of his torso, leveraged his younger opponent's weight against him, *aikido*-style. *Thwack, thwack, thwack, thwack.* The grizzled *oyabun* sat back on his short haunches and smiled down at his "little brother". In return for *giri*, Takahana exhibited the *ninjo* compassion of a great samurai.

Roman peeled off his latex gloves. "That's it for today, Monsieur Shino."

Shino could see his *nakama* badge of loyalty to Takahana was now a neat square of swollen, diffused discolouration. Shino felt bereft, a *ronin*, a masterless samurai of days gone by, lost in this sombre small city. He had never lived as an adult without a master whose respect he must earn, to whom loyalty was absolute.

Roman smiled, misunderstanding Shino's rueful expression. "Black always responds well. That will feel tender. Cleanse it with hydrogen peroxide or antibiotic ointment. I see some of the yellow around the buttocks is still floating. I'll touch that up next time."

Shino twisted off his goggles. Chantal helped him sit up on the bed. His chest burned. The paper underneath him crumpled and ripped. But the unfamiliar feeling of being cared for, rather than used, overwhelmed all physical pain.

Tending for a patient's discomfort was routine for Roman. "You have Bacitracin at home? Bactroban? Chantal will bring you tea outside." He rinsed his hands with a squirt of disinfectant.

Shino scratched a spider web tattooed in his armpit. The dragon lying below the freshly treated area snarled in anger at its owner. The points of its tail spiralling around one nipple twitched with wariness. Could the animal possibly sense the deadly laser's approach?

9

"These salads are so healthy, they disgust me."

Carlos shovelled *salade de printemps* around the industrial-weight plate. Carrot sticks, alfalfa sprouts and vine-ripened tomato swished through low-fat dressing. The main canteen of the WHO, or OMS in French, with its vaulted ceiling and tasteful potted palms was emptying out. Plastic chairs scraped back, trays of congealing sole croquettes smashed into each other on the kitchen conveyor. Sometimes the canteen basked under its glass-enclosed atrium like a vast sun-room promising relief for every ailment, but today rain drummed down on the roof over Isabel and her slouching Brazilian colleague.

She watched Carlos fidget, knowing if he hadn't been sitting in the heart of the WHO, he would have lit up a Gitane before she'd even finished her prim cottage cheese.

"Try the vegetarian lasagne next time."

"I'm sick of vegetarian anything," he growled.

"The lamb curry was pretty good yesterday, a trifle fatty."

"A trifle nauseating." Carlos mimicked her accent.

"Quite. You skipped the 'non-visible programme' meeting."

"No doubt also a trifle nauseating." Carlos shoved his tray to the far side of the long table. "I avoid those meetings like the proverbial plague, of which we have so many these days. I doubt I was missed ... " He glanced at her quickly, huge brown eyes filling with hope. "Was I missed?"

"Sorry."

"Hmmph. Nobody asked, where's Carlos with those Brazilian leprosy stats? Nobody asked about last week's meeting in

Rio to introduce five thousand municipal secretaries to our technical tools kit?"

"Not in so many words," Isabel hedged.

Carlos's scowl forced her to break cover.

"I don't recall your name coming up."

The two leprosy experts sat in dour silence, until Isabel's frustration got the better of her. "Even when Frank argued that just a little more support for resistance research and public health training would get us off the table three years early." Frank's defence of their department – its priorities and needs – weakened with each passing week.

Undiluted cynicism washed over Carlos's sallow features. "Why do we bother, Isabel? Bill Gates gives $200 million to malaria? Do we get a share? A tiny cut? *Poco* mosquito bite?"

"Malaria has chloroquine resistance going for it. A comeback disease, ergo more dead, ergo more money."

"Ergo, should we let leprosy make a comeback? Breed a resistant strain? You think I'm *loco*?" Carlos ran his fingers through his mop of unwashed chestnut curls.

"Carlos, I'm happy we stay under radar. Everybody scrutinizes the big diseases. Even if we get elimination on time, let's not look too successful or the NGOs will be right, everyone will cut their budgets and we'll look like fools. We need another twenty years of follow-up to global eradication."

"I wouldn't mind a little scrutiny now and then. You never get discouraged? Working eight days a week – dissemination, field trips, specialized NGOs coddling their stupid, stupid disease?" He fiddled with a surreptitious cigarette hidden under the table and watched her finish her watery crème caramel in its indestructible glass saucer.

Carlos rattled on, "I know why I do it – custody to Carmen, three kids at the International School," he ticked off the costs of his estranged litter – "plus something called *solfège* for which I pay five hundreds francs each semester. At least once a week, I ask Jaime, 'What the hell is this *solfège*?' And Jaime bangs on the table like this," at which Carlos clamped his lips over his unlit cigarette and banged on the table with his silverware, "*uno, dos, tres, uno, dos, tres, uno, dos, tres.*"

Neighbours looked up from their espresso dregs to watch Carlos Campagna drumming out his six-year-old's rhythm homework. Isabel burst into giggles.

Carlos improvised more Gene Krupa until a Haitian waitress swung her heavy frame from behind the cash register and personally extracted the knife and fork from his fist.

"So that's how to get service here," Carlos mugged at the retreating matron. "Now why regret my divorce when I can make you laugh so beautifully? Carmen did nothing but complain."

Isabel turned schoolmarm. "Because you still love her." She recalled a bird-like South American in flapping mules and a short skirt ushering three dark-haired urchins down the aisle of a WHO gala.

Carlos sneered. "Love, love, what is that?"

"Well, Roman looks Italian like his father, but he takes after his Swiss mother."

Carlos stared, "So?"

"So in the kitchen, I'm coping with an invisible mother-in-law, with his old-fashioned Swiss side. He can't recognize things right under his nose if he's not expecting them in his Swiss context, while things I hardly notice can obsess him. Like the order of the kitchen knives in that little block thingie. One out of place and he loses his temper, treats me like I'm thick or something. He throws a wobbly when he realizes I simply don't care −"

Carlos gazed at her through blood-shot eyes. "We were talking about love."

"Well," Isabel struggled, "I mean it's love that I've stayed married to such a control freak for eighteen years, isn't it?" She ruminated out loud, "Perhaps his work makes him worse, you know, because everything's measured in millimetres of pulses and micro layers of skin depth?"

Carlos shook his head. "How banal. English blood. That's

not love, that's tolerance. No passion. I need more. Does Roman love you because you rinse out your toothbrush better than his previous girlfriends?"

"I really wouldn't know, Carlos. Look where your hot blood landed you. The Swedish journalist? The Nicaraguan nursing administrator? At least Roman and I have been faithful for donkey's years. It wouldn't work if I couldn't trust him. I have to, travelling most of the time."

Carlos rolled his eyes. "Lucky you." He lit his Gitane as they crossed the frost-bitten parking lot. "Okay, but take a warning. OMS officially stands for *Organization Mondiale de Santé*, but these days it might as well mean *Organization Ménage Séparé*." Having played his oracular trump, Carlos loped ahead of her to their lair in Building L, home of contagious diseases.

Ménage séparé. Separated households, broken families, ugly divorces. Yes, the WHO was the global bastion of marital misfortune. She knew how lucky she was.

"I will have no regrets. Sex will be better as a woman," M Courtois sighed.

Roman demurred, "*Oui, Madame*."

"I'll just get – carried away in his arms. Whoever it is. I'll just let myself go, *non*?" Some months ago, this elegant middle-aged Genevan had been referred to Roman Micheli for massive depilation in preparation for his new life as *Madame*. Chantal's dossier tab read, "Courtois, Pierre/Patricia."

Yesterday, Chantal had thoroughly waxed the hair off his upper shoulders. This morning Lise massaged a black carbon solution into his thick follicles. Nothing was going to re-sculpt Madame's muscles into sylph-like curves, but at least the hairy thicket would be dealt with *en permanence*.

"Wipe," Roman signalled Lise. She swiped a soft sterilized cloth across the patient's flabby back.

"Ahhhhh," sighed Courtois. "I thought it would be more painful than that. The waxing was worse."

"We haven't started yet. Please just relax."

Courtois's mouth made a small "oh". He came from another of the Vielle Ville's "old families", and was accustomed to people who found his opinions interesting without fail. Downcast that neither the doctor nor assistant joined his ruminations about sex as a man or a woman, he thrust his chin back into the treatment pillow.

"Could you place your arm, like this? Just so ... missed here," Roman indicated an overlooked strip of solution. Lise worked in silence, concentrating on each square centimetre of freckled skin.

Roman checked the setting on the Q-switched Nd:YAG, and handed Courtois his goggles. The treatment began, working the centime-sized spotlight at the black lotion. A crackling sound, like a bug hitting a light bulb, made Courtois twitch. The disabled hair roots detached as Lise wiped in Roman's wake. Courtois's shoulders emerged, strip by strip, smooth and hairless.

Chantal had scheduled a whole hour for Courtois. The gentleman's amber cologne mixed with the smell of nervous sweat. Roman's mind wandered as he worked up and down.

Was sex better as a woman or a man? Did Isabel enjoy it more than Roman? Half his thoughts were on the skin stretched under his laser, but half his mind wandered to Isabel's soft thighs opening for his familiar entry.

Where were Isabel's thoughts during love-making? He, the middle-aged Roman, listened and smelled. He liked to look at his wife's tender spots. As a young man experimenting a bit on a tiny allowance and even less time, he imagined himself comparatively abandoned – a master, if not of outright ecstasy – of a physical release that was natural and good for the body. Yes, sex for Roman was healthy and relaxing. It was like coming home after a long storm, a wearying hunt.

Isabel was absent, pre-occupied, even frigid with her focus on work, that is, until the decision for sex was made. When it was over, the memory of her enthusiastic, almost sporty surrender was forgotten. Her energetic efficiency at sex had first frightened Roman, challenged and excited him, and at the same time, left him wondering now in his early forties, whether there wasn't a gentler and deeper kind of love-making. But was it necessary to be a woman to experience that? He was aware of many kinds of sexual thrall – states of subjugation or submission to overwhelming drives. As a doctor who'd studied psychology until it was textbook rote, such surrenders hadn't personally interested him. What passions, confusion, discord or desire drove the sixty-year old Courtois into signing up for total excision of his manhood and painful cosmetic follow-ups to end up a mere imitation woman?

Roman winced at the thought of squeezing his own feet into Courtois's handmade crocodile heels, size 44, aligned under the stool in the changing corner. The laser zapped on and on, as if on auto-pilot, and Chantal came and went, attending to other patients and calls, passing on instructions to Lise. A rare break of sun through Geneva's December fog blanket moved across the slatted blinds and crossed the wall until, arms aching, Roman stood upright. He surveyed the swathe of Courtois's finished dorsal terrain, gleaming pink and moist.

"*Monsieur. Pardonnez-moi*, we've only got the hairs in the active stage. Some are resting, others are falling out." Roman waved his hand in the direction of the hairs in transit some-where towards St Pierre Cathedral up the hill. "We'll see what is remaining as the waxed hairs grow in – "

"More of this?" Courtois's temples were now dotted with sweat, his expression white from endurance.

"I explained, you'll need at least two more sessions to remove the remaining hairs. Expect a little inflammation around the follicles. Lise will give you some steroid cream."

Courtois twisted his heavy torso, with its newly inflamed breasts, to survey his silky shoulders.

"*C'est beau*," he marvelled.

"It is so nice when the patient is satisfied," Roman re-sponded. "Not every treatment offers such immediate results. Unfortunately, you'll find your facial hair is more stubborn.

We will see you again in six weeks."

With this reprieve, the affable Courtois regained some of his *joie de vivre* until he bumped his head on the overhead spotlight. "Oufff," his hand shot up to test the bruise on his dripping scalp. He towered over Roman by at least seven inches.

The laser machine hummed in the corner. Still rubbing his forehead, the good-natured man-woman disappeared behind the curtain to pull on his tights and carefully ease his bra over the depilated skin. He chattered, "I have a dinner rendezvous on Saturday next with the most amazing new man. Works for *La Banque Pictet*. Could I go strapless by then? Just a little bolero to hide the biceps."

"You will be a vision, *Madame, sans doute*," Lise tittered. Roman raised a warning eyebrow at the girl and calmly updated Courtois's file with copies for his surgeon and general practitioner, and *mon Dieu*, a gynaecologist newly-hitched to Courtois's medical parade.

"Madame Olivier is ready in the next room," Chantal interrupted. "And the Studer child and mother are here early. I'll pull out the toy box."

"I'll go and mix your cream, Madame," Lise told the towering figure emerging in a pink wool suit.

Roman took a deep breath. Courtois extended an enormous paw glittering with a fresh manicure in metallic lavender. "*Merci, Docteur Micheli*. With me you are always the complete professional."

"*Mais bien sûr, Madame*, that goes without saying."

Courtois shook his head. "Geneva has changed, Doctor, and I am sorry to say that the decencies of mutual respect can no longer be taken for granted. *À la prochaine*."

Isabel often complained Roman's fixations threatened to turn him into a bore. He wasn't obsessive, Roman protested to himself, locking up the clinic for the night. On the street the homeward bound were bent over double against a bitter wind riding the lake's rippling surface and rolling along the pavement. Shivering commuters crammed the trams heading out to bohemian Carouge. Expensive cars forced their clotted progression eastwards to the sanctuary of hillside villas in Cologny. The Pâquis streetwalkers were rising from naps for a quick *goûter* before the clubs opened. Roman turned his collar up and strode past the gleaming display of Charles Jourdan shoes and headed up the steep blocks towards the Old Town.

He was not obsessive, *non*, *non*. Accuracy, precision, caution, weren't they the bedrock of a doctor's practice? For the second time in a row, he found Lise had misplaced the Studer child's psoriasis records. She must be more careful. Precise. Perhaps there was a touch of the father's military backbone running down the son's spine. There were better or worse ways to do things, proper methods worked out. Why call them into question?

And things that weren't correct should be put right. Things that weren't good should be bettered.

Roman always noticed small things out of place – like that public bike provided by the city elders propped on the rack by a thoughtless borrower instead of slotted in between the steel railings at the entrance to the Mont Blanc car park. Or those tattered yellow flyers for the Knie Circus left flapping around the base of the trash bin. The Knie had moved to Lausanne two weeks ago.

If told a treatment "worked", Roman wasn't satisfied without the details. He wanted to know why, before he used it on a patient. Immunologists would put Roman's chronic urticaria patients with high counts of thyroid antibodies on synthetic hormone – and hope for the best. *Why?* he asked the endocrinologists, why does it work for this patient, but not for the other?

Roman passed a Gypsy in frayed jeans and a worn denim shirt under his jacket sawing away at a dark red violin. A few coins sat inside his case "*pour encourager les autres*". The Vivaldi player who'd serenaded passers-by when Roman had stumbled into Mira Sullivan was nowhere to be seen. Some arm-twisting over choice kerbside prime property had no doubt transpired between the ruthless busking schools of Romanian and Ukrainian string-playing.

For example – was it healthy that the Sullivan girl refused treatment? Were there any recent studies of people who looked to their malformation for reassurance or identity? Roman's mind tussled with the girl's childish arguments of gratitude for her talent, her mother's love – all that rubbish. He wasn't convinced. Had that spooky Hawthorne tale been translated into French? Yes, subconscious fear was a likelier explanation than gratitude. Perhaps she guarded her portion of bad luck as a talisman against more misfortune. Surely her birth defect was a sufficient allotment of unhappiness? He'd read case studies on the psychology of the birthmark – he must fish them out of his files.

His feet slid a little on the smooth cobblestones of chemin Perron and he braced himself against the wind slowing his progress uphill to St Pierre's Romanesque arches. With raw breath, he reached the ancient wall of the cathedral plaza and paused. Would Col Sullivan leave things as they stood? Did the doting father have no influence on the girl whatsoever?

Roman had to guess at the parent-child relationship. His thoughts veered off again to that imaginary offspring, that youth who resembled himself. He tried to imagine a teenager with face mottled and unsightly. Would Roman reassure his own child that all was well enough left alone? Tell him looks didn't matter, what counted was brains, charm, virtue? Or would he urge him to remove it, insist that the path of his young life could be made easier, should be put "right"?

He passed the lawyer's office on the ground floor of their building and trudged up the heavy granite stairs, passing the lawyer's private apartments and the German banker's lacquered front door. When he turned the key in his own lock, he couldn't remember for a moment whether Isabel was away on mission or not. He crossed the sitting room at the end of the long book-lined entrance corridor to find Isabel working at the table. Where a hot dinner was no doubt waiting in the dining rooms beneath their floor, Isabel had scattered a rainbow of paper over every inch of varnished oak. Their greeting was perfunctory but not indifferent. Roman raised his eyebrows at the mess.

"We're in trouble," Isabel announced. "Right here in black and white."

"Pink and green," Roman corrected her, flipping a finger through the mess, "and yellow."

"It's not funny, Roman. This evaluation team must've injected their interviewees full of truth serum. Look! Their findings! – laying out all our bickering with the private leprosy groups in public! In print! On the internet! Even the fallout with the International Leprosy crowd. Here – just look at this paragraph. It's from a Reuters interview."

She thrust a page at Roman, still wearing his raincoat.

"*Cara*, did you ever hear of a leper who refused to be cured?" Spaghetti curled around his ankles. Isabel had forgotten to feed him.

His wife looked up, a finger marking her place on the page. "Please say leprosy patients, not lepers. Never. Unthinkable. Even if he didn't care that his toes were falling off, his family would object to the smell. Why did the Book of Job call it the Firstborn of Death? Because you're not just sick, you're decomposing right under everybody's nose –"

He cut her off with a mock gesture of thanks and went into the kitchen to put water on the boil. The doorway framed Isabel's coppery head catching the low lamplight. The russet glow against the burgundy chair upholstery, the evening darkening all around her – all those rich jewel tones – reminded Roman of the apostles that catch the rays of dusk through a stained glass window or El Greco's spotlight of divine illumination on Saint Peter ascending from the darkness.

As he watched his wife that night, Roman suffered a premonition that this image of her bowed head would return to him later. He stored the shimmering reflections to memory against a long separation. This eerie foresight shook his practical soul. He set about dicing plum tomatoes into geometric perfection.

To see Isabel under such pressure pained Roman. If bureaucratic sabotage frayed the leprosy campaign, Isabel herself might unravel. He understood better than anyone the nature of the private crusade that had set the bookish English girl-child in woolly knee-socks on her path to an office at WHO headquarters. By no coincidence had Isabel selected the Firstborn of Death as a foe worthy of her metal; a millennial disease so terrifying it had spawned an offspring disease of its own for psychiatrists – leprophobia – the irrational fear of leprosy.

Oui, his beloved Isabel was as devoted to her elimination target as to a battle campaign.

Listening to the indignant muttering outside the kitchen, Roman thought better of introducing any small talk of his own. He didn't air his professional frustration with the Sullivan girl's obstinacy. A healthy girl with a flush of purple down one side of her face was no big deal. You needed a lot to impress Dr Hanford – the official elimination of leprosy in all of Bangladesh or maybe three dozen new motorbikes for the Kothara Hospital's outreach programme.

They ate by the fireside – the table was still serving as Leprosy Central – after which Isabel spent much of the night reviewing the disastrous "independent evaluation" and jotting notes for an emergency conference call scheduled for tomorrow by Frank Norton to WHO regional officers.

Roman spent his following day less dramatically than Isabel. He shuttled between precancerous lesions, rosaceas and psoriasis, varicosities and photo-ageing. For once, the African diplomat arrived punctually, only to be told that his residual scarring was untreatable. On a better afternoon Roman might have been intrigued by a new referral of undiagnosable rash. Today he brooded, restless and irritable. Could he admit to himself that he enjoyed the god-like power he had over all of these souls and that the thought of one straying American sheep in a mulberry muffler drove him crazy? All day he saw the reception counter lined with other patients desperate for help, relief, and a return to the best possible option. And if sometimes they sought him out for the wrong reasons – didn't his misguided Siamese pray to the Refrigerator God for a downpour of mice? – they sought him nonetheless.

Roman fought off the temptation of hubris. At best, his was a pedestrian divinity that stopped short at the epidermal layers. Even when the reflections of Original Sin or the traces of venial peccadilloes lay bared for his sideward glance while he jotted down notes or scrubbed his hands, his laser couldn't penetrate deeper than the body's surface. Many a night he laid his head on the starched linen pillow next to Isabel and murmured half in wonder, "They bring me their skin problems, but want me to change their life."

Of course anyone could see that Mme Olivier would keep smoking no matter what; that after laser excision of her crusting, black mole, Mme Gistaing would head straight back to the chaises longues of Biarritz to roast more incipient basal cell carcinomas; that little Mlle Gruber's psoriasis was triggered by her domineering mother, not her baccalaureate exams. Causes were harder to remove than keratoses.

"I can't laser their lives clean," he would sigh to Isabel.

"More likely they should just get a life," she snorted and rolled over to sleep, thinking of her own patients, hundreds of thousands shivering in shacks and rice paddies from terror of their lesions, nodules and crippled muscles.

Yes, there were limits to what Roman could do. However, the Sullivan girl's medieval tryst with Gypsy fatalism overrode the obvious, easiest course – that offended every assumption of Roman's training! He had said that the patient was free to leave well enough alone, but did he really believe it?

As the dark nights crawled towards Christmas, he lay awake, revisiting this particular birthmark behind his closed eyes. He measured it again, considered the depth of colour in heat and wind, recalled the slight thickening of the epidermis. It would take at least eighteen months to lighten it, but that alone might transform her future. Yes, he thought, drifting off at last to the cadenzas of her fiery violin, the wrist bending upwards, the flexible perpendicular that kept the bow pointing heavenward, that taut, mounting energy – *oui*, this time, Roman was convinced he could change a patient's whole life.

Alone and locking up his private office in the season's early nightfall, Roman fished through Chantal's curtain of manila folders suspended in an open closet behind the reception counter. He found no "Sullivan" under "S" recording his odd consultation with the lumbering military man. Chantal's abandoned computer screen saver blinked like a seeing eye in the subdued hush of the waiting room. The fish tank bubbled turquoise at the opposite end. Roman's casual perusal of the labels became a careful search, then a file-by-file hunt, to no avail.

He smiled at his own stupidity. *Mais oui*, there was no record because there was no patient.

Roman dug out the Geneva telephone directory and looked up "Mission to the United Nations of the United States of America." He dialled the number and waited. After two rings an American voice asked, "US Mission, how may I help you?"

Roman hesitated, riffling the edge of the thick volume with his thumb.

The voice repeated, "May I help you?"

"Colonel Sullivan, please?"

10

"Not even one day's notice? Is that part of America's latest security precautions?" How irritating that Roman should accept a diplomatic invitation in less than an hour! Redolent with aftershave, he was already relaxing on their sleek suede sofa out in the living room. She emerged wearing her loose travel suit, just back from the dry cleaners. She'd been keeping it fresh for her flight to London on Monday.

"There, I'm ready." She straightened her elastic waistband and read his nuanced reserve. "You're not happy."

He looked her plain outfit up and down. "*Non, non, cara,* you look fine."

"My beige wool has a coffee stain."

"The green suit with golden threads?"

"On an ordinary Wednesday night? I'd look like a walking Christmas tree."

Marriage offered its silent smoke signals of peace or hostility and a row between such good friends could simmer or die on the strength of the oxygen one fed it. Roman enjoyed an Italian's innate sense of style and a Genevan's preference for sober attire. Unfortunately, Isabel was one of those English-women who was voluptuous with her clothes off but would never cut a "*bella figura*" when dressed. Her utilitarian dress sense came from generations of Westcott and Earnshaw women who needed sensible shoes that wouldn't fall apart in monsoons and Hanford men whose tweeds were made-to-order in youth, then worn for decades until they drooped loyally off osteo-porific shoulders stooping toward the deathbed.

Roman drove with the commuter flow across the Mont Blanc bridge, and turned along the quai du Mont-Blanc for the route de Lausanne and out of the city. Isabel stared across the water as if regretting already the distance between their Saab and the Vieille Ville. Motorcycles dodged in and out of the lanes. Behind thick windscreens tired women mouthed into mobiles their instructions for microwaving dinner.

The colourful neon letters that rimmed the rooftops lining the left bank bounced off the surface of the dark lake in primary colours: Pictet et Cie, Rolex, HongKong and Shanghai Banking Corp. Isabel brushed and twisted her hair into a tortoiseshell clasp at the back of her head and pulled a few tendrils loose to attempt a casual-dressy look. Bollocks, she'd forgotten earrings. Her nails needed varnish. She applied lipstick in the neon reflections.

"Anyway, what's so frightfully important about this dinner? We don't know anyone at the US Mission. Roman, you don't even like Americans."

He fixed his eyes on the bumper ahead. "I don't know why you say that. I made lots of American friends."

"In America. Student life doesn't count. We hardly left the hospital. We don't have a single American friend in Geneva."

Roman shrugged. "Anyway, it was a different America then. The country changed, not me. I don't want to talk politics now –"

He remembered Jonathan taking a post-midnight dash on a bet across the darkly threatening street to a Korean deli. The muggers didn't get him, to the laughing relief of the staff. A nurse had been raped outside that deli a week before.

"So, who invited us? A Mr Sullivan?"

"Colonel. The father of ... a patient."

"You never socialize with patients."

"Well, not exactly a patient. You'll see."

"I don't see at all. Why are we going?" Isabel was desperate to revise her response to the evaluation criticisms before next week's conference on advanced diagnostics at the London

School of Hygiene and Tropical Medicine. She was to moderate one of the panels. She needed to make at least three follow-up phone calls; perhaps the American residence had a sound-proof bathroom nicely tucked away down some corridor. What a waste of time – an entire evening spent with people she'd never see again and surely would never want to see again. Would anyone miss the English doctor if she spent a penny for, say, forty-five minutes?

They rolled along the lake road following the cavalcade of working weary and reached Crans. Roman checked his instructions and slowed until he spotted the discreet walls and heavily-guarded gate of the Permanent Representative's villa.

The Michelis' American experience had been limited to a dilapidated, debt-ridden pre-Giuliani New York, a concentrated dose of student camaraderie, cheap meals, and the odd blast at a jazz club. They'd survived a few blurry years on caffeine, diet pills and other experiments in sleeplessness. Their "America" stretched between Isabel's cheap and narrow studio and Columbia Presbyterian Hospital. The faltering city, itself not in the best of health, had welcomed them, educated and exploited them, turning them into a single, shared identity – doctor. At least they harboured a grateful affection for that.

The Michelis now entered the Swiss enclave of a different America, armoured in fear. The cranky Isabel noted with satisfaction that still outside the gates Roman was commanded to pull his car over by four Swiss soldiers. They waited for the ear pieces and walkie-talkies of the American guards inside the walled and barbed wire perimeter to spring into excessively polite and efficient routine; Roman handed over his driver's licence, name card, and a "photo ID", while the host country subjected his car to a rip-roaring, mat-lifting search of the Saab's back seats and boot.

"I thought we were guests, not suspects," Isabel quipped as Roman slid back into the driver's seat. "What would have happened if your Colonel had left us off the invitation list? Full body search? Fingerprinting? A nice friendly frisking spread-eagled against the wall?"

Roman endured her jibes in patient silence. He drove around the majestic curves of a landscaped driveway until sighting a large building overlooking a lakefront lawn. A trim aide wearing a dark suit waved a pair of ping-pong paddles to guide their parking with the frenzy of an airport ground staffer directing a B52 landing.

A smiling Filipino took their coats, directed them to the guest book, then showed Isabel the powder room. It was commodious enough for whole hours of useful telephoning.

Inside the door of the gargantuan sitting room, Ambassador George Kress-Parker greeted Roman as warmly as if the name Micheli stood at the top of his guest list. The diplomat was a familiar figure to many Genevans, not least because he was a Southern black topping six-foot-four of ostentatiously low-key deportment. His mere appearance connoted democracy, equal opportunity, and post-colonialism to enthusiasts. To the more cynical, his noncommittal, articulate charm fed suspicions of a polished mediocrity. Around the Palais des Nations, the serene Kress-Parker stood apart from the nervously jovial Africans in their French-cut double-breasted suits. While those elites animated cocktails with energetic hand gestures and vividly dressed wives, Kress-Parker travelled solo with imperial ease.

The orange juice looked reconstituted and the California red was no doubt going to remain on offer all evening. Clutching a tepid ginger ale and managing a fixed smile, Isabel returned from reconnoitering the powder room and observed their host introducing Roman to his guests of honour. Meanwhile, she herself was quickly relegated to the care of the birdlike Elsie, an Englishwoman assigned to look after her fellow country-woman. She noticed with irritation that Roman had wangled a flute of champagne.

"The official line is that the Ambassador is a political appointee," Elsie whispered to Isabel, "but Trevor says he actually came up through intelligence channels."

"American Intelligence? Didn't someone once call that an oxymoron?" Isabel joked drily over the tinkling hubbub, but Elsie shook her head, shocked, "Well, no, no, Trevor insists he is really quite bright ... "

Isabel longed for a proper gin and tonic but couldn't extract herself from Elsie's solicitous care. Roman looked pinned down in front of the grand piano by Kress-Parker's deputy, his curiosity about the Geneva laser specialist piqued by Col Sullivan's last-minute insistence the Micheli couple be invited. Other guests were filing in, so the junior diplomat excused himself from this "fascinating cram course" in lasers. A large hand on Roman's shoulder announced the appearance of the Colonel. Roman glanced over the now-familiar looming shoulder in search of the Sullivan daughter.

"So glad you could make it, Doctor. Your wife still freshening up? Let me show you around." A dining room of tennis court proportions beckoned through an arch leading off the reception room. Roman met some two dozen various diplomats, wives and assorted "regulars" assembled for an ordinary week night in the diplomatic calendar. Isabel was far beyond reach, sequestered with a mousy woman in pearls at the French windows leading to the lakeshore.

Roman caught names and shook hands. The Sullivan daughter seemed not of the party. He felt his shoulders drop an inch. The room's proportions, which had struck him as vast and portentous only minutes ago, now seemed banal and cramped. The paintings on the wall were forgettable abstracts, a cut above Holiday Inn art. The beige damask upholstery and the potted plants stood at attention.

Isabel sat next to Col Sullivan during dinner. The cold terrine in aspic with its soggy parsley came and went. The obligatory salmon course was almost finished before the Colonel got into his stride.

"Here's my theory, Missus Micheli – "

"Actually, I prefer Doctor Hanford – "

"Even better! You don't mind my talking to you about it?

Even though it's your husband I've set my hopes on?"

"Well, his practice doesn't involve me, you know. I work for the World Health – "

"I've always loved Mira as if she were my own. No question about that, even though it was my wife that found her at the orphanage. We talked about it a lot, of course. I was all for it, especially if it would make Lorraine happy. She needed something to do, someone to love while I was busy with postings all over. You know how that is, I guess – "

"Actually, I do," Isabel persisted. "I work in leprosy policy at the World Health – "

"You do now?" The Colonel nodded. "Well, it was Lorraine who picked up on this music thing, built the child's confidence up, so to speak, getting her past the disfigurement – "

"Disfigurement?"

"I think that Mira's stubbornness is somehow linked to her mother."

"Oh, I see," Isabel sliced her potato into minuscule discs. What was he talking about?

"My Lorraine always insisted she work hard, not make excuses for her face, get good grades. Real strong mother-love, the one thing that Mira needed. I reckon she associates the most important love she ever knew with how she looks – "

"Yes, I think I follow – " Isabel pushed her salmon bits through the lemon caper sauce.

"But if this goes on, she'll never really mature, you know? I'm worried she'll always be a little girl in a woman's body, because everybody feels sorry for her, see? Now that wouldn't be healthy, would it? Might have even spoiled her in a way." The Colonel took a large draught of his iced water.

Isabel grasped at this passing straw, "Is she spoiled?"

The Colonel looked up from his tumbler. "Oh, Mrs Micheli, don't think I don't love my daughter. I've loved her from the moment they put that poor little purple-faced girl in my arms and said she was mine. Of course, Mira's not consciously selfish. We never indulged the child."

Isabel brightened. "I work with children quite a bit. It's always the smile that gets to me – "

He sighed, "Now Lorraine's gone – "

"Oh, I'm sorry – " Not to mention bewildered, Isabel thought.

"Well, she died a couple of years ago. Anyway, somehow, it's all linked up, only I just don't know quite how."

"You've talked it over with your little girl?"

"Well, sure. When your husband rang me up this afternoon – "

The guilty party Roman was safely beyond Isabel's reach at the opposite corner of this table as vast as Texas. He was chatting happily in Italian with a woman who, if Isabel had got the high-speed introductions right, was the wife of a Swiss Foreign Ministry officer. She saw with chagrin the Italian woman's chic layered haircut, the old-rose bouclé suit with its fashionable fringe.

When had Roman acquired that distinguished, suave, extremely irritating poise? He was only a few years younger than Isabel, but looked far, far more attractive tonight than she herself. She'd heard warnings – had it happened to the Michelis? She didn't need a mirror to reflect such an annoying cliché, but there it was. Most of the time, she only noticed the changing shades of Roman, fleeting layers of "the older man" overlaying the short, shy, fellow medical resident – like transparent onion skin she could always see through. While this elegant doctor in a well-cut suit, his black hair brushed back from an intelligent brow, charming his dinner partner with twinkling black eyes – this person was an opaque, provocative stranger. It was Wednesday, after all, and soon, surely by eleven, everyone should be tucked up in bed. Nevertheless, Isabel was nagged by a lust running through her tired body, lust for her own partner of twenty years. On a week night, imagine.

She scraped the last of the mango sorbet off her plate and strategized how to place those overseas calls. The clinking cocktail glasses being cleared away from the room behind them signalled Act Three of the tedious evening.

"We're going to have a little concert, which we hope will make up for our plain American cooking," Kress-Parker joked. "First I'd like to offer a few comments while they're getting things ready next door." The American graced his way through obligatory thanks to the ministry couple visiting from Berne and a "special" welcome for the newly-arrived negotiatior for the International Labour Organization.

Toasts downed, the group discovered the various sofas and armchairs of the reception room rearranged into a mini-concert setting. A flushed Roman joined Isabel at the end of the second row.

"Do you think I could slip out now?"

"It would be very rude," he retorted.

A resentful Isabel mentally ticked off the catch-up phoning she would now have to do from her office tomorrow – Delhi first thing, and South America in the late afternoon. Just to listen to some little kid scrape away on her fiddle.

A scowling young man emerged from a book-lined study that served as backstage. An older blonde in a beaded blouse and black slacks with a little folder of music followed him. The two of them settled on the piano bench and waited. The woman grinned a mouthful of scraggly teeth at Col Sullivan. She couldn't be American, Isabel pouted. They don't let you graduate from an American high school with a bite like that. They'd report your parents for child neglect. Not far from her, the Colonel sat twisting his hands, his heavy torso at the very edge of a gilt chair too flimsy for his bulk.

A hush of anticipation settled over the group. Isabel's watch read exactly ten o'clock. Despite the informality of menu and dress, with what invisible precision Kress-Parker conducted his evenings! A violinist entered the room and stopped only a few feet from Isabel's chair.

Isabel saw immediately that the young brunette's complexion, flawless on the right side, was discoloured on the left by a plum birthmark running over her cheek to the upper-part of her throat. This was the Sullivan child? Some light powder dulled the unsightly shine. She wore her thick curls fastened at the nape of her neck with a sequinned white square of Indian cotton to match a white crepe jacket with gossamer sleeves like wings covering her slender arms. Her matching trousers swam dangerously in a pool around her ankles. Isabel was surprised the girl didn't trip over their diaphanous hem.

The elastic of Isabel's waistband had twisted over again. She'd eaten too much, too fast, too nervously. The string player's white get-up triggered thoughts of dry cleaning. Was there time before the London flight to run her black trouser suit through the shop? There was never enough time for anything at all. She glanced at Roman but he was staring rather idiotically at the musical trio. He didn't drink much on week nights, but Parker's mediocre wine had given Roman's tawny skin a post-prandial glow. Well, he'd been so keen on this evening, let the poor boy enjoy himself.

There were a few polite coughs, some foot-shuffling. The violin was tuned to the piano, string by string. The girl's dark brows rippled with concentration as she plucked once or twice very gently, while her right hand fiddled with the tuning pegs. Lord, why didn't she do all this while we were having dinner? Isabel thought it a cheap sort of stage business to enhance the suspense. She glanced down the row at the heavy Sullivan in his ill-fitting suit so uncomfortable on his twee chair.

At last, Kress-Parker straightened his jacket and beamed at his guests. "I suspect many of you know already, despite the natural modesty of my colleague here, that his daughter Mira just won first prize in a major violin contest – " polite applause, " – so before some greedy impresario sweeps her off," he glanced at a note cupped in his palm, "Mira's going to favour us tonight with *The Fantasy* for solo violin with piano accompaniment from Bizet's *Carmen*. This arrangement is by the German composer Franz Waxman, who emigrated to the United States in 1934."

Isabel braced herself defensively, a tone-deaf wanderer in enemy territory. She really would try to listen for once. Focusing with impatience on the violin player placing instrument to shoulder, Isabel nearly fell off her seat when the pianist unexpectedly bolted into the score, crashing into twelve bars of the *Toreador's March* before Mira Sullivan even touched bow to string. A few bars of demonic piano pounding followed. Before Isabel could burst into horrified giggles, the violinist dived after the piano, racing her hands up the violin's fingerboard and down again.

Well, she'd tried. Isabel surrendered to ennui and headache. Clearly this game of virtuoso tag was the order of the evening; the piano flailed away at the familiar themes and the girl threw herself, body and soul, into the doomed character of the seductive Gypsy cigar girl, frowning with the slow discovery of death in her fateful cards, then the demands of what quickly became a high-wire piece, sometimes at various points plucking at the strings with her left hand – the left hand? Could that be right? – even as the bow played away on other strings. Then followed what to Isabel looked like nothing more than pretty determined sawing. The violin trilled at high notes like a tin whistle. The girl plucked her punctuation marks at all the predictable moments.

The pianist's pages flipped wildly under Isabel's dizzied gaze. How much had *she* drunk? How many times had her glass been refilled over dinner? Isabel's stomach turned queasy. Had the salmon been all right? Perhaps it was just motion sickness – virtuoso vertigo. She tried to count her alcohol intake through a tornado of noise as the Sullivan girl's hand swept up and down the violin so fast there wasn't a hope in Hell of actually catching her playing something so *ordinary* as a single note. This German Waxperson had left nothing of the notorious cigar girl's habenera unadorned. Where a few notes had carried the tune, there seemed to be twelve, no – sixteen – oh *dozens* – the transparent sleeves whisked around in all directions.

Frankly, music had never been Isabel's thing. Why hadn't

Roman warned her? The violinist was departing from the realm of after-dinner entertainment to imitate the death-throes of some demented moth. Again Isabel turned to Roman for some sympathetic gesture, but he was staring straight ahead, wearing a rather imbecilic expression.

Finally, with a triumphant crash of chords and bow, the show was blessedly over. Isabel's mouth dropped open with relief. She checked the time on her mobile. The ordeal had lasted only ten and a half minutes. There was much applause and congratulations for the violinist and a few courteous pats for the piano team, but Kress-Parker stood up to play the girl's protective champion before anyone could suggest an encore. For that alone, Isabel loved her host.

The tall man's grey gabardine arm encircled the panting violinist as if she were a child of eight. He hugged her, sweat and powder smearing all over his dark lapels, but ever the polished professional, he took no notice. Would he next wring and twist the girl, maybe rinse her out like a face flannel? Isabel looked to Roman to join her in a conspiratorial smile, but he was staring at Kress-Parker crushing the petite musician in his avuncular embrace.

What had Roman said during the drive here? That this musician was his patient? Would he laser off the birthmark? Isabel prepared to say congratulations or thank you or something appropriate to the girl's guardian or step-father – just a quick word – and then they'd slip out. Roman looked determined to talk to the young Sullivan woman before they left and there was such a gaggle around her, they'd be simply hours getting out of here. She'd better make the first move.

While waiters distributed liqueurs and coffee, Isabel lost sight of her husband between the perspiration and perfume emanating from winter suits mixed with the aroma of strong coffee and at least one cigar. There were the perfunctory handshakes with all, the exchange of cards, demitasses downed. Kress-Parker slid into position near the front door and the Filipino magically dished out the correct coats, one by one. A clock in the entry hall chimed ten-thirty.

Roman edged his car between the gates where the clean-cut aide waved them off with Boy Scout glee. "You look tired, *cara*. What did you think of the girl?"

"God, I thought it would never end," Isabel groaned. "Her father's a bit thick, but determined. And why does everybody keep calling her a child? She's a full-blown woman."

"It's a textbook port-wine stain. Her playing is *extraordinaire*, *non*?"

"Oh, that. Well, Carmen's a bit obvious these days, don't you think?" Isabel shook her hair out of its barrette and fluffed it with her fingers. "I mean all those flamenco flourishes, those – I don't know, improvizations – "

"Cadenzas – "

"Yes, well, it's pretty kitschy stuff, hmm?"

"She is the dark type. Everybody loves Carmen. Nothing too *cherché*, perfect for such a dinner."

"Yes, we weren't a terribly musical lot, starting with myself."

"I agree. Mademoiselle Sullivan was a bit wasted on the labour lawyer."

" . . . pianist was rather dishy, in an Eastern sort of way."

"She looked more French to me."

The overhead street lamps of the route du Lac lent a foreign cast to Roman's profile at the wheel.

"Darling, I think you're talking about the page-turner. The person playing the piano was a man."

Roman tried to recall the piano team. "Of course, *cara*. I must be the one who's tired."

"Just wait 'til tomorrow morning when Spaghetti starts scratching at the kitchen window."

Isabel's victorious note didn't dampen Roman's customary enjoyment of the glide back into a silent Geneva, never more so than tonight. He loved the way the mammoth neon letters on the rooftops cast their primary blues and yellows squiggling across the lake's black waters like spilling oil paints. Geneva was such a small town of three hundred thousand souls. In its expensive way, it managed to be both stubbornly staid and provincially corrupt, with pockets of bourgeois decency sandwiched between the Arab-owned hotels and cool-eyed investment banks.

As Roman drove past the Pâquis district, he imagined that even the hookers of the *Salon VIP* were safely ensconced for the evening with their various Korean trade diplomats and Russian watch buyers. A lone North African in a caftan under his ill-fitting woollen coat made his way home across the pont du Mont-Blanc. Over-lit mannequins in shop windows panto-mimed across the empty streets in vain. Roman headed for his parking space rented in a basement of the Old Town.

Tomorrow's patient list flipped through his elated mind, the morning wizardry so predictable to him, so miraculous to patients. He hesitated to share the reason for his good humour with Isabel. She sat so warm and relaxed at last, her hair loosed in soft waves, those lush, familiar breasts underneath her sturdy suit. Roman liked his wife most just like this – when there was nothing she could manage, no one to telephone, no obligations distracting her from his company in the soft leathery sanctuary. Would she understand his newfound contentment? After all, Isabel was a doctor, like himself.

What was most satisfactory was to know that human nature was so predictable, after all.

What exactly had Mira Sullivan said? Yes, she would call Chantal tomorrow. She'd promised. He'd see her Monday evening, whenever the last appointment happened to finish. In only five days, Mira Sullivan would come to his office.

11

The quiet weekend flowed ever forward under the Michelis like a river tows flotsam below its surface. Roman spent Sunday afternoon watching Italian soccer on television. Isabel scoured field reports on leprosy prevalence in their bedroom. Freezing winds swept the elevated *quartier* and drove away the last customers from the outdoor tables of La Clémence downstairs. Isabel slumped into a doze just as a rainstorm washed all remaining signs of life from the narrow streets below their apartment.

Snow fell on the slopes of the Jura as low as one thousand metres' altitude above the city. Slimy leaves stuck to the four mounted cannons opposite the Restaurant Hôtel de Ville, leaving those coarse, iron behemoths looking like dedraggled pensioners. The soggy Sabbath suspended the hibernating Michelis in preparation for the demanding new week, passing from a grey afternoon into a charcoal evening. They made a supper of cheese and fruit because even Roman didn't feel like cooking.

Isabel set off for London before dawn on Monday in her practical raincoat and last winter's knee-high boots for peace talks with yet another hostile leprosy foundation. Her commutes were so frequent that when the taxi's diesel engine rattled away at five a.m. in the wet street downstairs neither husband nor wife even bothered to measure the distance that would soon stretch between them. Their kiss was that of a professional couple pressed for time.

She marched away as if on command, her sensible carry-on

suitcase bumping its wheels behind her, leaving Roman enveloped in her wake of lemony scent, minty toothpaste and coffee breath. He heard the taxi chug off for Cointrin's slick runways.

The downpour hammered the skylight window in the corridor where Roman straightened an inky sketch knocked out of alignment by Isabel's departing shoulder. The gutters overflowed in a curtain of water dropping four storeys to the inner courtyard behind the row of old buildings. The cozy kitchen was filled with a gushing sound when Roman squeaked the window back and forth to summon his errant cat and awaken his German neighbour downstairs.

In the microwave's reflection, he caught sight of the husband Isabel had just embraced: rough stubble over an expensive dressing gown, a man more eighty-three than forty-three, an echo of his late father. This frightening phantom of the future – impossible! If that old man lurked in the wings, when would he be visible to others? Roman splashed cold water on his face and flexed his torso. Ah, there he was, brisker and alert, the vigorous vision he carried of himself, especially on such a special start to the week.

Days with Isabel assumed certain aspects – warmth, conversation, and sympathetic undemanding companionship. The many solitary weeks of her absences guaranteed Roman the obscure pleasures of the monk *manqué*; an indulgence in discipline, the zen-like calm of doing something well, the submersion of ambition into professionalism. The orderly tyrannies of the appointment book actually beckoned. Had Roman Micheli not been raised a Catholic, might he not have been reincarnated as a wandering Buddhist married only to his meditations and beads? He grinned ludicrously at the microwave and wondered how he would look with a shaved cranium.

With this overly-flattering vision of himself as a mendicant in saffron robes setting out before dawn furnished with nothing more than a begging bowl, the well-dressed, freshly-shaved Dr Roman Micheli descended the narrow streets to arrive in the gold-mirrored foyer of his building. He pressed the code that called the lift and rode to the quiet sanctuary of his multi-million franc clinic.

Fuzzy-eyed Chantal, her bare feet in rubber-soled nursing mules, had made the coffee, fed her fish, set the DVD player on mute, and fanned the morning's medical records across the counter in order of arrival. Her make-up could wait until nine when the society types took their appointments with Lise to blast away liver spots.

Roman smiled to see it was once again a Shino morning. After so many sessions made possible by strategically jumping from one gaudy limb to another, there was no doubt that Shino was his least talkative but most colourful and amiable patient ever. Roman looked up at the sound of a Japanese conversation outside the reception room. Was the always-apologetic patient early for his six-fifteen? Shino nodded to Chantal and ushered an even smaller Japanese into the clinic. The pin-striped newcomer radiated so much pent-up energy that Roman had the impression a new model of Japanese compact had motored into his premises.

Both men bowed to Roman like hinged bookends. With hands outstretched, the stranger offered up a card embossed in an elegant font, *Kazuo Ino, Consulat Général du Japon, ch. des Fins 3, le Grand-Saconnex*. His position wasn't mentioned: Roman surmised that the vertical Japanese characters on the back disclosed more information. He escorted both men into his office to the smell of fresh aftershave, lingering floor wax and sterilizing liquids. After jockeying with Shino over the choice of chairs, Kazuo Ino took the padded chair opposite Roman's desk, leaving Shino to make do with the plastic chair usually occupied by the lunch tray. With more bobbing and ducking, Kazuo and Shino waged a showdown of throat-clearing Japanese, pregnant with promise.

"Coffee?" Roman interrupted.

"Nooo, thank you," Ino sneezed out. "Doctor Micheli. Pardon please such an unannounced intrusion at the hour of dawn ... " The brisk little man spoke quite acceptable French, almost too diplomatic.

Chantal flip-flopped in bearing two sturdy mugs filled with tea, soggy bags floating on milky water. To Roman's amusement, Chantal bowed and managed to exit backwards in her thick-soled flippers. Kazuo managed a smile drenched with distaste at the liquid, and exiled his beverage to the centre of Roman's desk.

"The Japanese Consulate in Geneva handles many responsibilities that are obvious – banking and trade duties, various official matters for our commercial and tourist community ... "

Roman glanced at Shino who bore an inane grin.

" ... and we are most interested in Shino-*san*'s case."

"He's getting the most expert treatment available in Geneva, I assure – "

"We express our confidence, total and complete." Ino replied.

Roman nodded and glanced at the clock. Did the Japanese realize courtliness equalled billable consultation points?

"Doctor, Shino-*san*'s treatment will terminate in exactly which week?"

"The patient's circulation suffers from smoking side-effects, but so far the pigmentation is resolving itself satisfactorily. I estimate at least nine more months to a year at our current scheduling, which given my case load is very generous."

"Not satisfactory," Ino growled. Shino shot a worried look.

"Pardon?" Roman's eyebrows rose.

"Not satisfactory."

"Patients with much smaller tattoos normally allow at least two years. I have over eight hundred patients under my care. With such demand, the timing is our decision."

Ino exhaled hoarse displeasure. "Doctor Micheli, I must request on behalf of the Imperial Government that you proceed faster."

"That is a private matter between a patient and his practitioner."

There was an awkward pause filled only by Shino loyally tackling Chantal's muddy brew. His gagging only drew a contemptuous glance from Ino.

"Doctor, do you not wonder about your patient?"

"I am satisfied that medical reasons for treatment are sufficient."

Ino barked at the perspiring Shino, who exited the office with an obedient jerk of the head.

"May I ask your indulgence for only a few more minutes, as His Imperial Majesty's government is paying for your very expensive treatments?" So Ino too was watching the clock, this civil servant on a distasteful mission. The visitor pulled out a sleek folding mobile phone from his breast pocket. He flipped open the high-tech clam shell to reveal a tiny video screen.

He turned the instrument to face Roman who saw a series of miniature photographs scroll under his fascinated eyes with each press of the Japanese's slender finger.

Fishing out his reading glasses, Roman could just distinguish a section of a foreign street where a flimsy white cloth with Japanese characters hung across the lintels of a low doorway.

Various men came and went in dark suits. Wearing sunglasses even in the rain, two struggled to open an umbrella. In another image, three men emerged from a white limousine, a fourth waited in the snow, still sporting the incongruous sunglasses. All the shots were taken from the same angle, through a one-storey window where a sliver of house plant protruded into the corner – a homely touch of domesticity framing the sinister images.

Roman discerned one foreshortened figure in particular, his dark sleeve inching over the same bracelet tattoo he'd seen on Shino. The man resembled Shino – a brother, perhaps?

"These photos were taken by teenage grandson of old woman resident in Ebitsuka, neighbourhood of Mamamatsu, southwest of Tokyo. The people of Ebitsuka disliked criminal activity in their *quartier*. This building became a *burakku biru*, as we say, a 'black building'."

Roman nodded.

"So. Boy passed the originals to Tokyo police who seek this man," Ino pointed to the lower half of a man emerging from the limousine, "for many bad crimes." Ino smiled coldly. "You've noticed your patient, here?" Ino indicated the man standing to one side of the vehicle.

"A resemblance, but surely – ?"

Ino coughed slightly into a linen handkerchief. "Doctor Micheli, Shino-*san* approached authorities with the wish to join normal society. We have government re-entry programme with cooperation of reputable companies. Fortunately for our Ministry of Justice, Shino witnessed the murder of an important politician in our Liberal Democratic Party. He offers useful information."

Ino gazed around the office for a moment before continuing. "Our government is very grateful, but this is delicate matter. As far as his employer knows, Shino is safely occupied in the syndicate's Geneva offices, busy with routine activities he learned in Paris." Ino continued, shrugging as if Japanese mafia expansion in Europe was common knowledge. "You know the sort of thing: shakedowns of Japanese banks, little gossip sheets to blackmail Japanese expatriate businessmen and naughty diplomats. That sort of 'squeeze', I think they call it? It can happen that some of my colleagues are very vulnerable indeed."

"Once Shino gives evidence, suitably protected of course, the man in the white car will recognize the error of his complacency – but too late. The prosecutors will have their testimony and Shino will have launched a better life under a new identity." The diplomat examined his elegant hands.

"This is why you sponsor his removal?"

Ino's eyebrows shot up at the word "removal".

"I refer to the tattoo, of course," Roman explained.

Ino smiled. "Of course. Part of his new identity. Since his arrival in Europe, Shino-*san* has also undergone plastic surgery."

"*Ah, oui.* And now the tattoo. I find myself in the middle of a thrilling *policier*," Roman observed noncommitally.

Ino's sinuous hand dismissed the doctor's wary coolness, "Two worlds, *non*? Tell me, you are an educated man, did you not recognize the rice pot?" Ino's voice quickly turned steely, "The pot is gone, I hope?"

"*Oui.*"

"Very good." Ino leaned back. "I tell you, *Monsieur le Docteur*, Shino-*san* is not the only small potato this syndicate has hustled out of Japan. The days when the gangster lords handed over their henchman to the police as part of an honourable understanding are long past. Now the henchmen turn in their bosses to wipe their record clean. It's almost religious, *hai*?" Ino reflected, "You're cleansing Shino-*san*'s exterior to mirror his inner redemption?" His thin lips curled downwards, "But redemption according to our Imperial Majesty's timetable."

"Please tell the Japanese Emperor that this melodrama is of little concern to me. Medically speaking, I do only what is possible. The tattooing is extensive, deep and professional. Eradication is by no means assured."

A Japanese could read a foreigner's face-saving assent. Making a deep bow, Ino swept his arm across the desk, retrieving his calling card and mobile to the safety of his inside pocket.

"Your work, Doctor Micheli, no doubt often demonstrates that surface appearances can deceive." He glanced in the direction of the waiting room. "Shino-*san* is a very low-born man, an untouchable by birth. He is lucky to be a high school graduate with a certain talent for foreign tongues and an adaptable spirit, but until now, an unfortunate weakness for loyalty. We Japanese have an old saying, 'If the boss says a passing crow is white, you agree, it is white.' However, such loyalty to orders may lead to nasty things. Now Shino has proved himself a man of honour and undeserving of death."

He bowed again, deeply. "Please complete all tattoo removal before summer and we will be most grateful. Even owe you his life."

"So he said," was Roman's dry farewell.

They found the hapless gangster fiddling with his crumpled Marlboro pack in the group of bored patients.

"Can we do something for Monsieur Shino?" Roman asked Chantal. Her eyes, puffy from tears, hinted at boyfriend trouble. "Move up his appointments? He's transferring away from Geneva earlier than expected."

She bit her glossy bottom lip and flipped through page after page of pencilled names blocked off in sections of twenty, forty, sixty minutes. She threw an irritated glance at the Japanese duo already exiting the clinic door to the lobby. They were punching at the lift button like impatient punks in a Tokyo *pachinko* bar.

Roman crooned at Chantal in playful placation, "If we move up his appointments, he will owe us his Honourable Life." It was a futile attempt to cheer her up and recover the day's elusive anticipation of routine ease. He resigned himself to the dictatorship of manila folders towering on the counter.

"You have made absolutely no effort to stop smoking."

Mme Olivier pursed her lips, only deepening the objectionable furrows. Her pout was shiny pink, the creases running from nostril to lips slightly softened this morning by Roman's exertions. Her nervous hands fumbled – this being exactly the stress she ordinarily relieved with a nice cigarette – as she whined, "But I pay you, Doctor! And it's doing some good, *non?*"

"*Non.* Everything will be undone within a year by your compressing your mouth around cigarettes all day." Roman held up a mirror to the woman's bronzed face, expertly plucked eyebrows, eyelids gleaming with expensive moisturizer under the merciless clinic lights.

"Stick a cigarette in your mouth," he commanded.

"Really, Doctor Micheli, I don't think it's necessary –"

"Please. If you insist on taking more of my time."

"Well, your fees are certainly expensive enough," she

sniffed. Even an unlit cigarette was better than none. This doctor's rejection was almost too much. Stretched out on the treatment bed, Mme Olivier usually felt cossetted in a rare moment of *détente*. And on today, of all days, when her fourteen-year-old had phoned in the middle of a performance review with her boss.

She looked at herself in the doctor's hand mirror. The lines were bad, even after five thousands francs' of lasering.

"I warned you that I could improve the appearance somewhat, but only if you stopped your tobacco habit. In my opinion, Madame, you are no longer a candidate for the laser."

Roman laid aside the mirror to avoid the sight of Mme Olivier's eyes filling with tears, her eyeliner seeping into her crow's feet.

"I am sorry, Madame."

"If there were anyone else with lasers in Geneva, why, I'd –"

"There is the hospital for more serious medical needs and Doctor Baumhofer, a laser specialist in Neuchâtel. But only a charlatan would continue." Roman opened the door. "I recommend you spend your hard-earned money at a health spa. Chantal has some brochures." He led the weeping woman to the counter and thrust Chantal's entire tissue box into her hands.

"Monsieur Stratford?" A pale, weedy English type in blue blazer sat next to the aquarium, his large blue eyes glued to the DVD, where a young woman's armpits underwent laser depilation.

"Monsieur Stratford!" Roman repeated at the top of his voice. Charles Stratford stepped forward with a flowering, oozing eczema. A plastic supermarket bag dangled from one bony hand. He looked vaguely familiar, but then Geneva was such a small town. Roman extended his hand and mustered his kindest professional smile for the newcomer.

"How do you do, Monsieur. You have brought your

creams, I see? Yes, we shall first review your case in my office. I see you were referred by ... "

There was still the full-face lasering session of Mme Dupont scheduled after that. Already Lise was prepping the elderly *grande dame* ...

Roman's lunch of avocado and fruit salad discoloured while he struggled with the unstoppable conveyer belt of patients – emotional, stoic, embarrassed, ever hopeful.

The morning visit of the two Japanese left Roman pondering his lack of curiosity. Didn't a good doctor stay aloof from non-medical affairs? Or was his world-view so narrow, after all? Roman watched himself like a twin sauntering with quiet mastery from room to room, greeting patients, reviewing treatments, pinching skin thicknesses, testing circulation patterns, scraping lesions. He marvelled anew at his own neutrality.

What did he know about any of these people? Was he turning into an automaton – a mere extension of lab results, drug prescriptions, X-ray and laser machines? The antagonistic, sceptical Bouviers of Geneva had scoffed at the new lasers, criticized their cost and their glamour. Roman had spent more than a decade proving them wrong. He'd worked hard to set himself in a different class from so many other doctors; he never passed the laser too often, he read the chamois-colour of the reticular dermis in time; from behind the safety of his goggles and mask, he monitored the contraction and shrinking between the second and third pass, before it was too late.

It wasn't merely a question of avoiding over-heating the skin, of scarring – any first-year rookie could read those danger signs. No, Roman Micheli had become a conscientious artist. Yet, underneath the well-practised cool that carried him from session to session, a perturbed Roman walked from the first treatment room to the one next door, from one waiting body to yet another, now questioning whether he really knew where to mark the borders of professional involvement.

During the CO_2 laser resurfacing of Señora Esmeralda Puig of Barcelona for depressed acne scarring, the electricity supply faltered twice and then utterly failed. The uneven surge of current triggered the machines' safety devices and the battery of wonder-machines locked down. One minute the clinic rooms were filled with comfortable mechanical humming, Roman merrily zapping the laser wand along Señora Puig's pits. The next minute, a shudder, a wheeze, a second shudder and a heartstopping thump jolted the floor. Then Roman looked up in dismay at Chantal as they heard the pitiful whoosh of the cooling system dying away.

Chantal called the building's concierge. She called the management. She called the proprietor himself. The circuit breakers were in use, she cried, flip-flopping from room to room in utter dismay. Roman inspected the control bank and all the connections. They let the machines rest for ten minutes, and then attempted to restart them, to no avail.

Roman called the machine distributor in Berne where a slow-talking office clerk promised two men would come immediately, but *la circulation* between Berne and Lausanne was bad. There was a *bouchon* of traffic near Morges. They would be there in a few hours.

"I've contacted the seven other appointments or at least left a message." Chantal sighed. "They'd better get it reset overnight or – " Desolate, she flipped to the next day's double page of appointments – twelve hours of lasering stretching from six-thirty to six-fifteen. She scraped her hair back off her tired face and waved her hand in listless futility. Chantal took the derailment of her appointments more personally than being stood-up by her Thibault.

Roman nodded his dismissal. The rooms cleared of disgruntled patients. Chantal recorded a special message for the answering machine and left. Through the quiet hours of waiting, he took advantage of his unexpected solitude to review the month's billing but he felt ineffective and insubstantial. Did a real doctor stand by, merely close up shop, when his equipment died under him? Was he was no better than a truck driver, a lathe operator, or, God forbid, an orthodontist?

At last two young technicians arrived and started work chatting happily in sing-song Swiss-German mixed with techie English jargon, exhibiting the bonhomie of men who can be sure the sight of them is always welcome. They seemed to inhabit not only a different dialect, but a different time zone – two jolly aliens in yellow jumpsuits alighting on planet earth in the winter's dusk of Roman's clinic, already radioing back to their UFO.

It was nearly six-thirty. The rue du Rhône below was alive with the criss-crossing headlight beams of commuters struggling out of Geneva. The drug addicts and homeless would be installing themselves for warmth about now in the underground parking of Cornavin train station.

Would he have to sit through the night with these two repairmen, authorizing spare parts and answering insurance questions? He heard the lift rising. Prepared to greet another repairman or disappointed patient, Roman leaned on Chantal's counter top in wretched exhaustion and saw the lift door slide open.

To the welcome sound of a laser machine starting up again behind him, the profile of Mira Sullivan slipped into the frame of the full-length antiqued mirror outside. She stopped, unsure which way to turn. In that instant, Roman caught her normal right profile paired with its reflection to make two sides of an exquisite face. For one moment, he'd glimpsed the perfection that hid beneath her birthmark, waiting only for him.

12

"I'm too late? You're already closed?"

The contrast between the girl's exotic looks and her flat American vowels struck Roman anew.

Chantal had turned out the waiting room lights. The girl looked past the foyer mirror's glimmer at Roman standing in the clinic entrance, backlit only by the surgical glare of the treatment rooms beyond. The doctor and his new patient shook hands in the shadowy twilight of a reading lamp casting a puddle of illumination over the appointments ledger.

"*Non, non*, come in," Roman switched the overheads back on, flooding the waiting room with antiseptic uniformity.

Mira huddled under a shearling coat, a hippie affair in beige suede trimmed with goat fur similar to one Isabel had worn back in the seventies. The American carried the look off better now than Isabel had when the style was fresh. Still, the effect wasn't fashionable: with all that dark hair and unruly fur flurried around her cheek, purply-black from the cold, Mira looked like a startled woodland animal.

He took her coat to hang in the cupboard and explained: "We had a problem with the machines – "

"Oh." She paused. "Should I come back another time?"

"Not at all. We'll start your file, *non*? First, please wash off your make-up without scrubbing too hard."

He waited in the main treatment room and prepared his digital camera. He set her high on top of the stool and aimed the arc light on her left cheek, tilting her face upwards to meet the glare. She recoiled just a touch from his scrutiny.

"I like wintertime, when I can wear a muffler," she apologized.

Roman pressed her cheek with his index finger. He watched as the young flesh cleared to white when the blood was forced from its abnormal web of veins, only to return to a dark purple blotch in seconds. He compared the skin texture and epidermal thickness of the normal cheek to the stained one. She sat braced, hands gripping the edge of the stool, her wide black eyes fixed on the wall behind him.

"Have you noticed any changes over the years?"

"That's hard to say. Maybe it's a little thicker than when I was a kid."

"Yes, thickening is inevitable. Now, I want you to hold that position, *comme ça!*" She sat taut while he ran off a quick series of photographs. "No, don't smile, just stay still. No one ever sees these but my staff and myself."

"Do you have many patients like me?" Mira asked, her pupils tracking his progress from one side of the small room to the other.

"Very few as old as you. Parents bring their children before school starts, at around five years old. The earlier, the better."

"Girls like me?"

"*Oui*, maybe a dozen with facial marks this extensive, over a decade."

Mira hesitated. Was she trying to imagine this hidden society so secret they never met, but communicated on waves of telepathic sympathy?

"Will you get it all off?"

Roman finished his shots and set the camera next to the sink.

"Your mark is slightly deeper than I suspected. You disguise it expertly. I think I can at least lighten it so thoroughly that only a mild blush remains. If your circulatory system responds very well, we might erase it altogether – except for those special occasions, perhaps the encores you choose to perform standing on your head?"

She burst out laughing and the mark deepened. "My birth

mother abandoned me because of this. And my real mother chose me for the same reason."

Roman nodded. "Wouldn't any mother want this treatment for you?"

Her troubled eyes roved across the row of sterilizing trays. "My mother taught me that my face was the window through which I saw the world. What other people saw was their problem. That taught me to judge people."

"By their reaction?"

Roman scrubbed his hands, though they weren't dirty. A tiny connection, a *petit indice* eluded him. What had Col Sullivan told him?

"Mademoiselle, why did you decide against treatment when you were – what age?"

"Thirteen, maybe fourteen."

Roman chanced it. "What did your mother die of?"

"Cancer."

"What age were you when you learned this diagnosis?"

Mira's eyes welled up.

"I see. She fought a prolonged battle, but your loyalty to her love couldn't save her?"

He heard an intake of breath and felt the air suspended around them.

"No." Mira collapsed from within and crumpled into the depths of her sweater. Roman could only reach for the tissue box next to the dressing corner as she let out gulping sobs, a sort of animal wailing, hunched over her precarious perch.

Roman felt perplexed. He'd elected a career as The Renewer of Flesh dispensing mostly good news, shining rays of rejuvenation on ageing and disease. People cried with relief after his dermal absolution. He now saw that other doctors, delivering a fair amount of bad news throughout each day, were more accustomed to outbursts of sadness or shock than he.

Mira's tears were spilling on to her jeans, plopping all the way down to the linoleum, no longer lady-like drops, but streams of grief. Finally, the girl's heaves slowed down. She wiped her face and forced an unsuccessful grimace of apology.

"I do not wish to upset you, Mademoiselle. You consider yourself lucky to be so talented, so promising, that you don't want to tempt fate by making yourself normal. I believe that was your version."

"But you think I refused treatment to keep faith with my mother?" Insecurity cracked her forthright American tones.

Roman delayed his honest opinion. "Are you still ready to start? We can do half an hour tonight, if you wish."

"Right now?"

"Why not? The first thing I must do is a short test of your response to different laser pulse depths. That is, unless you have a performance or important engagement in the next week or two? The laser will leave spots the colour of aubergine which fade after about ten days."

As if she knew further hesitation might be final, Mira blurted out, "All right, let's start. But after you answer my question. What is it you're not saying about my mother?"

Roman bent his head slightly in deference. "If you agree to go ahead, why explore the obstacles that – ?"

"I said I wanted treatment, didn't I?"

"*Oui*. I only observe that the deepest love you ever knew came from someone who preferred your frailty, so visible, so obvious in a child. You cling to that frailty, quite understand-ably, even across the grave."

She stared at him, ruby-faced, indignant.

"Yes, but there is irony here, *non*? The average girl, she says, 'Nobody loves me because of this mark, *eh voilà*! I remove it to be loved.' You say the contrary. I was loved *because* of this mark. Without it – perhaps I am unlovable."

"I never thought that!"

Roman added, "I think you fear, Mademoiselle Sullivan, to test a different love, not based on pity or protection."

Mira sat erect and challenged Roman from the height of the stool, but bit back a retort.

"*Allons-y.*" Roman led her into the treatment room where the purring machine waited. He directed her to lie down, batting down the hard pillow to receive her head and helping her to don the protective goggles.

"Please, if you would be so kind, remove your sweater and you may have to unbutton the blouse slightly around here," he pointed to the lowest part of her birthmark, lying close to her collar.

Smouldering, she obeyed. "So, Doctor, why am I finally here now?"

"I don't know. *Eh, bien,* Mademoiselle, we shall spend many, many months together. I have no doubt you will tell me in good time." He gently pushed her shoulders down to the pillow.

For long silent minutes, Roman poised, just inches above her brow. He pressed and released, watching the colour resurface through its cavernous map. Finally, he put his index and middle finger down on one particular spot at the red edge that bordered her lower neck. He would try the birthmark's response to two different pulse depths, filling in two test patches, ten centimetres square, side by side. He set the digital read-out at the first setting and enjoyed a surge of control up his spine; he'd navigated the breakdowns of both machine and patient back into smooth open waters, the shallows safely sounded and left in their wake.

Mira stared up at him through her purple lens. He fished for the thread of the lost conversation. "Perhaps, you have glimpsed a different kind of love, *non*? One that could replace the maternal love that sustained you all those years? The love of the audience for your violin, perhaps?" Roman hesitated, "or perhaps something more personal – ?"

"If you mean a boyfriend, there's no – "

Roman brushed this away. "Not my business. Mademoiselle, this," he stabbed at the air with the point of his laser gun, "this is my job, to remove the mark. Once that is done, it is not for me to say how or even if it will change your life."

Roman's clacking zaps echoed down the corridor of the empty clinic. There were all kinds of patients; Mira Sullivan was of the stoic variety. She twitched only at the first spurt of the icy water, then at the burning ray's snap.

"Could I bring my Discman next time?" she asked.

He worked the shots five millimetres along an invisible grid towards her ear.

"You can listen from one ear only. I can't bear wires in my way." Placing one finger on her throat as if marking a line on a book page, he smiled at her through his purple lens. "I will be jealous I can't listen, too."

He felt ambitious with this case. The lonely night stretched out in front of him. He calculated that she could tolerate about fifty points' worth. He switched the pulse depth and continued working up and down the soft throat that gulped down the tension.

"What school of music do you like?" he asked to distract her. He smoothed her hair out of his way. Lush, springy hair.

"I perform a lot of romantic works, flowery stuff, you know, so when I relax, it's Mozart, some Bach."

"Please be more polite. My roots are Italian."

She rallied through the rackety shots, "Don Giovanni?"

"You like Don Giovanni?"

She laughed under his steadying hand. "Well, nobody *likes* Don Giovanni, even the women who loved him. He's a complete creep."

A sense of humour in a patient was a good sign. It eased the long sessions and aided healing. If the outcome wasn't perfect, it allayed disappointment.

"Please turn your head away from me, there, *merci*. You know what I meant, do you also like the opera score?"

"It's awesome. 'Specially Elvira's aria." She started humming a bar of Mozart to herself for comfort which was nice for a change. The Japanese Shino sucked the pain in and out, like a pregnant woman training for natural childbirth. Some other patients, even men, couldn't control their silent flow of tears.

And often the children just bawled, children young enough to fear his laser even more than the playground taunts that scarred their hearts. His office was full of medical papers describing the psychological damage of birthmarks. There must be layers upon layers of defence mechanisms inside this girl too.

Mira retreated into herself, eyes squeezed tight under the absurd plastic bug-eyes. Roman felt her warbling through the throat's quivering muscles, but under the rhythmic shots of his laser, he heard only snatches of song – as if he had a trembling sparrow rather than a human girl under his care.

He finished for the evening. The left side of Mira's face glistened, swollen raw and horribly dotted with perfect blackish circles of deadened blood. As bad as she had looked without the CoverMark plastered over her skin, she looked monstrous now. She stared into the mirror he held up to her, shocked and speechless. Children were fascinated, but Mira was no longer a child.

"I look ghastly!"

"The surface distension will subside. The spots will start to fade by the end of next week, as your circulation washes away the destroyed blood cells."

"And then, when it's faded, you'll start all over again?" she asked with dismay.

"You can stop at any time, but we need many such sessions for full removal."

"I'm going to spend months looking like this?" Mira's voice rose in alarm.

"With a break for the summer. Yes, Mademoiselle, at regular intervals there will be a few weeks when you will look like you took a blast of – what do you Americans call these tiny pellets shot from a little boy's? –

"Beebee gun? Everybody will think I've got AIDS or leprosy!"

Roman suddenly thought of Isabel. She was supposed to be, wait, where was his wife? Her absences were so routine, he'd forgotten where she'd gone. How astonishing. Surprised at himself, his thoughts raced across a map of Isabel's usual destinations: Delhi, Kathmandu, New York, Vienna. He knew the conference in Brazil was finished . . .

"Doctor Micheli?"

"*Oui, Mademoiselle?*" In the mirror over the sink, evening stubble covered his jaw and unruly black strands of hair stuck straight out over his ears. He looked like a maddened marsupial with violet eyes.

"You've been very patient with me, Doctor. Instead of nearly screaming, I should be grateful."

"Your distress is temporary. And we will both look better without the goggles." He pulled off his pair and extended his hand.

"Oh! Yeah! Sure." She extracted the elastic headstrap from her thick hair with some difficulty. He aligned the two pairs of protective lenses in perfect symmetry on the counter and switched the laser machine back to nocturnal sleep. Mira recovered her sweater while he entered the number of points and response of her delicate skin on a virgin sheet of her new dossier.

"Please call Chantal for your next appointment. Tell her you want a one hour slot. We prefer to take the long medical appointments in the morning, starting at six-thirty."

Still, all was not yet back under control. Before he could stop himself, Roman had lifted the girl's delicate right hand – the same that had clasped her wondrous bow of wood and horse-hair – and lifted it to meet the brush of his lips.

His gallantry echoed their first meeting at Victoria Hall and transformed the girl. The anguished patient standing one foot away vanished. Before his eyes, a diva straightened her shoulders and accepted his tribute with a smile. The untouched cheek flushed with pleasure, acknowledging a different birth-right.

He flicked on the corridor switch to light her exit and helped her into her shaggy coat. She waved a brave, conspiratorial goodbye and pressed the lift button.

The aquarium's green glow illuminated the eerie silence. Roman checked the dawn appointments. M Shino was already pencilled over Mme Olivier, booked to submit another of his body parts for erasure. The doctor smiled to himself; Chantal's pencil could be more ruthless than any laser.

Roman tossed his white coat into the laundry bin and fetched his coat. For a moment he stared at the angel fish circling its glassy kingdom. Spaghetti would pity that fish. The Siamese would laugh at his scaly victim's entrapment, paw the glass, marvel at such stupidity while he, the free and worldly feline, danced nightly from roof to roof, from furry butt on heat to bloodied mouse corpse.

Roman locked up the clinic and thought he heard a gale of light laughter echoing down the empty corridors. Cleaning ladies arriving for night shift? Businessmen finishing late after a drink in the basement bar? Had the taunting ripples sounded male or female? The laughter was already gone. He must have been imagining things. There was no one there.

Part II

"Be careful what you wish, for you may surely get it."

Chinese proverb

13

The panhandling fiddler had turned subtly aggressive – Isabel considered that a sure sign of Christmas approaching. He leered at her through dirty, broken teeth as she rode up the escalator from the Mont Blanc car park. When she didn't toss him so much as a centime, he brushed her passing shoulder with his battered violin. The last time she'd shopped on the rue du Rhône, his gaping instrument case lay close to his ankles. Now it blocked all access to the pavement beyond. Isabel shivered as she navigated around him. He was like one of those lurking trolls jumping out from under bridges to demand tithes and forfeits.

She could deal with leprosy, for God's sake. She hardly need justify her rung on the human sympathy ladder! She just didn't like – was *like* the right word? – didn't feel *comfortable* with unwashed men scraping away at *La Vie en Rose* in public places. She couldn't stop thinking of this man as a Gypsy – ruddy tinker – her father might have muttered. Now such people were not only officially "Roma", but in a UN population report about the Balkans, Isabel saw them categorized as *Egyptians*, because they claimed lineages running from India to Egypt.

The lamp-posts sported green lights swagged into the shape of Christmas trees. People manning charity tables thrust brochures headed, "During this season of giving ... " at passers-by. Isabel headed into a department store to use the ladies' before browsing for Roman's Christmas present. She had to admit her prejudice: she didn't trust people who lived on the street – Gypsies, Roma, whatever. Oh, Lord, suppose any day now a file labelled, "Communicable Diseases Among the Roma Population" landed on her desk. It wasn't impossible. She had to face it sooner or later: her caseload of leprosy, her life's work, was drying up. New diseases circled the airspace over the WHO building, "like stacked-up planes", she muttered out loud.

The department store sound system bounced manufactured Christmas carols through the walls of the ladies'. Despite herself, Isabel irritably translated the clumsy French lyrics into English as she emerged from the cubicle, insisting in a mutter, "Angels we have heard – "

"Excuse me, did you say something?"

A haggard mother in fashionable jogging clothes had materialized out of nowhere to change her baby's nappy.

Isabel set down her groaning briefcase and perfunctorily washed her hands. "No, just talking to myself. Sorry."

The young woman looked disappointed. She'd offered Isabel a bright smile, but in the mirror facing them, Isabel saw dark shadows circling the stranger's eyes. "Oh, for a minute I hoped you were talking to me, because you were speaking English."

Oh dear, Isabel panicked, another desperately lonely wife transferred with her husband to Geneva by some bank or agency. While he spent his day in a familiar corporate office, this abandoned creature paced the isolated, invisible cage of the language barrier, lost among the machine-gun barrage of French-speaking females.

Isabel felt no sisterly compassion. In all her years in Geneva, she'd avoided expat spouses like the plague. Or rather, she preferred plague to post-natal depression. While she loved children, she loathed the prospect of joining the ranks of their marginalized mothers. This woman would no doubt end up lunching at the American Women's Association or taking a quilting class or struggling through French conversation classes at the Migros night school.

"Lovely baby, got to run," Isabel fled the smelly infant and his watery-eyed mother clutching his heels mid-air. The stench of baby poo stuck in her nostrils, she escaped to the street with just over half an hour left for her gift hunt. She inhaled the chilly street mix of diesel fumes, freshly-brewed coffee and grilled kebabs with relief.

It was nice to put the Rhône between herself and WHO headquarters. This morning's meeting had ping-ponged between inconclusive and fractious. Isabel pulled back as a tram car slid past within inches of her shoulder. Got to be more careful. Her mobile rang, but it was only a call from Carlos, so she ignored it. Carlos believed that no more than ten minutes should pass between the springy little conception of a shiny new idea and its proud delivery to someone else, usually Isabel.

She didn't want Carlos's input right now; she needed a Christmas present. She was hardly likely to find it at the toy emporium of Franz Karl Weber but she halted, mesmerized by their Christmas display, a miniature hive of automated twitching and nodding. A Harry Potter Lego train pulled into its tiny platform over and over and over again. A green dragon swooped down a wire to the roof of a miniature Hogwart's where in the dungeon, a mechanical Professor Snape in a rigid plastic black cape twitched back and forth between his minuscule vials of potions. All that busyness, but nothing changed.

She moved on at last, working her way down the shopping boulevard, dwelling on what she had said, what Carlos had explained, how Frank had waffled, as usual. It wasn't only in ladies' lavatories that Isabel mumbled to herself: she had an unfortunate habit of rehearsing dreaded confrontations or re-staging unsuccessful arguments under her breath. She would often defend Carlos by comparing his Brazil frustrations with her setbacks in Goa or Kashmir. This morning it had been Isabel, not Carlos, who needed defending, Isabel who was battling the fiercest resistance in her region. Somehow, in his haphazard but charming way, Carlos was making better headway than Isabel in shifting leprosy administration from private hands to the public sector.

She threaded her steps through the bustling lunchgoers to Touzeau's glassware display and peered at an exquisite wine glass – an outrageously priced gold-and-platinum etched vessel. Roman's Christmas present? What a perverse idea. Roman favoured sleek Italian designs. What was she thinking?

She was thinking, actually, that in a few weeks' time, the draft budget would be finalized for February approval. Quite possibly, the tiny leprosy team would be downsized yet again. People were jumping ship anyway. At the drinks party to celebrate reduced prevalence in Bangladesh, Viviana had announced her decision to leave leprosy for good and "work the sugar angle" with the preventive nutrition team. In the midsummer, Phitphong had flown the coop to Bangkok to manage bird flu outbreaks.

So Frank was left with just Isabel and Carlos. Certainly Carlos couldn't bail out, not with all those school fees, Isabel argued in a half-breath to the faceless shoppers ignoring her. No one had his handle on the Portuguese-language leprosy sector. For that matter, was there anyone else at the WHO who could match her three generations of Earnshaws and Westcotts and Hanfords scorching away their youths in the former British Empire of South Asia?

Yet one of them – she or Carlos – was in jeopardy. Her stomach had lurched when she glimpsed the personnel budget waiting for Frank's signature – dramatically smaller than the earlier figure bandied about.

Suddenly she knew how Father Shardar must be feeling. Right about now he'd be tucking into his supper of dhal and vegetables boiled up by Mrs Chitra. Isabel made a mental note to re-invite the crotchety old priest to Geneva, walk him around the corridors, pull him into what Jonathan Burden would call The Big Picture. "Get him on board," she muttered sarcastically.

She still didn't have a present for Roman. The Cyrillus Boutique's Scottish tweeds tempted her, but her blood boiled at the price tags. Happy faces bobbed and chatted behind café windows or queued along glass counters bulging with ready-made ham or cheese sandwiches and croissants stuffed with mayonnaise. Isabel's stomach rumbled at the rippled rows of tempting fruit pastries, their glaze melting in the *pâtisseries'* indoor heating, then glimpsed her reflection in the window-pane – no room for pastries on those hips.

She fingered a navy cashmere jumper in Bon Génie and knew she could do better in Hong Kong Duty Free, only that trip wasn't until March. A rather dishy youth on a men's cologne ad caught her eye – his pubic hair creeping suggestively around his navel. Probably gay, she sighed. She spritzed and sniffed the cloying scent. Onwards.

She didn't trust herself to select a CD. Roman chose his own novels from the French racks. She'd given him cross-country skies only last Christmas. Her thoughts drifted back to the toys up the street. How delighted some of her littlest patients would be with just one of the single-figure sets – a dragon or a Snape. Was there time to go back and order a dozen? Better yet, would those Danes at Lego donate a few thousand?

She tested a second, then a third after-shave. Roman was wedded to his Yves St Laurent, but there was always room for change, wasn't there? He was getting set in his ways. (She'd caught him the other day adjusting the alignment of her electric toothbrush to stand exactly two inches from the edge of the basin in parallel to his own.)

What did Roman want, anyway? Whenever Isabel put the ritual question, Roman answered with something infuriating, like, "More time with you, *cara*." Useless man, she snapped into an anonymous pedestrian flow. Why didn't he help her out just a teensy bit, just once?

They'd done the sentimental presents (resetting her grandmother's engagement ring), the pet present (Spaghetti), the luxury goods presents (his beloved leather coat), the sexy lingerie presents (she still received the catalogues five years later), the surprise holiday-for-two ticket (which had to be rescheduled twice), the art book presents, the DVD box sets, the annual magazine subscriptions, the over-priced and under-used health club membership. Noel Nausea swamped her empty stomach.

Driving back up the rue de la Paix with a gift-wrapped coffee table book of "Floating World" Japanese erotica, her mobile trembled in her jacket pocket.

"I'm just pulling in, Carlos."

"I need to talk to you. Where did you eat? I searched all the canteens – "

"I skipped lunch. I've been testing Christmas aftershave. I smell like a gigolo."

"I need to tell you something."

"Hang on, Carlos. I'll come to your office."

So it was Carlos after all. If Frank hadn't renewed his contract, how would he keep up custody payments? How many kids did he have, anyway?

The omens were bad. Carlos had shut himself in. When Isabel knocked, the lock turned, the door opened a crack, and one brown eye met her green-eyed gaze. She slipped into his narrow room.

His office had started out like everyone else's – a long, narrow coffin of a space ending in a pane of glass sheltered in an irrelevant gesture from Geneva's winter fog by Venetian blinds. There was scarcely enough room for two people to sit in this space; the architects of WHO headquarters had conspired that claustrophobia would squeeze any staff ranked below P6 back into the field.

After that, depression was Carlos's personal decorator. Cobwebs draped his dying house plant. Tell-tale scorch marks notched his desk's worn edge. A box of maté stood empty, waiting for some caring cousin in Rio to replenish his stock. Even the Club Med photo of his family waving on the sill, as if they were all about to jump from the window, even that was outdated – Isabel seemed to recall that one more infant had joined the Campagna litter before the divorce.

She averted her eyes from the mouldy husk of an ancient

ham roll lurking under the wall heater only to take in a sight more shocking still; Carlos was openly smoking a cigarette inside the boundaries of the world's largest institution dedicated to *health*.

"I have some terrible news." He exhaled smoke and tugged at his curling moustache.

Isabel stabbed in the dark, hoping he might not have been sacked, "One of your kids got hit by a car? Carmen's going to remarry?"

Carlos picked away the rim of his emptied polystyrene coffee cup and let the plastic crumble to this feet. "Unbelievable news."

She closed her eyes. "Oh, Carlos, Frank called you in."

"It's the last thing I expected." He shook his head in disbelief.

"Oh, Carlos, I am very, very sorry." His hands were shaking. There was no mistaking the exhaustion creasing his weathered face.

She'd dreaded this, but he had no one else to comfort him. "Maybe it's for the best. You need a fresh start with some other disease. Something sexier that'll get you the credit you deserve. Have you thrown out any lines to other departments?"

Open-mouthed, he listened to her nervous babbling: "Sooner or later we all have to move on. That's the point of elimination, right?"

He sneered, "Isabel, what are you talking about? How many diseases do I need?"

"Frank told you. About the cuts."

"*Que pasa?*"

"Didn't Frank sack you?"

"No! Isabel, shut up. I've caught it."

"Fired, then." Agency-world English was such a Babel of idiomatic confusion.

"I've caught it. Leprosy! Look!" He reached around his left shoulder and jerked his damp shirt collar away to give Isabel a peek at his back.

"There, no, no, farther down."

"Have you done a skin smear for acid-fast bacteria?"

"Not yet."

"Oh, Carlos, come on, that's just an allergy. Urticaria."

"It is NOT an allergy."

The two doctors stared at the lesion in fascinated silence.

"Well all right, then, close your eyes and turn around," Isabel commanded.

Both knew the drill, the simplest of clinical tests for impaired sensations on a red or white patch, a thickened or tender cutaneous lesion, a nerve losing sensation. If you wanted to be really picky, you could go all the way with a smear and if you were totally bonkers with terror, insist on a biopsy. But why fuss? The free drugs were so efficient, it was cheaper just to gulp down your medicine and get on with your day.

Isabel grabbed a ballpoint pen and poked it randomly on Carlos's upper arm. "Ouch!" he flinched. Then she placed the tip on his right shoulder and he winced under her impatient pressure. She pushed hard in the centre of the lesion and he evinced a slight reaction.

"I didn't feel that."

"Quite. Then why did you react?"

"You pushed too hard."

"Well, if it were leprosy, you wouldn't have said anything."

"Well, maybe I just knew it was coming. I have an idea. Have you got a feather in your office?"

"A feather? For Christ's sake, Carlos, you have one suspicious lesion. That's all."

Carlos cursed under his breath, "*Puta de madre*. You know what I think? I'm quitting. *Adios*."

"Oh, Carlos. You can't quit on me. The only reason Brazil and Angola and Mozambique are still on the endemic list is because we didn't have a Portuguese speaker until Frank found you. I'll be shattered, absolutely shattered, if you bail out on —"

"Oh, Carlos, don't leave me, I'll be simply shattered —" He

crossed his eyes ceilingward and clasped his hands in prayer like a triptych of the martyred St Stephen shot full of arrows.

"All right, all right, all right!" Isabel stood up and dragged her hair back from her forehead, steeling herself for action. "You're a leper. So bloody what? You want a sterling silver bell under the mistletoe? You know one little ROM dose'll fix you. Show me your sample packs."

She rubbed her hands together. "Carlos, this is going to be the shortest case of leprosy in the entire history of mankind, quicker than Jesus turning wine into water." She waved an impatient hand. "Well, you know what I mean." She flung open his cabinets. A deluge of WHO-issued travel kits tumbled on to the carpet around their feet – dusty pill bottles, fistfuls of expired medical samples and cigarette butts tossed to the back of his shelves. Dented Novartis cartons and Nippon Foundation brochures flew over her shoulder.

Carlos stared down at Isabel's bustling derrière.

"Yiiiick. When did you last clean this place?" Isabel fell back in disgust on her haunches and slapped the grime off her palms. "You're disgusting. August 1999! I should make you swallow this entire box of useless stuff."

A dejected Carlos swivelled round and round in his chair, the WHO's answer to Miss Haversham – betrayed, embittered, forgotten, nursing his wounded psyche.

" I have loved you like a sister – a sister-in-arms – a guerrilla fighter against the evil forces of," his forbidden cigarette waved in the air, "of global bureaucracy, superstition and medieval prejudice, of all things cowardly and passive, starting of course with Frank Norton. Only now, Dr Hanford, I see you have ice in your veins. You are a cold Anglo-Saxon bitch." He shook his head. "Don't expect to see me at next Monday's meeting," he muttered.

"Carlos – for my sake –"

"You fight the good fight. Did that Maxwell Foundation come through?"

"Not yet." In fact, Isabel hoped that before the Monday

showdown, she'd have a last-minute commitment out of her New York pilgrimage to offer as ammunition to Frank.

"I will say a rosary for you." He contorted his torso to gaze at his lesion in the reflection of his dark computer screen. Isabel caught sight of an airline ticket peeking out from under a pile of unread documents. She seized it and waved it under his nose in accusation.

"You're not even staying long enough to give your report?"

"*Esta aqui*. You deliver it for me." He shoved his summary on South American case loads and multi-drug distribution into her hands. She couldn't help but notice with envy that his leprosy prevalence rate was less than half her region's. What did he have to be so sour about?

She rose to leave him there, her eyes filling with reproof. "It's an allergy, Carlos. You're allergic to the fight. Sloping off just because – because you've got a little leprosy – that went out with Ben Hur. You're just a malingering coward."

He feigned macho indifference. "Whatever."

Back in her office, she rested her throbbing head in her hands. Her computer monitor blinked at her, *Expert Reviews in Molecular Medicine, Cambridge University Press by Vishwa M. Katoch*. ". . . The success achieved in growing leprosy bacillus in the mouse foot has galvanized leprosy research, leading to extensive work in different animal models . . . "

Her desk phone rang. "Isabel, that you? This is Jonathan. Hey! I'm in town!"

"In Geneva?"

"Where else? Like I promised. Only sooner."

Jonathan. Here? Throughout Isabel's entire adult life, she'd enjoyed an invisible force field, a Buñuel-esque wall that prevented her old boyfriend Jonathan from entering local airspace.

But here he was. Jonathan Burden, who left no opportunity unanswered, in the city of Calvin. Incongruity defined.

"That's g-g-great," Isabel stuttered at the appalling possibility of Jonathan as house guest. "Where are you staying?"

"The President Wilson. With a wonderful view of the lake. Gorgeous room, great service. I'm looking out my window right now at this amazing sprinkler thing shooting up – wow! And I thought Calvinists hated sex!"

"Jonathan! Well! Yes! Will we have any chance to see you?"

"Howbout tomorrow night? I'm lined up for this evening."

"Well, yes, quite. How about tomorrow night? Indeed. Um, why don't I just give Roman a tinkle to make sure – "

"I love it when you talk dirty, Izzie – "

"I'll call you right back. Give me your room number. Right. Your mobile number, then."

Isabel hung up and gazed, unseeing, at Dr Kotch's mouse paw waving to her all the way from India via her screen.

Carlos had leprosy? Jonathan Burden for dinner tomorrow? She couldn't have been more surprised by the day's events than if Roman had suddenly announced he was having an affair. She chuckled and speed-dialled her husband's direct line.

14

"What if he asks me right away, *cara*?" Roman shouted from the kitchen. "We can't begin dinner with a flat refusal." He set the timer for the rice and addressed his conspiratorial twin in the smoky glass of the wall oven, "Not that Doctor Burden would notice anyone's manners."

"He won't be that crass, Roman. You'll see he's smoothed out considerably. Well, I mean, he must have, considering his clientele." For the third time, Isabel adjusted the narcissus perfuming the living room windowsill and glanced down at the empty pavement below. Jonathan pushing back into their placid lives after so many years felt very odd.

"I suspect all he wants is a free meal." Roman measured out his salad dressing. "Perhaps he won't even bring it up."

"Well, then why was he so anxious? I had the impression he called before he'd even tipped the bellboy."

"Not anxious enough to give us the simple courtesy of some advance warning – "

"Well, he's afraid of rejection. He always was insecure – "

"You said that twenty years ago when he took up with that intern – "

"Pharmacist – "

"Under your nose. That your relationship was too intense?" Roman licked a drop of balsamic vinegar off his finger. "That he was afraid of rejection?"

"Afraid of commitment. I'd just finished that trendy book about American men all playing at Peter Pan. Someone left it in the Residents' Lounge."

"Probably Jonathan. He'd think it was flattering."

"Just try to be generous, Roman. Oh, there's the door. He's early."

Jonathan heaved his well-buffed frame into view at the top of the wide marble steps and sucked in the cooking aromas. He slumped on the door jamb for comic effect, his corduroy bulk panting with burlesque staggering. "Well, Roman, hello, hello, hello, it's just great to see you, just great."

Roman took the bony hand extended in mock appeal for support and shook it once. He glanced up from the level of the American's shoulders and tried to summon the same bonhomie.

He recalled Jonathan Burden only too well. Until Isabel's recent foray into their Manhattan past, Roman had relegated Jonathan to one of the dustier shelves in his personal Cabinet of Wonders – the corner where the glass was never washed and mental mouse droppings collected. There Jonathan was frozen in time, dishevelled from an all-nighter waged on diet pills, standing in the corridor in Columbia Presbyterian's gynaecology ward. Roman could still hear Jonathan hailing Isabel – actually waving his stethoscope at her like a limp dick – while he, Roman the Conqueror, strolled towards Radiology's swinging double doors with the red-headed Tropical Diseases resident on his arm. A Triumph worthy of Pompeii.

Jonathan had accepted defeat gracefully. He'd even stopped taunting Roman with the accusation that the quiet Swiss had snagged the indomitable Isabel Hanford on the rebound. If the memory culls images for a mental album, Roman's retained only a fuzzy freeze-frame of Jonathan, his white coat stained with pizza sauce, baying his futile regrets in Isabel's direction.

"Beautiful apartment, Roman. Very quaint."

Isabel handed Jonathan a glass half full of Roman's better Merlot. "Well, it's not supposed to be quaint. The only way to make these old spaces work is to make them as airy, as light as possible. Roman's a modernist, if ever there was one."

"Well, that's what I mean. I mean, modern is period, now,

right, right? I mean, even Martha Stewart was getting into Neutra before she started doing time." Jonathan stretched out on Roman's Corbusier chair, his lanky legs six inches over the end. He bestowed a grin of lavish affection at his host as he addressed Isabel, "You know what we used to joke about Roman back at Columbia? Over-educated, over-sexed, and over here. Romeo Roman."

Isabel and Roman laughed politely at this inversion of reality. Jonathan was trying to inflate Roman into some *personnage* requiring courtship. To paint the medical resident Roman as a compact Casanova – now that was desperate flattery. Catching each other's wary glances, the Michelis stayed on their guard, knowing Jonathan's mission was to inveigle Roman into partnership.

Roman fled to his German appliances and Japanese knives, leaving the two Anglophones to exchange brittle quips. Tonight, Dr Jonathan Burden – who'd kept a running account with the McDonald's near Columbia – tonight that New World Philistine would taste a delicacy relished by the Caesars. Roman lifted the lid of an enamelled casserole and prodded his wooden spoon at two octopi simmering in rosemary-flecked wine broth. While he'd been examining the satisfactory improvement in M Schwaeger's precancerous neck lesion thanks to a new five-per cent imiquimod solution at his clinic, the dependable housekeeper Mrs Siskovitch had followed his written instructions to the letter. Jonathan would think twice about suggesting Roman hook up with his franchise of medi-cated beauty salons.

Tender purple tentacles beckoned up from the bubbling sauce. Flaring his velvety nostrils to catch the fishy scent, Spaghetti purred from his basket near the dishwasher.

" – I told you I was coming to Europe, Isabel! I told you over lunch. I'm planning to expand here."

"Well, you did say you'd fancy it. I assumed you were building castles in the air," Isabel faltered.

"Castles in the – man, Izzie, you don't know me! Most guys

in New York would jump at the chance to go into partnership with me. We've taken the business out of the clinics and put it right into the malls. We've got space now in three locations in LA, two in the Bay Area, one each in Houston, Kansas City, and Chicago, as well as the three original places in New York, one right above Armani."

"These are certified medical treatment centres?" Roman interjected from the kitchen doorway.

"AMA approved. Anything too serious, I refer to Arkadash-ian – 'member him?"

Roman did recall a bookish youth who lived with his mother in Queens. He carried a homemade dinner in a paper bag to night shift. But perhaps that was not how the hardworking Armenian would want to be remembered:

"*Oui*, he did a brilliant paper on new treatments for Nevus of Ota. You know, *cara*, I brought that *Lancet* home to show – "

"That's the guy, down on Thirty-third! Takes a lot of skin cancer off my hands, so to speak." Jonathan clownishly examined his palms for melanomas. "Meanwhile, we concentrate on the money-spinners. You should see the bookings for our Botox and Sushi Lunch Specials – you know, group sessions maximize the economy of cracking open a vial. Right now we're building an ad campaign for our preventive-care massages. We hook the shy ones when they come for something medical – suspicious mole removal, crusty wart – and throw in a free massage. After that they sign up for a whole season."

Isabel wriggled a little. "Massages?"

"Well, don't laugh, but in Geneva we want to start a new programme called *Massages du Monde* for a touch of – "

"Globalization," Roman quipped. Isabel shot him a foul look.

"Massages such as?" She started chirping like a talk-show hostess. Jonathan pulled himself out of the black leather seat and leaned over to confide his wares.

Roman felt his upper lip curl and went to uncork a second

bottle of wine. "Don't worry about your trade secrets here. The apartment's not bugged."

Jonathan ignored him. "Thai, based on the principle of stimulation and harmonization of the body's energy network. Takes 'bout an hour and half. It's really good for muscular and joint pain or nervous stress, you know. Big with stewardesses these days. If they're not under stress, who is? Right?"

Isabel nodded. Roman thought of his boyhood days, when a certain butcher on the rue de Lyon had sweet-talked his mother, the elegant Madame Micheli, with expert dissertations on the quality of his beef, only to lean more engagingly from behind the counter to stare down his mother's generous, if discreet décolletage.

" . . . Ayurvedic is for fatigue. Offers total relaxation. In fact, some ladies say they get a little bit more than they bargained for, if you know what I mean." He had the gall to wink at Isabel! "It's a massage with perfumed vegetable oil. Oxygenizes the tissues, eliminates the toxins . . . "

"Sounds marvellous," Isabel sighed.

"Well, I'm sure with Roman on the job, you don't need it as much as some of those old girls do," Jonathan chuckled.

He was as obnoxious as ever. *Aucun doute*. Roman set his casserole on the dining table and hacked up a crusty baguette for the bread basket.

" . . . The Brazilian massage is pretty lively. We work out the cellulite with caffeinated cream, throw in a waxing or permanent laser depilation. Then we wrap you up in clay to drain out the toxins – "

"Oh, God, I'd love to be mummified for an hour, just to avoid Carlos's phone calls – " She laughed in Roman's direction.

"And the latest is massage with heated oil and warm, smooth stones resting on the energy points."

"*À table, s'il vous plaît*," Roman called to the two ex-lovers.

"Oh, thank you, darling. Doesn't it all sound sybaritic, Roman? Really, Jonathan, I wonder why you even bothered with med school. Obviously, you've got a knack for this sort of thing. No wonder the ladies flock to you."

"Well, I don't do that end of it, of course. I'm handling the serious stuff, the injections, the diagnoses."

"The serious stuff . . . " Roman muttered. He uncovered his casserole.

"Wow! What's that?" Jonathan ran one manicured hand across his moist pate. "A squid? Andrea and I ate squid rings once in Greece. We sailed around a lot when we were first married. 'Course Andrea kept making excuses why we couldn't pass through Geneva. I guess she couldn't cope with seeing one of my old flames, huh, Izzie?" Jonathan leaned over the pot with apprehension to examine the simmering pods.

"Octopus, an ancient Roman speciality," Isabel explained.

"Oh, Roman's not that ancient!" Jonathan snickered.

The conversation drifted a bit. Jonathan's workaholism, Andrea's defection to Miami, alimony, custody. With a little more wine and warm solicitation from Isabel, Jonathan announced he'd moved on, with a glancing allusion to a new "relationship option that might work out". Roman imagined the said "relationship" pumping barbells in a West Side gym at this very moment, building up the strength to handle Jonathan's neuroses. Jonathan drew a discreet veil over further details, as "there was a third party involved".

It was now Roman's opportunity to update Jonathan on his career, even shine a little. He delved into an explanation of Genevan attitudes towards optional cosmetic surgery – not yet a middle-class phenomenon, but common in the moneyed circles of watches, jewellery and banking. Anyway Roman kept busy with medical and remedial cosmetic dermatology for a constant flow of patients – some travelling substantial distances – to try his laser techniques.

Jonathan asked about the money side. Roman waded into the chillier waters of machine and insurance costs. It really wasn't any of Jonathan's business, yet it would seem unfriendly to be coy to a colleague.

Even to himself, Roman's conversation sounded dry, almost withholding. Isabel looked desperate for Roman to lighten up. The more she squinted and frowned cross-eyed at him, the more Roman began to enjoy boring the flaky American. A perverse glee filled his European soul as he watched Jonathan struggling to sustain his frozen smile of porcelain veneers. Roman fought back any hint of a joke and kept up his po-faced account until Jonathan looked glazed enough to tumble into the octopus leftovers.

"Uh, that's great, Roman, just awesome." Jonathan took a deep breath of relief as Roman grinned with less-than-virtuous complicity at Isabel's stony expression.

There was a long pause while Roman sopped up delicious bits of garlicky sauce with a thick crust of bread. "More octopus, Jonathan?"

"Oh, uh, no, thanks, I couldn't eat another, uh, tentacle. Jonathan puffed out his stomach to make his belt strain around the middle. "I had a big business lunch."

Isabel cleared their plates and set down Mrs Siskovitch's fig and almond cream tart. "So." She flapped her linen napkin back into her lap with an irritated flourish, "Your turn, Jonathan. What are you really doing in Geneva after twenty years? I don't expect it was just seeing me in New York that inspired this visitation from the heights of High Society Dermatology!"

Jonathan looked hurt. "Why won't you take me seriously, Isabel? I've told you twice. Roman, help me out, guy. Is she always this deaf? I'm canvassing the possibilities of expanding into Europe. The hitch is medical certification, which I'll get round by bringing in a local doctor. The rest is easy, the money's set aside. All I need is the right location and partner, plus new advertising to suit Les Continentals. Less of the before-and-after garbage you see in the back of English women's mags. Something classier, more like an ad for Yves St Laurent men's cologne. Yeah?"

Isabel thought of the nude Adonis advertising aftershave.

"I'll go and make coffee," Roman said. He retired to the kitchen and loaded up the espresso machine. He heard Isabel and Jonathan sitting out a lengthy silence punctuated by pistons of steam.

Isabel joined him in the kitchen and uncovered a tray laid with cream, sugar and chocolate mints.

"I thought you told him already I wasn't interested," Roman whispered.

"I jolly well DID tell him. And I should think any partnership was an obvious nonstarter after your scintillating performance. I've heard of Boring for Britain but what was that? Death by Droning?"

"Why? Am I so passé? You think I couldn't cauterize the eighty-two year-old Madame Aliberti's bleeding varicosities at one end while she enjoyed orgasmic massage – if I wanted to?" Roman smirked.

"You've no interest in that kind of thing."

"Of course not. Although it's flattering to be asked. Certainly, it's going to be delightful to say no."

"I had hoped it wouldn't get this far." Isabel clenched her hands. "This is so embarrassing. How do we put the poor man out of his misery?"

Roman glanced into the living room. "He doesn't look miserable to me."

They found Jonathan by the mantelpiece, fingering Isabel's favourite sculpture from the Seychelles.

"Aaah, that's great. Yeah. No cream for me, thanks. You see, I wanted to talk to you about it first, Roman. Because without your input, I couldn't go ahead – no, wait, let me explain how I see this. There's some rentable space on both sides of the river. I looked it over this morning – "

"Jonathan, you know – " Isabel started.

" – and found eleven hundred square metres not far from the train station, quite close to a department store, what's it called? Mansion? – "

"Manor, but – "

"Near the Payot bookstore," Jonathan pronounced Payot with a hard "t". Roman closed his eyes in distress.

Isabel frowned. "Not too near the train station, I should hope. The Pâquis is full of drug addicts and prostitutes over on the other side – "

Roman stared at his wife. Was she assisting this madness?

"No, closer to the lake shore. Discreet, needs a lot of work and all new wiring, considering the machinery. Now, over on this side, the agent showed me something near the place des Eaux Vives, but I wanted to be closer to the big hotels."

"Near Escada? That is a bit out of the general flow."

"Yeah, not as good as Roman's location, right smack in the centre of everything ... " Jonathan's plaintive tone drifted across the coffee table.

Roman stuttered, "It was difficult to get that space. I'm afraid it's not expandable."

"Well, that's too bad. You know what they say about base-ball, offer them free stone massage and they will come." Jonathan's confident gleam disconcerted Roman, left wondering how baseball came into it.

It was high time to arrest Jonathan's daydreams. Roman gathered himself up. "Jonathan, I appreciate your approaching us, Isabel and myself, with this offer. No doubt Isabel would like a holiday from her leprosy patients to lie naked under a pile of hot rocks – "

"Oh, that's a good one!" Jonathan laughed too heartily.

" – but I'm afraid there is no way I could go into partnership with you."

"Oh, I guess I realized that." Jonathan made a show of brushing some lingering tart crumbs off his lips. "Great dessert, Izzie. Relax, Roman. I've already started lining up someone else as a back-up option. You can't be the only derm in town ready for a great opportunity. I just thought I owed it to you to explain in person, you know, as an old friend and all."

That night the Michelis lay side by side in the dark, long-marrieds reading each other's thoughts. Isabel felt the heat of

Roman's indignation over Jonathan's deft charade. Roman felt the mattress settle only after Isabel slowly relinquished her tension from the dinner.

At last she spoke, "He should have said something right at the beginning."

"He did, *cara*. He said, 'Hello, hello, hello.' As far as I'm concerned, that was already going too far."

15

"To laser a patient is a responsibility, a privilege," Roman protested at dawn the next day, his strained voice reverberating around the quiet clinic. A solemn Chantal, hair still wet from a rushed shampoo, nodded a face bare of make-up.

Roman railed on, while his assistant lined up the sterilized tools. "After all, any laser treatment is an intrusion, a repeated intrusion, into someone's most sensitive organ, the skin. It is not like a barber's shave or ... or a massage. It penetrates the surface. The body feels it as an aggression."

Chantal helped ease Shino's bruised limbs into a crisp white gown. How much could the little man take? His back was still inflamed from a previous session. He shifted his hips gingerly across the medical bed. Chantal helped him ease his weight on to those buttocks where the glamorous apron of tattooed pleats had given place to a mass of purplish and white circles, colours bruised into blackness, dyes draining away their morbid life.

Roman flipped through Shino's file, then scrubbed his hands and drew on his latex gloves. "Each case is unique. I remain objective and dispassionate, but at least I try to understand why the patient seeks me out. I feel an obligation to explain the medical limits or possible side effects. Someone should tell Doctor Jonathan Burden that laser medicine is more serious than blowdrying someone's hair."

Roman glanced at Chantal for sympathy and she looked down at the docile Japanese between them, it was Shino who nodded eagerly. Roman suppressed last night's indignation and turned to the task at hand.

"Yes, Monsieur Shino. Please forgive me. This morning we put out the dragon's fiery breath. From here," he ran his fingers between the man's rib cages, "to here."

Shino bowed from the waist.

"Would you like to remove the nipple rings yourself? It's a bit delicate. *Non*? Chantal?"

Chantal gingerly fingered the eight concentric thread-like silver rings piercing Shino's nipples. She looked for a clasp or catch but found none.

"We'll have to cut them off," she ventured.

"All right. Monsieur?"

Shino sighed. The little that remained of his emerald dragon uncoiled its scaly torso with each inhalation. The animal's eyes rolled in turquoise and vermilion agony, as Roman thrust the goggles at Shino and slammed down his own pair, obscuring his angry scowl.

Laser gun poised at the hip in cowboy defiance, Roman stared at Chantal through his violet lenses.

"How could anyone think of opening a laser beauty clinic five blocks away as if he were opening some – some nail salon on the Upper East Side, *eh*? *Non*?"

"No, *Docteur*. I mean, yes, *Docteur*." Chantal swabbed Shino's nipples with numbing gel, then used medical shears to snap the hair-thin rings one by one. She extracted them with excruciating care. Shino exhaled deep rushes of nicotine breath. He fixed his narrow black eyes on Roman's explosive expression.

Roman attacked the dragon's tongue, the crack of the laser's regular pulse accompanying his outraged asides. *Thwack, thwack, thwack.* "Imagine, Chantal, our Monsieur Shino taking this artistic triumph by the Master Horrobin's needle, this tattoo that deserves museum *hommage*, to some despicable storefront called the Beverly Hills Beauty Beam salon?"

Shino shook his head, protesting over the mechanical thuds, "Hori-*jin*, Hori-*jin*!"

"*Exactement.*" Roman pressed at the treated area. "It would be an insult to his genius. Can you imagine just strolling in and letting some *stagiaire* or *manicuriste* tackle this beast, unique and treacherous?" *Thwack, thwack, thwack...*

Shino nodded, "*Hai, hai.*" The doctor's hand stretched the dragon's scales wide to meet the laser's obliterating flashes. For many minutes, the only sound was the hammering of the white machine cube standing waist-high in the corner and its snapping appendage in the doctor's grip.

Roman stepped back and squinted through his goggles, like a frenzied portraitist at his easel. He peered at Shino's pectoral muscles. The greens weren't picking up enough light. The yellows were even less cooperative.

"I, too, am a master. I have used the laser now for almost twenty years. I apologize for being indiscreet, Monsieur, but can you imagine? Half a million francs of advertising to plaster Geneva with the name of Burden, Burden, Burden. Prepare to see helium balloons trailing the name Burden over Mont Blanc and into France!"

"*Mon Dieu.*" Chantal swabbed with agitation at Shino's chest.

"Yes, somebody should warn the French authorities. I'm afraid it's too late to save Geneva."

A fascinated Shino listened to Roman. Should he ignore the doctor's indiscreet complaints uttered underneath the laser's percussion and pretend to count the ceiling holes? Or should he struggle courteously to respond as part of a horrified trio? He understood this much – that there was an enemy doctor named Burden from Beverly Hills invading his doctor's territory. These things happened often in Japan, between the *Inagawa-kai*, the *Yamaguchi-gumi*, even overseas where the *Jigyo-kumiai* was expanding. Too bad Dr Micheli didn't have an umbrella federation like the *Sumiyoshi-rengo* to sort out rivalries. Shino felt a wave of empathetic *ninjo* for the embattled Swiss. Unfortunately, this benign moment was shortlived, dispelled by a sensation like burning pellets rolling in formation just above his abdomen.

Shino closed his eyes. Was this excruciating lasering worth it? Could he really start life anew with a pay-off large enough to start a DVD rental store, to go home to his deaf mother in Kyoto to watch her orchids grow in peace? What if something went wrong? Was this doctor really the measured professional he claimed? The great Horijin had meditated before his private shrine for half an hour before tattooing that dragon. Even washing his bamboo needles was part of an honoured ritual. Never had the Master behaved so distracted! Tattooing *irezumi* gave you no opportunity to rip off the skin, bow and say sorry, come back tomorrow with your spare body for another try! *Hai!*

The Japanese fantasized about a calming cigarette and his solitary lunch to come – some *inari-zushi* or *tekka-maki* – bought at an upmarket hotel bar overlooking the lake. For now, he was drifting, hungry and lonely, under a medical lamp, far from all he knew.

The doctor rattled on about this Burden man to his distressed assistant. A lock of her hair scraped the unflattering brown sun marks on her cheeks. Shino fancied rice-white skin. He'd entrusted his own skin, his future, to this *gaijin*. Ah, to be charitable . . . Forgiveness enlarged the spirit. One must fight to keep the nobler values alive: dignity, compassion, duty, obligation, even now that the last of the Occupation bosses lay in his grave.

Yes, an era had finally ended, but debts must still be paid. Shino thought of Kurosawa's movie heroes – monosyllabic, patient and just. And his *oyabun*, the god-like Takahana sitting, thinking in silence behind Shino's shoulder as they cruised Rippongi district in the graceful white limousine. He thought of the five hundred million yen hush money covering the deal between Tsusho Realty and the Houston people linked to the White House, that squirt of a president's son whining he'd had no idea that Tsusho was controlled by the *Inagawa-kai* mob. Someone died to pay for that screw-up . . .

The wide fluorescent arc light shone right through Shino's goggles. His eyelids watered into amethyst puddles. He smelled a flowery scent mixed with Western woman smell as the two *gaijin* chatted back and forth in agitated French.

" . . . Ahh, maybe it is a big bluff. *Oui*, he thinks he can frighten me into fronting for his overpriced massage parlour. Hah! Think of Madame Olivier – ?"

"*Oui, Docteur –* "

"How contented she will be, getting her smoker's lips lasered every week, while she enjoys an Indian sex rub-down! I am sure that Doctor Jonathan Burden won't tell La Olivier to stop smoking. *Mais non.* He will sell her a lifetime package of Botox and Sushi Specials. What a sad day for Swiss medicine."

The doctor's distress was about some professional rivalry. Shino had never tasted botox, but the doctor's reference to *sushi* made him think of varieties he couldn't get fresh in Geneva. He'd been nibbling *gunkan maki-zushi* out of his lacquered lunchbox at noon on the day Takahana scanned the morning headlines and strode red-faced with rage from one room to the next. *Ieeee*, Takahana's short kimono flapped around his powerful, hairless thighs: he ranted they'd be tied up in lawsuits by Onishi's devious lawyers and his young financial brats with their American MBAs. *Ah, so deska*, and that might leave the field open for those trespassing bastards from Kobe.

At that fateful moment, Shino had bowed to Takahana's call, laid aside his lunchbox and gone into the inner office for instructions. He loved his usual duties: delivering laundered funds, smuggling porn featuring schoolgirls in white ankle socks, and his personal specialty – threatening shareholders' meetings with embarrassing disruption, publishing incriminating titbits of business blackmail in *sokaiya* newsletters. Shino missed the great days of Takeshita's government, when they held even Japan's prime minister by the balls . . .

Ah, but Shino was pretty old-fashioned still to like that sort of thing, Takahana chided him more than once. Shino's little extortion deals would die off – younger Japanese businessmen cared less and less about saving "face" – why couldn't Shino get into the *shabu* amphetamine traffic? The rocket launcher deals? After all, Takahana cajoled, the boss had noticed Shino was cleverer than he looked, self-taught but discreet. Shino always understood more than he let on; small wonder Takahana trusted him like a son. That's why on that particular day, Takahana had given him a much more important assignment...

"Turn over, please, *Monsieur? Merci.*"

The doctor was finishing up. "The reds are almost gone. *Eh, bien*, we'll address those stubborn greens next session."

Shino didn't bother to glance down. After so many sessions of the laser's staccato jumping between his shoulders and arms, his lower buttocks, his thighs front and back, the small of his back, he knew what to expect. The brutish dragon's dance with the impudent carp was no more. Master Horijin's needle had etched shimmering silvery apricot scales down the carp's swishing tail and the doctor's laser had blasted that magic into a dark fragmented mass, a betrayal of Horijin's work.

Shino struggled to camouflage his distress. Dr Micheli was doing his best. Wasn't he forever in the debt of this Italian-Swiss, operatic temperament and all? If *oyabun* Takahana blew up for fear of losing a billion-yen kingdom to that scarfaced brute Onishi, *so deska*, why shouldn't Micheli-*san* blow up at an invasion by this Beverly Burden? Shino bowed his head and looked away. Ingratitude over losing his dragon was inappropriate. He must acknowledge his debt, his *giri*, to the hard-working doctor.

All men were brothers under the skin, Shino concluded with primitive satisfaction as he pulled on his trousers behind the changing-corner curtain. Dragons of all nationalities fought other dragons. Sometimes it was the loyal carp swimming alongside who set things right, the little fish no one noticed.

"Roman, you won't believe what just happened."

Roman was examining a Bosnian child. When his mobile rang, he feared the worst. A call on his private line interrupting work must be important; he often imagined an accident. Nothing like that ever happened, of course, but it was a recurrent fear that sprang up, complete with screaming ambulance, a frantic bystander poking for help at Isabel's autodial,

Chantal's cancellation of his straitjacket of appointments, the arrival at *Urgence* to take charge of Isabel's care not as a doctor, but only as a husband standing by, heart in throat.

Why did he entertain such fantastic forebodings about his wife? Why was it so familiar, this panicked sensation that flitted by for no reason as he took her calls? His left palm palpitated the spread of freckles cast around the boy's tiny armpit, moving on to the fleshy bumps on his shoulders, while his wife's crisp consonants in his ear competed for attention down the line.

The anxious mother watched doctor and boy from the visitor's stool. She picked at the fringe of her woollen head scarf and stared back into her child's moon-saucer eyes. The woman's shoes were worn, her skirt soiled, her attitude listless.

Isabel never called on a whim. "Frank quit this morning. All this time he's been nurturing an offer behind my back to move to the Hong Kong regional office. Technically it's a downgrade from P6 to P5, but with the overseas housing and perks ... He needs more money. He needs more space. Needs to be closer to his ex in Australia, rhubarb, rhubarb, rhubarb. He says, 'It's for the kids, Isabel. You wouldn't understand. You don't have kids.' Which only makes me more furious. He's abandoning ship, positioning himself for the next big chicken flu panic. He's not making a big enough noise for himself in leprosy."

"You are upset, *cara*? Can I call you back?"

"No darling, not upset. But could we meet at lunchtime? With Carlos on sick leave, the Director General wants a decision out of me this afternoon."

Roman laid a gentle hand on the head of the two year-old shivering in his pathetic cotton underwear.

"You'll tell me all about it at 1:45, *non*?"

"Café Central?"

Roman turned back to the glum Bosnian woman waiting in front of him. "Madame these *café au lait* spots alone wouldn't worry me, but I think need X-rays of his skeleton and an eye examination."

It was too early to diagnose the rare Recklinghausen's

Syndrome definitively, but some symptoms of Elephant Man disease were undeniable. He gently suggested the woman summon her husband from the waiting room. He would not say more than necessary until he was sure.

Shortly after, he found himself drumming on the table after rather brusquely ordering two plates of oysters. Both the oysters and his wife were late. He glanced at his watch and repressed the suspicion that he wasn't reacting correctly to Isabel's good news. She was long overdue for a promotion, even a temporary one. His stomach rumbled. He'd eaten a light breakfast before dawn; no doubt this disgruntlement was mere hunger. And there was that last appointment: no doctor enjoyed diagnosing serious disease, so tragic in a child. In self-reproach, Roman conceded that he'd chosen dermatology to avoid the messier options, only everything in life turned out to have its messy side. *Regardes*, he scolded himself, dermatology could be undeniably superficial, so finding a serious anomaly should be professionally satisfying, *non?*

If Isabel was held up, why didn't she call? He'd never figured out the politics of that eight-storey rectangular empire of plate glass stretching the length of two soccer fields, surrounded by vast parking lots and housing room after room for conferences where participants were reduced to plaques: Non-Government Organization, Foundation, Burundi – not individual doctors or patients. Isabel's colleagues didn't treat individuals with Recklinghausen's or Sturge-Weber – they juggled whole volumes of statistics with container loads of pharmaceuticals. They treated entire countries, not rashes or moles. They didn't have a case load, they prioritized whole disease families, corralled plague regions, commandeered their legions of anti-biotics against barbaric germs, like Caesar taming borderless Germania.

"'Lo, darling."

She looked harried and middle-aged. When she pecked his cheek, her roughness brushed his own. The raw lake winds rushing through the place Molard scoured her Celtic skin. No doubt, Roman reflected, if she'd married the wonderful Jonathan, she would look ten years younger. She'd resemble some intelligent version of "Doctor Barbie", those wrinkles and freckles lasered off so often that her features would seem wrapped in cellophane.

Isabel dragged herself heavily across the wooden banquette to face him just as the oysters arrived. They declined wine and the waitress frowned. Acrid cigarette smoke mingled with fried fish fumes wafting out from the kitchen.

"... I had no idea what was coming. I thought it must be Carlos's little crisis, you know, asking me to take over Brazil until he regained his senses and came back to work – or asking me to supervise some git seconded from bilharzia, and I was jolly ready to tell them where to stuff that idea, when Frank announces *he's* jacking it in, only of course the weasel called it 'transitioning' – isn't that just like him?"

She nibbled a fingernail. "And I always thought Australians were supposed to be so straightforward ... "

Now why did Roman recognize a young man who'd just come into the restaurant that moment, his coat collar pulled high and a pink-red scarf twisted rakishly around his unshaven chin?

"Roman?"

"Yes, *cara*?"

"Are you listening?"

He squeezed lemon juice over a succulent oyster and couldn't help but think of his wife's more delicate parts. Had he ever treated this sallow young man taking a window table? Roman was a doctor who remembered his patients, not the kind who boasted at how many he'd forgotten.

"... I was floored. Flabbergasted. Stunned. I'm not ready. I have half a dozen things to follow up on the fund-raising, not to mention reining in a few diehards in the field who were resisting the downsizing ... "

Roman liked his world and its people as well-classified as his instruments. He filed away deformities, nevi, kerotids, measured nasal labals. He did not know this young man, and yet he did, he did, he did. Like Spaghetti eyeing a new insect invading a sunny corner of the pantry alcove, Roman watched the skinny stranger out of the corner of his eye. He registered the rather oriental cast to the eyes, the full lips. No, Roman didn't know him and yet...

"... So after a fair amount of badgering on my part, I'll get P6 pay for as long as I take on the lion's share of Frank's workload, but not the accounting supervising, that'll be farmed out to the girl who does the number-crunching for some of the other communicables ..."

"That's wonderful, wonderful news, *cara*." Why did this youth perturb him? Why did the flamboyant slinging of that scarf, the playful disregard of the printed menu, the confident flirtation with the waitress who practically dashed off for the boy's white wine, why did these gestures irritate Roman?

"... and I'll be given some start-up leeway to clear off my desk, and take a trip to Delhi, etc., to get that whole end of things into some kind of holding pattern until ..."

Roman thought of the last time Isabel had been promoted. With more warning, he'd taken her out to a dinner of truffled risotto. It had taken him four attempts to replicate the dish at home, but he'd mastered it. Isabel deemed it was lovely, but not quite the same without a job promotion as garnish ...

"... do you think so?"

"Absolutely, *cara*."

"Good. I just wanted to hear you say yes. I'll tell the DG's office right away. There'll be more travel, of course, a bit more work at the coordination level, maybe a trip to Atlanta –"

"When do they make the final decision?"

"Confirmation to P6? Well, I suppose," her brow clouded over, "I suppose, sometime in the spring."

"And what are your chances?"

Isabel sucked on a mollusc. Roman saw she hadn't even considered not getting confirmed. "Quite good I should think.

I've got all of December and January to make it stick. I'll wrap up the field work over the next few weeks – you don't mind postponing Christmas, do you, darling? Everything around here slows down, so I won't be watching my back until the New Year and I can get so much done out there."

No, he didn't mind. Truly he didn't. *Franchement*, it was all a bit silly celebrating Christmas without a manger or toys.

"Of course they'll post the opening and advertise in the *Economist* and all that, but who knows the work as well as I do? And who's as big a Charley as me to think that there's any career in leprosy?"

She chortled with self-derision and downed the last of the oysters. Roman suspected she'd been turning leprosy's unpopularity to her advantage for some time.

He took her lemony hand in his. "So the only worry I have – that you might have a terrible disappointment after all the work you'll put in – that's nonsense?"

"They wouldn't dare. Oh, darling, you're very good at homing in on things. You're such a good listener . . . "

By tacit consent, the meal was brief. They were both busy and fulfilled professionals. Roman imagined his coming Christmas endured alone.

"Isabel," Roman asked, pouring out the last of his San Pellegrino, "do we know that young man sitting at the window? The one with the reddish scarf hanging over his chair?"

He took Isabel's sturdy black overcoat from the maitre d' and laid it over his wife's shoulders. Isabel surveyed the dining room as she thrust her arms into the sleeves, and then turned back to him, proud of herself.

"Oh, yes, darling! It's that pianist boy. The one I thought was so dishy? He is quite sweet-looking, don't you think, sitting there all by himself? I wonder who's keeping him waiting." She waved her thanks to the head waiter.

Of course, of course. Roman knew that mulberry scarf very well.

16

"And how is the world of music?" Roman pressed on the treated skin of Mira Sullivan's throat. He released the spot to observe how the deeper veinage below the laser pulse's depth responded. Her skin was velvety and resilient. There was young skin, younger skin, skin like M Shino's which was smooth but doughy –

"I'm working on something quite modern," she mumbled, wincing at his methodical prodding under her left earlobe. "There's a contest coming up where you get extra points for something Swiss and extra points for something modern, so I went for both. It's a bitch." She glanced up through her goggles. "Sorry, my father hates it when I use language like that; that's probably why I do it."

Roman recalled student conversations in New York, the repetitive, scabrous dialect of residents' frustration, the way Isabel's English had shifted into rhythm with Jonathan's "shits" and "fucks" and "mothers" and then faded back into Hanford propriety when she took up with Roman.

"Well, I'm not your father."

"Ummmmm," her mouth avoided the press of his hand. "Although I suspect you share his love of machines. Anyway, I figure that if I play a piece of music unintelligible to the most expert judge, not to mention absolutely unknown to civilized man, woman or beast, I might win. I mean, who's to say I played it right or wrong? Who dare argue with total dissonance? Right?" She smiled that open, American grin.

"Hold still, please. Are you playing with your usual accompanist?"

"Anton? He's not interested in anything but romantic music. He's got no modern ear."

"With your talent, why bother with contests now? Wasn't Sion enough?"

"Hardly. You have way no idea about the competition out there."

"Oh, there is competition for all of us." He pushed a clump of her thick curls away from her ear. "Do you recall Doctor Burden in New York?"

"Sure," Her eyes were squeezed tight against the encroaching zap of the laser beam.

"He is opening one of his clinics here, which will be competition for me. No, don't open your eyes, not yet, please. I'm coming very close to the upper edge. Is the discomfort making it difficult to practise? We'll take a rest before your next big performance, *non*?"

They chatted as Roman continued lasering, filling in the pearl-sized spaces left between the original patterning, like the witch doctor who had pricked the ritual grid of scars across the forehead of the Honourable Elangu Wanga, Roman's unpunctual African patient. The machine zapped and snapped rhythmically over the girl's chiselled cheek. The flashing ray crawled millimetre by millimetre towards her nearly invisible Adam's apple. Her mane of black curls splayed out behind the goggles' elastic band and cascaded over the hard pillow.

As Roman circled the treatment bed, he noticed her feet were pressed together and pointed slightly downwards in the posture of a carved saint or queen stretched out on her granite sarcophagus in the silence of a medieval crypt. Those extraordinary dexterous hands rested like two tranquil lilies floating on a pond of sandwashed denim skirt.

The clinic had fallen still, leaving Roman to work with more than his practised concentration. Only when he escorted Mira Sullivan back to the waiting room, did he notice the uncommon hush.

The DVD screen was silent. A blackening noon of ineffectual light strained through clouds that could not decide whether to rain or simply swirl in wetness up and down the street around the last holiday window-shoppers. It was day, but dark, the middle of working hours, yet no more patients looked up at Roman from their ranks near the aquarium. With incongruous embellishment, Chantal had traded her clumsy nursing flipflops for a pair of black velvet party shoes sporting a coquettish purple satin bow at the back of each heel.

"Chantal?"

"*Oui, Docteur?* – I'll be going now, *ça va?*"

Of course, of course, it was Christmas Eve already, the start of his silent vigil leading up to the scheduled phone call from Isabel, followed by a modestly festive supper with his brother and sister-in-law in Cologny.

"I'm not sure the shoes go with the uniform," he evaluated with mock sternness from a distance. "They are intended for the lucky Monsieur Thibault?"

"I'm breaking them in for *le réveillon, Docteur.* Tibo and I will go dancing."

So, another year was over, another New Year's Eve of salsa and Tibo for Chantal. As usual, Roman and Chantal shared a formal kiss on both cheeks and exchanged presents. Roman's was another crystal liqueur glass in the set Chantal had started for the Michelis eight years before, Chantal's a bottle of Anick Goutal perfume Isabel had picked up duty-free in Heathrow transit a month before.

Holding her shearling coat over a crooked arm, Mira smiled politely at Chantal's frivolous footwear. One side of her face wore a thick bandage over a glaze of cooling gel but a staccato of black dots peeked out from under the cotton gauze.

"They're very cute," Mira spoke up. Her hesitation was obvious; she hoped to linger a little in the Christmas spirit, soak up the protection of the medical sanctuary before facing the stares of uncomprehending strangers on the pavement outside. It was always like this, Roman thought. Whoever it was – man or woman – the patient who landed the last appointment of the year fell in with the happy collegiality of Roman and Chantal closing up for the holiday week, chatting to the Serbian cleaning ladies about the fish feeding, exchanging modest presents, pulling the plugs on all the machines and on the year itself.

The departure rituals performed, Roman and Mira waved Chantal off in the arcade lobby and emerged on to the street. Dancing sparkles of reflected red and green braved the drizzling mist obscuring the thunderous sky.

"How do you get home?" he asked, unfurling his umbrella.

She wrapped her mulberry scarf more tightly around her chin to shelter the bandage and with the other hand pointed out a bus stop down the street.

The vision of her riding home on crowded public transport offended Roman's sense of gallantry. "*Non, non,*" he shook his head. "It was a very long and painful session. You can't ride the bus looking like that. Couldn't you telephone your father or a friend? Here, use my phone –" He fumbled for his mobile.

She laughed, a little amazed. "No, thanks, I've got my own. Anyway, people have always stared at me."

"Your bandaging might be displaced by the crush. Where do you live?"

"Petit Saconnex."

The pavement was overflowing with bodies pressing to get home. Suddenly he yanked her towards him, out of the path of a speeding tram. "*Regardez,* that one was so full it didn't even stop. The buses are worse. The whole city is going home."

She laughed again, crumpling the gauze of Chantal's skilful nursing. "Don't worry, there'll always be more."

Roman took the girl's arm and steered her firmly uphill, towards the garage where the Michelis rented their parking space.

"Do you open presents on Christmas Day or Christmas Eve?" Roman meant this as polite conversation – it had always been a point of contention in his own marriage – as Mira and he settled into his car at the back of the dank basement. Too late he realized his thoughtlessness. Given Mira's deceased mother, the subject of family celebrations might pain her. He felt relieved when the girl seemed not to have heard his question.

He inched his car down the narrow byways of the Old Town, working his way towards Mira's suburb. A long uneasy silence settled between the two of them. In this unfamiliar intimacy, Roman feared a sudden appearance of her former prickly antagonism. In their numerous sessions at the clinic, Mira had relaxed into the Americanisms and nervous friendliness with which she habitually protected herself.

The Saab's cozy interior enveloped doctor and patient in the smell of leather and traces of Isabel's lemon and verbena. Now Roman's nostrils picked up a third *mélange* – of antiseptic gel and wet goat fur, and escaping from beneath the shaggy coat, the veil of amber and vanilla he'd come to know from Mlle Sullivan's appointments.

If she still mourned her mother, a sudden comment from the safe depths of the passenger seat disguised her grief:

"When Mom was still alive, we'd go to an Embassy cocktail or whatever they laid on at the official residence. Dad didn't care much for it, but Mom always got gussied up, wanted me to bring my violin, perform seasonal stuff in churches and clubs, you know the kind of thing. In Beijing, the Chinese put up decorations and then leave them hanging for weeks and weeks until it's time for the Lunar New Year," she glanced at Roman's appreciative chuckle, "kind of cost-effective, all-purpose winter festivity. They're wonderfully practical, the Chinese, and so you have all these big SALE signs everywhere, so everybody can get new clothes which is absolutely part of their own New Year tradition. And then lately there was this surge of Christian evangelism that was popping up all over the place, kinda weird and intense and superstitious. Very Chinese."

"You went shopping on Christmas Day?"

"On the actual day? Oh, no, we'd just go to a noisy restaurant for a ten-course banquet with other diplomats. We've always been overseas. I guess that's why I can't associate Christmas with a big family reunion."

She chatted on while he concentrated on the impossible traffic. No one would let him change lanes. The other drivers exhibited all the indecision and unpredictability associated with two-bottle holiday lunches. The girl would never have got home without his help.

"... when work slows down and things become very –"

"Very what?" He'd lost track of her conversation and he glanced at her while waiting for the street light to change. All he could see was that monstrous white bandage under the curly fringe.

She sighed. "Well, I guess – and maybe I think this only because I'm me – but I think I like Christmas best because everything turns very musical." She paused. "No, that's not exactly what I mean. Everything turns musically forgiving."

"Forgiving?"

She nodded, the cruel gauze tugging at the down of her unmarred upper cheek. "I mean, all year, in the stores they play this crappy wallpaper rock or bland Musak. Then for a few weeks, the sound systems play nothing but Bach, Handel, Mozart, and all these musicians jockey for position on the sidewalk around the stores," she lowered her head confidingly, "and for once, everybody gives them lots of money."

Roman nodded and smiled.

Encouraged, Mira turned full face to him and continued, "And, you know how everybody sings, even people who can't hold a note? You know how they start going, "Gloooooo, orrrrrrr, orrrrrrr, orrrrrrr, eeEEEEE AHHHHH!"

Roman laughed at her choral outburst. Miraculously, a Volvo let him shift lanes.

She laughed too. "You know? These people completely forget they can't sing, maybe they're even totally tone deaf, but they belt it out in full voice anyway. People make complete fools of themselves at Christmas-time, like they're children again. It's wonderful, beautiful, as Thomas Carlyle said: music may well be the speech of angels. At Christmas, the world turns into a whole choir of angels — imperfect, human angels, warbling lovably off-key."

Roman laughed in recognition of himself — he who had inherited the Italian love of singing, but no voice. Christmas Mass — something Isabel attended peevishly as a concession to Roman's sister-in-law, allowed him a chance to belt out his would-be Pavarotti guts. Thinking of his relatives, Roman glanced at his watch. Fede and Liana's dinner wouldn't start for hours and hours.

The thickening fog slowed the outward flow to a crawl. By the time Roman descended into the car park under the Sullivans' building, Mira had chatted them both into the assumption he would share a holiday toast with her father. Although he protested as a matter of form, Roman was himself wondering why a short drink was not an appropriate bridge-building gesture with the Colonel's alien imperial culture. This offensively inoffensive, strategically innocent American father would no doubt see the doctor's brief appearance as a show of complicity between two men who only wanted to bless Mira's New Year.

Roman was appalled by the Sullivan apartment. He'd never bothered to imagine Mira's dwelling; it could be called little more than that. How could she possibly "reside", "live", or "make a home" here? The bare walls were a utilitarian cream slapped on for rental purposes. There was one sofa covered in a nondescript flowered pattern, probably ordered from a cata-logue by a US Mission personnel clerk from Kansas, with a coordinated armchair that looked fresh out of its factory packing.

By comparison, even Roman's minimalism, the carefully chosen chrome and calfskin Corbusier chair, the abstract oils on the walls, the bordeaux, jade and fawn paint offset by white trim, Isabel's hand-woven Kashmiri throw, the spotless crystal and hand-painted Ticinese pottery shining on his dining-room walls – everything in the Micheli home was richly chosen.

No such discretion had been exercised in the Sullivan flat. Even the carpeting – so blandly beige, so modestly mediocre – receded beneath Roman's gaze. There were no books or paintings, only an elaborate exercise bicycle standing in one corner. A wide, flat-screen TV with built-in DVD player dominated the open space. In front of it stood a functional coffee table the right height for a spread of potato chips or pretzels while "watching the game".

It looked like a fresher version of that sterile Residents' Lounge in Columbia hospital – an unloved space for waiting, wasting time, coming down from, getting up for – a pit belonging to nobody and everyone. There were no Christmas decorations, not even a calendar, just this neutral holding zone. He'd stayed in hotel rooms with more personality.

From where he stood, Roman detected only one sign of real life – through a bedroom door at the end of a short corridor he could see the metal scrollwork of Mira's spindly music stand with sheet music scattered around the flat carpeting.

Mira laid Roman's coat on a dining chair lined precisely with five others standing at attention around a bare dining table. Roman guessed the father and daughter grazed at the kitchen counter.

"Your father, perhaps, he is not here?" Roman asked, unsure whether to crease the fresh chintz of the sofa.

"I thought he would be. I don't know . . . "

She pulled a mobile from the bottom of her fringed suede satchel and punched at the buttons with both thumbs displaying the dexterity of her generation. She talked in casual, flat American vowels to a receptionist in Americaland. Roman pictured a woman protected by her mental seat belt in some enclave linking the US Mission and its bowels of military intelligence to this sterile apartment and onwards to the elaborate impersonality of Ambassador Kress-Parker's lakeside villa and the entire barbed-wire world of Americans abroad.

Nonplussed, Mira folded up her phone. "Cindy says he's stopped off at Beth and Rick's for an eggnog on his way home. Too bad, he didn't mention it this morning." Her social graces were failing her by the second. Roman pitied her, standing dwarfed by the vast beige space. He felt that to walk out right away would consign her to this anonymous desolation.

"Let's see, what can I offer you while waiting for him?" She pulled herself out of her shearling and scarf. Her bandage's rough edges snagged on the goat fur. She marched into the galley kitchen and soon Roman heard the impatient slamming of cabinet doors as she hunted for something to drink.

"It's not important." Roman called. "I really must be going." He was acutely uncomfortable, as much for himself as for this young woman audibly floundering; indeed, what might Col Sullivan think if he walked into his living room right now?

The unwelcome bullet-pop of a cork snapped Roman to attention. To his deepening dismay, Mira emerged from the kitchen bearing a frothing bottle and two grocery store wine flutes.

"Champagne? Really, I don't think – " he begged off.

"A friend gave it to me when I won Sion. Did you meet Charles backstage? Probably not. It's been sitting in the fridge for months 'cause I can't drink it alone. Dad always sticks to beer – champagne gives him acid. Please ... it's Christmas Eve." She poured his drink and sipped from her own.

"*Santé*," he toasted her, and tasted the stinging bubbles with embarrassment for her loneliness.

"Do you and your wife celebrate a traditional Christmas?" she asked.

During one of their sessions, Roman must've mentioned there were no Micheli children; now he couldn't remember the exact day that information had passed. Mira sipped again at her wine and, pulling her rumpled sweater to order and smoothing her skirt, settled down on the overstuffed sofa. The glass in her hand transformed her bearing. Roman marvelled at this sudden glimpse of that other Mira, a sighting of the hidden diva who listened like the mistress of a flock of forest animals to an entire orchestra, merely waiting for the right moment to cast her melodious spell over them.

Her duality unnerved Roman. He looked desperately for a formal, temporary seat and at last placed one of the rigid dining chairs opposite the girl. He explained Isabel's workload and constant travels, mentioned his pride in her imminent promotion to Acting P6. His words thudded on his own ears as if they were wadded in cotton batting as thick as Mira's bandage. The girl nodded, yes, yes. Despite her comparative youth, Mira's own competitive drives recognized Isabel's story. Roman saw with a little awe that underneath the girlish conversation and the diffident air, Mira Sullivan's *daimon*, her soul *intacta*, was far more sophisticated than her years or upbringing. An inner woman sipped champagne and sat poised on that appalling sofa for her personal circumstances to catch up with her God-given gifts. There was a Mira-spirit that already assumed the gaucheness would wear off, the face would resolve, and the well-meaning father would be accounted for, somehow.

Roman scrutinized his glass, unsure where her easy conversation about teaching part-time while building a concert repertoire was leading them.

The American drawl, so different from Isabel's precise diction, lulled him in the fading dusk. He wished she would turn on some lights. He felt trapped in a timeless gloaming with this girl, making surreal conversation about his wife's drive and speed – as if Isabel were an exhausting make of car. He felt more and more like an attendant page at Mira's feet or a courtly visitor to her impersonal dominion bringing news of a distant adult kingdom of responsibilities and routine. With each sentence, the blurry picture he painted of his wife in perpetual motion only underscored the embarrassing stasis of his own existence.

Mira sat very still, listening to Roman expand, despite himself, on the topic of marriage between two professionals, in terms as loyal as possible. Her black pupils widened as the sinking darkness enveloped them. Mira's prickly forest of protective reserve, her tangible anxiety that the deliverance of her music wouldn't hold, that the cloth of love wouldn't cling – he'd fought that battle. Now in this premature twilight of a featureless apartment, there was an air of passive reception settling about her. He saw her form reflected in the darkening pane of the living room window like a fairy-tale illustration in pen and ink. Her thorny soul's hedgerow unfolded its branches towards him while she sat serene at the centre of the un-explored woodland. The dark bandaged beauty was sleeping more fitfully, tossing, a restless spirit waiting to assume her rightful throne.

How long had they sat there, sipping and confiding? Roman could hardly make out the hands of his watch, " . . . well, now, I must depart to my sister-in-law's roasted capon and figs. *Merci, Mademoiselle*, with a Merry Christmas to you again, and please convey my best wishes to your father."

Making his lame speech, he rose knowing that his own protective reserve felt threatened. The wine curdled his stomach, collapsing in on itself for want of lunch. Outside the windows, thick-banked yellowish fog had blackened the sky, leaving only one's ears to report on life outside – the swish of tyres on wet asphalt, a stereo thumping away in some adjacent apartment.

Now Geneva social custom dictated that having shared a glass on such a sentimental evening, Roman and Mira should exchange light, formal kisses on both cheeks. Medical protocol recommended a handshake be the limit. Roman collected his coat and moved towards escape, extending his large hand to feel the pale, agile fingers grasp him back. She presented her good cheek to be pressed against his. His reflexes were too slow, his solitary being dizzied by the eerie sense of a command perform-ance descending from the footlights just for him. The long-forgotten sensation of a female reaching *up* to him intoxicated him. He put his hand out to protect her bandaged cheek, but his fingers slipped into the thicket of wild, moist hair.

179

She launched into a flurry of kisses brushing his rough cheek and with a start, he felt her tongue searching his wide lips. She was his patient – this was all quite ridiculous, he thought as he tried not to kiss her back, but in fact, let her explore his mouth with an unexpected hunger. In fact, he enjoyed the sensation more than he could have imagined. He could only stop her by embracing her tightly, holding them both, her full breast to his chest, murmuring, "Shush, shush," as if to a child waking from a nightmare.

He smoothed down the springy tumble of hair and breathed with her in deep rhythm, his day's growth of beard catching at the bandage, all the while, the thumping of some manic rocker vibrating the floor under their feet.

After a few minutes, he drew away. His collar had got stuck to her adhesive tape, so this extraction required a slightly less passionate degree of concentration. He avoided her gaze until he saw she was trying not to giggle.

"It's all right, it's all right," he laughed, to reassure them both. All this for Christmas! – he was flooded by the boyish sensation of unwrapping an unexpected present. The power of knowing that all this energy and hope was his – just for the asking – filled him with undeserved joy.

He zipped up his coat, rescued his cashmere scarf off the floor, and left the apartment; he carried away an image of Mira still standing where he had embraced her – in the nucleus of nothing, an indistinct figure retreating into a dreamy void, one hand outstretched in a wave.

Stirred and confused, he stumbled his way back to the car park. He rested for many minutes, safe in the familiar womb of dashboard and leather. Looking outside his marriage had never occurred to him. The dangers of adoring patients were obvious from the start of his career. Moreover, he was a contented man. "Other women" carried obvious complications, implications, and consequences.

Why risk career and security? Why should Mira Sullivan seem any different? Only because she beckoned to him from a strangely private place? She was his patient, he reminded himself, yet she had already set herself apart in his mind from that tiresome caravan of surnames and complaints that tramped through his hours. A neutral emptiness revolved around her like formless clouds circling a heated core.

The holy evening's blessing succoured Roman's hesitations. He set off for his brother's predictable supper surprisingly serene, even exhilarated. He looked forward to Isabel's telephone call. Of course, an embrace like that was not meant to happen and must be slotted into its appropriate place. Being Dr Roman Micheli, he only needed to integrate this new, intriguing element into acceptable alignment with the rest of his ordered life. He hummed a Christmas carol to himself, off-key. Everything would be fine. *Parfait.*

17

The city's first serious snowfall hit after midnight on what Isabel always called Boxing Day.

Genevans woke up to an urban precipitation – lacking the countryside's conviction – mushy plops rather than the powder flaking down on the higher elevations. The December morning promised more a suggestion of light than the real thing. Indoor lamps would burn all day. Snow tumbled and melted on cobblestone and granite for hours after dawn, leaving stubborn white patches covering Geneva's half-tones of pewter and slate. The trams' rumblings were muffled to a slither.

Alpine foothills ringed the southeast of the city and the slopes of the Jura slumbered to the northwest – the razor-sharp ridges of the younger range so exciting, almost religious in their heroic visions and fatal risks, while the older Jurassic hills sat wiser, softer, worn down by time and familiarity. Two tectonic options – like two recumbent women – each so different from the other.

The fresh cityscape inaugurated the beginning of what Roman would later recall as a gloriously empty week spent in exotic, semi-innocent suspension. Having cancelled their Tunisian break in the sun, Isabel set off to canvass Carlos's South American territory before the WHO family began its new year in earnest – unsheathing the bureaucratic daggers for the pitched battle to succeed Frank Norton.

His wife's starched Provençal pillow lay undented next to his unshaven cheek. Roman wallowed under the duvet and watched the snow climb by inches up the window overlooking the lake. Half-asleep, he gloated over the unexpected victory of wresting his deposit back from the travel agency.

He breakfasted in luxuriant ease, forgetting Spaghetti out on the shingles for more than an hour while he read *Le Temps* from front page to sports, *Espace 2* dribbling on Isabel's bathroom shortwave usually tuned to the BBC World Service. Throwing open the living room window to the wintry chill, he gloried in the raw winds rushing up off the shore, thick cloud blankets rolling one over another double-speed across the skies all to the soft accompaniment of a city bundled up.

Spaghetti scrambled in at last, shivering his sleek wet coat in rebuke. Roman obediently trailed the indignant furry rump down the corridor to the kitchen.

"Look at me." Roman stared at his rumpled reflection in the chrome face of the coffee machine. "I keep wondering, what is the Darwinian triumph of human beings? For the sake of the universe, I certainly hope something better than me is evolving – somewhere, somehow."

Roman patted the soft brown marks above Spaghetti's beige face. The cat's orange eye slits followed the can opener in Roman's gesticulating hand.

"The question is: do better forms of life ascend all the way to a God? Does He exist? Where is the proof? Could I see it if it were under my very nose? Or am I half-blind, only sensing an explanation just beyond my peripheral vision?" He thought of his Iraqi patient, Ayad Salim, fumbling for his jacket which lay unseen only inches from his thin hips.

The cat miaowed languorously.

"You pray for proof that a Higher Good exists? Despite all the cruelties of your world? You witness evil, let's say, the dog who bites the cat next door. An atrocity, I agree. And yet no whiskered angels descend bearing tidings of great catnap? You pray for a mouse in your basket, but no miracle mouse appears. And though I am a higher being and could report that vicious dog or set a mousetrap, I don't even notice the dog bite or the missing manna of mouse. I do not answer your pathetic prayers. And so in disappointment, you turn atheist. Even though I am right here."

Roman scooped out gelatinous offal. "Here you are, you horny furball. I touch the wall and giveth light. I transform cans into *viandes*. Let there be tuna nuggets. *Bon appétit*."

The week's empty days revealed themselves to Roman like treasure being unearthed. Monday, Tuesday and Wednesday passed uneventfully. He shaved by the dim daylight each morning, had his hair trimmed or his shoes reheeled, collected his croissants and loaf, salad and cheese, even dialled a few neglected friends to convey holiday greetings. To his relief, he heard only the canned cheer of answering machines.

He spent Thursday afternoon wandering through a Hodler exhibition at the Musée Rath but the images struck him as romanticized and false. By Friday, he felt restless where he'd expected to feel soothed, so he drove up to Martigny and mingled with the crowds viewing the Phillips Collection touring from Washington DC – until he caught sight of a former patient gazing at a blue Picasso bather in the distance. He skirted that side of the gallery, returning to it later.

He passed an idle Saturday revisiting Voltaire's old mansion on rue des Délices. He hadn't been there since his *gymnasium* days. The old man's pistachio and yellow salon hadn't changed, but the upstairs was freshly whitewashed and sleek. Voltaire grinned down from his bony Houdon statue, his skeletal hands gripping the armchair tightly, facing yet another century of *infâme*.

Only the charcoal haze dampening the Calvinist city drained Roman's holiday mood. On Sunday, he fled in his car up the twisting curves to the ski village of St-Cergue. When the nose of the car pierced the fog cover he felt renewed by the unmarred blue sky.

On a café terrace, he bathed his pallor in the brilliant mountain glare. Huge drifts of snow lined both sides of the main street, forcing passing cars to the middle. The village teemed with overclothed families, sports tribes identifiable by their gear: middle-aged couples in downhill boots and puffy neon suits, rowdies in snowboarder elf-hats and hang-dog sweatshirts, or sinewy cross-country loners in Lycra tights.

Roman nestled among them, a civilian in mufti, a Rip Van Winkle returning to life. He pulled off his sheepskin gloves and ordered a San Pellegrino. He observed the passersby: teenagers joking and shouting, competitive athletes laden with purpose, harassed families stripping the padded layers off their toddlers like unrolling cocooned pupae to dry them out in the warmth of the sun.

He basked in the company of so many healthy people, feeling a strange new affection for them all, just content to sit on the margins unencumbered by their social rites. Life was complicated enough without all that.

At a nearby table, a young father knotted up a soiled nappy and headed into the bar. Roman's secret son-vision, that congenial, articulate tousle-haired treasure of a non-being, Micheli Junior, had skipped toilet-training. Conveniently, that fantasy occupied an eternally sweet-smelling stage somewhere after nappies and before pimples.

Here and now, at this café, Roman might have bought *figlio Micheli* a soft drink, just as his father had so many years ago. They would have debated in mock-seriousness the merits of skiing versus snowboarding and why it was still important to study Latin and Greek. Such imaginary arguments entertained Roman, whether he won them or not. Of course, his son always stood up for himself.

The important thing was to keep all things, real and unreal, possible and impossible, well compartmentalized. Roman imagined a strong locomotive pulling many times its weight in cars. If the rails were in good shape and the signals clear, a single engine could pull vast loads unimpeded across many miles.

Yes, Roman must keep the signals and crossroads clear in his mind. The red lights must be observed. He was the doctor,

Mira was the patient, Isabel was the wife. *Bien*, his wife, nothing so impersonal as *the* wife. He was hardly your average fool to be tempted by some middle-aged crush, some mid-life infatuation! Yet ... yet, wallowing today in the holiday clamour for pasta and fondue warmed by table-top butane burners, how his sun-drugged thoughts kept flying off the rails!

Since that heady fondling of the trembling Mira less than a week ago, Roman couldn't pass a boutique or jewellery shop without spotting some treat to shower on her, some marvellous bauble the prosaic "intelligence" officer would never notice. How had a girl so brimming with exquisite music managed to attain near-womanhood under the guardianship of that khaki bulldozer! Roman felt an urge to fill her beige cell of an apartment with delights for all her senses − fragrant flowers, inspiring art, more books to keep company with the ones she quoted so endearingly. He felt like ripping up that wall-to-wall mediocrity she called home and laying down carpets of culture and cuisine cooked up with his own hands.

His mind's nose recaptured the whiff of the cheap amber and vanilla coming off her shearling collar and he thought of the locked-up Guerlain counter he passed every night as he left the clinic. Had Mira ever inhaled Egyptian rose, tonka bean, iris, heliotrope, amaryllis, the wondrous complexity of a classic French perfume? He imagined her in the rainbow colours of Fogal tights, cashmere sweaters, silk lingerie encasing those breasts underneath her violin. All varieties of Italian unmentionables winked at him from shop windows and he also imagined − despite himself − Isabel sneering at how anybody found the time to hand-launder such things.

In short, he dreamed of reclaiming the girl Mira for Europe. *Oui*! Surely that was it. Not a personal desire, *non*, more an artistic imperative, practically a political mission. Wasn't Mira essentially European like him? Her music defied all the banality of her adoption. Her ancestors bred mystery and song in their bones fed deep by Romania's forests where bears and Gypsies roamed. Anyone could see that rich legacy must be suffocating under a tasteless American veneer. Outrage over the cultural kidnapping of Mira Sullivan surged through Roman with a selfless fervour – yet didn't it also make his balls ache deliciously, such as he hadn't felt for years and years?

Oh, the florid images flew at Roman – so inured to scarred, tattooed, discoloured and oozing flesh; his imagination seemed to be declaring a vacation all of its own. Dazzled by the sunrays ricocheting off the snow, all Roman could think of was this particular skin, the blotchy new whiteness revealing itself week by week underneath the wine-dark cheek. Symmetry restored from nature's fairy-tale curse at birth. What power! Had he ever imagined what happened to people once they finished his treatment? He had never even tried to find out. Only two days ago, he'd avoided a former patient in the museum as irrelevant and intrusive. Wouldn't it really just start with Mira once he'd finished her treatment? Wasn't there so much more to do?

He already imagined her as he relinquished her back to the world. Only a blush down the cheek might remain once he had finished. It was too early to say. Not all cases were *évident*. Now thanks to him, there would be beauty to spare. Would that be the end, as usual, or would it be only the beginning?

Roman glanced at the menu weighted down on the metal table. He could order or not. No one waited for him. No one stretched their legs with impatience next to the aquarium or thumbed through old copies of *Bilan*. He was liberated – from the shackles of Chantal's infernal appointments book, from the machine insurers' monthly bills, from the – no, no, he didn't need liberation from his marriage. He was bound to Isabel by love and loyalty, not handcuffs. He closed his eyes against the sun and let the warmth of self-knowledge soak his soul.

Indeed, it was a comforting thing to know he would not fall prey to a childish enslavement that endangered his hard-earned serenity. Any masculine weakness could prevent him from making sure that everyone was happy in the end. He imagined

Isabel, Mira, the Colonel and himself, warbling an aria in four parts, like his father's Mozart 78s.

Nonetheless, there were so many things one could have done, perhaps still could do, for a girl so exceptionally gifted. Mira was a butterfly awaiting release from her chrysalis, ready to share her fire on the world's stage, her blood rushing through those pounding veins with each cadenza. He recalled the strength of her upper arm, firm and white, making arcs with her bow, her face pressed sweetly against the instrument, rapturous expression on her –

"Doctor Micheli?" A man standing above Roman cleared his phlegmy throat.

Roman squinted into the slanting rays. A spectral shadow towered over his table. He lost his image of Mira wearing something diaphanous, playing Elgar in front of hundreds of people after dedicating it to the abashed dark-haired doctor sitting third row centre.

"Well, it is you, Doctor Micheli! I guess we haven't seen each other since that polio reception."

Roman grasped the freckled hand and tried to make out the interloper's features.

"I guess Isabel's running around as usual, leaving you all alone?"

Of course, that multi-syllabled "alone" took some struggling with, those Australian vowels that wandered through three phonetic backyards before deciding where to settle. Roman took in the over-worked frame in the drooping brown ski suit, two sunburned pre-teens lurking restlessly behind him. How unlucky to discern the rangy features of Frank Norton, Isabel's defecting department chief.

"Ah, Doctor Norton. *Mon Dieu*, these are your twins, so tall? Please sit down. Can I offer you a coffee? A Rivella for the children?"

Norton exuded relief at stumbling into a familiar face. With sullen shrugs the Norton boy and girl accepted drinks. The sapphire sky washed the other holiday-makers with a forgiving radiance and on all sides of Roman's table, families peeled off Goretex and sweatshirts. The Nortons, however, lips blue and cracked, noses dripping, displayed their gloom like damp dogs left leashed outside a liquor store. In a forced gesture of affection, Norton tousled the hair of the boy, who pulled away.

" . . . said I'd take them for the hols, and we're having a fine time, right, Brian?" He confided to Roman, "Lana and I used to bring the kids up here when they were little for sledding, had a fine old time over at Basse Ruche. Said they didn't remember it much when we got here this morning. The last few winters we took 'em over to Chamonix for some big skiing, but I'm pretty busy this winter with Lana gone, and the move to the new department . . . "

This offhand reference to abandoning Isabel was slipped in under radar, but Roman couldn't resist inserting a wicked, "Transitioning?"

" . . . In more ways than one. It's been eighteen months now since the divorce. Lana's set up her own practice in Perth, but you know, these things take time . . . Gone to Phuket with her new boyfriend for Christmas, helping a bit to resuscitate the tourist economy, you might say," Norton explained, "Gary's a bovidine obstetrician – "

"*Pardon?*"

"Ah, well, just a jumped-up vet specializing in artificial insemination, I reckon." Norton fingered his beer mug, "And that's more polite than some other things I've heard those guys called back home?" Roman struggled to understand Norton's antipodean vowels, " . . . but they make millions down there delivering lambs. The kids say he's a nice guy? I guess I owe her that much. It means a lot more air fares back and forth . . . ?" Roman nodded to Frank's string of interrogatives. "I had to make the jump for the money alone . . . hope Isabel doesn't feel I dropped her in the . . . Ah, well?"

Norton sucked at his beer foam and gazed at the customers clumping *heel-toe, heel-toe* in their rigid ski boots towards the restaurant. Some teenagers pushed past their table and a snowboard caught Norton's ear lobe, followed by a flurry of insincere apologies. In a startling outburst of animation, the twins burst into giggles, sputtering their drinks all over the table when their hapless father apologized back to the snowboarder. Roman offered a paper napkin, but Norton refused, brushing the slush off his temple in hangdog resignation. He did seem the kind of person who got hit by heedless snowboards or rival diseases with fancier budgets or wives absconding with millionaire vets. When the restless twins had finished slurping, their father shooed them off.

"I tell you," Norton said, leaning across the table with watery eyes, "never get a divorce. Kills 'ya, it does? Everything goes rotten during the Christmas season, no way you can make it all right for the kids. Keep that in mind, you and Isabel, if you ever hit a bump. You take it from me."

"We have no children."

"Aw, yeah, I forgot. Sorry," Norton looked only momentarily embarrassed, "lucky for you. Well, kids aside, it's still lousy. When you're in it, you can't wait to get out, anything to clear the decks. Lana was angry at all the travelling I did, never home, you know the story. Now nobody's home any more, because there isn't any more home. Where did the divorce get us? Now the kids are collecting all the miles. Messy."

Roman half-listened to Norton's dreary litany while an interior French dialogue lured his thoughts back to those two white arms wrapped around her violin in passionate embrace, that challenging stare over their accidental coffee, that figure lying calm through the painful laser sessions, eyelids fluttering under the goggles, taking quiet deep breaths to calm herself . . .

" . . . Isabel's ready to lead the team − not that there's much of a team left, with Carlos off sick − ?"

"Yes, I heard the news about Carlos," Roman commiserated.

"Well, yeah, it's still a little early to say for sure, but so far, the Ridley response to the lepromin smear is negative."

"Negative −"

"– So it's not multibacillary, and possibly not even pauci-bacillary."

"Curious."

"Ah, yeah." Ah yeah seemed Dr Norton's view of most things, but he startled Roman with a sudden rap of his knuckles on the tinny table. "You know, I'm glad I bumped into you? You tell Isabel to watch out over the coming months. Cover her ass, you know what I mean?"

"*Pardon?*"

Norton's tone hardened: "They're giving her a temporary fill-in to take over some of her workload. If Isabel's not careful, this little lady'll run rings around her – she's Hong Kong Chinese, third generation medical, made a big splash in SARS. I bought her a coffee the other day. Good-looking, co-operative, understated, but underneath all that Oriental dress-ing, a real talented toughie. Headed for the top, I reckon. Better remind Isabel that her P6 isn't a sure thing. Not that we all don't think very highly of your wife's work, but you know, these days," Norton hesitated before adding, "what with political correctness, donor sensitivities, and all that . . ."

Norton gathered up his hat and gloves. "So tell Isabel, it's not a sure thing, but then, it's the sure things that bore us to death, right?" With that the Australian Ghost of Christmas Lost rallied his offspring, rustled his family SUV into reverse through a sooty snowdrift and headed out of the municipal lot for the descent to Geneva.

The sun dropped behind a cloud and a steel shadow swept the emptying tables. The digital clock on the police station flipped its read-out to 3°. The undiluted joy of Christmas rebirth, the thoughts of gifts and love and a fresh new experi-ment that had flooded Roman's soul all morning fought against the sagging end of an ordinary afternoon. He pulled on his heavy gloves and paid the bill. What had he been thinking?

18

Isabel lugged her battered suitcase out of the taxi sideways to spare the wheels further damage. With a zombie's tenacity she scaled the familiar marble steps. She was green-gilled from jet lag, too tired to open the elegant Christmas presents waiting on the mantelpiece. She received her husband's embrace with numb gratitude and sank her exhausted frame into the narrow antique bathtub foaming over with fragrant bubbles. Outside their tiny bathroom window, the Geneva sky looked the colour of tin.

"It's so lovely to be home, darling, you can't imagine," she called to Roman reading in the bedroom. They shared their relief, as usual, to be together again; air travel on Isabel's scale begged eventual disaster, but the gods of the tarmac still smiled on Dr Hanford. Her luck was not only holding, but generous; nary a bag had been misplaced or a departure delayed. So now she was back again, safe again.

She worked the elastic band out of her hair, sank her gnarled mane under the water and rested a steaming flannel on her sore eyelids. Her tour of Carlos's territory had been fraught with misunderstandings; even when his field staff hovered at her elbow at every turn, she was drowning in missed cultural nuances. She was running up against some post-colonial Latin fatalism that even her customary Hindu or Sikh interlocutors would have deemed defeatist. She began to view the leprosy campaign through the prism of Carlos's quotidian despair.

Her body felt flabby and worn out. She surfaced out of the froth to find Roman, clothed in his slacks and a soft pullover, poised on the closed toilet lid, a glass of red wine in his hand. He was gazing down at her, his expression pensive. She waited for him to say something, but he only pondered the suds floating over her generous belly.

"Roman?"

"Hmm?"

"What did Frank say again about – "

"The Chinese *doctoresse*? Not much. I'm confident you can manage her."

"Funny, him mentioning her to you, of all people. Nobody said anything at work." She brushed some soapy froth off her breasts. "I don't want to get paranoid or anything."

"No, *cara*. It was just small talk, polite conversation."

"Polite conversation?" Isabel sniggered. "Not Frank Norton. He's got no social nous at all. Whatever he says pops out of his subconscious like one of those comic strip balloons. Once he called Carlos 'Che', right in the middle of a heated argument about leprosy vaccine trials. I can understand why Lana Norton 'transitioned' – "

" – for a bovidine obstetrician."

Isabel giggled. "You know, darling, while I was in Argentina, I had a scathingly brilliant idea. I will offer Father Shardar a short-term contract in Geneva to manage South Asia so that I can concentrate totally on the budget battle. And I'll put this dragon lady Cheong on Carlos's patch. That'll keep her – "

But Roman had wandered back to read. He certainly seemed distracted. She heard him fiddling with the CD player in the living room and then an Anne-Sophie Mutter rendition of Mendelssohn started up. At least she recognized that one as an old favourite. Isabel wondered if he was worrying again about his machines. Every call to the repair people sent him into a frustrated funk for a week.

"Doctor Hanford, the other night I reviewed the budget allocated to reporting and assessing cases in outlying regions and – "

Isabel glanced up from her pile of Frank's back memos. After much combing and sifting, she realized that Norton had spent days drafting arguments that amounted to nothing more than appeals for funds to finance fund-raising. A ream of circular waffle. She resented the Hong Kong doctor's intrusion.

"Yes, Doctor Cheong?"

"Please call me Cecilia."

"Yes, of course. Call me Isabel."

The good doctor poised herself on the edge of the visitor's chair in Frank's office where only weeks before Isabel had flopped down in frustration. The newcomer looked powdered, coiffed and immaculate in a lime wool suit with hammered leather piping set off by a jade brooch. The tiniest gold crucifix dangled on the ivory rectangle of her neck. A large mole grew out of her delicate chin. Isabel had heard that the Chinese revered such moles as hefty portents of personality and luck in Chinese culture, but she couldn't help thinking that Dr Jonathan Burden would have lopped it off with Frank's letter opener here and now.

Isabel braced herself for this morning's bright idea. Cheong seemed to have learned English by listening to inspirational radio shows – everything came out informative, upbeat and totally patronizing.

"Isabel, this budget shortfall gives me a good idea. As you may have guessed already, I love a challenge. I've had some experience with the problems of demographics and contagion on the mainland. During the first SARS outbreak in April 2003 – "

"Yes, Frank said you were one of the key people – "

The doctor started tapping on her clipboard with a tortoise-shell fountain pen, "Of course, SARS was highly contagious – nothing like leprosy. In Hong Kong we designated all of Princess Margaret Hospital and Prince of Wales as SARS-only. But how to arrest transmissions all over the mainland? Terrifying! Health providers falling sick as fast as patients! The Chinese health communications infrastructure was very ill-prepared. Mainland officials don't like to release bad news."

This woman was all defined lines, her blunt haircut of black brush sweeping the collar of her hard-edged suit, her impeccable pale tights running down to the polished Italian shoes.

She ran the top of her Dupont back and forth across the upholstery of her armchair. " . . . In Beijing, we persuaded the AsiaTel-China joint venture headquarters to pre-program their cheapest model of mobile phones. AsiaTel shipped them to the hinterland for reporting directly to our disease control mappers."

"My goodness."

"Yes," Cheong continued in her mix of British and Chinese accents: "Immediately on diagnosis we interviewed victims long-distance about contacts. We collated pertinent data on possible transmission. We alerted adjacent districts – "

"You're suggesting we use mobiles to support the blister pack programme and follow-up medical checks – ?"

"Exactly! Reinforce motorcycle and foot-doctor visits. Yes! Especially in the mountain regions."

Isabel pondered this.

"How many mobiles did these telephone people provide?"

"To cover the entire network of mainland health centres, we started with three hundred thousand."

Isabel gasped, "Three hundred thousand?"

Cheong's glossy lip curled with distaste as she chuckled, "China is so big, yet so backward. Company could give us old model. Mainland consumers are earning more money now, only accept latest technology. Howbout I work up a proposal to assess the needs in a priority target country and a second list of possible suppliers? We persuade them to donate first-generation smart phones with still-photo capability for long distance examination and diagnosis?" The Chinese sniffed, "Nobody buying that model any more with video-capable phone prices dropping fast."

Isabel softened a bit. "Well, it might work in India or the Philippines where the villagers are tech-savvy, but I can't see it working so well in Sudan or Brazil. Wouldn't they just get stolen?" Isabel's memories of South America were painfully fresh.

Cheong ignored the awkward suggestion of Third World vandalism. "Isabel, this is the sure thing to back-up the accompanied-MDT cases. Maybe that would shut up your missionaries who want everybody to come to the clinics."

Isabel smiled despite herself. Imagine Father Shardar 's scorn at the idea of treating the hill patients by SMS and smart-phone photos! Oh, let Cheong run with her idea. What was the harm? No doubt by next week the Hong Kong woman would be distributing diagnosis demos on portable DVD players.

"I'm afraid you've forgotten one thing," Isabel said with a note of sympathy for Cheong's enthusiasm. "You've spent most of your career in Hong Kong and perhaps haven't spent much time in the remote field. You must realize that some of our villages don't even have electricity. Wouldn't these phones need recharging? Where would our more isolated patients plug in?"

Cheong practically jumped with glee. "I was hoping you'd ask! No problem, Isabel! I thought of that already and ordered these gadgets for testing under operational conditions." She reached into her Gucci briefcase and pulled out her own mobile connected by a short cord to two AA batteries housed in a sort of lipstick case. "Latest device for using ordinary radio batteries to recharge. No need for charger. For sale on internet." The Chinese winked, "But of course, you make them donate."

Isabel's mouth hung open at the sight of the clever little cables dangling over her desk. The most remote village shop-keeper sold transistor radio batteries. She swallowed her pride and asked, "When do you think you could have a draft of this, Doctor Cheo – sorry, Cecilia?"

"Oh, here's my draft. I'll keep you updated."

Isabel took the printout and nodded, "Thank you, Cecilia."

"It's my pleasure." Cheong's eyes crinkled with anticipation and the powdery little mole twitched its hairs like a mouse's whiskers. She glanced at her Rolex and started in surprise.

"Wah!" she said, like an excited winner of a television quiz show. "Not too late to call Reykjavik!" And with that, Dr Cheong was off like a sprinter at Happy Valley.

Isabel blinked once or twice and blew her nose. She'd caught a cold on the long flight from Rio. She glanced at her watch, sipped her cold tea and read more of Frank's pathetic memos. She had half an hour left before her first appearance as Frank's replacement at a morning meeting of department heads. Judging from the paperwork, there were huge gaps in the stats coming in from the Congo, Mozambique and Niger. Carlos had spent thrice the time on South America than on sub-Saharan Africa over the previous eighteen months. She suspected that the Sudan made Brazil look good.

There were only a few weeks before the next big reporting roundup. Under the current budget, the Technical Advisory Group had asked for two more years to develop new diagnosis tests and employ them in the field over five years.

The money just didn't match up. Damn Frank! Damn! Damn! Isabel had calculated the figures twice over. Frank must've hidden this shortfall for months; and made sure he wasn't around to announce the bad news when the deadlines fell.

With a practised gesture the discreet Chantal interrupted Dr Micheli's session with M Emmenegger to slip the doctor a hand-written note – not on the clinic's plain notepaper – but on blue stationery framed by a girlish wreath of embossed pink and yellow daisies.

Dear Dr Micheli,

I hope you and your wife had a really good Christmas vacation. I'm sure we didn't intend to mess up our doctor-patient relationship when you accepted my invitation for a drink, but I guess that's what happened. After thinking things over, I've decided that maybe I need a break from my treatments. Maybe after a while I'll change

my mind, but I can't say right now. I'm really sorry about
disrupting your scheduling, so please bill my father extra for any
inconvenience the cancellations cause you. Anyway, I've got a few
concerts coming up that I should be better prepared for, and as you
said, the inflammation should be down in time for a public
appearance. It's probably all for the best.
Thanks for trying to help me,

Sincerely yours,
Mira Sullivan

Mess up our relationship! Maybe this and *maybe that*? What was
the idiotic, gauche, inarticulate girl thinking? Roman crumpled
up the page of schoolgirlish lettering. Professional indignation
and personal disappointment clutched at his chest. Somewhere
muddled under these adolescent phrases was a fully-fledged
woman, but the utter lack of finesse in this pathetic girl's
withdrawal stood between that adult and her doctor. He'd
detected the *femme complète* in the light of the Victoria Hall
footlights, felt her embrace him, admired her courage under
the painful laser, imagined her – well, he couldn't hold her
accountable for what he'd imagined. Nonetheless, this hovering between fey child and breathtaking brilliance was maddening, maddening –

"Can I get up now, Doctor?"

Roman glanced at the patient Emmenegger in the protective
goggles, goggles that should be wrapped around Mira's head in
less than an hour.

"*Non, non*, we're not finished yet," he muttered. "*Pardonnez-
moi*." He opened the door to the reception area. "Chantal,
please try to telephone Mlle Sullivan. It's about this afternoon's
appointment."

Against his better sense, he'd marked off the days and then
the sessions in a countdown towards Mira's first appointment
of the new year. Would she mention their embrace? Or wait
for him to take command and assume responsibility for what
happened next?

Why should anything else happen? He should finish her treatment and then perhaps, no longer patient and doctor, they could be friends. After all, he admired her musical genius. What stamina! Memory! Discipline! Roman shivered with pleasure thinking of the rigour of her *formation professionelle*, the precision, exactitude, (all those traits in himself that Isabel mocked.) But this had nothing to do with Isabel. Husband and wife were getting along as usual. The remaining days of the holiday had passed contented. Roman admitted that his favourite new pastime, playing Sibelius, Schubert, and Tchaikovsky CDs while imagining Mira rendering each piece while wearing considerably less than most virtuosi had a rather obvious adolescent aspect – but surely listening to music was harmless?

He couldn't wait to see the real Mira again – by now his thoughts of her fluttered and flapped happily around their secret cage locked off from the rest of his mental routine. He commiserated with Isabel about Brazil, whisked up creamy pasta to soothe his wife's ragged soul, fed Spaghetti veal left-overs – all the while anticipating his next encounter with the musician.

There would be a touch of awkwardness, of course. His professional calm would ease that away. Then would follow the delicious intimacy of the treatment itself, where, with all medical proprieties observed, he was still free to hold her face in his hands, carefully rearrange her hair to accommodate his beam, lean close to her, see those miraculous hands resting on her skirt.

Everything would return to normal, with a *promise*, but of what? At his weakest, he'd dared to imagine a second kiss. He'd worked out in his mind the words with which he would fix her into some kind of emotional holding pattern allowing him time to sort out his own anxious feelings. Somehow, he was sure, once back on his territory, he'd reclaim authority over the situation; all the usual professional ammunition stood on his side of the siege – his spotless white coat, the hum of machinery, the antiseptic air they inhaled together, the reassuring slap of Chantal's slippers in the corridor outside the closed door.

He'd wanted to safeguard his sweet confusion for as long as he could; now this infernal blue letter punctured all fantasy. It was exactly one-thirty and by cutting ten minutes off the Weilhand case and pushing a fifteen-minute delay on the two-twenty-five consultation, Roman calculated on eking out thirty minutes to persuade Mira to change her mind. Throwing on his coat, he fled the clinic's supportive warmth – bubbling aquarium, DVD drone, and Chantal's dove-like cooing down the telephone – for the frosted city outside. Pedestrians, cars – even the flags lining the quai du Mont-Blanc – were chilled into a slow-motion still-life. The ragged street violinist had abandoned his parking entrance enclosure and loitered outside the Paillasse bread counter, clapping his chapped hands together over a steam ventilator. With little more than the consolation that Mira had agreed over the telephone to receive him, Roman nosed his car downhill into the midday crawl. He was long past perceiving the incongruity of a doctor navigating quai Gustave-Ador to personally retrieve a patient.

He'd scarcely touched the bell when she opened the front door and stood back to let him pass. This Mira Sullivan was not the pliant fantasy he'd nurtured over solitary days, but a resolute flesh-and-blood person who met his irritation with undisguised exhaustion. The Christmas Eve laser session had left a square of ten rows of rust-coloured spotty tracks covering her downy cheek. Roman was tempted to test the resolution and examine a slight crusting that was forming on one of the small areas – some Vitamin E and arnica salve would speed the healing – but Mira had already sensed his desire to touch her and moved slightly away.

His indignation was enormous, a stew of anger and relief such as might be felt by a parent retrieving his toddler from a dangerous ledge. Cloaked in silence, Mira looked set on meeting his emotions with a resistant, almost absorbent passivity.

He hovered near the door and twisted his driving gloves.

Unable to find the right beginning, he hesitated lest he lose his bearings further by venturing deeper into that impersonal expanse.

"You shouldn't have come. I wrote you why." She swallowed and slumped down on a barstool facing the open kitchen counter.

He could only see her defeated shoulders and bowed head, but mustered, "The treatment can continue as before. There is no problem, and I assure you, no, no complication." He found the crumpled letter in his pocket and thrust it back at her, as if rejecting the words themselves.

Her answer came as an unexpected slap. "I might believe that. Maybe it would be easier to continue, only not with you. I'll find a different doctor. I can't come for session after session and feel the wrong way about you, a married doctor. I think there are rules about that from your side." She hesitated, "Believe it or not, I have my own rules, too."

Roman's chest constricted. Find another doctor? His starched white coat, his professional armour deflected nothing? Protected him from nothing?

"Really, Mademoiselle, there's no need to dwell on it," Roman demurred. Her flat, clumsy allusion to Isabel, even indirect, already panicked him. Wasn't it easier to stay in that fantasy bubble that had floated so cheerfully throughout his holiday week alone?

Was it ignorance or innocence that drove her dolefully on? "I mean, well, it's obvious that something's happened, right? I feel so close to you. I feel very comfortable, very safe when I'm with you. Apart from the unendurable agony, of course."

She touched her cheek in a light comic gesture and despite their dismay, both laughed. She added, with an imperial defiance that shocked him, "You could send me to another specialist, couldn't you?" She folded her arms in front of her chest and squeezed herself for support. "Wouldn't that be more appropriate?"

"*Oui*, I'm a happily married man." How trite. How banal.

Imagine referring her all the way up to Neuchâtel to see that mechanic Baumhofer. What a ridiculous idea. "Let's not be so troubled by what happened." He saw she was starting to cry. "You know, you are young." He cleared his throat. What an old man he sounded. "Perhaps such things seem more important to the young. *Merci* for the kiss, but let us just say, *bien*, it was the spirit of Noël."

She proved more honest than he. "I didn't hang any mistletoe. I'm not looking for an excuse. I wanted it to happen."

He sucked in a deep breath and offered her another chance at escape: "Sitting in this lonely, impersonal apartment, a little champagne, these things happen, *non?* It is of no consequence, shall we say?" He worked up a smile but it froze, silly and impotent, on his lips.

She looked confused at this dismissal. He blustered on: "Let us continue as before, finish your treatment, putting that little *lapsus* behind us?" *Merde*, now he was speaking Latin to the girl! If he'd pictured something, it was not this – these patronizing older-man excuses parading as sophistication in a dead language!

Mira's eyes narrowed, glancing from his helpless grimace to his hand, stretching out to her like an independent party to their conversation. He could not command the damn thing to return safely to his pocket.

"You don't understand, Doctor Micheli. It's not like I'm, like, in love with you or anything – "

"Oh, *non, non, non* – " He shook his head in one direction, then another, encouraging, discouraging, with all the coherence of that patient Shino.

" – You see, I just want to make sure that I don't fall in love with you later. I mean, I've heard about women having a thing with their doctors. It's normal, you know, for a girl to get a crush on her doctor with his powers to transform you, cure you." She shrugged. "You look okay for your age. You're probably used to it. That's probably why you say nothing happened – "

"Well, of course, a *thing* happened – " Was he trying to retrieve or release her?

"You see, it's not normal for me. Now you've held me like that – " she gestured feebly to the spot where they had embraced only ten days before – "I couldn't, you know, go on . . . " her voice trailed off into a helpless whisper.

Roman dreaded another doctor treating Mira Sullivan. He, Roman Micheli, was the man destined to remove the birthmark from this miracle of talent who would go on to do wondrous things. She was *his patient* first, he would not relinquish her to anyone else. He must say anything to keep her. If she denied being in love, then she possibly loved him already. She defended herself with lies, outright lies. Yes, yes, that was it! She was in love with him, it was obvious – her denial was the very proof! He felt elated, charitable, and secure once more. All he had to do was bind her to him, act on it, *for her own sake*. That was the best thing for everyone.

"You have no reason to fear anything," he said, his wayward, disobedient right hand still wavering in mid-air. If she shook it now, they would have settled it, forever after, doctor and patient.

Instead, she reached with her left hand like a partner taking up the offer of a dance. The air collapsed between them as she sank into his confused and hapless embrace. This time there was no rough bandage preventing the brushing, rushing kisses that covered her cheek. She felt so small in his arms, so round on top, so slender below. Her mouth was full, dry lips bitten and chapped with tension, now swollen with crying. And suddenly everything felt swollen and full and too muffled underneath coats and tights and shoes and slacks and –

Roman was a married man and Mira was confirmed within twenty blissful if awkward tender minutes as most inexperienced. He was not an overeager boy. Everything was in his control again, normal. Everything fit as exactly as he could have designed. So, there was no need to let things get out of hand, after all. She'd said she didn't want to fall in love with him, and he was so very much in love with his wife. They understood each other perfectly and how she melted so sweetly despite all that!

Tumbling through the ticking seconds of his stolen lunch break, half-on half-off that virginal sofa, so stiff from its factory delivery, Roman felt an almost comforting sense of sin, his own Original Sin, envelope him. No longer the cleansing god, he was merely a man after all. Who could say from moment to moment who was the patient and who the healer? This was the most delicious thing that had happened to Dr Micheli in twenty years of touching other people's skin.

19

Yoji's letter arrived in Geneva the first week of February. He relayed rumours bouncing around the karaoke and strip clubs of the Kabuki-cho district and the Golden Gai alley bars – including Shino's own beloved hang-out, the Ginger Gin. And not just rumours. Last week Yoji dropped off Takahana at a shareholders' meeting, and went to pick up some chicken *yakitori* takeout from Hoku's, where he was elbowed aside by two guys leaning across the grill right into the chef's face, right in the middle of his customary welcome yell, *"Irashaimase!"* They wanted to know where they might find Takahana's "so-called driver", Yoji warned. "They looked like Onishi's guys."

Shino deciphered Yoji's heartfelt scribble while perched on the edge of Micheli-*san*'s treatment table, legs crossed tightly under the thin examination gown. His body resembled a half-finished jigsaw puzzle; his upper arms and groin sported discoloured rectangles at various stages of pigment dispersal, advertising the relentless work of previous weeks. He folded the letter into tight little squares just as he saw Dr Micheli pulling on surgical gloves tighter than a condom in a Chiangmai cathouse.

"*Bien*, Monsieur Shino, this tattoo is so private, perhaps you have changed your mind? Prefer to keep a little souvenir? Then this must be the most delicate of our sessions, *non?* You insist this is necessary? *Allons*, Chantal. Please terminate the cigarette, Monsieur. *Merci*. Perhaps I will administer an anaesthetic? It would be best."

Shino felt the doctor press on his genitalia with discreet, but obvious medical curiosity. It isn't me insisting, Shino protested silently – in fact, his penis tattoo was his greatest vanity. He hadn't collapsed when the two tattoo assistants held his foreskin taut so the master could work. He hadn't fainted afterwards from the pain, like that famous wrestler Heikuro – such a wimp. And as tribute, hadn't Horijin tattooed the two characters for *shino-bu*, "endurance" and "living in concealment" where Shino's pubic hair would grow over?

Nevertheless Tokyo had decided for him, decreed that he would only be safe once every tattoo, the last trace of *Irezumi* Shino was erased. Admittedly, his face was much handsomer than before. He'd emerge from his Purgatory almost a different man. *Hai*, he owed them everything – and yet? He couldn't help but resent the one thing that would never change: back home he would remain forever *eta*, unclean, the descendant of generations of undertakers, the lowest class of *burakumin*. Ironic to think now that his untouchable status was the very taint, the permanent and invisible stain, that had pushed him inexorably into joining up with the likes of Takahana. Why be thankful for that? As if nobody needed an undertaker sooner or later! At the end of the day, even the Emperor needed burial.

The only undiluted gratitude he had ever felt was to this strange doctor, a true gentleman who treated Shino for the first time in his grovelling, bowing, subservient life with straightforward respect.

How disloyal, Shino! Think of something else, *hai*! This Chantal woman never wore any stockings, even in winter time. Her legs weren't smooth and manila white, but brownish and stubbly. Shino preferred nurses in white stockings. Micheli-*san* smelled of fresh lotion rubbed all over the freshly-shaved facial hair that invaded half his throat. Black fur blanketed the sides of the doctor's neck, his wrists, even his Adam's apple. The Japanese closed his eyes and thanked the gods he didn't have to shave every single day.

The doctor was so relaxed after his religious break! Shino

had once taken the horse-faced whore from the Ginger Gin to a western comedy where the American mother went on Christmas vacation without her little boy. For some reason, the whole family lived in some kind of institution. (No single family dwelling could have so many rooms – even in America!)

Shino lay back on the examination table, straining to connect the slapstick "Boy Stays Home For Burglary" to the likely festivities of his sober Swiss doctor. No, no, instead this European would ask for a blessing for the new year in a church somewhere. Perhaps Micheli-*san* even spent the anniversary making an offering at a shrine? Had the honourable doctor enjoyed a special fish dinner with his mother to show respect? Had Shino already committed a discourtesy by failing to inquire after the old Mrs Micheli's health?

Anyway, the clinic's atmosphere was much calmer now. At least there was no further comment on the hated Burden person challenging the doctor's medical domain. Shino knew Europeans had their own means of dealing with intruders. On a train ride to Kyoto, Yoji had regaled him with the grisly details of how an Italian mafia contact had returned a favour for Yoji's uncle in Yokohama. Shino listened to the murmurs of doctor and assistant.

"Monsieur, we leave you for a few moments while the anaesthetic takes effect, *non*?" The doctor patted his arm. The two starched figures left for another treatment room, leaving Shino prone with the massive laser machine warming up at his side.

He was so glad Geneva had finished Christmas. Shino hated the gloom of the Swiss December with its underlit dead-empty night streets. Winter was hard enough during holidays even back home. Shino stood in the rainbow glare of Takashimaya Times Square, a riotous blinking and flashing, and tried to wish away the palpable lull that hung over Lunar New Year – the filial obligations, the bowing and scraping, the well-wishing and blessings. Humid smog shoved Tokyo's pollution right up his nose. Braziers filled the alleys with the smoke of low-slung bars and their fishy smell clung to his jacket, no matter how he tried to mask his discontent in wreaths of cleansing tobacco.

How he missed that homey stench now! Shino had endured two dreary weeks in his apartment in working class Servette, staring up from his IKEA futon at Yoji's gift from Tokyo – a poster of the legendary Blind Swordsman, Zatoichi. His long hours were peopled with fantasies culled from lurid French BDs, *bandes dessinées*. He liked to spin stories in his head, and now they assumed not the childish, bug-eyed bright-coloured look of Japanese *manga* comics, but the more sombre *noir* images of the French graphics kings. Lately he imagined himself as the trench-coated and mysterious Shino seeking justice and revenge in the dark alleys of Paris, Warsaw, Budapest, Prague . . .

The young computer geek living on the floor below had draped Christmas fairy lights across his balcony rail. Their glow rose and fell in cascades of red and green against the frosty mist swirling below Shino's railed ledge.

When he got tired of dreaming up BD storylines, Shino tossed an overcoat over his bathrobe and sought the fresh air of his balcony to smoke a cigarette. *Thumpa thumpa thumpa.* A guitar bass rumbled through his slipper soles. Right underneath him, a gaggle of western kids shrieked to their impenetrable music on and off for days, like ritual ghosts.

Shino rolled out his bedding, each night testing yet a different corner of his apartment for sanctuary from the noise, but tormented by pounding, he lay aroused by the vision of the Swiss girls' roly-poly tummies jiggling to the music downstairs, belly-buttons bulging out from under glittery stretchtops.

Shino had nobody to gamble with and nobody covering her giggles with her hand like his Ginger Gin girl. Alone in his bathroom, he massaged arnica oil on his bruised skin, wondering if girls sporting navel piercings would have fancied his nipple rings. What about that girl ferrying party treats across the car park the other night? Shino hadn't been able to make out her features, but her spiky hair was dyed *Hello Kitty!* bubblegum pink. Did she colour pink between her legs, *hai*? *Hello Kitty, Hello Kitty* . . .

He tossed the empty bottle of duty-free Suntory into the trash. The honourable thing was to clamber over this flimsy railing and let himself fall to the asphalt, politely avoiding Hello Kitty Girl's yellow Opel if possible.

Honour or shame? His suicide would only grieve and further impoverish his widowed mother and hadn't she worried enough, without more questions being asked about him? He imagined his final moments, a foreigner in Air Tokyo slip-ons splat face-down outside the dry cleaners. Honour in that?

His office stayed open during Christmas, but no lassitude on Shino's part could lower the energy level of Minami Publications SA. Each morning Shino browsed *Asahi Shimbun Online*, culling court reports for tidbits. Or he pecked and poked at the keyboard calling up the latest sumo results. After a few hours of this tedium, Miss Dejima would boil water in the cordless kettle and fill three turquoise bowls with steaming noodles – shrimp for Shino, beef for herself and chicken with spicy sauce for Kakizoe who slurped as he totted up figures on a spreadsheet. The only fun left hitting up "subscribers" was in Paris – even in hiding, Shino was industrious; he'd fleeced Geneva's Japanese community of face months ago.

He saw out the European New Year's day watching Ozeki Tochiazuma's battle for the Emperor's Cup by satellite re-broadcast from the Kyushu Grand Sumo Tournament. The Mongolian grand champ looked nervous. The hairless mountain of gentlemanly force patted his flattened ponytail, brushed rice powder in an offering to the spirits, and then squatted, waiting. Two false starts, ahhhh – then he charged in low, ramming the *yokozuna* Asashoryu right over the edge of the mat! Shino could practically smell the sweat reeking of wasabi and mirin from his lounger in Servette!

At last the medical duo was returning. Shino glanced balefully between his legs. His arms were covered with tracks of rusting brown blotches. Swathes of his chest and stomach were flesh-coloured once more, but here and there resistant yellow-ish greens streaked across his skin.

"Chantal, remove Monsieur Shino's ring, *s'il vous plaît?*"

After today's session the only remaining tattoos were the spider webs lining his armpits and the jealous *oni*, with his lethal horns and vicious fangs over a row of blackened teeth. Jealousy, intrigue, all of life etched by Horijin would meet the fate of his snarling dragon, his *koi* fish dancing in the turquoise waves, the mischievous Benten Kozo and today, even his snake.

Chantal gingerly lifted the glans and its reptilian green eyes fixed her gaze. Halogen light glinted off the metallic dye covering the shrinking tube, silvery green scales recoiling from her touch until the snakehead, wearing its golden collar, flopped from between her latexed fingers.

"*Pardon, Monsieur,*" she blushed.

"A mind of its own?" Roman joked from the basin over to Shino, who managed a nervous chuckle. The Italian's sympathetic comment meant to say that the penises of all men formed an international fraternity? Though Shino wondered how European husbands could possibly survive without the relief of karaoke salons and the girls of Dogenzaka Hill.

Chantal worked the tips of small surgical scissors under the gold ring. She clenched, but the metal was surprisingly solid. The blades slipped sideways and jammed hard into the sparse bristles edging Shino's testicles.

"*Aiiiigh!*" The Japanese screamed, clutching at his balls. Chantal jumped away in shock. Roman attacked Shino's fat thighs with more novocaine spray. The Japanese's hairless torso rasped in and out, emitting tobacco-tainted squeals.

There was an awful minute of frozen staring at Shino, crumpled over and gasping with pain.

When the trio had recovered their poise, Shino nodded frantically and Roman injected a needle-full of lidocaine with such deft expertise that Shino could do nothing but wait for the anaesthesia to kick in. That stupid Swiss cow didn't even bow in apology. The doctor was searching out a stronger pair of clippers among his instruments – they looked capable of slicing through bone – and Chantal sterilized the shears carefully. At last the gold circle dropped into the nurse's palm. Roman detected a shiver cross her shoulder blades. The wounded snake lay prepped and flaccid.

Roman had never lasered a penis before. He considered himself sensitive to the feelings of patients exposing their sexual parts. He'd lasered off radiation markings from many breast cancer patients, their suffering organs lopsided by lumpectomy, tender and maimed, or sadder – the merciless zipper scar of a mastectomy running flat across the de-sexed ribcage. Despite himself, Roman was happier to remove radiation marks when he could see the friendly tattooing of an artificial nipple on a reconstructed breast. After all, he was both a man and a doctor – recurrence of the disease was everyone's first concern, the woman's survival the imperative. The oncologist's scalpel, the chemotherapist's exhortations, the radiologist's pulses – these activities relegated Roman's laser gun to the bottom of a woman's priorities.

Now, transforming a snake back into a penis – it was indeed a first.

"*Ça va mieux?*"

Shino managed a tiny grunt of assent.

Roman explained the problem of skin sensitivity, the pulse required, the risk of blackening. He tested the efficacy of the deadening spray. Shino pressed his lips together as Roman injected a second jolt of painkiller.

Shino emitted a slight whimper, a farewell to any chance of hearing ever again the feminine titters elicited by his erect snake, its head swelling lubriciously against the squeeze of its necklace, veins bulging down his shaft, scales throbbing up and down in ecstasy, and then, the triumphant spit – SNAP! The laser beam hit the base and Shino held tight, revisiting his snake's past conquests. How the saké waitress at the Ginger Gin trembled in play distress! How the raucous gambling downstairs punctuated the eager thrusts of his happy snake – how its triumph banished the shy Shino from the shadows, raised the lowly *burakumin* to heights of ecstasy! Shino's snake, bold and curious, tickled as the horse-faced girl's flattened ass bumped hard on the tatami mat. And how she had resumed her shift afterwards, hiding her giggles behind her work-roughened hand! She pretended to be on the game and Shino played along to give her face, but in fact he was her only client, the only one who came back.

Shino focused through his goggles on the doctor's head bowed over his work. Now there was no pain, only awareness, as if the dentist had decided to work at the bottom instead of the top. The assistant stretched the snake towards her as the gun approached. *Thwack, thwack*, no pain, only the cooling water's spurt, then the laser's snap.

All this – the demise of his snake, the erasure of his rice-pot, the finale of his dancing carp and dragon, his exquisite sumo apron – all gone. *Sayonara*, Superboy Kintaro. Shino's body surfaced slowly, restored from the grave of distaste and cowardice where he'd buried it years ago in favour of joining the select band of the *irezumi*. Here was the older, very ordinary *burakumin* returning to life – with bowed legs, stubby torso full of tobacco, saké, abuse. He was just an ugly, sallow, scarred, unfit leftover of a life of *giri*, duty and obligation, to *oyabun* Takahana. Where had his loyalty led?

As never before, Shino felt how much he owed Dr Micheli and in almost the same breath, realized he was sick to death of moral debts. He could not return to Japan only to hide, beholden and cowering. He would repay this doctor, yes, but with a gesture so grand, he could stride into the sunset like Toshiro Mifune's Sanjuro and never look back. Shino Watanatra would throw off a lifetime's chain of bending his soul at the waist before it was too late.

But how?

20

To bid farewell at the end of their "lunches" felt like an offence against their passion, while to share that passion was a sin *tout court*. Of course they didn't have any time for actual food and Roman had to admit to himself that he missed the ceremony his generation associated with love, the niceties of companionship beyond the carnal. Were it not for his afternoon schedule, they might have shared a fine Margaux. (The girl's knowledge of wines had been criminally neglected.) He could have prepared fresh tortellini from Épicerie Pizzo with a homemade *sugo* and a grating of fresh *parmigiano*. (Fetching himself a drink of water in the Sullivan apartment, he'd discovered a bright-green cardboard canister of pre-ground "parmesan cheese" on the shelves. He still shivered at the horrible memory.)

Not that he could drink alcohol at midday. He faced a full queue of patients each afternoon. Anyway, his poor Mira didn't seem to eat regular meals. Apparently, when he wasn't serving as a "spare man" at diplomatic dinners, the Colonel snacked in front of what Mira called "ball games". The Sullivan's gargantuan refrigerator tumbled forth ice cubes and housed Diet Pepsi and banana-flavoured low-fat yogurt but there was no fresh pasta or ripened cheese in sight. Worse, the Colonel's laundry alcove *cave* contained no wine, but enough crates of Jack Daniels and Coors to quench a thirsty platoon.

"What will you do this afternoon?"

Mira whimpered, "Don't remind me." In the twilight of her curtained bedroom, she pulled the sheets up to her chin. "I'm giving lessons for Graziella who's having a baby, and then another rehearsal with Anton for the charity function. Brahms' Second, written in Switzerland – "

"I should listen to that?" He traced the damp curls veiling her brow. Since January, Roman had spent many hours adding to his CD collection.

"Anton does a Liszt solo and then for an encore we play Schibler." Her black-lashed lids fluttered a little. His darling was dozing off.

Beyond her pearly shoulder the clock-radio read 14:17 in digits large enough to launch a bombing sortie. Rising from his pillow, Roman knocked his temple on a goose-necked studio lamp dangling from a loose hinge. He rubbed his bruises and gazed at the flowered bed cover. The harder Roman's eyes searched out the secrets of Mira's private chamber, the more he felt an intruder waking up inside a magician's box of tricks.

Mira's dressing table, flounced to match her awful quilt, was littered with eye-shadows, body talc, mascara wands and blusher brushes, hair elastics, clips, that cheap amber cologne and foundation tubes. (Imagine trying to fit a fraction of that retinue into Isabel's spartan sponge bag!)

The dermatologist in Roman detected a deodorant powerful enough to mask the exertions of the entire *Orchestre Suisse Romande*. The girl's bra lay across a tufted pouf. Roman cupped his hand over its owner, and caressed the soft hillock. Mira murmured.

Her mustard-coloured violin slept under an acrylic scarf on a side table. The rubber padded chin-rest looked greasy with make-up. Its flanges and screws pointed in the air like little squirrel paws. A misshapen lump of resin and a handkerchief smeared with make-up lay in the violin case. Her *archet* stood propped against the wall, its cable of horsehair resting limp. This humble mess moved his whole being with its disregard for anything but the final, glorious result, but also warned him he'd fallen in love with a rather sloppy person – all right, a total slob – quite unlike himself. Roman only wished he could share his amusement with his best friend – Isabel. Too bad they couldn't laugh together at the incongruous sight of his hairy frame navigating a sea of scattered sheet music in a boat of tacky chintz.

Mira's mark was resolving well; the surface was less pebbly already. He ran his fingers down her jawline. "What are you doing, Doctor?" she whispered coquettishly. She squeezed his thigh in return. He played with the close-cut nails and the bird-like wrist of her left hand. Such pleasure she gave as she learned new exercises to play on his torso! Yes, the girl was a quick learner. Why had Isabel never found that secret spot?

He thought of Shino's scaly snake. Did every man's penis command its owner? But why resort to such puerile excuses for his fallen state? The miracle of Mira's gasping caresses left him questioning that semblance of "order" guiding his life. A few weeks ago, he'd lorded like an omniscient, mocking god over Spaghetti's ignorance of the larger planet. Like Spaghetti waiting every morning on the window sill, Roman clung to the delusion he controlled the mysteries of life with systems and schedules. Now the tomcat fumbling across the roof tiles in all weather was none other than Dr Roman Micheli.

To have mistaken the petty technocracy of his previous life for morality! Everything he'd done "right" only buried him under an empty conformity. At last, he'd done one huge thing wrong – something risking career and marriage – only to feel redeemed.

"What're you thinking?"

Even spoken in flat American, her banal question was novel enough. Isabel never asked what he was thinking – she knew. She thought it for him.

It was a bit embarrassing to say he felt redeemed, so he settled for: "I have to go, *chérie*. How I would love to hear you rehearse the Brahms with your boyfriend."

"You silly old man. You know Anton's not my boyfriend." She yanked a T-shirt over her head to cover her abundance and all but naked, twisted her bow strings tight and tuned the violin. Roman listened to the sweet vibrato of the opening measures.

"Here's where Anton comes in − " she hummed and swayed her hips. Roman marvelled again at the blue veins rippling through the translucent back of her knees. He loved to hear her play for him alone. Yet his fantasy of a Mira perfected by his laser, radiantly costumed before an adoring audience of up-turned faces excited him even more.

They parted with an indescribable sweetness at the last possible flip of the clock's digits. Roman raced through the cultural Kalahari of the living room, casting a guilty glance at the studio portrait of the Colonel in uniform on a bookshelf devoid of books. Once again, he would be late for the afternoon line-up. Sweat broke out on his upper lip as he adjusted from his hot shower to the car park fumes followed by a fresh breeze off the lakeside. He had no time to return his car to its usual spot uphill and dived into the Mont Blanc car park, then rode up its infuriatingly slow escalator lined with watch and jewellery advertising. Did Mira really like her childish Swatch with its cartoonish face? Wasn't it time she wore a timepiece worthy of − ?

Could that be right? He glanced back down the ranks of glass-covered ads lining the escalator's wall. He twisted to stare back and found himself looking right into the forehead of a startled businessman on the stair behind him. At the top of the moving stairs, Roman stumbled over the case of the Gypsy violinist, overturning the man's pathetic few coins on to the sidewalk. In contrition, Roman emptied his pockets of spare change into the scuffed case. He rushed to descend again and remounted for a second time, riding past the offending poster.

There was no doubt.

He donned his reading glasses just to make sure and circled without pause in front of the bewildered Gypsy to repeat the upwards journey a third and final time. The grizzled news vendor stared up from her magazines, a cigarette hanging off her lower lip. The moving stairs now seemed to race, not crawl, past the transfixing poster:

"Laser Away Years in a Lunch Hour! Smooth Skin in a Single Afternoon! *Massages du Monde* and More! The internationally-famous Beverly Hills Beam Laser Clinic and Spa arrives in Geneva!"

Smaller print read, "Yearly memberships available at introductory rates for a limited time."

More cosmetic blurb than medical announcement, the offending ad featured the soft greys and silver of fashion photography. Lettering spanned the androgynous chest of a long-haired Adonis, seemingly oblivious to a bare-shouldered blonde goddess resting her head on his rippling abdomen. Their two bland faces challenged the onlooker with the arrogance of clean-jawed perfection. Very fine print running along the edge read, Dr Jonathan Burden, 022-897-7346. A head shot of Jonathan himself wearing a white jacket over a black turtleneck grinned at Roman from the bottom right-hand corner.

The bastard had done it.

Roman scoured his pockets for a scrap of paper to no avail, then hunted for a coin. All his money now nestled on the stained velvet of the Gypsy's case. With impatience Roman yanked a *Tribune de Genève* from its roadside dispenser without paying. He scribbled Jonathan's number across the masthead.

He felt murderous. Yearly memberships to a doctor's practice? How did that *con* Burden even get such an idea past the medical board? It'd taken Roman Micheli – Genevan-born and bred – two full years to wring a licence clearance for the city's first laser clinic from those sceptics. He'd been discreet, built his practice into a sober, reputable credit to the conservative powers that governed the canton's medical borders. Others had followed in Zurich, Neuchâtel and Lausanne, but he was the pioneer who'd refined the machines, reported the cases, fielded the constant challenges of that insurance Cerberus, Dr Ferdinand-Emmanuel Bouvier.

Roman marched through his reception area past Chantal's

gaping mouth into the safety of his inner office, slapping the newspaper into his fist. Chantal glared at a mother, complacently absorbed in *Luxury Goods*, while her brat kept banging a wooden horse at the aquarium glass. Why was *le cher docteur* ignoring his lunch trays week after week? Why was he taking calls on his direct office line, even when *la doctoresse* was out of town and the aged Madame Micheli certainly enjoying her daily siestas in Lugano? Why did the doctor now lock the right hand desk drawer where she needed regular access to the billing adjustments? If he had taken up showering at the gym, why didn't he ever need a change of sports clothes?

In fact, half the time he didn't even take his gym bag to the gym. Why?

More than once since the turn of the New Year, Chantal had suffered the frightening sensation that Dr Micheli's clinic was running on autopilot – and losing altitude with each passing week. Chantal had only two sure things in her life – Tibo and the clinic – if you could call Tibo a sure thing. Glancing at the slammed door of Dr Micheli's office, the assistant's eyes brimmed with tears.

The doctor was dialling out on his private line. Again.

"Hey, Roman! That's just like you, always the gentleman, first to congratulate me. That was Colette just now, my new receptionist. So tell me, how does she sound? Quadrilingual. Puts me to shame. So, you've heard the good news, huh? I've nailed down that partner...You can't say I didn't make you the first offer, right? ... Pretty soon. The doors open in a couple of weeks, provided we get delivery of the machines on time. Listen, lemme pick your brains for a sec. Back in the States, we've got a national Laser-for-Life deal guaranteeing priority appointments, discounts on facials and follow-up photo-ageing creams with customized moisturizer, sunscreen factor 1000, baby – hang on, just let me run this past you – Do you think that kind of thing would fly here? I mean, does Geneva have enough executive types to pay a premium for cutting in line?...hmm, no comment? Maybe we'll wait 'til we get the founder list built up, then toss the database to our marketing people in LA ..."

Jonathan prattled on in parallel with Roman's racing thoughts. Who was qualified to partner Jonathan in a new clinic? Not the two dermatologists in nearby Nyon who did acne and allergies. A new woman in Coppet had settled in a partnership with an immunologist next door – she did a lot of biopsies for hives and skin cancers. De la Crecy at the Cantonal would retire in a few years and anyway, he approached any laser procedure with the fanfare of a mission to Jupiter. Some dissatisfied youngster from Lausanne Cantonal looking for a funding angel? Hôpital LaTour?

Roman ran down a mental list of names, until Jonathan startled him with –

"Bouvier?"

"Yeah, Roman, yeah, that's what I said. *Bou-vee-ur.*"

Roman's heart pounded. "You do not mean Ferndinand-Emmanuel Bouvier, the gatekeeper for Albion Assurance?"

"Well, Ferdinand-Emmanuel? Ferd – , that's who I mean. I tell you, that guy is one fast worker. I'd love to sick him on a few insurance fogies down in Pasadena. He pushed the paperwork through in record time. I'm lucky I stumbled across him, practically by accident."

"I wouldn't have recommended him myself," Roman struggled out.

"Well, in fact, nobody proposed him as a potential partner. Somebody said that if I wanted to scope out the compensation position here, you know, get the narrowest benchmarks set by the insurance honchos ahead of time, I should check with this Doctor Bouvi-*ur*. He and I started talking machine costs, premium increases, the framework for approval – man, have you seen the mahogany walls of his office, Roman? They're, like, museum-quality – and anyway, one thing led to another. Then all of a sudden, I saw a teeny-weeny flicker of interest in his eyes – "

"I don't believe it," Roman mumbled to himself.

"So we hashed out the terms and agreed to split responsibilities down the middle – I manage the machine purchases and advertising campaigns, vet the masseuses, apply for cosmetic imports, handle rental and installation, and he lends his imprimatur for the local medical requirements, licensing – "

"It's impossible!" Roman exploded. "Bouvier denies laser coverage at the slightest excuse." The fat folder containing his enemy's terse letters glowered even now from the top of Roman's filing cabinet as he heard Jonathan's voice protest, "Whoa, whoa – "

"Jonathan, you and I are not best friends, but as you would say, we go back a long road. So I will tell you outright. Bouvier is dishonest. Through his family, he controls shares in Albion that he doesn't declare. All he wants is to keep Albion costs down and dividends high. He comes from an old Genevan family and would no more do a favour for an American *arriviste* like you than swim across Lac Léman in ski boots. He is setting a trap for you."

There was a long pause before Jonathan responded, "Well, frankly, Roman, I think you've lost a little of your famous Latin charm. Bouvi-*ur* assured *me* that he didn't see a problem, as long as there was valid medical reasoning behind the treatments – "

Roman shook his head in frustration. "Yes! And everything short of metastatic cancer and – and – and gangrene is unnecessary cosmetics to Bouvier. *Bouvi-ay!* You would not believe the birthmarks and disfigurements he's turned down for treatments. I've sent at least three cases to lawyers in the last year and a half without success."

"Hmmph." Roman could practically hear Jonathan processing this unexpected new slant on things. The American finally retorted, "Well, he's hardly going to refuse treatment at a clinic where he's a silent partner, now, is he?"

Another pregnant silence stretched down the line.

"This is an absolute conflict of interest!" Roman insisted. "Besides, Bouvier can't possibly defend any involvement in something with 'spa' in its name!" Roman shuddered. "No one in Geneva will believe this!"

"Well, as long as he's not directly involved in my diagnoses, I'm betting that Geneva won't see it your way. Anyway, Bouvier already cleared it with them – now how did he put it? – 'In all *transparence*', before handing over the licensing fees. So Roman, if you don't like the competition, maybe you better take it up with them."

"I shall."

"They might take a dim view of you trying to hog a virtual monopoly in this town on a cutting edge speciality. Swiss medicine has an international reputation to keep up."

"This isn't about medicine," Roman growled.

"No, it's the fall of Roman's empire. The Beverly Hills barbarians are pounding at the gate – with an insurance gate-keeper in their pocket."

"You won't last, Jonathan. This is the city of Calvin, remember? Sheer boredom will force you to close in a year."

"Times change. Even Genevans might change. *Wellness* seems to be the buzzword around here. Prevention's a recognized aspect of medicine – it's not all expensive prescriptions and high-tech machines. Who says a few aromatic massages won't prevent more immune collapses or stress lines than you treat? Don't turn up that noble profile of yours at a holistic approach – "

"Holeeestic? The only thing holistic when you finish are the holes in your patients' wallets!"

"Seriously, Roman, Switzerland can't stay a closed shop for guys like you forever." Jonathan clucked. "Oh dear, I was afraid you'd take it this way. Relax. At least I'm the devil you know. What can I say? That's the way the gravity belt unbuckles, buddy."

"I beg your pardon?" Blinded by fury, Roman couldn't process Jonathan's Americanism.

"And there's one other thing I might as well spit out. The last time I saw you two together, I realized Isabel didn't dump me for you, she dumped me for her burning missionary call. You were the kind of high-minded schlemiel who wouldn't get in her way, expect her to have children, or stay home to be a mere wife. At least when I had a wife, I had the real McCoy. So that's off my chest and now I gotta go. Our soft-opening's in two weeks, so let's say we make peace with a free Early Bird massage on the Businessman's Special – ?"

Roman slammed down the receiver. With some effort, he directed Chantal to prep Mme Boehlen and concluded the fidgeting child's consultation in record time. Why hadn't Jonathan Burden stayed in New York to fluff up Fifth Avenue's lips and empty Broadway's mink-lined pockets? Like a maniac mowing down weeds, Roman ploughed his laser gun up and down the bewildered Mme Boehlen's labal folds.

He squeezed in calls – to the board of medical practitioners, to the insurance tribunal and to Zurich for sheer sympathy from Kessler. There was nothing anyone could do. He finished his last appointment in a state of nauseous indignation.

He heard the dying wheeze of the lasers as Chantal shut them down for the night, then the recorded cadence of her departing gesture – the answering machine check. For ten minutes or more he sat alone, in the dispiriting glare of a solitary desk lamp, pulling at his temples. He felt a little better when he started pounding his fist on his desk, repeating under his breath, "Burden, Burden, I detest you, Burden and everything you represent."

A polite grunt interrupted his chant.

Shino stood silhouetted against the glow of Chantals' reception lamp glowing behind his back. He clutched his empty *portefeuille* to his stomach and bowed twice.

"I, uh, forgot ring this morning. For keeping, memory."

"Your ring?"

Roman glanced at the intruder's left hand. To his recollection, Shino wasn't married, but he'd heard that Japanese businessmen often lived overseas as "grass bachelors".

"Oh, yes, the – ah – of course. Didn't Chantal return it to

you?" Silly question, or why would the poor man be here after six?

"On the telephone she said it was safe in your desk." Shino nodded respectfully.

"Ah, did she? *Pardon*." Roman opened his centre drawer and saw the gold of Shino's pitifully narrow penis ring shining through a single layer of tissue.

"*Merci, merci, merci, merci*."

At last Shino reached his final bow, but the stubby man paused before closing the door after him. He pulled himself up straight to attention, as if about to salute the waiting doctor, then settled for yet another bow, and left with the most unnerving smile of sympathetic commiseration the trembling Roman had ever seen on a patient's face.

21

Pebbles of excitement skittered down Isabel's spine as she lowered herself into the upholstered chair behind a small placard printed, *Dr I.K. Hanford, Leprosy*. The round conference table in the centre of the small rotunda was surrounded by four stepped banks of arm chairs dangling earphones for the translators' dulcet whispers. A communal writing shelf fronted each tier of seats. So this was how it felt to sit at the very core of power! Like a mini Security Council, the central table bristled with changeable cards. For once, the name Hanford was stencilled on one of them.

Indifferent to Isabel's stage nerves, WHO minions crisscrossed the muffling carpet and slotted in other names. A graceful Sri Lankan girl slipped between the chairs, her plait of oiled black hair brushing her waist. She counted out exactly three virgin pencils and one yellow legal pad for each place with the concentration of an acolyte setting an altar. For a moment Isabel was back at Father Shardar's, watching the swinging coils of women working in the paddy fields below his clinic.

Too bad Roman couldn't escape his crammed schedule to cheer on Isabel from the stands. Poor boy, so fagged out week after week by his relentless workload. He never turned off his mobile these days for fear of missing a distress call. He hid from his troubles under his Discman earphones all weekend. Spirits flagging, he even asked her to cook Sunday lunch for a change so he could go for a run along the lakeside. The brisk weather had done him good. When he came back, skin aglow, he didn't say one picky little word about the charred chops. He must be fretting about Jonathan's opening, but being Roman, he'd manage somehow.

God knows, even when relaxing, Roman was the kind of man who needed structure. His latest idea of signing up for Saturday gym sessions got her full support. She'd investigated a "couples package", but Roman argued it wasn't practical with her travel schedule. He was such a good sport, pointing out the obvious before she started feeling guilty about her frequent absences. So responsible, so sweet. Imagine, after all these years. She was so lucky.

"*Pardonnez-moi.*" A clinking jug of water landed at her elbow. She must look a bit of a swot, arriving simply eons before anyone else, but she'd wanted to settle into these rarefied chambers – reserved for gladiatorial battles like today's.

Some things never changed. Isabel thought of herself at eight, the only child of ageing colonial servants, always the first pupil back at school. Wasn't she still that child, with carrotty hair scraped into tight plaits pulling at her temples, the elastic of her new navy socks digging into the fat bit behind her knees? She could hear Miss Mellins' echoing heels rounding the corner, she saw the amused smile on the young teacher's face at blue-faced Hanford catching her death cross-legged on the corridor lino, hand-me-down chemistry books nested in the pleats of her uniform.

Test signals whined down the WHO sound system. When the ringing in her ears subsided, Isabel straightened her progress report already sliding across the polished oak.

As the case numbers dropped, her leprosy map shrank. Bureaucratic pressures mounted, private NGOs turned nervous, corporate impatience grew. Today leprosy earned Isabel a prominent place at the table, but only because of the approaching target – one patient per 10,000 population. She was sure they could succeed, but at what price? How many other disease advocates panted to declare leprosy a premature victory just to push Isabel into institutional oblivion, abscond with her budget and relegate her to the back row of the upper circle? Dozens of contagions clawed after her money – oh, God, it wasn't *her* money. They weren't *her* patients. She mustn't, mustn't sound like her father huffing on about, "my natives, good people, sound characters if you handle them right".

She ran her eye down the speakers list. Who might stab her from behind? Boast bigger resistance? Fatter numbers? Brandish knock-on damage to agriculture, labour? Retarded growth? Security risks?

Poor old leprosy, with only Isabel to fight for it. She would always be, despite Father Shardar's disdainful rejection, "one of them".

Dr Ralph Philips and team arrived at their seats facing the chairman's throne. "Knew some Philips in Lincolnshire. Solid family," her father had barked at her on one of their companionable Sunday walks to digest Marjorie's reheated tiffin.

Stress was etched all over Philips's craggy face this morning. Should he make his polio eradication deadline next year, it "might be mankind's single most ambitious accomplishment" – well, at least that's what *The New Yorker* had said. "Mankind's most ambitious accomplishment." Better than a moon shot? Cracking the genetic code? Eclipsing the smallpox victory?

Ralph leaned towards Isabel across the yawning surface, incanting with an encouraging smile, "*I saw in heaven another great and marvellous sign; seven angels with the seven last plagues –*"

Isabel whispered back, "*Last, because with them God's wrath is completed.*"

Ralph rapped the table with the approval of a supportive prefect and turned back to his papers. Were Ralph and Isabel the last of their kind, the vestige of old-fashioned disease warriors tracing back through fanatic field researchers, no-nonsense army medical officers and pious kamikaze missionaries? Back to those faceless Knights of St Lazarus, back into medicine's darkest corridors, to the nameless caregivers – candle lamps and begging bowls in hand – illuminating the seventh-century abominations of the ancient leprosaria of

Verdun, Metz, and Maestricht? In their stead came a new, antiseptic breed – nuclear lab technicians, computer geeks, genetic whiz kids and mobile-phone mavens. Such people spawned around them exponentially.

Well, you could quote all the Revelations you wanted, but it was jolly well obvious that God's wrath wasn't completed just yet. Polio might yet beat even Ralph. After all, the yellow fever virus had hidden in mosquito eggs until the doctors abandoned the dream of eradication. Yaws proved intractable. They'd spent futile billions in the 1950s and '60s hoping to drive out malaria once and for all – but tell that to three million sufferers today.

Still, a wistful Isabel ran her eye down Ralph's polio stats . . . India 214 cases left, Pakistan 96, Afghanistan eight, Egypt and Lebanon one case each. One lousy case . . . numbers to make an epidemiologist drool.

After sixteen years of fighting disease, Philips looked a case himself. One polio victim missed, one fever misdiagnosed, and his five billion dollar house of cards threatened to collapse. His team faced a post-tsunami outbreak in West Java, but the Indonesians were managing well, vaccinating five million children in one month. But there were still frustrating cluster mop-ups in Benin and Cameroon because of a political foul-up in Nigeria. One Muslim doctor – the president of the Supreme Council for Shariah, no less – had claimed polio vaccine made little girls sterile. So new cases cropped up in sixteen countries.

Suppose some fanatic called Isabel's blister packs of antibiotics a Western conspiracy? A First World plot?

Nervous, she yanked down her skirt hem and concentrated on the tiny print of the new draft budget. The dreadful digits had not miraculously improved overnight. WHO money for "communicable disease prevention, eradication and control" was down *twenty-four per cent*, slashed by eight million dollars. Every dollar less under Isabel's control only fortified the NGOs holding $70 million and bolstered their priorities and agendas over Isabel's.

"I have every confidence you'll find outside money, Isabel," the Director General had purred at her during a chance encounter outside the WHO travel agency. "You'll excuse us, now," murmured the Director's assistant, his South Korean shadow, always at his side.

Sadly, Isabel hadn't found enough – not by travelling to New York or London, not by phoning appeals from Okinawa to Arizona. The proposed budget still fell short of her needs by seventeen per cent. What would they do to her today, where the indirect lighting only enhanced the room's aura of intergalactic autocracy? If she wanted to throw a departmental wobbly, it couldn't be in front of the Director's financial man.

How she missed Carlos's running commentary as the two of them witnessed Frank roll over and wag his paws in the air for the few seconds he gained the floor. There was something about the yearly gathering of the Communicable Diseases Cluster that the acerbic Carlos always managed to make hilarious:

"Lighten up, Isabel. I like to imagine it's one of those Star Wars councils, only with really lousy costumes." His hand traced an imaginary marquee in the air, "*The Phantom Funding, Episode Seven*. Thank you, Planet Leprosy, for your progress in fighting the Dark One. As a reward, the Empire decrees more taxation for you!"

She fought back her giggles while Carlos wheedled, "But without money, how can we eradicate this scourge from the Galaxy forever, oh, Queen? Settle for elimination, leave total eradication to the Jedi knights from Planet Polio! Ssssht. Stop giggling, *por favor!*"

Carlos was at it again the next year: "Hey, Isabel, let's issue headdresses to all the 'communicable' chiefs, you know? Like Carmen Miranda used to wear? With condoms and syringes and snails trimming their sombreros? No? You think this is a bad idea? I think it is a brilliant idea. *Si*, Frank could wear bells on his hat band, you know, to warn everybody that he's coming. In fact," Carlos widened his eyes, "why wait for the budget meeting? Let's make it official! Hat regulations year round! C'mon, shush, stop laughing."

Dear Carlos, this was the year you threatened to distribute headdresses and now you're not here.

The room slowly filled with the wise men and women of the Communicable Diseases Cluster. The Hepatitis alphabet – Doctors Levant from "A" to Wiersma from "E" settled along the west wall, followed by the worms – hook, tape, guinea and heart – slinking to seats along the north wall behind Isabel. The more venerable incurables – like typhus, yaws, mumps, scarlet fever and whooping cough – were tough old birds with stable, if unspectacular, allowances. They sent deputies who greeted their doyen, the majestic "Dr Sdawala, Syphilis and Gonorrhea", as he strode in carrying a hand-carved pipe – unlit of course – before him like a totem to ward off budget cuts.

The fever crowd – Lassa, Crimean Congo, Rocky Mountain and Rift Valley – scattered to various geographic corners of the room. Around these centres of gravity the parasite people – cestodes, nematodes, and snails – attached themselves where they could.

The headliners arrived last. The sinister anthrax duo, two ex-military doctors, looked no one in the eye. The Mad Cow trackers trailed computer print-outs of feed flows and cullings behind them. The newly-installed Ebola beauty, Oxford-trained Dr Elizabeth Ngono, cut a swathe with her regal smile. As she inched her admired derrière to a seat, her wooden earrings clacked like clappers of death.

Tiny, snowy-haired Dr Rupert scuttled in as if he hoped to go unnoticed. Hunched over his thin smallpox brief, his narrow shoulders bore the perverse glamour of controlling a historic scourge turned weapon of mass destruction. He ignored the eager nods of the anthrax *arrivistes*.

Now, the big guns from tuberculosis and malaria and HIV-AIDS filed in. With much clearing of throats and straightening of ties, they took their reserved seats as barons of the round table. Ah, what glory for the malaria team this year – with sequencing the *A. gambiae* mosquito and pinning down the 12-amino-acid peptide binding to the mosquito mid-gut and salivary gland! Isabel had heard joyful shrieks coming down the corridor at the news. Her natural goodwill struggled with envy that morning as she thought of the new money siphoned their way to annotate the whole genome sequence.

"Every dog has his day," the voice of her father's ghost consoled her.

The donor countries and well-barbered private money lounged in a boxed-off loge like Roman tribunes attending the Games. The tidy bald man from Aventis Pharma plopped down his briefcase of two billion dollars to shake hands with the jolly Japanese representing heavy donations from Tokyo. The Asian was a recent object of sympathy, forced to pledge almost five billion to save his "number one face," when The Bill & Melinda Gates Foundation surged to four and a half billion.

Isabel came after the introductory remarks, opening salvos on more money for the new 24/7 SARS Response Centre, and the revision of the biosafety manual for possible biological and chemical warfare. Listening to the Financial Secretary outline the usual forecasts, her chest tightened, and stomach nerves curdled her morning coffee. Maybe Carlos was watching from somewhere in the shadows? In vain she searched this gallery's cavalcade of disease, death and dollars for her comrade's face.

Instead, she spotted that defector Frank Norton. He was preening himself like a rooster under the Fire Exit sign, courting his new flock, the avian-flu team advised by a Swede fresh from a culling in Cambodia, still garbed in his tropical suit. Isabel had no champion today, and only one silent ally – the supportive, gentle Dr Chizamba, the Novartis leprologist from whom all free medicines flowed – for now.

The words "Hanford" and "leprosy" announced down the microphone straightened her spine. She heard a voice from the speaker system sounding awfully like her mother Marjorie dictating to the house servants:

"... control of leprosy still eludes six countries: Brazil, India, Madagascar, Mozambique, Myanmar and Nepal ... we cannot afford complacency ... Although the reduction in prevalence is dramatic in historical terms, we're seeing a worrying drop-off in the reduction curve, even some regional surges. Moreover, even the global prevalence rate of 1.4 per 10,000 is short of our goal, and in the top 13 countries, it is unreachable in the short-term (e.g., 5.9 in India, 4.3 in Brazil) ..."

She was aloft: "While broadening our reach through provincial and municipal health care systems is producing results, we are mindful of the continuing need for social rehabilitation, genome analysis, immunological research, and alternative drug therapies."

She aimed one of her big guns with her most convincing glance at the chair; "Even if we meet our deadline, and I believe we shall, leprosy will continue to require the WHO's full attention –"

After five minutes the reedy voice of that stranger – that Englishwoman who was her official self – reached her closing remarks. Isabel landed her courageous single-engine appeal for an injection of new funds for mobile units on the last paragraph. Hands trembling, she switched off the ignition and wondered: had she managed to read her pages in the right order?

The chair called for questions. Her battle was engaged and the frontal assault came at her full throttle.

The results of mobile units?

"... using mobile units by air and road we reached beyond out-patient departments of leprosy hospitals to patients living in difficult-to-access areas ...we're moving in this direction in India, and especially Kashmir, the conflict and earthquake damage permitting, applying past experience in Angola and the Congo in collaboration with NGOs on the ground, including those not involved in leprosy control activities. Mobile units enable us to supply drugs and assist provincial health services down to the village level ..."

Isabel felt her voice settle down. She was actually relishing her moment. Ralph beamed brotherly encouragement from across the table.

"Brazil? Decentralization is under way in the north-east. Yes, well, Mr Secretary, if Doctor Campagna could be here this morning, he would echo my dismay that Brazil is proving such a hard nut to crack – "

That drew a bit of a laugh. Sorry, Carlos –

" . . . we must convince those NGOs who raise money by advertising the horrors of the disease to redesign their approach, to despecialize care, destigmatize leprosy, encourage people to seek diagnosis and treatment – "

She was almost home now. The surge in prevalence?

" . . . a substantial proportion of fresh cases are presenting with single lesions as they are being diagnosed earlier, but in India in particular the rise in prevalence is due to several operational and administrative shortcomings, rather than epidemiological factors."

Isabel was still explaining South Asian delays when she heard the chair recognize an intervention. Was that not a familiar Australian drawl breaking in from behind her? " – not so much a question of money as cooperation. The global leprosy movement has had to reckon with the very public disagreement between ourselves and some of the traditional NGOs over the speed of decentralization and shortening treatment duration – " The traitor Norton nodded to Isabel and added, "With respect, Doctor Hanford."

For a full thirty seconds, the assembly sat in silence, watching the financial officer review his copy of Isabel's report. She noticed with alarm that the Director's shadowy assistant placed the independent evaluation report at the Secretary's elbow, pointing to a paragraph. In the second row, Dr Ngono murmured to a companion, setting off the ominous clack of her earrings.

The Secretary cleared his throat, "Doctor Hanford, the independent evaluation of global leprosy work highlighted a lack of collaboration between our administration and outside actors." He peered through half-moon glasses as if deciphering a classical Greek passage, "If I might quote, 'Relations among some collaborators at the global level are very bad. Concerned NGOs, physicians, and scientists have raised important questions about technical, operational and strategic matters that have not been resolved. Some of these concerns are related to the WHO leprosy team and perceptions that it focuses too exclusively on meeting public health targets for leprosy control'." He peered at Isabel over his delicate lenses. "I read that you even expelled the International Association of Anti-Leprosy Associations from our working alliance?"

His piercing eyes bore through her.

"Mr Secretary, some collaborators have stalled their implementation of our decentralization programme. They voice doubts about the long distance use of multi-drug packs and the shortening of treatment duration – "

"Doctor Hanford, in your report you called for more money, for rehabilitation, research, etc.? These outside actors have ample funds. Is the problem that you can't persuade them to push your target through? Is it really money you lack, Doctor Hanford," he paused to take aim, "or merely diplomatic skill?"

Isabel laid both her hands flat on the smooth table like a drowning woman losing hold of a rescue boat. "The so-called specialized clinic tradition versus our public health approach may drive some differences. There might be personal misunderstandings. But most of our setbacks are caused by protectionism – the ambition of certain leprosy organizations to retain their constituencies."

The Secretary flipped through a few pages of her report and laid down his glasses. "You are requesting funds for more mobile units?"

"Not just for mobile units. We need more funds all round. Despite policy disagreements that have unfortunately become only too public, our department remains committed to the

233

targets set and the priorities of early diagnosis and shortened treatment. We will work harder to allay the fears within the research and rehabilitation ranks, fears stoked by certain NGOs who feel threatened by our less traditional and, shall we say, secular approach?"

The Secretary fingered his knife-sharp lapels in feigned apology. "We understand, Doctor Hanford, but for the moment, the WHO's bottom line won't improve – "

She added quickly, "Now, in most endemic countries, drug services reach patients through the health care system or the uneven geographic reach of leprosy clinics. However, elimination campaigns have to mop up undetected cases that accumulate over a period of time. We need vans, cars, and motorcycles to reach these remote areas, places disrupted by earthquake, armed conflict, poor transport, areas of illiteracy where cases are locked away out of fear – "

She was flailing. There were impatient coughs and whispers. Frank was on his feet again, using that conciliatory tone: "So sorry, but might I contribute just one more tiny word?"

The Secretary sighed into his mike. "Yes, Doctor Norton?"

"We all want to see Doctor Hanford prove the more recalcitrant NGOs wrong. So isn't the question not whether we reach these hidden cases, but how? Obviously at minimum cost and maximum safety?"

Where was Frank going with this, Isabel wondered?

" . . . Now our new colleague, Doctor Cheong here, brings impressive experience gleaned from the SARS campaigns, remarkable success using the latest telecommunications in quarantine circumstances for gathering data. She has suggested that with video-capable cellphones donated by the private sector, leprosy diagnosis could be carried out long distance. Drugs could be distributed according to the guidelines of our Accompanied Multi-Drug Therapy while visual phone contact with the patient would help reassure those Doubting Thomases in the missionary clinics."

The chair pinched his eyebrows together as if tuning into a

hidden frequency through his Third Eye of Accountancy. He spoke in the low tones of a father too disappointed even to look his disobedient child full in the face: "You didn't mention this idea, Doctor Hanford. Any estimate of savings under this alternative proposal?"

"We haven't got donated phones yet. It remains a suggestion –"

"It sounds very promising."

"Of course it's under consideration –"

"Good! I look forward to hearing soon from Doctor Cheong and yourself as to how it works out." Putting pen to paper, the Secretary drew a line through her name.

"Let's see, now we're on to – right! Doctor Philips. How is the new Sanofi Pasteur vaccine doing? We're all ears! Please, Doctor?"

Isabel examined a hangnail on her left thumb carefully for a full five minutes before she could appreciate Ralph's flawless summary of the uptick in caseloads spreading from Nigeria to Saudi Arabia.

She felt Dr Cheong's heated enthusiasm from high above singeing the back of her scalp. As soon as the Secretary announced a break, she ignored Dr Cheong's collegial wave and made her way up the slanting aisle to the padded doors to escape into the lobby's wintry daylight. Roman's mobile was busy again. She reached the toilets, locked a cubicle door against the world, hung her new blazer on the hook, knelt down on the sterilized tiles, leaned over the perfumed blue waters of the toilet bowl and threw up.

Part III

"One of them, when he saw he was healed, came back, praising God in a loud voice. He threw himself at Jesus's feet and thanked him. He was a Samaritan. Jesus asked, 'Were not all ten cleansed? Where are the other nine? Was no one found to return and give praise to God except this foreigner?'"

Luke 17:15–18

22

Roman's life had acquired a delectable charm that withstood Isabel's grating job complaints, tedious clinic routine, even the few second-hand accounts of Jonathan's obnoxious "soft" opening that reached his ears. An underground spring of pleasure and purpose gurgled unseen through the subterranean caverns honeycombing Roman's staid terrain. Illicit love, sweet as it was secret, irrigated the familiar pavements of Geneva.

The city itself was thawing out. Some of the tarpaulins came off the sailing boat yardarms clanging in the freshening *bise*. Patches of brown earth showed between frozen snowcaps above the city.

The clinic's tempo shifted into spring. Chantal returned with a sun-parched smile from a skiing weekend. She eased a pair of dancing clown fish into the aquarium's luminescent waters and buried these scaly acquisitions under office expenses as air freshener replacements. When co-signing the end of month payments, Roman pretended not to notice.

Even the winter's ambitious caseload loosened its grip on the appointments book to make way for a season of short-term treatments. The Japanese Shino had only a few sessions each month now. Mira would take a break from treatments to allow for her performance schedule over the summer before returning to the clinic in September. Roman's other patients deliberated longer when fixing their future sessions. They peered over Chantal's counter at the appointments bible, already spread-eagled to dates for June and July. They equivocated, made calls on their mobiles, tapped and thumbed self-importantly through leather-bound agendas and electronic diaries, trying to post-pone or move forward those unsightly, radical treatments until the summer's ruthless exposure was safely over.

In anticipation of competition from Jonathan's lavish "hard" opening, Roman cancelled a whole afternoon of appointments to film the latest in permanent depilation techniques. He cast his cheerful, if hirsute Iranian patient Falooz Mahoubhi as his satiny star. He added a segment showing the removal of *lentigos solaires*. Thereafter, he strode into his clinic every day at dawn, heart alive with vengeance, to slap his custom-made DVD into the monitor. He instructed Chantal to let the infernal thing run all day. He invited a consultant to suggest a new promotional campaign, but blanched when the young man – seizing on Roman's insistence that he was a true Genevan and a traditional professional – unveiled a poster reading, "The Enlightenment Returns! Let Our Laser Enlighten Your Life", with a grinning Voltaire wearing Roman's white jacket and purple eye goggles.

There were limits, even with Beverly Burden, Bouvier and Company lowering standards across town.

Meanwhile, Roman had partially reclaimed the normal sanity of his weekly schedule. He met Mira every weekend. He still saw patients on Saturday mornings but, as he'd explained to Isabel, the best time to grab the right gym machines was a full hour before the lunch rush, so Chantal and Lise now closed up for the weekend without him.

The new DVD must be running its final cycle of the Mahoubhi armpits this very minute. Roman snuggled down into the delicious folds of Mira's bedclothes. He heard her humming her Brahms' Second in the shower, the splash of hair rinsing, the echo of her perfect pitch against the linoleum. It was like digesting a fine meal, Roman thought, sniffing her lingering aroma on the sheets. A long dark hair on the pillow-case tickled his ear and he enclosed the strand with a hairpin hidden in his tracksuit pocket, another item for his cherished collection of souvenirs: a single hair from her violin bow lay looped and tied in his desk drawer; a snapshot of the seven-year-old Mira in Beijing; her quarter-sized violin pressed against the ruby cheek, her curls festooned with a monstrous red bow; the Victoria Hall programme of that confused night with the Colonel; a haunting digital snap, eyes closed, reposed on the clinic pillow.

Had he fallen in love with her from the start?

From where he lay, Roman saluted his gratitude to a framed photo of Col Sullivan astride some intricately piped and polished motorbike. How convenient that every single Saturday Jack Sullivan cruised the mountains with fellow expat road warriors, Bud and Henley.

Roman sipped some cool mineral water he'd set by the bedside through force of habit, then sank contented back into the percale fluff. He sighed, replete with physical luxuriance, dozed off, for three minutes? five? seven? half-covered by the no-iron sheets. At first they'd felt like whisper-thin damp face tissues. Now he would suffer a great deal of polyester for the sake of passing his *grasses matinées* tangled between Mira's graceful limbs.

"I wish I could stay forever," he called. She didn't answer.

He dozed in this indulgent haze for a while. Surfacing again to the sound of a hair dryer, he considered, was he addicted to the girl? She emerged more beautiful each week with the glow of passion, not to mention the gradual fading of her mark into a rosy sheen. She was all softness – not with Isabel's nervous flab – but firm to his touch. He savoured the sight of the dimple at the top of her buttocks, the soft dark down between her thighs, the velvety folds above.

Still humming, the girl herself emerged from the misty bathroom and he heard the generous *ssspritt of* the Guerlain perfume they'd purchased after a laser session. In the end, Mira chose Mitsouko, "a kowtow to my itinerant Asian childhood".

For years, Roman had glimpsed the stretched and painted Guerlain saleswoman dusting off bottles opposite his lift bank, never imagining ... but there he was that day, darting nervously around the counter, afraid of being seen in Mira's company.

"In cash?" The saleswoman had glanced at the girl's bare ring finger and Roman's guilty gold band, then directed a mean, knowing smile at Roman. "Would you like that gift-wrapped?" With his hairy arms a tell-tale garden of Chamade and Shalimar he'd hurried past Chantal to fumigate himself in time for the next patient.

The risk was worth it the next Saturday as a Mitsouko-drenched Mira murmured, "Imagine I am your concubine, strumming my *p'ipa* in the hidden ear of your heart." To see her bloom like this! He had made her so truly, so obviously happy. How could this be wrong?

Over only a few months, they had developed an intense companionship. True, Roman chose the time, but the girl dictated the tone. She completely understood Roman, wanted everything for herself that he wanted, but happily, no more. Her simple plans matched his – music and passion. Even the inexpressive vowels of her prosaic conversation turned more poetic with each meeting, as if his touch brought forth sentiments that only her violin had voiced until now. Such communion had nothing to do with mere friendship, he told himself; surely it was a merger of souls, a wedding of artists.

Mira glanced down at his listless form stretched out on the limp sheets. She rubbed the fur across his shoulders.

"You coming to rehearsal? Just once?"

Roman glanced at his watch curled on the night table. His "gym sessions" ended at three.

"*Oui*, but just for an hour."

"Well, *bouges* your butt, Doctor. Anton's getting hysterical about this sonata. Don't take anything he says personally. It's not my fault he can't master the second movement." She rolled her eyes with comic impatience. "Maybe you could turn pages for him? It would make you look a little more useful."

"If he needs it, I don't see why not. But I can't read music, *chérie*. He'll have to elbow me when he gets to the end of a page."

Mira stopped short, her blouse half over her nose and stared at him. "You can't read music?"

Roman reached for his underwear. "No."

"Oh." She recovered sufficiently to joke, "You can read, can't you?"

"Books? Yes, as long as they're in big print, with pictures."

She played with his hair for a moment and seemed plunged into thought.

He sighed, "Am I not useful, *chérie*?"

"Totally useless, apart from changing my face and my whole life. Those are nice pants." She looked intently at him. "Does your wife pick out your clothes? My father said after that dinner party she was a nice woman. I feel guilty about her."

Roman recalled Isabel's frosty dismissal of the Colonel. "She *is* very nice, very dedicated to her work. We won't talk of her. She has done nothing for me to hurt her. If you are happy this way, so am I. It's best like this."

Mira looked less than consoled, "Here's your sweater. And for sure, don't forget your gym bag."

She twisted her damp hair into a turban of soft apricot and pulled on cabled woollen stockings and embroidered flat slippers under a flounced peasant skirt. Mira wore everything so well on those generous breasts and narrow hips – Chinese silk, Turkish vests, weird *mélanges* of sports gear and Afghan fashion from the street markets – these pieces sadly reminded Roman of Isabel's unconvincing attempts at bohemian wear during those distant med-school weekends in New York. With her purposeful girth and functional waist set below her open face, Isabel had finally reverted to tweeds – no doubt on the echoing suggestion of Hanford *père* tamping down his pipe to boast that his little redhead had grown into a handsome woman who "scrubbed up well".

Of course, Mira had the colouring that gave her the allure of the Gypsy camp, the Mongolian steppes, the windswept alleyways of dusty Beijing. Roman imagined galloping across open tundra with his chameleon lover astride the back of his steed. This necessitated fantasizing that he could ride at all, but no matter – Roman wasn't ready to admit that his inner life had taken a vacation from reality weeks ago.

Tying up his running shoes, Roman saw the supply of cotton squares tucked next to the rosin in her violin case; they protected the instrument from her make-up oil. This time next year, she would hardly need them. He stroked her pensive cheek for a moment. "No longer afraid? Of being beautiful? Of bad luck?"

She shrugged. "I was, like, so neurotic, I can't believe it. Haunted by Nathaniel Hawthorne. Geeesh." She hunted for her keys while he dragged on his shoes.

"Ah, yes. Your American story. Tell me again."

Like a babysitter repeating a bedtime tale that no longer held any terrors, she recited, "Aylmer loved his wife, but her birthmark challenged his faith in science. He started to hate her mark, and she worried that sooner or later, he'd hate her. So she agreed to let him experiment on her, just to keep his love."

"That made you afraid."

"He decorated a special bedroom with ruffles and curtains, and behind it he installed this scary laboratory with a kind of Igor assistant. He finally emerged with his potion. So, despite all her fear, she drank it out of love for him. The mark disappeared, but the potion killed her."

Roman imagined the effect on an impressionable adolescent.

Mira rallied, "I'm sure my teacher hoped I'd accept my birthmark. But why did Hawthorne write it? Removing the mark was a way of draining his wife's female nature, you see, her red-blooded humanity. Sort of like an abortion. He wrote it when his wife was pregnant. Do you think Hawthorne was afraid of her fertility?" Mira busied herself with zipping a dog-eared copy of Brahms into her case.

"You're turning very literary on me, *chérie*."

"Oh, stop smirking. I've always loved literature, especially Austen and Twain. Don't make fun of me if you can't read music. You seemed so educated, but in fact, maybe you're just over-specialized." She made a mocking face at him.

"*Merci beaucoup.*" He stuck out his tongue.

Such typical little jibes wounded his feelings; he had assumed a cultural superiority over her as his birthright.

"I thought you loved me for all that."

She chortled. "You thought I fell in love with you because of your Europeanness?"

"Well, yes," he stammered. "And because deep down you yourself are European, in your blood, in your art – "

"Oh, right." she scoffed. "My early years in Romania were really wonderful – "

"So why – ?"

"You silly man, I fell in love with you only because you were so lovable, and – so lonely."

She ignored his stunned silence by squeezing him play-fully, "And of course, you're so good at certain, nonverbal things."

He could barely manage a smile. Lonely? Dr Roman Micheli? He was surrounded all day by colleagues and patients. He relished his hours alone, and his hard-earned monastic solitude. She made him sound almost pathetic.

Seeing his scowl, she added, "Of course, it's lovely that you're so sophisticated. It's just so hard to catch up. My German lessons aren't going very well," she laughed ruefully, "and my French and Italian are limited to music terms."

"What about your talent? The contest? You mustn't stop striving – "

Mira laid the bow into its velvet nest. The acrylic scrap covering the mustard violin was gone. Roman had bought a Hermès silk scarf printed with medieval musical instruments while getting Isabel a birthday wallet.

"Oh, the Sion thing isn't such a big deal, not like the Wienawski or Menuhin competitions. I've been thinking about it all, looking at the music business, what's ahead – getting the right management, contests, niches, marketing. Let's face it, I'm not that good. It's too late to try for the top."

Crestfallen, Roman took advantage of one more lingering

kiss, not enough to soothe his pervading disquiet. He reached for his gym bag.

She bustled into the kitchen. "Hang on, I'll just make a quick sandwich. Love makes me hungry these days, but then I'm too nervous to get it down. Must be the spring air," she flirted at him.

"Shall I make it for you?"

"Don't be silly. Some gourmet concoction that'll take hours?" She squirted mayonnaise from a tube on to spongy white bread, slapped on iceberg lettuce and slipped in a slice of processed cheese.

"I'll make one for Anton. He'll be mad we're late. Want one?"

"No. Thank you, *chérie.*"

In an underheated rehearsal room the Slav raised his thanks to heaven for their arrival and clumped across the battered parquet to offer the doctor a perfunctory handshake. The pianist's greasy brown hair hung from a centre parting down his temples. He smelled of cheap food and tobacco – a sullen hound waiting for his mistress to take him for a walk. Anton's origins in Kiev remained unclear to Roman, and Mira hinted that the murky business of establishing a tenuous residence in Geneva was "better not spoken of".

The girl stood on tiptoe to bestow a conciliatory peck on the peevish boy who pulled at the khaki threads straggling off his sweater hem.

Was Roman's memory playing tricks or had Isabel called this raggletag student "dishy" that day in the Café Central? The accompanist's truculent charms certainly eluded the older man. Now devoid of his shoulder-padded suit, not to mention a clean collar, the round-shouldered Anton easily looked five years younger than he had that night at Kress-Parker's mansion.

"Right. We start. Okay?"

The boy unfurled his sheet music, eight pages reduced by photocopier and taped together edge to edge into a miniature imperial decree. He tested the pedals. Mira rosined her bow until white dust powdered her skirt. Roman's antennae, so good at picking up a patient's unspoken worries, sensed a young man's machismo chewing on something unsaid.

Roman unfolded a chair in the corner while the two musicians conferred. He calculated on thirty more minutes before he was due, buffed and toned and utterly guileful, to make *salade niçoise* for his wife.

Leaning intently over the keyboard, Anton closed his eyes and articulated Brahms's introductory chords as a sort of question put to Mira. She answered with four descending notes, smiling to Roman over the heel of her instrument.

The pianist repeated the phrase, twisting his torso away from the keyboard to gaze up at Mira.

She dipped her upper body and the violin answered the piano more emphatically.

Roman loved the lilt of her wrist bone poised above the strings. He sighed when his own thick fingers circled that magic joint. He worshipped the little knuckles that flexed back and forth, the way her index finger and little finger balanced the bow with a seesaw pivot, the way she angled the taut hairs inward as if to carve the song out of the violin's belly.

He watched her sway into the air, retrieve the theme from Anton and send the notes skyward until she gathered them up in a sequence of double stops. Roman watched those tapered fingertips pressing and releasing until Anton introduced a second theme. No doubt this was the centrepiece of Brahms' composition; Mira seized the new melody, exploring it with a lyricism that –

"*Merde!*" The boy exploded. "What you are doing? You take off like that without me? This is not big American space-shuttle!"

"It says allegro."

"It says, allegro *amabile.*"

"Okay. Okay. Start at fifty-four." She lifted her bow.

"No, no good. Go back to thirty seven."

"Anton, you're pushing too hard on the crescendo –"

"I am not too hard. I support you even when this is both of us, not me just accompanying you. You see here?" He jabbed at the title, *Sonata for Violin and Piano*. You don't meet me, even half the way!"

"You're just too loud. When you do the variation, you drown me out – " she hummed her counterpoint and tapped her bow tip on his music.

"I'm drowning you? Keep swimming better! Or maybe you have not so much energy this morning?" Anton arched an eyebrow in the direction of Roman's corner.

Mira exhaled. "Okay. Thirty-seven."

"Thirty-seven. No, no, even better, from beginning."

"Ahhhh, Anton, c'mon."

"From beginning."

His expression suddenly turned from wrathful keyboard king to hopeful puppy. "You bring sandwiches? Good. Mayonnaise?" He shot an apologetic smile across the room to Roman, "Students, always hungry!"

"At this rate, we'll never get to the second movement, much less the mayonnaise. Did you work on those arpeggios? Your fingers were like chopsticks last week."

Anton insisted on going over his solo bars three times. Roman marvelled at Mira's patience. She listened to each rendition as if it were for the first time. She responded with her single bar again and again until finally the two musicians swirled off in tandem through their web of notes.

Forgotten on his folding chair, conscious of waiting wife, Roman observed the two artists burrow into their task. As his final minutes with Mira crept past, a painful sensation slunk into his heart. Watching Mira partnered by Anton was like eavesdropping on lovers from behind a locked door; he was here with them, wasn't he? In fact, they no longer saw him. He wanted to be their one-man audience, their sounding board, but they left him unacknowledged, like a peeping Tom, an intruder, a voyeur.

He hadn't suffered while watching their duet at Kress-

Parker's house. It wasn't as if he felt jealous of their work. At times they even scrapped and bickered like a tired married couple. *Mon Dieu*, what was this poison lapping at the edges of his joy?

The two players shifted from a minor key back to major. Mira's solo passages soothed Anton into a repeat of the piano's opening bars, but this time the violin's response was fuller and multi-dimensional. Roman lingered dangerously, reluctant to leave the other two entwined in their staves and staffs.

Mira's fingers picked up tempo as Roman folded up his chair. He had to run. He had to dash. He looked at her for a signal affirming her devotion. The ferocious Anton clasped the girl tightly to each phrase and captured her in his net of Brahms while Roman crossed the bare boards, aching for Mira to stop playing. She nodded a matter-of-fact farewell as the doctor descended the marble stairs of the Conservatory two steps at a time. Up the stairwell, some unknown girl's laughing outburst accompanied his harried exit.

23

"These *cornets* are not resolving so well as expected. I said at the beginning I relished a medical challenge, but . . . "

The obedient Shino jerked his head down to examine the fading remnants of his jealous *oni* devil's horns. Their glorious reds and yellows were gone but traces of blue cones, now impotent and slightly ridiculous, still remained.

"Your tattoo master surpassed himself with the mix of dyes, here," Roman traced one latexed finger down the discolouration rippling along the muscle lining the inner leg. "I wish I could ask your Monsieur Horijin what exactly he used there. *Tant pis*, we'll just have to experiment a little more. We'll try a different machine."

Roman pressed Shino's thick flesh. Doctors could never guarantee eradication would be complete, but Shino had placed all his trust in Roman. The diplomat Kazuo Ino had certainly assumed that Roman's treatment would result in a complete restoration of Shino's original hue. To have pounded into obliteration the poor penis snake only to see defeat hanging by a horn tip! These protuberances mocked all Roman's skill. It felt like trying to outwit the poison of jealousy itself. Roman promised the Japanese that he would persevere.

A discouraged Shino shuffled away. Roman flipped through his medical reference books, but his thoughts rattled away from the challenge of the stubborn tattoo pigments to the problem of Mira.

In fact, he was reeling from their first lovers' quarrel. He was more certain with each passing day, wasted in secret replays of her every word, that she'd provoked their spat. Why else had she seized on Roman's few incautious comments about Anton's temper to defend her accompanist so ferociously? Anton had had a hard life. Roman couldn't possibly understand, but an abandoned Romanian orphan could. Roman flared at that suggestion. Genevan society regarded him as a *secondo* on his father's side – sufficiently "second-drawer"? (somewhere he remembered Marjorie Hanford naming social drawers) to know that immigrant or refugee status didn't excuse uncouth behaviour. Mira accused him of Swiss complacency, of assuming too much, taking the good things of his life, even taking her, for granted.

Enraged at the suggestion he was interfering in Mira's friendship with the gloomy pianist, Roman called her an ungrateful brat. She flared back with surprising independent fire, labelling him "jealous and possessive". He declared her "childish".

For twelve days, he'd heard not a word from her, only received a terse note calling off last Saturday. He'd thought the days of prevaricating little blue notes and sudden cancellations were long past. He'd thought their Saturday trysts were inviolate.

Roman stewed at his desk. Only two weeks ago, he'd listened over *spaghetti al limone* to Isabel's latest run-in with her energetic Hong Kong colleague while silently congratulating himself on the relaxed way in which Mira embraced their affair. Her maturity on that score had made it so easy to keep their passion a secret. Even Chantal, whose every pore was sensitized to the doctor's moods and needs, seemed unaware of anything but trust and kindness between the doctor and his American patient.

Better yet, how naturally Mira had seemed to accept the limitations of his married status, as if she, too, preferred to keep their public lives distinct from their discreet affair. Not for the first time since their row, a poisonous bile rose in his gorge: yes, their affair was certainly discreet. Perhaps too discreet? Discreet even from Anton? If so, why?

His fingers furled and snapped the page corners of his medical volume. His lunch tray sat on the plastic chair near the door, the avocado slices browning under plastic wrap. The doctor's mind festered with questions about Mira's hidden hours; suspicions popped up like troublemaking gossips hanging over the garden fence. What was Mira doing right now? Whom did she see on weeknights? Maybe she'd gone away last weekend. Alone? Why was her mobile always turned off? Should he leave a message at the Conservatory or risk sending a letter that the Colonel might see?

The days passed while he waited out her silence. The chattering whispers became harsh, hammering hisses. Was Mira as innocent as she seemed? Was there a more worrying explanation for the delight he discovered in her ever more skilful caresses? What did she scribble in that locked diary on her sloppy dressing table and whose idea was it that she always perform with that slouching creep? Weren't there any women pianists in all of Geneva good enough for her and did Anton have to be so tall?

The hisses mounted into a taunting chorus of La Scala dimensions. On Thursday he punched Mira's number into his mobile, not once but a dozen times. On Friday he grew careless and added her number to his auto-dial list, stabbing at the redial button between every session. Phone to ear, he paced the corridor outside his treatment rooms while the patients undressed or while Chantal cooled inflamed skins with aloe vera gel. The silent phone nestled in the pocket of his white jacket while he sleepwalked through consultations, aimed one laser after another up and down faces and limbs with drone-like precision.

"Any calls, Chantal?"

Chantal shook her head, "no". Her pert face was suspiciously brown. Roman suspected she spent her lunch breaks paying hard-earned francs to step naked into a *Bronzage Magique* booth in Jonathan's hardly-opened spa. Here Roman spent every waking hour warning his patients of the dangers of bronzing and his own assistant was parading the complexion of an artifical Tahitian.

Saturday morning, Roman's mobile vibrated against his groin at last. He lit up at the longed-for digits of Mira's apartment phone number. Rushing to safety behind his closed office door, Roman answered, "*Bonjour?*"

"Doctor Micheli!"

Roman started at the rough-hewn salutation. Col Sullivan needed to talk to the doctor. Was an invitation to lunch appropriate? (This was a personal matter concerning Mira, not a medical question. He didn't mind paying consultation fees, but figured a man-to-man chat was better over "a few drinks and a steak".)

Roman's torrid visions of Mira and Anton exploring kamasutra positions now flipped to a Sergio Leone showdown with bikers Bud and Henley in the car park of the working-class "Buffalo Grill" just across the French border. There Isabel would be summoned to pick his leftovers off the tarmac, one eye bloodied and possibly a broken –

"The Hilton?"

"The first floor restaurant? You know where it is?"

"*Mais, bien sûr.* The Hilton. Of course."

Roman was the first to arrive, even though the Hilton lay only a few blocks down the hill from the American Mission. Like a condemned man Roman marched across the pont du Mont-Blanc through spring gusts that lacerated his lungs and sent his leather coat lapels slapping reprimands at his reddened cheeks. His stride was deliberate, but his mind full of trepidation. He practically counted each sailing boat, nodded good morning to each passing stranger, all the time fingering the mobile hoping for a last minute reprieve for a freckle crisis or deadly wart at Geneva Cantonal emergency.

The welcoming bustle of the Hilton lobby, the sound of a "nice day" at the magazine stand, the bellhop dragging a Samsonite mountain through the lobby – these signals warned Roman that he'd left Geneva proper and had crossed into the hostile territory of another republic's Founding Fathers and Freedom Fries.

A beaming Chinese waiter escorted Roman past a buffet table groaning with perfect fruit, fans of cold cuts and whole turkey legs glazed in maple syrup Bar-B-Q sauce. He took his seat at a sunwashed table next to the plate glass window and stared down at a steamer pulling out from the quai du Mont-Blanc across the street. No, escape on a sightseeing ferry wasn't going to help.

He ruefully surveyed the waiting duelling field of white linen and ice water. Did Mira know about this paternal assignation? Had she triggered her father's vengeful wrath? How would Roman face the father's accusation or at least limit the appalling repercussions on his professional credentials? Roman must exercise what the Americans called damage control –

"Would you like a drink while you wait, sir?"

"*Non, merci.*" Perhaps a blindfold and a cigarette?

He'd been a fool to imagine the only illicit romance of his married career would never be discovered, but now he perceived how truly cavalier he'd been with his entire life – his joyful scenarios had never included such a phone call from the Colonel, only a hazy lifetime of listening to Mira perform in public and luxuriating in her rippling, slender arms every Saturday lunch until – *non*, Roman couldn't come up with a single defence for his infatuation with a patient. Infatuation, *merde*, a full-blown affair, an unforgiveable breach of every code. He tried to recall what the medical authorities had handed out to that rogue obstetrician Charbonnier up in Rolle with his Leporello's list of conquests.

Guilty, as charged. Roman glanced around for the looming American's bulk to shadow the sunny dining room. All he saw were fresh flowers, waitresses in shiny black skirts. He overheard jet-lagged businessmen placing calls to check on car tune-ups and Little League games back in Wisconsin and Omaha. *Mon Dieu*, these people called long distance just to ask after their pet vaccinations and ensure their lawns were being watered? Surely no real harm could come to Roman, not here in this bastion of Midwestern decency with the spring light sparkling on the lake, the sound system playing Gershwin –

"Well now, here you are! There's only one guy more punctual than an American soldier and that's a Swiss doctor, yup?"

The Colonel glanced at Roman through a weekender's sunburn, the white mark of biker glasses lining his meaty cheeks. Strawberry hair covered his enormous arms sticking out from knife-pressed short sleeves. Around his beefy neck he sported a thin chain ending in some sort of ID card tucked away behind a row of ballpoint pens clipped across his shirt pocket. With dispatch, he flapped a white napkin into his lap and ordered a beer. The Chinese waiter was "already on it, Sir."

Roman realized he had not only crossed into hostile territory; he was sitting dead centre in enemy headquarters.

"I presume you don't mind being my guest?"

Roman shook his head, masking his panic. "No, no, no. It's a privilege, considering the circumstances."

The Colonel looked puzzled, then snapped open the gigantic menu to order. Roman dithered over his Last Supper. This was no time to advertise his Italian gourmet tastes if the Colonel's kind incarcerated Martha Stewart with a toss of the finger bowl. Roman settled at last on a simple Caesar salad for symbolic fortitude while he ranked his priorities in terms of troops about to be sacrificed. He faced the implicit possibility of exposure. If Isabel had to learn of the affair, so be it, but he would defend his professional licence to the death.

The salad ingredients rolled forward on a chrome chariot laden with an armoury of spice jars and pepper mills, but the Colonel's bonhomie and small talk about new barbed wire and security detours around the Mission drowned out the waiter's extravagant lettuce tossing. The Colonel's sizzling steak arrived on its iron platter, spitting noisy indignation over its slaughter.

Roman pecked at his soggy croutons while he watched his host cross-hatch the beef into an aerial bombing grid and dice it into neat and bloody cubes.

" . . . a miracle, that's what it is, not just the improvement in her face. That's fantastic, I can see what a pro you are, even though I know there's a lot more you could do, and no doubt about that, but the change in her personality has already been real noticeable."

"I'm so happy you're, uh, pleased – ?"

"Well, I admit I hadn't foreseen all the consequences of your treatments, not all of them happy." The Colonel's eyes narrowed. He cleared his throat. "That's what I need to talk to you about. Salad okay? Good, good."

"This is awkward for both of us, but I wonder if – " Roman seized the Colonel's pause, knowing in the same breath he had no plausible line of defence.

"Well, it is awkward, at least for me. I'm talking to you straight because, frankly, I don't like to entrust my family problems to colleagues or outsiders. Around the Mission, that kind of thing is seen as unprofessional, especially for a man in my position, but as you're a *doctor* – " the Colonel's stress gave Roman shivers, "I knew that at the very least, you'd be interested in my little girl's overall welfare."

"At the very least."

The Colonel leaned over his foot-wide platter, dangling neck chain tinkling on his jumbo water glass. Roman heard the last sizzle die into an ominous quiet as the Colonel confided: "Doctor, I hope what I'm going to say to you now remains off the record, so to speak. I mean, off the medical record."

Roman exhaled eager relief. "I would also prefer it off the record, all records."

Sullivan nodded. "Good. When I first suggested to you that it was essential Mira be treated, I was thinking of her future, maybe recording contracts, tour possibilities, you know, the kind of thing they call in music circles, The Big Career. Not just teaching all week, with dinky chamber music performances at retirement homes on Sunday afternoons. We're talking CD covers."

Sullivan was talking money of course, Roman realized. Here before him was an American. Sullivan wasn't seeking some Italian patriarchal revenge at dawn. He wasn't provoked by parental outrage into a revocation of Roman's licence. He was after compensation. Francs, dollars, lire. What Jonathan Burden used to call *moolah*. If Roman pinned Mira down in Geneva, did the Colonel fear it might smother her chance at the Big Bucks?

Roman scrutinized an anchovy. "I see no reason why she shouldn't have the career she dreams of."

The Colonel huffed, "My little girl has to stay unentangled, unburdened with emotional relationships."

"She is no longer a little girl. Of course, I agree one hundred per cent that anyone involved with Mira should be content to occupy, uh, as you would call it, the back seat?"

Col Sullivan's face flushed beet red. "Doctor, that's just why I called you. I don't want anyone in the back seat, particularly the back seat! I don't want anybody in the whole goddamn car!" Sullivan exploded at a piece of gristle stuck on his fork and tossed it back into the congealing gravy.

"Surely a supportive relationship could help her succeed?"

"Not when she's doing the supporting!"

"I beg your pardon?"

"Doctor Micheli, my little girl is like a flower to me and I want to see her bloom into a strong, successful woman, un-en-cum-bered." The Colonel stabbed his steak knife at each syllable. "One day she'll get married and have kids. Sure. But she's got enormous talent and right now she's gotta put that to work. That's what Lorraine and I dreamed of. Having the mark removed from her face can only help. But not if we make her beautiful and then she falls into the arms of the first male who preys on her new-found confidence, a man who lands her with – "

"Did you say preys?" Roman straightened himself to face

257

the firing squad, eyes open, hackles raised.

"That's exactly what I said. Preys. People take advantage at times like this, just when she's feeling good-lookin' and sexy for the first time in her life – "

"And you regard someone who loves Mira and whom Mira loves back as nothing more than a – ?"

"If she meets that man in a professional context and he twists her trust and inexperience into a sexual relationship, I don't call him a man, I call him a predatory son-of-a-bitch!"

"And how would you deal with such a predator?" Roman waited for the bulky shadows of Bud and Henley to fall over the sunny tablecloth on cue.

"Well, unfortunately, things've already gone too far while my back was turned." The Colonel drained the bottom of his beer mug.

Roman pushed his damp romaine leaves through a pile of grated cheese. Over the Colonel's shoulder, he spotted an "exit" sign next to the toilets at the far end of the dining room. If he excused himself . . .

The Colonel glanced over his shoulder, then leaned across the table. "You better finish that. You're sure you don't want a beer? Or a glass of wine? You look a little peaked to me. You want us to open this window?" He glanced around for the Chinese waiter.

"No, thank you." Roman had never credited American sadism with such subtlety. Even Spaghetti offered his mouse victims swifter mercy.

"Mira has told you of an affair?" Roman ventured at last.

"Not exactly, but a father knows the signs. Even a DIA knuckle-dragger like me can tell when a male intruder's been hanging around my home while I'm not there."

He'd gone too far. A mere ten years' seniority gave this man no right to reduce Roman to the status of a burglar –

"Nothing I can't deal with in good time. I'm gonna have that little weasel Anton served up on a platter, just like this one here."

"I'm sorry?" Roman knocked his glass, sending crushed ice slopping over his untouched bread roll.

"Of course, you wouldn't know, Doctor. Sorry. Let me put you in the picture."

"Please do."

"You probably don't remember that Ukrainian twerp who played piano with Mira at the Ambassador's dinner? I've seen this kind of guy before in Beijing, Warsaw, Romania – talented, underfed and deeply, *deeply* in love with his new American girlfriend." Sullivan smirked, "Oh, and by the way, not exactly about to refuse a green card if it should just mosey his way – " Sullivan's paw slithered suggestively toward Roman.

"And you intend to separate Anton from Mira somehow?" Roman fought back the broad smile. Through no fault of Roman's, this glorious misunderstanding could result in permanent exile for the sorry Slav.

"Only after we've dealt with this baby business. That's what I wanted your advice about."

The word "baby" shot into Roman's forehead like a bullet.

"I could see the minute you showed up at the concert that you're not just a medical man, but a guy with heart. A guy who'll go the extra mile. Nothing to do with her birthmark. Now I want to minimize the repercussions of this. Are you Catholic?"

Roman demurred. He hadn't attended regular Mass for over twenty years.

"I don't want to offend you but maybe you can understand the sensitivities of our situation. I'm not a practising Catholic any more myself, but Lorraine and I raised Mira in the Church and she's bound to have mixed feelings about this for some time to come. What we need is some counselling from someone you can recommend here in Geneva, once she gets back from New York – "

"She's in New York? – "

" – We can pull her through this crisis together. I can tell you've had a steadying influence on her, the way she talks about you. I've really appreciated everything you've done for us."

Col Sullivan waved at the hovering waiter. "You got lemon meringue today? Sorry, Doctor. I'm afraid I've shocked you."

"*Non, non.* If I understand you — " Roman's thoughts frantically raced across the Atlantic.

"I know. The A word. It's hard for me to spit out, but let's face it, times have changed. Even an old altar boy like me can see that an unwanted pregnancy is just something we've got to get behind us. My younger sister in New York wasn't shocked when I phoned her. Would you believe, she confided to me that it wouldn't be the first Sullivan abortion! Well, considering our older sister's a Carmelite, she knocked me over with that little item of family intelligence. I just want to make sure Mira comes out of it A-okay. That scum bag Anton wouldn't be able to support a wife on what he earns, much less a baby. There's no way he's knocking up my little girl just to wangle a passport out of me."

The dessert cart rattled up to Roman's elbow. His numb reflection, distorted into a fun-house figure by the silvery curve of an ice cream bowl, pointed to a fruit tart. He finally found his voice.

"I think, uh, I know of a therapist who might help her if there are any problems. This woman often works with families at the International School. Um, when is the, uh, procedure scheduled?"

"Oh, she'll be over there for a couple more weeks."

Roman forced his most professional smile, "Perhaps I can do more? It's a happy coincidence that I may go to New York for a conference on laser techniques. I might meet her briefly, see how she's doing?"

The creases relaxed a little across the weather-beaten forehead. "Oh, Doctor, I'd be so damned grateful if you would take the time. I have my sister's address handy. She works at the York Street public library on the Upper East Side. Here, borrow one of my pens."

Col Sullivan pressed on the curling "O" of a dog-eared black book to locate a Mrs Mary O'Neill on 434 E. 77th Street.

At a moment like this, Roman hardly trusted his usual handwriting. With shaking hand, he copied every line in big block letters.

"And people say you can't read a doctor's handwriting! They never met a Swiss medical man!" Col Sullivan chuckled his palpable satisfaction with his Mission Accomplished.

Roman closed his eyes and prayed he would reach New York in time to save the life of his only child.

24

"You sure you don't wanna Coke?"

"No, thank you." Roman waved off the soft drink with a bend of his right wrist, shackled by handcuffs to a hard steel bench. He shivered in the air-conditioning blowing across his perspiring brow. "I don't . . . drink Coke."

"Hey, man, everybody drinks Coke. Even foreigners like you. Shit, even Arabs drink Coke. Only they call it something else, uh, Koranic Coke or Moronic Coke, or something like that. Anyway, under the rule on refreshments, I'm supposed to make sure you get offered a Coke or a snack or something."

Roman stared at his laughing captor through lids heavy with jet lag from behind the screen of a chain-link holding cell. The pimply boy in his mid-twenties grinned back for a moment, and shrugged shoulders so narrow that the epaulets on his security uniform slipped on to his upper arms.

"Knock it off, Mike." A prim young woman, her thick brown wavy hair lacquered back into an expensive hairslide, shot Roman's jailor an exasperated frown.

"Okay, no offence, Yolanda. Just trying to make our guest feel at home."

The boy's pale blue eyes roamed the video monitors hanging above his seat at the elongated countertop running the length of the underground security room. There were half a dozen other department store staff in office chairs facing the surveillance monitors stacked four deep up to the ceiling.

Roman checked his wristwatch. For more than an hour he'd been detained in this room below "Pantyhose and Lingerie", watching Mike and his colleagues stretch and swivel, sip soda pop through straws, all the while flicking at hand controls. They spied on the bald scalps, crooked partings, bad wigs and spring hats slipping underneath the cameras' range on to the monitors of someone else sitting around the room. The shadowy shoppers flitted and sauntered at unnatural angles in choppy segments scattered across the narrow security room.

Roman studied the monitors too – there was nothing to do but observe the grainy shadows grabbing and poking at shelves and chatting soundlessly to salespeople. How long had these youngsters watched *him*? Because in this room, any member of the public was a thief until proven innocent, until he or she had disappeared from the fat eye hanging over their heads back to the anonymity of Times Square. Had they lingered over his crumpled phantom dragging his flight bag through the Kids Krazy Korner? Had he looked as dishevelled as that matron now working her way past stationery goods, or as disreputable as that tall father extracting toy cars from his toddler's grip? Which one of these hidden sentries had witnessed his unwitting – ?

Roman wanted to rinse out his eyes gritting up with the sand of aeroplane air and New York pollution.

"This is all a misunderstanding. I told them at the door. I meant to pay for the baby suit. I was merely looking for a telephone. I'm very tired, very jet-lagged. I just arrived from Geneva. Someone's expecting me."

"I had a cousin who went skiing in Geneva," Mike said, as if this might relieve Roman's plight. He dragged his gaze for a second away from the monitors to glance at Roman. "Or was it Genova? No, they made that up in the Princess Diaries. Maybe I mean Genoa?"

"Could I make a phone call, please?"

"That's in a regular jail they promise you one call. Only one call. Like the joke about three wishes and no wishing for more wishes, right? Heh, heh. People confuse us with a real jail, but man, the NYPD are busy boys. They've got more serious

263

headaches than shoplifters. Hey, man, this is just a department store detention room, not Alcatraz! If you gotta cellphone, make all the calls you want. I'll be happy to punch in the numbers for you. You're not officially arrested, only detained on suspicion.''

"Are you sure this is legal?" Roman tried to suppress the astonishment in his voice.

"Merchants' Privilege — that's the lawyer's term.'' Mike nodded to himself, happy to have clarified things. He squinted and flipped through out-of-focus perfume counters, men's shoes, ladies' lingerie racks. Roman stared with Mike at the rows of thongs.

"Don't get hopeful," Mike winked to Roman, as he flipped back to the bra racks. "Yolanda over there gets ladies' dressing rooms, and if you ask me, she likes it just a little too much. But I bet a Swedish doctor gets to see a whole lot of interesting things.''

"I'm not Swedish. I'm Swiss, a Swiss dermatologist.'' Roman's mouth felt stuffed with cotton batting.

"Oh," the boy seemed disappointed. "Cool.'' He steered his surveillance camera by remote control across the Oscar de la Renta boutique, fourth floor. "I know the difference between Switzerland and Sweden. One's in Scandinavia. When the girls from Kids brought you in here, they said you were Swedish, even though I could've sworn your name sounded Italian. But you know, that's the kind of mistake they make up on the baby floor." He rolled his eyes.

"Please, I don't have a cellphone. Is there a telephone for me to place a phone call?"

The boy shook his head dismissively. "Phones in here are all part of the house circuit. I mean, what do you expect from Babywear? I'd go retarded too, if I had to work with Sesame Street reruns playing all day right next to the cash register. Hi Ernie! Hi Bert! All day long. My people were Dutch way back, in upstate New York. Van Heusen, Mike Van Heusen, like the shirts.''

"Nice to meet you." He longed for the Dafalgan somewhere in his carry-on case at the far end of the room, still open from the search for hidden weapons, dangerous explosives, and contraband baby clothes.

"This is my first week on the job. You're my sixth catch. Whoah! Got one there! Numbah Seven!" Mike grabbed a hand-speaker and punched in a two-digit number, "Hey Esteban, Mike here. Girl, minor, green windbreaker, black cargos, blond extensions, juuuuusssst leaving Accessories, direction Hosiery, with a hairbrush in her pocket."

He smiled over at Roman. "So. Skin doctor, right? True what they say about sun factor 30 making no difference? 'Cause I got a Northern European profile, so I gotta watch it."

Roman's taxi had crossed the bridge into Manhattan only three hours ago. Just yesterday he'd confirmed his tickets, informed his office and started packing for "his New York conference".

Isabel wondered how she'd managed to forget Roman's plans. She also felt secret relief that for once, she wasn't the one neglecting their marriage for professional reasons. Her flagging energies – sapped by Frank's public betrayal – lodged her knee-deep in office troubles. She would go back to India on Sunday night for a week and had to prepare for the Midrand conference coming up, but of course, her mobile would work practically anywhere, so Roman didn't need her hotel number. She wished Roman a quiet journey over the Atlantic, free of buzzing Walkmen and screaming brats.

"Remember they have a different phone system, so rent one at the airport and call me as soon as you've checked in, darling." Bleary-eyed, she added "You need a little break. Make the most of it."

Roman's flight featured a double bill of Hitchcock classics he'd seen decades ago and blockbuster garbage he'd avoided ever since. Wherever he cast his tired eyes, images of the same tiny starlet crossed and uncrossed her legs on his neighbours' seat backs. He tried dozing, but finally lifted his eye mask to watch the endless dawn unfold as he was borne eastward towards Mira and his child.

The pink and rose skyline should have heralded the beginning of this new life in his mind, but he was beset by fears – for his marriage, for Mira, but most of all for the unborn Micheli. Oh, the diseases and malformations that suddenly haunted Roman's encyclopaedic medical imagination, not to mention the unknown Sullivan congenital curses that might already threaten his perfect boy! How long had Mira carried his child without taking vitamins or folic acid? Was she stuffing herself with those awful white bread sandwiches? Was she getting enough exercise? Getting rest? Getting an abortion?

He battled these demons all the way to Shannon airspace, although he did apply himself for as long as ten minutes to the happier task of thinking up possible first names. On the scrap of a cocktail napkin, he tried to list all the things they would have to sort out, both practical and paradisial, but emotionally exhaused, he fell at last into a daydream of tactile memories of Mira soft-bellied in bed as he stroked the down lining her navel and the sight of her sucking mayonnaise off her fingers. She must stop eating that processed poison. And then his fevered imagination came up with crazy fantasies of a broadminded, even contented Isabel wrapping up Christmas toys for the first time. Christmas, a real Christmas with a tree and a child. A Madonna Mira, his Isabel an understanding Anne.

Despite all the most consoling fabulations visiting Dr R. Micheli bolt upright (reclining his chair felt like slowing his progress to Mira's side), his confusion redoubled with each hour spent in the vice of seat belt 12C.

He landed, dry-eyed and frantic, in something he'd never heard of called "Terminal Four". An Hispanic immigration woman warned him he'd be delayed by his lack of a new passport – his sturdy red Swiss booklet wasn't "MRP" – didn't work without a new computerized magnetic band – but he'd get in "just this once" under the "one-time exemption".

A rumpled Roman searched out the taxis and when his case

flipped sideways on its flimsy wheels, a courteous black guard righted it for him while a second armed airport security officer held open the sedan door. No one palmed him for a tip. This was not the New York he recalled.

Braced for the assault of that excitement of grime and offensive smells he'd once revelled in as much reviled, he shied off asking anything of his Egyptian taxi driver, Mr Abdul Fariz, licence number 3458 who immediately warned him not to smoke, "In case you might want to, my friend, because that's against the law now, my friend." He chauffeured Roman down the middle lane of the Long Island Expressway to the strains of Bach for a pre-fixed fare right to Mrs Mary O'Neill's front door.

Roman combed his hair and brushed croissant crumbs off his lapels. He lugged his case up the stoop of the four-storey brownstone flanked by rubbish bags and battered cartons. In preparation for Mira's startled face, her tumble into his arms, the happy ending that looped like fraying celluloid on the seatback of his own imagination, he braced a heroic smile.

No one answered his buzz at the door. He knocked until his knuckles turned red with chafing, his smile freezing into a grimace. The flutter of a white curtain in a third-floor window made his heart leap, but only a tabby cat settled on the sill.

Resting on an upturned milk crate, he counted sunflower-gold school buses dodge and swing around 77th and York Avenue – little stubby ones, long unwieldy ones, their windows full of round, staring faces. He imagined his son ferried home in one of them.

Of course, Mira and he must talk about nationality. Roman's son had to be Swiss. What did that mean for military service? Weren't they reinstating the draft? Oh, God, that damned Colonel wouldn't have anything to say about that, not if Roman could help it.

A Korean crone emerged from a laundry two doors down and stared at Roman. Hiking up the elastic waist of her turquoise jogging pants with authority, she told him "sitting on crate was against law".

Confused by the immigration lecture on magnetic strips, he'd rushed out of the airport without renting a phone. Now he realized his error. Checking into a hotel would be admitting failure; it might mean segregation from the welcome flutter of those white curtains. He scrawled a desperate "I'll return in an hour" on the blank side of one of his name cards and wedged it into the crack of Mrs O'Neill's front door. Flapping in the breeze off the nearby East River, the little scrap hardly seemed adequate to the mission of saving a life.

Dragging his case to York Avenue, Roman braved the double doors of a Duane Reade Pharmacy with the vague objective of unclenching the migraine fist squeezing the back of his overheated thoughts. He focused his dry eyes on the rows of bulky Pampers and Clairol rinses, Pringles cylinders and St Patrick's Day paper plates for a simple bottle of paracetamol.

He cursed his failure to get a phone. Not only could he not try Mrs O'Neill's telephone number, Isabel might start calling the Drake Hotel. She might ask for the conference. He hurried with his pills to the cashier.

"You gotta a Member's Card?" A tubby brown teenager smiled down at him through an orthodontic brace arched around her chin. She stood on an elevated platform behind the cash register, so that her broad bosom loomed over Roman's aching head.

"No, sorry. I'll just take the aspirin." He fished out his credit card.

"You sure wanna Member's Card. Lotsa discounts. Here." Her white-mooned inch-long talons thrust a flimsy plastic card under his nose.

"Just the aspirin, thank you."

The girl took a step back and waved a scanning device across Roman's box of Tylenol, then paused in her practised dance. "Shee-it. I entered that. This here ain't no aspirin. You said you want aspirin, you shoulda got aspirin."

"It's what I want. Thank you."

" 'Cause there's a difference, you know. Some people can't take aspirin."

"Yes. Yes, I know," he nodded, counting the seconds to escape. "I am a doctor."

She waved her head in exasperation. "Well then, you oughtta know the difference. You said aspirin."

"I meant to say paracetamol."

"But you *said* aspirin. I can't read your mind, man. We gotta be careful here that people don't buy things they shouldn't be taking and we get sued. That's why you should get a Member's Card. That way the pharmacist can enter your contra-indications in our database and whatever branch you go to – "

"Well, as a sort of simple reference, I did say aspirin."

Her eyes narrowed. "You dissin' me?"

"I do not think so. I'm not sure."

"I am not simple-minded. You got cash? Our computer's down and I can't call your bank, 'cause it's overseas. Thanks. Here's your change. And here's your paracetamol. Wait, Mister? Hold on, you forgot your Member's Card."

Roman hunted for a drinking fountain, but was told by a store manager doing his homework in Duane Reade's back room to buy a can. For this he stood in line all over again and very politely paid cash, again, as the computer was still down.

Fleeing to the street in search of a bin for his dripping can of root beer, Roman hit a buffeting wind that roared unimpeded from miles farther south along Manhattan's asphalt corridors. It sent his plastic pharmacy bag flapping around his knees and whipped his case one hundred and eighty degrees around. Brains fried with frustration, Roman tried to think of some-thing manageable or just doable before he returned to his vigil at Mira's door. He would buy her a present, a baby present, and return before six. At least Mrs O'Neill would be home from work by then. He waved at taxi after taxi, but the heedless yellow beasts bounced and braked past him, their tyres thunder-ing and clanking noisy indifference over a loose manhole cover.

A very tall black man dressed in a dark overcoat and smart

silk tie arrived at the corner where Roman flailed away. The man carried an over-sized computer case brandishing a sticker that read, "Software Savior, Prayers and Repairs, 1–800–RESCUES". He lifted a white-gloved hand to shield his face from the gusts lashing at a row of newspaper vending machines chained to the lamp-post.

Together the two men stared up at the "Don't Walk" light. The stranger glanced at Roman's waving arm and bequeathed in a confiding Caribbean baritone, "Changeover time, mon. You never get a cab this time o'day."

A Cadillac town car with the dead eyes of smoked glass windows and a driver wearing reflector sunglasses appeared on the crest of 82nd St and cruised slowly down York Avenue. "You take it, brother," offered the Jamaican. "You were here first." The car's tyres skimmed the concrete kerb.

"Are you sure?" Roman himself wasn't sure. Would the town car overcharge him? Was there something illegal about the driver? Was there some reason the gentle-faced computer repairman stepped back from the idling sedan? Its silent Charon waved him into the capacious low-slung backseat. Roman asked for a department store he'd frequented long ago – the only address he could think of besides Columbia Hospital, Isabel's old apartment, Lincoln Center, and the Central Park Zoo.

Inside the car, the driver turned up the eerie New Age music. Roman sank back and hugged his case closer under his chin. He watched the city blocks bounce down their neat Dantean numbers until the car slowed to circumnavigate the Helmsley and Grand Central Station and then, at last, after a disorienting circling through back and side streets, the driver held out his gnarled hand for Roman's cash.

Roman yanked his case from the bowels of the boatlike interior on to jostling rush-hour Times Square. He stared through the failing light at billboards advertising unfamiliar television shows. He passed a Victoria's Secret emporium and tacked past a spyware discount shop. His bleary eyes finally discovered the store's entrance, obscured by scaffolding and the wide flanks of delivery trucks. He untangled his case from someone's dog leash and pressed on.

He recalled a self-service cafeteria where the lost Italian inside him could enjoy a reviving espresso but he'd been wrong to imagine the store as a sanctuary. The ground floor crush was worse than the pavement outside. At least his pounding migraine filtered out the mobile-phone conversations conducted all around him.

Escaping the chatting salesladies in Cosmetics, Roman headed towards Mens' Casuals, when a thin-lipped youth darted at him and whispered, "Exanthus" in his ear. The dyybuk suddenly sprayed Roman's parched throat with the scent of freshly-mown dandelions.

Roman struggled upward by escalator, trailed by his rattling case, to the babywear department on the fifth floor. Apart from a giggling pair of young salesgirls, the only activity came from two hand puppets counting up to twenty in Spanish on a video monitor in the "Kids Krazy Korner".

He fumbled his way down the racks, pushing and pulling at tiny outfits on doll-sized hangers. In all his fleeting dreams of fatherhood, his son had never worn silly sausage skins of spongy stretch fabric, nor needed demeaning snaps at his crotch or matching socks with rubber footpads. Roman had never confronted the mortality of his unborn child or the terrifying vulnerability of all human infants, unable to run, forage or defend themselves. This once-in-a-lifetime embryo was somewhere on that island right now, beyond the reach of his desperate father. Roman had had scarcely more than a day to contemplate the reality of blood and flesh and – was it ten weeks already? – of a minuscule heart beating beneath Mira's protective shell. How protective?

The danger his baby faced at this very minute made Roman faint with terror, rally with indignation that anyone – Col Sullivan, some New York gynaecologist, even his tender Mira – would dare harm this child. He must hurry. Why had he let a

Korean biddy shoo him away from his siege of the brownstone? Panicking anew, he yanked a sea-foam scrap printed with dolphins and, stomach sickened by "Exanthus" fumes, searched for the cashier. He felt ill with deceit, yet awed by what he'd wrought – to Mira, to Isabel, to himself and now his son. He stopped for a second to catch his breath on a pint-sized stool in front of the puppet movie. He mopped his brow with the babysuit and knew; only sleep and a smile from Mira would relieve his torment. He glanced at his watch and saw that Mrs O'Neill might be home by now.

"Mister? Are you all right?"

A sales girl, arms full of toddler jeans, bore down on him.

"Yes, I'm fine. Pardon me. Is there a public telephone?"

"Next floor down. Off the toilets near the truck entrance. Use the staff exit. You can pay for that at the cashier's on fourth."

In a sprint that required all his concentration, Roman found the stairs and headed for the exit sign, repeating Mrs O'Neill's telephone number, over and over.

The battered phone was out of order. When he leaned against the wall next to the graffitied plastic booth, he took a deep breath, but the stench of the men's room nauseated him so much that he plunged out of the double doors left open for unloading deliveries. He emerged into the blessed early evening breeze sweeping up the sidewalk. Was that a pay phone he saw at the street corner – ?

25

"I just stepped out for some air," Roman insisted.

"With the baby suit in your hand? I gotta be fair but firm here."

Mike Van Heusen ticked off the stringent guidelines of his recent training – a paralegal in the Bronx had filed a lawsuit, still pending, against the store alleging wrongful arrest. Mike intoned his mantra, "Fair but firm, fair but firm."

"I was looking for a pay phone outside. Yours is broken."

"You left the store without paying. That's a no-no." What was worse – this boy's pity or his baby talk?

"I intended to come back. I just needed air. Could I please place a telephone call?"

"No lawyer needed here. If you insist on a lawyer, then I gotta call the police. That's always a drag."

"I have no lawyer in the US."

"Well, we're instructed to offer you a list but I'll tell you as a friend, they're not the cream *de la* cream. You know what I mean?" Mike threw in a grimace. "You don't need one unless they press charges."

"Then, please, please, just return my passport and use my credit card to pay for the baby suit and then, please let me go."

"Well, looks like they got some problem with your credit card over there. It's on a foreign bank right? You got cash on you?"

Roman fished through his wallet full of Swiss money, but found only one American quarter. Where had it gone? He'd paid cash for the ride from Kennedy Airport and then for his paracetamol and then for the town car to the department store. Now he remembered that he'd planned to get more cash at an automated dispenser on his way out to dinner to discuss Mira's pregnancy. It was dinner time now.

"I don't want the baby suit any more. Just let me go."

Mike smiled, fairly but firmly. "That's what they all say, man. Forget the earrings, forget the Judith Lieber rhinestone clutch. We get two thousand a year like you, but unfortunately," Mike looked so sombre Roman thought of his own countenance when explaining the possible side effects of a much-needed treatment, "unfortunately, guys like you gotta make up for the ones we didn't catch. You pay the penalty whether you want to make your purchase now or not. Anyway, I can't let you go until you got cleared. They punch in your Social Security number yet? – "

"I am not an American. I haven't got a Social Security number." Roman was so tired, he was having trouble forming the English words.

"Oh, yeah, yeah, yeah. Yolanda phoned in your passport number already, didn't she? See, your number goes into this national database and, then assuming you're not some terrorist wacko, you just sign our confession form, and pay five times more'n what you stole. You want me to add that up for you, to save time?"

"I would appreciate it."

With a helpful nod, Mike searched for his calculator across a counter cluttered with printed forms and store directories. "Hey, no problem. Okay, lemme see that tag. Stu? Lemme borrow your scanner for a sec? Okay, that'll be sixty-nine ninety-nine, plus sales tax times five – hey, wait. Yolanda? We figure penalty before or after tax? I forget every time. Well, brace yourself, it's more'n four hundred dollars."

Mike busied himself with the paperwork of Roman's Purgatory with such relish that had he been in better humour, Roman would have asked whether the boy received a commission for each collar. The store's "Shoplifting Confession Form" chugged out of a computer printer that had seen better days while Mike carefully checked the detainee's signature against his passport. He commented that Roman didn't look his age – probably because he was a skin doctor and knew all about that "Botox shit and all".

While Mike was rubbing Roman's credit card up and down his denim-covered thigh and running out to see if the stubborn little plastic would work better "over in Pantyhose", Yolanda stood up at the far end of the room to greet two newcomers – a Chinese-American and an Hispanic wearing windbreakers and pressed khakis, sombre-faced smooth-skinned gentlemen. They resembled each other so closely, they might have been separated at birth somewhere midway across the Bering Straits.

She escorted them over to Roman. Officer Chuck Merguez and Officer Thomas Heong-King Lam flipped plastic-covered IDs under his nose. They were from the downtown Manhattan branch of the Immigration and Naturalization Service and having run his record through their national database, enhanced, upgraded, and updated since the tragedy of 9/11, were sorry to inform Dr Micheli that it appeared according to their best records that in 1975, May 19 to be exact, Roman had failed to extend his student visa as required by law after two repeated notifications sent by registered mail on February 7 and March 13, 1975 to 426 West 116th St – well, Sir, that was your then-registered address whether you'd already moved in with your girlfriend on 92nd or not. Neglecting to respond, and having failed to apply for further legal permission to stay in the United States of America – well, Sir, whether you knew it or not – you have been in a long-standing position of default – yes, Sir, even though you freely left the country six weeks later in the spring of 1975 – a default that left you recorded as overstaying your student visa by some *decades* – Sir, I know, Sir, but this is what our government records show –

"Could I make a phone call?" Roman blurted at them, in a voice strangled with panic.

Officer Merguez looked at Roman with the same professional sympathy Roman himself assumed when delivering bad news.

"Why, certainly, Sir. If it's a local call, you can use my cellphone."

With shaking hands, Roman dialled Mrs O'Neill's number now engraved on his feverish brain. He heard the telephone on 77th St ring three times, imagined the fat tabby opening one dozy eye and then heard a click as the answering machine began in a nasal, business-like, middle-aged female voice: "I am not available right now. Please leave . . ."

Officer Merguez folded up his cellphone with the air of a man who had seen all this before, too, too many times. He nodded to Officer Lam, who resumed his recitation without further ado: Roman would now be required under the laws reviewed by Congress to be escorted back to Kennedy International – yes, Sir, I know that is where you just came from – and to rectify your overstayer status in your country of origin – well, yesssir, where you're more than welcome to reapply for a tourist, professional or business visa at the United States Embassy in Berne or the United States Consulate in Geneva.

Now. With or without legal representation, Sir. With or without a call to the Swiss Consulate in Manhattan which, we might advise you Sir, is now closed until Monday. Up to you. Catching one of the last flights to the Continent would be a helluva lot more comfortable than sitting in an INS holding cell downtown for the weekend. You can trust us on that, Doctor.

Merguez actually smiled. "Thank you, Sir. Cute stretch suit. My baby girl has one in pink, only with elephants."

They emerged on to the street where Roman might have expected to find the Software Savior beaming welcome next to the Stygian Cadillac, but apparently the Immigration and Naturalization people preferred to ferry their human cargo in banal minivans. Mike Van Heusen chased after the sad little posse, hailing them as they pulled away from the kerb.

"Doctor Micheli? Doctor Micheli?"

"Yes, Mike?"

"Do you think you'd be able to fill out this questionnaire on your trip back? Mail it to the address printed on the bottom? They kinda worry about more lawsuits, you know."

Mike's pleading eyes directed Roman at the sheet thrust into his sweating palm. It was printed in English, Spanish, Chinese and Arabic:

Dear Customer,

Your business is important to our store. In order to assist us in improving our customer detention service, we would appreciate your taking the time to respond to the following questions. 1. Was your detention officer available to you at all times? 2. Did he/she clearly explain the reason for your detention and answer all your questions? 3. Did he/she explain your various options with regard to legal assistance and payment of fines? 4. Did your detention officer offer you refreshments and toilet facilities . . . ?

Brisk spring winds whisked the last trace of morning fog off the striated slab of Mont Salève guarding the city of Geneva like a monumental Cerberus.

Roman inched his Saab back from the airport through a Geneva clogged with weekend traffic – cars topped with ski racks and motorcycles dodging from lane to lane. During the nightmarish British Airways "red eye" to London and the dawn connection by EasyJet to Zurich and the over-priced full fare Swiss shuttle to Geneva, Roman's stubble grew into bristle. He parked at the lakeside and headed for the safety of his clinic. He's go anywhere, face anything but the humiliating interrogation of his kind Isabel setting off herself that very afternoon for the same airport.

The battered wheels of his case clattered behind him through the empty shopping arcade. When his exhausted mind couldn't summon the digits of his own lift security code after three tries, he shrugged his guilty shoulders and dragged the case up the fire escape stairs instead.

With morbid resignation, he entered the haven of reception's darkness watched by the dead eye of his video monitor and the circling school of fish. The only comforting sound was the murky aquarium's bubbling. He dumped his case at the foot of Chantal's counter and rubbed away the sweaty leather particles clinging to his palm.

He ran hot water into an examination room sink and tried to scrub away his wretchedness. Throwing the used paper toweling in a bin, he hoisted himself on to his own treatment bed. The clean, crisp pillow welcomed his heaving emotions. His eyes felt too sore to close, so he stared up at the orderly holes of the acoustic tiles.

He must be suffering some kind of cleansing aberration. Nothing in life was sure, but Roman's every instinct hurried to reassure him that his last ten days of obsession exploding into full-blown insanity was the purging of an emotional boil, somehow "for the best".

Wasn't his fruitless pilgrimage to New York the needed proof that he'd succumbed to borderline madness? Surely the weird retrieval of some long-buried visa hiccough felt catastrophic now, but one day might seem a blessing in bureaucratic guise.

He would try to call Mira this evening. There was still a chance. He could still fight. The warning cries of "prudence" and "practicality" pestered his conscience. He battled off these sanctimonious harpies and tried to conjure up his baby son. He recited a prayer for his survival, but the impish murmurers wouldn't shut up: wasn't an abortion the easiest, the neatest solution – for Isabel and for Mira? Shouldn't he feel reprieved, even relieved?

Non, non, non. He felt robbed, cheated by life and of life. Surrounded by his expensive machines and medical diplomas, his tools and tissues, all the trappings of his infallibility, he felt punished. He pulled his knees toward his chin and sobbed in stifled gulps for his child-who-wouldn't-be.

26

A few blocks uphill from where Roman wept, Isabel pictured her husband relishing the overheated-coffee-and-Danish good humour of international laser colleagues. She could see him exchanging cards and papers with his peers, bustling back and forth between air-conditioned conference rooms. She imagined him fumbling with the spigot of an enormous American coffee thermos, his bundle of photocopied speeches and participant lists tucked awkwardly under his elbow as he was introduced around and agreed to meet up later – maybe after the new machinery exhibits or the side-effects seminar?

It wasn't just that it was his turn to get away from the Geneva gloom. He did seem in need of a change. Of late he hadn't appeared actually unhappy – no, quite the contrary – more disengaged, but curiously happy to be so.

Certainly different.

Yet his uncustomary absence on this silent Sunday made Isabel restless. Her solitary lunch – the fag ends of cheese, a last yoghurt and some leftover pasta she couldn't leave a day longer in the refrigerator – remonstrated that their apartment was more and more just a mutual way-station. Halfway through her ascetic meal, a shaft of light pierced the afternoon fog. Isabel bathed her eyelids in the warmth. Opening them again, she spotted a golden bolt of dancing dust light up a spider web in a far corner of the dining-room ceiling. One of Spaghetti's seasonal furball deposits lurked under the bookshelf. Mrs Siskovitch must have overlooked it for weeks. Isabel had never acquired her mother's knack with servants, but unlike Marjorie

Hanford, she hadn't been raised by them.

She measured out three days' worth of dry cat food in a neat row of plastic bowls and adjusted the kitchen window a crack to allow Spaghetti's morning slither. She plodded through her packing list with a sinking heart: she'd stocked her toilet bag one too many times. The flag of futility had shot up. An invisible expiration date had been breached. How confusing that just when her life should seem settled, it suddenly felt "off", like milk gone sour.

Was anything specific wrong? Nothing had happened, really. Frank's departure had been a setback, true. But nothing tragic or traumatic had hit her, nothing that could account for a winter-long sense of life disintegrating beyond salvage. Nothing more than that she was turning forty-four, Marjorie's feebleness was depressing, and Roman was going through some kind of phase.

She fished the door keys from the bottom of her shoulder bag and took a last look at the living room to imagine how in a few days Roman would find it on his return – neat but neglected.

A telephone's ring broke her restless funk. She dropped her raincoat at the front door, but half-hoped she'd miss the call. It might be a distant relative passing through Geneva, hooting a hello, darling, ready to barrel over for a chat. Her father used to say you had to be ready for that when you lived "out station". Her mother always had a sponge cake ready.

Not that anyone ever looked in on Isabel and her "Italian" husband. Whether distantly-related Hanfords actually avoided the Micheli apartment and skulked like guilty resistance fighters under the radar of her sober territory to the sunny slopes of Courchevel or the Valais, Isabel really couldn't care less.

In fact, why answer the phone at all? Who even used the land line these days? The Michelis were still listed in the directory only through sheer inertia. Who needed calls from marketeers – saccharine, presumptuous, intrusive – or lately, the German banker downstairs complaining yet again that if Dr

Micheli wanted to listen to a violin sawing all Sunday, he might be well advised to don earphones, or better yet install better sound-proofing and, no, he didn't care if it was Hilary Hahn herself, live, in person.

Isabel plopped on the edge of the bed to answer the machine-gun *tat-tat-tat* of a weekend concierge's rough, accusatory French. Could Dr Micheli please come to fetch his *truc* left for weeks at the *Conservatoire*? Having set it to one side, the concierge could condemn the expensive bag to the lost-and-found where Dr Micheli could bid *adieu* to *les baskets* and *le training* — so very elegant she, *personnellement*, would not trust these expensive temptations to fate — otherwise could she take them home where they would be safe?

Roman's gym bag, safe? Safe in some nicotine-rasping char's council flat somewhere in Servette? There must be some mistake.

The concierge recited word for word the *renseignements* on Roman's ID tag.

Roman's bag stolen?

"Our students are many things, Madame, but not thieves. Although I don't say they don't borrow chairs and the odd coffee machine from year to year," the old woman chuckled, "but at heart, we are not thieves. We are *artistes*. It is some weeks now I see your husband with his bag." She sucked on an invisible cigarette into Isabel's ear.

Isabel jotted down the address of the *Conservatoire de Musique de Genève, rue Petitot numéro 8, pas le Conservatoire Populaire, notez bien*. She assured the caller that she had taken note that it was the Conservatory for professionals, not the other one. She guaranteed Roman would retrieve his bag by the end of the week.

The hush of the apartment seemed to have taken on a buzzing of its own. Isabel sat very still on the bed for a minute, a plump woman with red hair whitening around the temples, puzzlement shadowing her open face, freckled hands folded in her lap. She felt called on suddenly in class, caught daydreaming without the answer to a question she hadn't quite heard. She

281

cast about for the problem lurking behind this little mystery, but couldn't wrest it to the surface.

The tags must've got changed or the bags switched when Roman was distracted. Why, on any given Saturday morning, the city of Geneva must be absolutely clogged with unshaven middle-aged husbands lugging those black nylon bags from their cars to locker rooms and back. Surely the gym bag – so similar to a thousand others – was spirited away by a Roman doppelgänger from the gym to the Conservatoire de Musique on the pont Neuf.

Roman would laugh when he found out, but he might be annoyed. After all, who had the time these days to fetch a stupid sports bag?

For the routine hours of moving herself from point A to B – for as long as she rode to the airport, finessed her upgrade to a better seat, and waited for her flight call – Isabel left the problem of Roman's roving gym kit in the locker of her sub-conscious.

An hour after boarding, she rolled up the shade of the plane's double-glazed porthole to watch the diagonal rivulets of rain driven by the jet stream. Her mind daintily stepped over the tell-tale lentils trailing down the path of deceit as she reviewed her files for the Midrand Conference – Africa's first leprosy convocation since 1938 – and concentrated on arrangements to be finalized with the London executives of the Asian mobile-phone company. Then she snapped her ring binder shut and thought of Roman.

He'd been going to the gym every Saturday since after Christmas but hadn't noticed his gear was missing for – what did the concierge say? – some weeks? Did he keep a spare bag? Certainly there was some mystery here, not noticed by Isabel until this minute, gazing down at the English channel through spinning drifts, a cloudy mystery that deepened when she realized that Roman didn't need his gym clothes laundered very often.

In fact, Isabel was hard put to recall his new navy-blue track suit in the laundry basket, ever. Did he give it to Mrs Siskovitch for dry-cleaning? Really, Isabel sometimes wondered what the cleaning lady thought of her employers – a finicky doctor who wanted her to dust off his collection of chrome sculptures on the mantelpiece not once but twice a week, and his doctor-wife who hardly noticed whether the dishes were washed.

Isabel exhaled relief at Victoria Station's familiar queue of black taxis grinding out their diesel welcome, the high-street ordinariness of the tree-lined streets of London at dusk. She shunned the cost-saving chain hotels with their business centres and airport cars in favour of a three-star brick affair in W11. The lobby smelling of humid carpeting and stale disinfectant felt safe this evening. Safe from what?

At last Isabel settled in her tights and cotton dressing-gown on the striped chair next to the window in the privacy of her hotel room. She reviewed her notes for tomorrow's meeting with The British Leprosy Relief Foundation to be followed by lunch reviewing the BBC World Trust's next regional campaign. For all his work-outs, Roman had not, in fact, become noticeably fitter. On the other hand, he was undeniably more relaxed . . .

Isabel poured herself a whisky and soda from the mini-bar, in one swig breaking three private vows – about WHO travel expenses, drinking alone on the road, and the fear of turning into her mother, right now out in the English countryside slowly pickling herself in gin. She must call Marjorie, but first she'd touch base with Roman. He'd scribbled out the Drake Hotel telephone number in New York, but the digits were quite illegible – even for a doctor's handwriting. If he wanted her to call, he might have made it a little easier. Was that a nine or a zero? A seven or a four? She hoped to catch him during a break between sessions, reassure him she'd landed quite all right, thank you very much, and how was he?

Somehow she got connected to the wrong Drake, a Drake where there was no laser conference that weekend whatsoever. Did Madame perhaps want the temporary registration desk for Motivational Mothering or the Alive with Alzheimers pre-planning seminar? No, there was no Dr Roman Micheli, M-I-C-H-E-L-I guest.

That could only mean there must be two Drakes in Manhattan, and could he give her the other number, please? With respect, Madame, there was no other Drake Hotel in New York City.

Isabel persisted. The young man sneering through snot on the other end of the line also persisted.

Could he pu-lease check the listings of functions and conferences and guest lists again? She snapped more like Mrs Marjorie Westcott Hanford every second. Imagine Roman's reaction when he realized he'd given her the wrong number. What a series of muddles were flying towards her, like dark birds in formation! Clutching her pen, she doodled an arrowhead of small black wings across the bedside notepad.

If she had misunderstood Roman's plans, there was no one to blame but herself. She hadn't paid enough attention when he announced this unusual expedition to the non-Drake Hotel. Once this London jog was over – no, of course, after she'd done the Kashmir field trip – then she must absolutely, resolutely insist that she and Roman take a holiday together, no matter how short.

Isabel rattled the ice shards at the bottom of her glass and just this once, poured herself a second drink. There was no point in ordering dinner; years ago the hotel had closed its "French" restaurant in the face of competition down the street from a noisy hamburger and salad joint, a Cypriot family place and a rather forbidding fusion-fashion palace. She'd make do with the mini-bar peanuts.

Sucking at an ice cube, Isabel pondered; had they chosen the right place to test the utility of mobile phones in strife-torn regions? She must remember to ask tomorrow for a list of technical questions to put to the communications officer in Delhi. Dr Cheong had argued for Mozambique, but then Dr Cheong wasn't going to have to go there, was she? Despite the

WHO's notorious lack of cross-corridor dialogue, Dr Cheong had finagled herself a timely, albeit temporary, secondment to battle a virulent outbreak of bird flu in Sa Kaeo, Thailand. If Dr Cheong was going anywhere, it was on a cushy Cathay flight to Bangkok with Frank Norton to measure the H_5N_1 viral count in mountains of dead chickens.

Carlos would have done Mozambique. Isabel missed Carlos.

The stats on leprosy up in the quake-torn territories beyond Father Shardar's district were sketchy. Leprosy was hardly endemic in this area, but they couldn't be sure, and that was the point, wasn't it? To get the kids – the blistered girls hidden under veils in back rooms, the scowling dusty little boys with numb lesions – and bring them down off the hills to tally and treat their lesions, or at least send them blister packs up the war-torn paths using diagnoses by mobile phone or DVD portables or – bloody hell – by mule, if necessary.

She could almost hear her mother laughing. *Ironic, isn't it, Isabel, you can hardly go up there safely now without a passport and an escort armed to the teeth? In the old days it was all one country, don't forget. It was the heat on the plains that drove us up there. Your grandparents married at St Fillans in Sargodha, then travelled up through Muree at seven thousand feet, then chugged down again along the Jehlum River. Then onwards to honeymoon in the Vale of Kashmir. All one country in those days, darling.*

We all hated that stodgy hotel. Can't recall the name now, but everybody hated it, so of course your grandparents haggled for a house-boat with two bedrooms, a drawing room and dining room. Just imagine, for three weeks they floated across the glassy reflections of peaks on Dal Lake. Pour me another peg, darling. Not so much ice, thanks ever so much. Where was I? They had two local boats tied to the back for the mangi's wife and baby – and possibly all his proverbial sisters and his cousins and his aunts, heaven knows – and the mangi poled away from morning to night, from mooring to mooring, and sometimes, just to get away from the smell of the cooking pots and the mosquito coil of punk dragging along behind, they'd set off by themselves on a shikara. No dear, not exactly a punt – where your grandparents would sit, well, lie rather, on cushions under a roof with curtains hanging down for privacy, just drifting along without a care in the world . . . Everyone said later that they were as happy as any couple could be for as long as it lasted. I can just remember my mother's laughter, drifting up to my nursery of an evening. And after they sent her to Delhi, they let me visit her twice, but only speaking across the length of the garden, of course. And then she didn't want me to come any more. You have to seize your happiness when it comes to you, Isabel, darling. Don't put it off for a rainy day. You just end up with rain.

Drifting on a crystalline lake. Isabel stared into the cubes melting at the bottom of the cheap glass. God, to think how the honeymooning Westcotts' idyll ended.

Evening traffic roared westward down towards Bayswater. She smelled the stale odour of frying fish. If it weren't for this unexpected mobile-phone trial, if it weren't for Roman's demanding practice, if it weren't for a thousand other things that always, always, always mattered more, Isabel could be showing Roman the relics of her family past. Well perhaps not in Sargodha itself – the old golf course, the overgrown tennis court, whatever was left of St Fillan's under the Himalayan snowcaps – all that was pretty much out of bounds across the barbed wire and the closed border – but at least the Indian-controlled territory.

Even if half the houseboats stood empty, permanently moored witnesses to the curfew and snap and bark of the hated Special Ops troops, wasn't there at least something to be shared, something to be rescued? Was it really too late to dispatch the ominous winged flock clouding her psyche back over the horizon?

Isabel slammed the empty glass back on the mini-bar hard enough to make the ice bucket jump. Now, right now, this was all going to change as soon as she got back to Geneva. The wounds from Frank's budgetary dagger had dripped for weeks until the good Isabel, the noble Isabel, the idiotically driven and blinded Isabel stood bled bone-dry of sentiment, of motivation, of the last shreds of loyalty. She and Roman had sacrificed everything marriage was supposed to mean to false gods – professional responsibilities, financial security, and social conscience.

To hell with that. With each week, Isabel saw herself ageing and drying up, while Roman sunk into his second adolescence, his head jammed between earphones when he wasn't trotting off with that ridiculous gym bag banging around his knees.

She flicked on Channel 4 and listened halfheartedly to the upbeat actuality of security preparations for yet another "peace-making" India-Pakistan cricket match, followed by the local news. Isabel ran her bath water with the dribble of English human interest gabbling through the rush of water.

Her decision to change her life galvanized her, or was that merely whisky courage? She would take action and declare her independence. Only a few hours ago, the strange problem of a wandering gym bag had distracted her, when all along she should have been diving to the lower, darker depths, to dredge up the lurking truths that never braved sunlight. Her inability to reach Roman by telephone – the silly man had forgotten to rent a mobile and would probably spend a fortune from the hotel only to say he was flying home the next day – all this was proof that they absolutely must stop living on phone calls and catch-up conversations.

The very first minute, the very second she saw Roman, she'd announce her plan to whisk him off to Kashmir with her. They would lay flowers on Grandmother Westcott's grave lying in permanent purdah, consoled only by the remains of her loyal Reggie, both of them interred an antiseptic distance from the other forgotten ghosts in Srinigar's colonial cemetery.

Trembling with the excitement of it, Isabel swung her heavy thighs over the edge of the high old-fashioned tub and sank into the warm bubbles. How many so-called friends had objected to her grandmother's burial in the sahibs' cemetery? Argued that "After all, Reggie, the doctors know so little, for the sake of all of us, one can't be too sentimental. In this heat, it simply pays to be careful."

No one intended to cast any slur on poor Lily's good Christian soul, considering all she'd suffered.

Isabel imagined her grandfather's miserable pilgrimages with tiny Marjorie to visit his wife, the child positioned off a safe distance, waving a brave hand towards the white-frocked nuns and their patient behind the gate. Marjorie rarely spoke to Isabel of the inevitable day her father announced there would be no further visits; "Mummy's not so well these days. Her sight ..." Feeling an unspoken contamination in the eyes of the pretty ladies around her, the child Marjorie had done her very best from then on to look especially clean and neat, for Mummy's sake. Even drunk, Marjorie was still the cleanest old lady in her parish.

It had taken all her grandfather's clout to wangle permission to transport Lily's ravaged corpse back from obscurity at the mission to a shaded grave in a lead-lined coffin under the Srinagar pines, before the alarm went up among the local gossips sheltering from the heat up in the cool hills. Some whispered over their evening drinks of religious propriety – given the whiff of suicide, after all – but of course, that wasn't the real reason the Sargodha Club had drawn together in a silent consensus against welcoming those desolate, dangerous remains. Srinigar was all right, if it had to be somewhere. Even so, some doctors believed the bacteria could survive in the soil for generations, especially in cemeteries.

Or course, Isabel mused in her dingy hotel bath, those ignorant biddies were quite wrong, medically speaking, to be so cruel in their polite caution, shivering over fearful descriptions of Lily's final disfigurement while they sat, powdered and perfumed, draped in flowery chiffons. They sipped champagne punch on the club veranda discussing what small kindness they might do for Lily's little Marjorie. And she heard her mother allow herself an occcasional sigh: "But you know, darling Isabel, as I grew older and wiser, I noticed that all my mother's former friends, those colonial gentlewomen, kept their white gloves on whenever they shook my father's hand."

27

"Doctor Burden strangled? In Geneva?"

Inspector Rémy Clerc nodded, "Yes, Doctor. Quite an anti-septic job – the *service d'identification judiciaire* even put in overtime but still came up empty-handed. This job seems impossibly professional – no saliva, cigarette butts or stray hairs for DNA analysis, no footprints, no fingerprints, no blood. *Très efficace*, even for Switzerland. Not even signs of a struggle, although the angle at which the neck was broken might suggest the killer was much shorter than the victim. Around the station, my colleagues call Doctor Burden the man who strangled himself."

Roman forced a tight smile while the cheerful inspector continued: "You see, our homicides generally fall into the predictable categories: the angry husband and battered wife, drug violence, rape. Last winter we had that banker wearing a rubber suit shot three times by his mistress. That was a nice change ..."

"*Oui, oui*, I so much appreciate your informing me without delay." Roman nodded, hoping to hurry the man along with his duties. What an intrusion at ten o'clock on a Tuesday morning, their busiest slot for extended sessions!

"Oh, it's not mere courtesy, Doctor. As I say, without fingerprints or witnesses, this is a murder case to be solved by people, not labs. We're talking to everyone in the victim's address book, that is, his Palm Pilot."

"Of course." Roman fingered the raised insignia on Clerc's calling card. He gave his best imitation of sincere regret, "I'm shocked, Inspector. *Profondément.* He was a successful doctor."

One didn't have to say *good*. Roman continued, "It was a memorable experience to share my residency with him so many years ago. I am, well, stunned at your news."

"You were close?"

"*Mais non.* We'd lost touch for many decades, but his accomplishments were well-publicized. His arrival in Geneva was an undoubted stimulus to our medical community."

Roman was indeed stunned, not by grief but by Jonathan's audacity, his sheer bad taste getting himself killed in the middle of Roman's crisis and on Roman's turf. Even the usually modest Roman felt that for once he had the right to be the protagonist of his own tragedy. He couldn't deny feeling, well, miffed that Jonathan Burden was so keen to force his way into the local spotlight, he would get himself killed. Roman had no attention or emotion to spare for Jonathan's admittedly permanent downturn in fortune.

Since his return Roman had abandoned any of the precautions second nature to the cold-blooded womanizer or even the Saturday afternoon adulterer. Sunday night he'd dialled Mrs Mary O'Neill from his mobile phone and from his office line Monday morning. Surely someone was sleeping in that mute brownstone on 77th? He programmed Mrs O'Neill's number into the bedside phone on Monday night so that his index finger could poke at the redial button without hindrance. His frenzied calls went unacknowledged, like prayers to a foreign idol. He craved the sound of Mira's voice, the smell of her bed, the fluttering of her fingers down the long neck of her violin. Mira now inhabited some netherworld, a limbo banked on all sides by answering machines playing a librarian's nasal invitation, "Please leave your message after the beep."

She must have left the brownstone – but not for the hospital, he prayed. Roman saw little choice but to leave his name with Col Sullivan's secretary. Surely the worried father was eager to hear about Roman's New York visit?

Apparently not. The Colonel's secretary informed Roman

that the military diplomat was in a meeting. Some hours and many tries later, Roman realized that this meeting never paused for coffee, never went to the washroom, and would never, ever break for lunch.

Clerc continued his clipped description of Jonathan's demise. An exhausted Roman listened through the dementia of jet lag, mired in a despair he couldn't confide to anyone. All Tuesday morning he had sensed the world recoiling from him – the disembodied aunt, the silent father, the anxious Chantal. Worse, Isabel had shuttled back from London late last night obsessed with the idea of some romantic pilgrimage to India.

Clerc had paused and was staring at him. Roman fumbled on, "You've informed Doctor Burden's American offices?"

"*Bien sûr*. They were in a better position to inform his family. Perhaps you know more about his private life?"

"He spoke of an ex-wife, grown children. It all sounded amicable."

"*Famille recomposée*? Second wife, step-children?"

"*Non, non.* Jonathan was always something of a bon vivant with the ladies. A born Romeo, you might say."

Clerc nodded and smiled: clearly he'd already had Jonathan's notoriety in the skin trade impressed on him. "We've already received calls from the *New York Observer*, calling him *le roi de Botox*. Clerc looked quizzically at his notebook for a moment. "I always thought it was the *New York Times, non*?"

"He was very *célébré* in the United States."

Imagine bothering to murder Jonathan! Of course, he was patronizing, vulgar, competitive, infuriating – but murder? Such a mortal sin for so venial a target, spiritually speaking. Jonathan's faults didn't warrant slaughter, although there were times back at Columbia when Roman had felt like slipping a Darvon in his Dr Pepper to shut him up.

Could Dr Burden have faced a money problem? Roman answered Clerc's questions about overheads, set-up costs, the improvements in machines since his own investments, you understand. Anyway, whatever Jonathan did, he was certainly transparent about it. He would broadcast his ambitions and feats within minutes of execution to anybody who'd listen – again and again.

A *crime passionnel*?

"After only a few weeks in Switzerland, Inspector?" Hadn't Clerc himself just said Jonathan's murder bore the signature of a cool professional, not a jealous husband or a patient with Botoxed brains?

Was Dr Burden prominent in religious or political circles?

Roman could imagine the deceased was an expert at tax-deductible donations and gala fund-raising events but he tried not to laugh out loud at Clerc's far-fetched theory that Jonathan's explicit ads for bikini-waxing inflamed Wahabist elements at the Sion or Lausanne mosques. An imam had been stabbed last year by a rival sect and one never knew –

"Surely you have better leads than that, Monsieur Clerc!"

"*Eh bien, Docteur*, even in Switzerland, we don't always solve a murder in the first few hours, unless we committed it ourselves, heh, heh – "

Roman stared down the chuckle dying on Clerc's lips. Chantal was settling the Englishman Stratford in an examination room while poor Mme Piguet fidgeting outside in reception faced impending news of a third malignant facial lesion. Roman snuck a glance at his watch.

Of course, this impatient *geste* was tactless – disrespectful to the deceased. It was indiscreet to signal to a Swiss policeman that there were other things more important to Roman than a janitor's discovery on a Saturday evening of blue-faced Jonathan splayed out on the spotless floor of his new Geneva waiting room. The victim's throttled neck resembled a sack twisted closed and secured by a lethal tourniquet improvised from a pair of surgical gloves, their packing talc still fresh. A second pair of gloves had disappeared, no doubt on the departing killer's hands.

At this description of the murder, an inappropriately funny memory flashed back – of Jonathan recounting his "Death by

Rubber" to Roman in the Columbia lounge one morning following his night shift conquest of an overweight, but hard-working orthopaedic therapist. Gloria Entermann's pent-up lust for the capable Resident Burden had used up "a whole pack of rubber precautions", Jonathan boasted. Gloria Entermann had been *très sympathique* and deserved better than Jonathan's locker room betrayal.

Alors, how ironic now – Jonathan had predicted his own end. Were all of us insentient oracles, blabbing and blurting the omens of our undoing in front of a banal snack machine? Perhaps Roman had already said or done enough to preordain his featureless future and unremarkable end as a long-married, respectable laser doctor. What if a person's path wasn't strewn with mortal temptations and path-breaking decisions pointing to a heroic or tragic destiny, just undeliberated little *gestes*, repeatable thematic stabs at absolution and redemption that added up to an obvious denouement?

Roman's thoughts wandered away from Clerc's recitation . . . Or were the Calvinists right and the Catholics wrong? Had God already decided who died by surgical-glove asphyxiation? Had innocent Jonathan long ago suffered a premonition of his final rendezvous with latex – hence the poor man's urgent need, even greed for reassurance that no matter how irritating, he was one of the Elect?

Oh, but the Calvinists could never answer the obvious question, why would God bother naming names, fingering souls? Roman preferred his first conviction. There must be cause and effect, even if undetected. Some inconsequential act by Jonathan had mushroomed into this fatality – that was more like it. Knowing Jonathan, the American had somehow soli-cited his own termination through some minor infraction, some thoughtless offence. That was the kind of thing that would do him in.

Poor Jonathan. Roman flushed with unfamiliar affection, if only for their shared past. Perhaps the chastened, heartbroken Dr Micheli was finally stumbling on some morsel of fellow-feeling for Jonathan's congenital foolishness? Suddenly even their rivalry looked fraternal in its longevity. *Le pauvre* Jonathan. All he'd wanted underneath it all was estimation. All he could offer in return was a kind of indiscriminate affection, the panting unselfconscious pushiness of an overgrown, over-groomed Long Island puppy. And in the end, all he promoted was making people more relaxed and more desirable, if only on the surface.

A stab of pity replaced affection. For the strangled Jonathan, or for himself? The shock of Mira's disappearance left Roman's emotions newly threadbare. Now Jonathan had escaped such ravages – yes, escaped! Mira's pregnancy, throwing open the glorious prospect of fatherhood, had offered escape from the futility of routine and impervious age. Then it had slammed shut, tossing Roman back into a life he'd once imagined was satisfying, even admirable.

The minutes ticked by as the dogged Clerc detailed the search of Jonathan's hotel room, his laptop files and new spa premises; medical books in stacks near the door, freshly deliv-ered laser machines in their bubble-pack blocking the reception area – too cumbersome to suggest attempted burglary – freshly varnished beauty counters and cartons of massage creams and fragrant oils.

"Did Doctor Burden follow any cults? We had some Satan-ists up the Rhône a few years back – "

"*Pardon?*"

"We found a crate of black rocks shipped from Hawaii – "

"Stone massage," Roman mumbled, rubbing his aching brow. "I believe one heats them to ease muscle tension."

"Oh." Clerc sighed, disappointed his Hawaiian cult theory led nowhere.

"I really couldn't say more, Monsieur Clerc. We hadn't kept up. Out of courtesy, my wife and I invited him to dinner at our apartment once last year. He broached the idea that I might even be his partner, but of course, I declined – "

"Of course."

"His approach to the use of lasers differed from my own."

"I see." Clerc made no move to go.

"You can understand I'm too shocked to discuss it further."

"Of course. It is the normal reaction, I assure you." The stolid inspector wouldn't unglue his bottom from the consultee's seat without *something*. He had his job to do, just like Roman.

"Ah, *oui*, I recall now, he told my wife about a lawsuit, but that was in New York – "

"*Ah, bon?*"

" – a malpractice dispute over a Botox injection. His American lawyers could explain, of course. It wasn't a Geneva affair."

Clerc scrawled a few more words on his note pad. "Can you tell me more of his social milieu? Personal habits? Gambling?"

Would this policeman never go? "*Pas vraiment.* He was prosperous enough to propose a European chain."

"But only in Geneva, so far."

Roman paused. "*Oui.*"

"Are there many laser doctors in Geneva?"

"*Non.*" Roman gave the investigator a frank gaze.

"How long have you been practising in Geneva?"

Roman waved his hand, "Oh, just under twenty years."

"Of course, I can understand you didn't need a partner – "

"Certainly not!"

"So he found a Doctor Bouvier." Clerc's eyes stayed fixed on the note pad balanced on his knee.

Roman hesitated. "So he mentioned." He dared to rise from his desk.

"Yes. In fact, we'll be speaking to Bouvier next. He seems to be our main lead. There are hints of some irregularities in the licensing arrangement, I'm told." Clerc flipped the notebook closed. "Mind you, I didn't say suspect. Friends are always anxious we find a scapegoat." He rose from the visitor's chair. "It helps to cushion the loss."

"Doctor Burden was a most colourful *personnage*."

"I begin to feel I know him. This morning my wife pointed out his posters along the route de Lausanne. Seems she'd already signed up for the *autobronzage.*"

Roman nodded, "*Au moins,* she'll avoid sun damage that way." He ushered Clerc closer to the door.

"Ah, you mentioned Doctor Burden spoke to your wife. Madame was also a personal friend?" Clerc had assumed a distracted air.

"A fellow medical student. She returned from a professional trip last night."

"Well, we'll drop into her office for a chat. And just for the record, Doctor Micheli, you were in Geneva this weekend?"

Roman's heart fluttered at the risk of explaining to Isabel anything the policeman might discover in confirming his story – the four-hundred-dollar baby suit, the mad shuttle from Terminal Four back to Terminal Four, Mike Van Heusen's absurd questionnaire crumpled in the bin only two metres from where Clerc now stood. Roman was trapped by aeroplane records and his silly story of the conference to maintain with Isabel.

"No, I was away from Geneva at a conference. Keeping up with the latest developments in medicine is a formal requirement for practising, you know."

"It must keep you very busy," Clerc smiled. "Please excuse my asking. A formality, I assure you."

Isabel's office was scarcely wide enough for all three of them, so Clerc's sidekick, a lantern-jawed woman in a bulky padded police jacket had to settle for a position in the corridor outside. Did she have to stand with boots rooted a foot apart, hands on hips, as if auditioning for an Inspector Morse episode? The woman seemed poised to draw fire on the upturned rump of Carlos's idle secretary bent over the 1992−9 filing cabinets in a futile display of filling her empty hours.

A rubber-necking Dr Cheong clicked past in her Italian pumps, slowing, to gape at the Praetorian Heidi. Isabel glared right back over Clerc's shoulder. She was sure that her P6 status would be confirmed by the end of the month and she'd sewn up guarantees of more London money at last. The elation of the second honeymoon idea had only risen higher on the unexpected success of her latest discussions. She'd landed home in Geneva on wings of relief and excitement – rehearsing her suggestion that Roman drop everything and accompany her to Kashmir in words that wouldn't sound either needy or bossy.

After a deep sleep, she'd left Roman snoring in bed to rush into the office before the sun had fully risen and – before this Clerc official had interrupted the happy momentum of her productive morning – pounced on the phone to nail down the difficult meetings in Kashmir and explore arrangements for an idyllic holiday for two.

"Jonathan, killed?"

Clerc sighed, "Didn't your husband even mention it?"

Isabel glimpsed her open-mouthed reflection in the dark screen of her computer. Jonathan dead. Dear Jonathan. Roman's concentration was growing more distracted with each day. Of course Roman had never cared for him, but she had, once. He should have said *something*. Left her a note.

"How sad. How did he die?"

The details were grotesque. Who in Geneva hated Jonathan? Who in Geneva even knew Jonathan? No, she had never met the ex-wife, hadn't kept up with Jonathan, certainly enjoyed lunch in New York after so many years and then hosting him in Geneva, but that was just catching up on things, you know.

"Everybody loved Jonathan in the old days." Isabel added sadly. "A bit of a clown, over-the-top with the nurses, but then," she added in a wistful whisper, "we were all so young."

Clerc scribbled a few more notes. *Crime passionnel?* Jealous girlfriend? Deranged patient?

"Oh, I hardly think so, Inspector. You see, Jonathan just wasn't the sort of man you'd get deadly about. I mean, he was quite lovable in his way, but rather, uh, lightweight. A bit flaky. Besides, I don't expect he's got any Geneva patients to speak of yet. Anyway, even Jonathan wasn't stupid enough to risk a new medical venture by getting involved with a patient." She tittered, "Nobody's that silly."

It was all over really rather quickly, considering Jonathan was dead. Isabel booted up her computer with relief as the door closed behind the two Swiss police. The screen hummed its steadying little whirr.

She was furious Roman hadn't even mentioned Jonathan's death. Roman hadn't been himself since she first told him of Jonathan's plan to expand into Geneva. He'd been absolutely shirty when Jonathan came to dinner and downright unkind when Jonathan named Bouvier as partner. He'd been broody and distant and uncommunicative for weeks and weeks, not to mention unloving, inattentive and secretive.

He'd become someone she didn't recognize. And somewhere along the line, Isabel suspected with a cold rush of hurt and confusion, he'd lied to her about something.

Starting with that blasted gym bag.

"Clerc said it bore all the marks of a professional killing," Isabel called to Roman as she set the dinner table. "That's the kind of thing you hear about in New York, or LA, or maybe London. Remember the Vatican's banker dangling from a noose off the bridge? But not in Geneva, of all places. Can you imagine. In Geneva? We live here our entire adult lives without so much as a stolen windscreen wiper and Jonathan gets murdered within weeks of arrival!"

"There are lots of elements in Geneva that don't pass through the WHO, *cara*. It only feels like a quiet town. I wouldn't be surprised to learn that the Pussy Cat Club in the Pâquis ushers dozens of cold-blooded assassins through its doors every night." Roman sliced two fillets for stroganoff, sautéed the onions, added sour cream, paprika and lemon juice.

"I still can't believe it." She returned to the kitchen for plates and paused, "I must say, you don't seem very upset."

"I'm not." Roman looked up, a butcher's knife in his hand.

Isabel was struck by the same sensation she'd felt across the long diplomatic table that night in Crans, but this time, Roman was yet a different man – not the elegant charmer of that evening – but someone hard-eyed and matter-of-fact, definitely older than his forty-four years. Was the case load taking its toll on his spirit? What was eating away at him?

"Don't you feel the slightest bit shocked?"

"Of course, I'm shocked. Not that Jonathan died, we all go sometime, but I'm not accustomed to a police officer sitting in my consulting chair asking why Doctor Burden imported Hawaiian lava. Or checking my height as I stand up to see if I'm as short as the suspected killer – "

"He didn't!"

"Or asking me where I spent the weekend."

Roman sounded as if Jonathan's death offended rather than saddened him. Surely Roman's aesthetic snobberies didn't extend to how people got themselves murdered?

They settled down to eat. Isabel changed the subject from Jonathan to her day in London. She chattered on about her meetings and the clever way she'd pointed out how only a larger donation would make a really visible difference to the rate of early diagnosis and how the cooperation with the phone people might bring other dividends to the trust. All the time she was talking, she was scrutinizing Roman's cold aspect, hoping for signs of softening. Was this a good time to discuss details of their trip?

"Roman, are you listening?"

"Of course, *cara*."

"Are you thinking about Jonathan?"

"I am not thinking about Jonathan."

"Well, darling, you look so far away, I thought – "

"I'm just pre-occupied, that's all."

"I made a few phone calls this morning to India and talked to the travel agency downstairs, just to suss things out. You know how while I was in London, I was thinking about this getaway."

"I just got away." His tone was as sour as the stroganoff.

"Well, darling, not for very long."

Roman concentrated on soaking a morsel of bread in the sauce. "What did you mean by that?"

"Well, Roman, wouldn't you enjoy more than a weekend cooped up with a lot of other doctors? A real adventure for the two of us?"

Roman shook his head. "Not right now."

"Well, you seem so distracted these days. So forgetful."

"Forgetful?"

"Did you get read my message about the gym bag?"

Roman blanched. "What about my gym bag?"

"Well, it's turned up at the music school on the rue Petitot and you don't even seem to have noticed it's missing, that's all."

Panic closed up his throat. He waited for something awful to happen, but Isabel's freckled innocence still queried him without accusation.

"You don't seem yourself at all. I really want us to take this trip together. It's important to me."

"Impossible, *cara*. impossible."

"Well, we should make it possible, Roman. We're not prisoners of our own lives."

Weren't decisions already taken, implanted like steel rods barring his view of the sunny spaces beyond?

"We are prisoners, *cara*, happy, happy inmates." He finished his salad and folded his napkin into precise quarters. "Our basic needs for food and shelter are met. We stick to our routine. We take our exercise. We work like the devil for the Greater Good. Most of the time we're separated by our professional life sentences, but from time to time we enjoy the odd conjugal visit in our low-security facility. Isn't that what they call it?" He gestured at the dining-room walls.

Isabel stared across the table at him. Her half-eaten stroganoff congealed in front of her. Roman fingered his place mat and poured them both another glass of wine. Isabel couldn't remember her husband ever talking like this.

"Is that how you feel?" she asked at last.

"Don't you? Or are you so busy flying from one airport to another, you've left your feelings in the lost-luggage department?"

"Don't sound like a trite radio play, darling. Of course I know what I feel. I know what you feel." She reached for her glass with a trembling hand and took a long gulp. "I don't recognize you like this. You're challenging me." She swallowed and added, "And I think you're lying to me."

His eyebrows shot up at her. *En garde.*

"Roman, why was your gym bag at the music school?"

"You really want to know?"

"We've never had secrets from each other. It's not that I don't trust you. I'm just confused, that's all. In fact, I've been confused for weeks. Maybe months, I don't know." She paused. "And I don't want to be confused any more."

The finality in that last phrase, the honest intelligent pain in her expression forced Roman past his protective guard. Roman heard his own voice tell her as much but not more than had to be told. She couldn't spend the rest of their marriage asking about an idiotic sports bag.

Isabel felt a surge of jealousy mixing with a cold nausea at his months of lying; she now knew the shape and size of the unseen thing occupying the empty space surrounding her for so many months. Now it had a name and an awful, detailed reality. She watched, hot-faced and humiliated, as Roman paced from the dining room to the kitchen and back, and eventually collapsed into his Corbusier chair, shaking and sobbing, telling her about all those Saturday afternoons and the not-wanting-to-hurt-her.

She burned at that insulting cliché, then turned faint as he revealed the desire for a son that had haunted him through the loneliness of so many years. And the guilt of the last months as he tried to reconcile his feelings for this patient. And just when Isabel was thinking she might be able to handle a meaningless affair, Roman blubbered on about a pregnancy, the beautiful

301

fleeting reality of a son. God, make him shut up. Not that too. A baby . . . his baby . . .

Isabel fled the living room. Her mouth made noiseless sounds of pain. She held her stomach as the stroganoff rioted and finally sought refuge in the toilet. Then she sat on the edge of their bed and panted to herself, make it not so, make it not have happened, make it not true. Undo it all. Make everything go back.

She heard Roman scraping off their plates at the sink. He was listening to her, waiting for her to break down completely, to wail, to scream hysterical questions and recriminations.

She supposed crying would come later. Nothing came now but short gasps of disbelief. First, she would have to abandon everything she had thought stood firm under her feet. These were not feelings she could label, but she felt them as a kind of death, a chasm of disappointment commanding her to step forward and drop into the unknown. Her next destination was the abyss of no longer being loved. He had pushed her off the cliff of twenty years' trust.

She wondered where each of them would sleep from now on. She wanted to tell her best friend and then realized that after so many years of continuous travelling, forgotten birthdays, cancelled lunch dates, all her old girlfriends had fallen by the wayside. Her remaining best friend was somewhere in their kitchen this very minute, awash in the horror of all he'd done.

She couldn't bear to hear another word from Roman's mouth. Even to look at him. She did not know this man, who had been the most intimate companion of her entire life. She could not go "home", this was her home; so she would go. She had to pack her bag and go – just go.

She looked into the closet for her suitcase but it wasn't there. It sat in the opposite corner of the bedroom, not yet unpacked from London. It gave off the conspiratorial air of a knowing accomplice, her last and only friend.

28

Shino wrapped his loins in a fresh *fudoshi* of fine white lawn. He'd always been particular about his under-wrap. He positioned the front of the sack for maximum ease and looped the braided ties snug around his waist. The gesture was second nature, yet now he felt a grudging tenderness towards his lasered body – demoted, denuded, yet still his soul's loyal servant.

He kicked the tufted futon back against the wall and lay down, resting his head on a scented pillow to drag on his Parisien. He scratched his contented groin. He wasn't accustomed yet to this hybrid vessel of a blotchy body. The eager-to-please *kobun* Shino had re-emerged with a washed-out echo of his glory days as Takahana's right hand. Some pigment traces were still fading here and there, but there was something miraculous about his renaissance as a naked, normal nobody. Shino savoured the innocent lassitude of a newborn.

A rush of hot water bubbling into his tub sent steam escaping under the bathroom door. The girl was singing a pop song, her thin voice echoing off the linoleum. Even for shower warbling, it sounded pretty awful. Shino smiled to himself and gazed up at Zatoichi, peeling off the ceiling in the April humidity. The next guy to move into this dump could have the poster; Shino would find new rooms soon. Now which Zatoichi incarnate was his favourite? Who was a better Blind Swordsman, the original actor when Shino was a teenager? Or this souped-up twenty-first century-retread, his hair streaked blond? Also *hara sho*.

Shino felt flush, even illuminated with grace. The harmony,

the calm and order of his little world, its *wa*, was finally established. He was an honourable man beyond reproach. He'd followed orders, fulfilled obligations, and even repaid one last personal act of gratitude with an original flourish of his own. Surgical gloves! Shino chuckled.

The Geneva morning was almost as damp as a lovely spring back home when the Tokyo traffic fumes, sniffed over the morning's first miso soup, hinted that summer's humidity was on its way.

Finishing his cigarette, Shino plugged in his red kettle and ripped open two packets of instant shrimp noodles. He plucked fresh chives from a pot on his balcony and diced them into the broth. The potted bulbs he'd carried off with his modest groceries from the Miyai shop on the rue de Zurich thrust green spikes out of the moist soil. Somewhere in Kyoto, his mother was locking up, unfolding her careworn cotton futon. The winter's ordeal was almost over. In a few months, with Shino's final traces of tattoo gone, his spider-webs whisked away by blood circulation and time as surely as victims of spring cleaning, he'd bow his indifferent farewell to Secretary Dejima and that slurping bore, Accountant Kakizoe. He'd pass back through Narita immigration with a new passport bearing his improved features and a new identity.

If only Kazuo had agreed to let him assume the name of his favourite sumo champ, Odeshawa. *Ah deska*, such little frustrations must be accepted. Everything had gone according to plan. Now there would be no *kobun* Shino on the planet to prosecute, just as there was no Onishi left to threaten *oyabun* Takahana's empire. Any other boss would have observed tradition between police and gang, handed Shino over for negotiated sentence – but not Takahana, a truly exceptional boss. He'd made sure no one would take the fall, not even his little *irezumi* extortionist.

Shino sniffed the fishy breakfast and rubbed his empty stomach. Within a few weeks Kazuo Ino – oh, his pose as a "diplomat" in Dr Micheli's office had been good! What a laugh! – would hand him new papers and a new future with Takahana's final thanks.

As long as he kept his refashioned head down, the Kobe Yamaguchi bastards would never, ever find him. Best of all, his fame as Driver Shino, the *irezumi* in the nondescript suit who took down rival lord Onishi, would grow into legend. Gossip and questions would harden into leaks and pay-offs. They would hunt for Shino, *hai*, in public baths, at shareholders' meetings, behind the wheel of a white limousine, his red beaded bracelet betraying him beneath a shirt cuff.

Wasn't it better than a Blind Swordsman episode, with only the final scene missing, the one where Shino receives the grateful bow of the laser doctor, dipping no higher or lower than Patient Shino's own nonchalant nod of acknowledgement. With a slight dip of his head, Shino practised his smile – subtle, assured, slightly ironic. As offhand as the unforgettable Mifune. Fade-out. Cue theme music. Roll the credits. Shino's mind ran this lovely scene over and over, while he waited for the girl to emerge from her bath.

Too bad Micheli-*san* was a westerner, more likely disposed to alert the police than to reward Shino's *bushido* spirit. An unseemly Swiss confrontation would only disturb the *wa*. Happily, honour was honour, acknowledged or not. Anyway, a foreigner's thank you carried no weight on Shino's moral scales; he only liked to think Zatoichi's grin beaming down from the mildewed ceiling signalled the legendary swordsman's beatification.

And now, for the future. What would he call his new shop? *Shino Kino*? *DVD Zatoichi*? His mother would make the perfect assistant. She could remove her hearing aid and not be bothered by the stereophonic booms of the action movie running all day on the monitor suspended over the check-out desk. He'd got that idea from the demo DVD in the doctor's waiting room.

At last, the pink-haired girl emerged, boiled to a lovely prawn colour from her wet curly head with brown roots just peeking out of the fuchsia spikes to her bare toenails varnished a glittery lime. Shino watched her wrap herself into his thin towel, inadequate to the task of covering her heavy breasts. He sighed with happiness and rolled over to offer her a smoke. This girl had such a circular bottom! Rounder than a sumo's stomach!

Hello Kitty girl settled down on the straightened futon. Her name, scribbled across the top of a discarded croissant bag, read "Lolie". Last night, Shino's efforts to pronounce her name had reduced them to leaning against her Opel in gales of laughter. Still grinning, Shino bowed and bowed until the girl accepted an invitation to watch his favourite Swordsman DVD upstairs. She was nothing like the horrible professional he'd tried once in the Pâquis. Lolie loved his set of Suntory bar glasses, his farewell gift from Yoji. They'd spent a delightful inarticulate evening miming Zatoichi sword moves, losing various items of clothing in their flirtatious exertions, until Shino was thrilled to discover that his new acquaintance could giggle as well as any Japanese.

He lit a Parisien for her, just like Tatsuya Nakadai did on screen.

"Punky Girl, *très bien*," he wagged his head.

She riffled through his CDs and chattered in French. Shino caught names he thought he recognized from various news-stand magazines. He offered to run down to the bakery for more croissants, but she gesticulated *non*, she'd have to run, *vite, vite*, she said, running in place like a jogging instructor on Nippon TV, but maybe he'd like to go with her tonight to a party in Eaux-Vives? She'd pretend he was some kind of Japanese gangster, *ratatatatata*, she imitated a machine gun, not an import-export man. *Ça va?*

He nodded in objection, with a vehement, "*Non, non, import-export, salari-man!*"

This mischief of passing off her gentle stubby salesman pal with the bruised torso as some kind of exotic thug on the lam seemed irresistible to the girl.

Shino sat cross-legged on the futon, watching Lolie clutch

his towel to her chest and act out this invitation. He improvised the words and gestures that said he'd play along, to make her happy as his contented mind contemplated spending the rest of his days protected by such charades. Why not rehearse on the arm of Mademoiselle Hello Kitty? His halting French tongue was loosened, almost fluent, in her company. Perhaps she'd enjoy the stories he was always making up.

His old plan of rescuing the horse-faced bar girl from a tiresome future to marry him and live together in obscurity with his deaf mother had assuaged his lingering doubts about losing the rice pot of his *nakama*. At least, there would always be one person in his life to whom he remained the swaggering *irezumi*, the legendary Driver Shino.

Meanwhile, why not assume a good, pronounceable French identity – Jacques was good – to go out on the town in his new Burberry raincoat to meet Hello Kitty's artistic friends? Tomorrow they were going to spend the afternoon reading BDs together.

He sucked in the idea with audible pleasure and picked the noodles out of his teeth with an ivory toothpick, one hand covering his mouth to show he was a gentleman. The gesture reminded him of his tiniest rebellion and most secret consolation. In his mouth Horijin had tattooed the Buddhist's Lotus Prayer in tiny black characters. *Hail to the Lotus Scripture of the Good Law.* Each sincere utterance of this single phrase ensured his rebirth into perfect Nothingness. Shino didn't need to chant his favourite devotion; his piety lay unseen, but always there, literally, on the tip of his tongue.

"You will be happy to hear you don't have leprosy."

Carlos twisted his contraband Gitane pack in his trouser pocket. He pulled on his moustache and fixed on Dr Johannsen's poached-egg eyes sagging behind his wire-rims.

"No shit?"

The Scandinavian smiled. "No leprosy. The smear is negative. The biopsy is negative."

"You know as well as I do there are no tools that can absolutely rule it out."

Johannsen sighed. "Carlos, as far as any laboratory in the world can detect, you don't have leprosy."

"Then what is it?" Carlos knew exactly where the thickening white lesion of skin lay under his cotton shirt. He'd seen those lesions in the field. He wasn't imagining this. It would be there after he left Johannsen's office.

"Any history of psoriasis? Eczema?"

Carlos rolled his eyes.

Johannsen threw up his hands. "So let's just say idiopathic allergic reaction." Johannsen tapped at the results with his ballpoint. "You're taking the medicine anyway?"

"*Si*. Turns my piss orange."

"So stop worrying. Come back in two weeks and we'll have another look at it."

Carlos glared in anger at his complacent colleague. "So why are you trying not to laugh, man?"

"Well, I was thinking you might drop in on Doctor Bovay downstairs." Johannsen buried his smirk behind a show of cleaning his eyeglasses with a tiny Wet-Wipe.

"She's a psychologist!"

Johannsen drew himself up. "And you're a doctor. You've heard of hysterical pregnancies, pseudocyesis, with all the symptoms of bloated stomach – ?"

"Hysterical – ! You – !"

"Well, if that's not acceptable to a macho like you, think of it as excessive virtue. You went to Catholic schools, right? Surely you've heard of the stigmata? Check your palms." Johannsen chuckled, "Nothing's impossible, although I've never pictured you wearing a hairshirt – "

"I am a doctor, man – and that's the only reason I don't slug you one."

"So, you know as well as I do that auto-suggestion is a well-documented phenomenon. Mothers break out in lash marks if they see their children whipped. Saints pray themselves into the bleeding wounds of Christ. Husbands develop lipopexia on their stomachs when they sympathize too much with pregnant wives. The Russians did a lot of research on – "

"You think this lesion is my imagination? You think I'm crazy? Are you crazy?"

Johannsen turned serious. "You've been under a lot of stress over in Building L. Don't deny it. Everybody in the main building's heard the stories. Infighting, tiffs with the NGOs – "

"Where'd you hear that?"

"Water Cooler News Network. You should be glad they're not selling copies of that independent evaluation report at the news-stand downstairs. I heard somebody say just the other day that leprologists usually have some kind of martyr complex, can't work with people, hey, I heard – "

Carlos cut him off. "Just a difference of opinion over integrating into public health services."

Johannsen sniggered with *schadenfreude*. "Wow! You leprosy experts are really falling apart . . . "

"Very funny. You just said I wasn't sick. Isabel can handle it, she just needs her P6 confirmation. She'll get the NGO people to come around. They can't own the disease forever."

Johannsen leaned forward, incredulous. "Doctor Hanford? P6? In her dreams, Carlos. Her name'll never get past the Japanese – she aired her views on their murky money a little too publicly. Besides, haven't you heard? Frank's sewn it up for his little friend from Hong Kong, the Empress of SARS."

Carlos fumed all the way back to his office, past the startled greetings of malaria and shistosomiasis. He unlocked his door to reclaim possession of his narrow domain. The only space this father of four could call irrevocably his own had been scoured during his sick leave with the vengeance of a cleaning woman scorned too, too long. That damn Moldavian bitch had even confiscated his secret ashtray, vacuumed the industrial carpeting until he could see his footprints in the nap and wiped years of tender fingerprints off his family photo. The only thing her vindictive scrubbing could not erase were the cigarette scorches on the edge of his desk. He leaned over and peered at the Club Med snap, realizing for the first time that it was years out of date – the youngest of his estranged litter was missing.

He fingered his lesion. Still there. Christ! Who'd ever heard of such a thing as hysterical leprosy? Still . . . he didn't feel sick. Wiggling all his fingers, he jabbed the point of a letter opener into his left thumb. "Ouch!" It hurt as much as the week before.

He unlocked his desk and dug out his copy of the embarrassing evaluation. He'd hardly glanced at it before he went on leave: "Misunderstandings include expectations of the leprosy alliance that were not clear, perceptions among some collaborators that the alliance was being managed by the WHO in a manner that was not sufficiently consultative, and the belief that a number of collaborators were behaving in a way that was not open, inclusive or collegial . . . panel was surprised at the vehemence with which some collaborators have attacked each other in public and in private, to a degree very uncommon among the many partnerships for health that exist . . ."

Was Johannsen right? Were they the laughing stock of the headquarters? The panel's conclusions reflected all the hallmarks of Frank's self-protective, dictatorial, antagonizing regime, and there was poor Isabel left to take the fall. Years of ramming through elimination targets without listening to the objections of Lopez, Cardona, Aguilar, *compadres* in the field. Wasn't Isabel's last memo full of some Jesuit named Shardar in north India complaining that Geneva's priorities were wrong for his region?

Isabel's voice-mail said she was available at a list of numbers – where the hell was she? – he got a busy signal, no matter how many times he dialled.

Carlos pulled at his moustache. He felt ready to fight again. He was damned if he was going to report to some doctor in Dior working her charms on the newly divorced Frank the Forlorn. He redialled again and again.

He reached her husband's clinic and was put through to a

dull-voiced Roman Micheli. Isabel had left for Delhi and Kashmir ahead of schedule. How was Carlos's health? He was very glad to hear it. No, he didn't have any local number for her. And the mobile-phone service up north was unreliable.

"Well, that's the point of her mission, to check it out," was Carlos's dry retort.

"Was it?" Dr Micheli sounded sad and preoccupied. He'd be sure to convey Carlos's message, if Isabel called.

Carlos dialled a new set of numbers in India, working his way from Delhi's WHO headquarters to some old mission in Srinagar. Isabel and Father Shardar were on a fact-finding tour for five days up to the border areas to test the viability of long-distance diagnosis and local medical capabilities.

Si, that's where Isabel was right now. Sent on a miserable truck ride to put mobile phones in war zones while Dr Cheong measured Frank's office for new curtains. Dr Cheong take over the leprosy department? With her high-tech donations and data banks and spreadsheets showing new leprosy cases down, one-dose treatment for all, and elimination a done deal? Isabel knew it wasn't that simple. Isabel would make the deadline *and* hang in for the longer haul.

The pernickety lingering headache of leprosy would be wiped off Cheong's map for sure within a year, especially if the elimination targets were met. Cheong would deliver the numbers but with that success she'd let leprosy drop right off the agenda. With Isabel dispatched to the field, Dr Cheong was already calling the shots.

That is, unless Dr Carlos Campagna stopped her in her stiletto tracks. Isabel wouldn't let them cut the budget, leaving patients without follow-up surgery, rehabilitative therapy or social re-integration. Isabel wouldn't forget the recidivist cases or the quest for better diagnostics and even a vaccine.

He dug out his list of Tokyo telephone numbers and started dialling. Stigmatization was a big issue with the Japanese and the yen tap showed no signs of running dry just yet. So what if it flowed from some thug billionaire aching to whitewash a lifetime of race-boat racketeering into a Nobel Prize? *Bueño*, Carlos was no goody-goody Isabel. He had no problem using tainted money to cleanse untouchables.

There was hope yet.

29

"Doctor Micheli has asked me to say a few words, for which I feel both grateful and honoured. I must start with a public apology to Doctor Hanford. I want to make full amends to my colleague and friend, Isabel."

Father Shardar directed his gaze at the pews filled with uplifted, waiting faces. He could not have felt more incongruous, a wizened, black-eyed septuagenarian risen to the heights of the lectern in a suspended pulpit on St Pierre's austere altar. His left hand fiddled with an unlit pipe in the pocket of his Delhi-tailored suit of summer-weight wool. He unfolded a thin sheet of paper and cleared his throat.

"In our recent encounters, Doctor Hanford tried to persuade me that times had changed, that the leprosy mission had changed – not out of failure, oh, no! Out of success! And therefore, that a stubborn old coot like me must also change with the times. I disagreed, vehemently. I admit I exploited some of her own unspoken ambivalence about policy changes. Standing here on this very sad occasion, I recall saying something rash that pains me greatly now. In short, I regretted out loud that I had ever considered her as one of us."

The old man paused as if refuelling his courage with a new supply of words.

"That was an unjustified rebuke borne of anger and hurt, sore feelings fed by an old man's confusion. And it was obvious to me during her last visit to India that my words had wounded her. Now it is too late to retract them, but to those that loved Doctor Hanford, admired and worked with her, I can only say

I would be proud to claim her as one of us, although I cannot be so presumptuous."

The stooped figure paused to look at his listeners. "She belongs to you here in Geneva, and everything your work stands for. And more than that, you should be proud to hold her up as a model of what a doctor should be. These days the leprosy campaign must speed things up, get a move on, de-specialize, as it were. The catch phrase is that 'the best is the enemy of the good'. Oh, yes," Father Shardar gave a rueful smile, "You will not be surprised to hear she tried that one on me, too. However, in Doctor Hanford's case, there was no contradiction between hurrying up leprosy elimination and taking time for each and every straggler. I know, I was one of the stragglers. She was a *good* doctor, and she was also the *best* kind of doctor. Perhaps it will help us all to understand and accept better her untimely and violent death."

Thank God this ill-tempered curmudgeon had come to Geneva, Roman thought. Shardar had witnessed Isabel's final hour; at least she hadn't died alone. He glanced at Marjorie, pressed against his side in the first pew, but the old lady's exhaustion seemed to insulate her, even from him.

The flight to India for Isabel's burial had been a logistical nightmare. and Roman had survived it numb. A practical fixer, his grief on hold, he'd held up through it all. By day he slept-walked, going through the motions. By night he lay awake, staring at his wife's pristine pillow, with no means of reaching Isabel, of saying he was sorry. He left her soap untouched, her toothpaste cap askew. Her hairbrush still lay on the floor under the bedroom window, forgotten in the wake of her white-faced, tight-lipped departure.

He wondered how he would make it to the end of each day. How could he ever mend this bleeding breach between them? He heard Chantal's hushed command of the situation outside his office door as Lise and she sorted out notes of sympathy, signed for flowers of condolence, made reservations and phoned in cancellations.

He asked Isabel where she was.

Lise delivered his sandwich and salad on a tray. He signed some *bulletins de versement* to clear away the bills. Chantal pushed patients from side to side, from this day forward to that. When his office door was shut, he dialled his apartment and listened to Isabel's recorded voice on the neglected answering machine they'd forgotten to disconnect. He listened to her again and again. Her message did not forgive him.

He conserved all his energy for collecting Marjorie from Suffolk on a few days' notice. He packed the old woman's summer dresses himself and held her arm as they boarded the long flight to Delhi. They made a strange couple entering Indira Gandhi International – the Englishwoman clutching a cracked plastic flight bag and the Italian Swiss with his calf-skin case. They emerged from Arrivals to face a frantic racket of arm-waving people, cardboard signs and cloying sweet smells that reminded Roman of exotic cut flowers that needed a change of water.

They passed a sleepless night in the Oberoi Hotel, thanks to a booking so last-minute, they had to make do with the disco bass rumbling through the floor of their rooms until three in the morning. Roman spent at least an hour waiting for the delivery of a "proper drink" for his mother-in-law in the middle of the air-conditioned night. He ran her bath and helped her to the bathroom door. Sat with her "to talk a bit", only to find himself watching her bewildered profile staring out of the window, her features that of the aged-Isabel-who-would-never-be framed by the fuschia dawn. Her lemon tea in its ornate silver service arrived at seven with echoes of colonial fanfare, then cooled untouched on its trolley. Neither of them mentioned Isabel. It seemed crass to discuss someone who was ever-present but unseen, unable to join in.

"So changed, dear boy. It's all quite changed. I don't see a single *tonga* down on the street."

The dithering old lady tried to telephone a girlhood chum, but the number was wrong or disconnected. They nearly

315

missed their connection to Srinagar.

Thank God Marjorie had agreed to a local burial. The alternative of extracting Isabel's remains out of the outstretched hands of the Indian bureaucracy didn't bear consideration. Thank goodness for a Westcott family plot somewhere on this noisome, dirty, articulate, beseeching continent of orderly mayhem and impenetrable tongues.

Still, did this pilgrimage make any sense? Was it a misguided obsequy to ask a half-gaga Hanford to accompany him all this way? *I am unworthy of you, cara, but I bring with me a blameless soul whose grief is unstained by betrayal.* Worms of guilt ate Roman's innards and turned these paralyzed hours into a private purgatory.

The most colourful country in Asia was all black and white to him. Yet swamped in remorse, he felt this river of people to be his only solace. There were so many anonymous faces and bustling bodies, grazing curry from a tin box while sitting on a bench, or kicking a football against a crumbling brick wall, or dodging traffic on a home-made crutch. Every one of them would follow Isabel – along with Marjorie, along with himself – sooner or later. Yet, none of these clamouring strangers seemed in any particular panic about their unavoidable departure.

"Marjorie, I want to tell you something. Isabel and I didn't part on good terms. I hadn't been myself, as you would say, for many months. She left Geneva profoundly distressed with me – "

"Oh, darling boy, don't, don't. Nothing matters now. You had as good a marriage as many. Neither of you paid much attention to it," she commented, "but that doesn't mean your marriage was worse than those who do."

He feared he was starting to break down, knew tears were too "Latin", something Marjorie wouldn't countenance. She was already thrusting a starched linen square from the breakfast tray under his nose.

"There's no point in regrets once they've gone. Believe me. You can't afford to be too sentimental. You'll learn that in time. Besides, it was so quick. At least she didn't suffer."

Of course, it had been sudden, but Isabel had suffered beyond contemplation. Such disasters could mean horrific and hopeless awareness. Father Shardar had told Roman the details, but Marjorie mustn't ever know, no mother could bear it. For good reason Marjorie would prefer anything to prolonged farewells and interminable suffering. A sun-mottled hand patted Roman's and reached for another gin and tonic, no ice.

There was little time between their journey in a battered taxi past the ramshackle rows of Srinagar's shop fronts looking over the floating gondolas of vegetable hawkers bumping against the docks of Lake Dal and Isabel's perfunctory burial. Here the press of the heat and the crowding of corpses – the week's take of illness, not to mention random explosions and sneak grenade attacks – moved such affairs along without apology.

Six days after Isabel's accident, Father Shardar led Roman and Marjorie down a path behind an elderly caretaker who extricated a rusty padlock from the bars of an iron gate. They proceeded in solemn, irregular formation to a weedy corner of the neglected old graveyard. A band of respectful Indians trailed along and whispered, hands muffling their questions and stares under the burning sun. Incineration was always so much cleaner, the caretaker had murmured within Roman's earshot; he was grateful that Father Shardar had at least commandeered enough district poobahs to pay tribute to Isabel's dignity and Marjorie's expectations.

Someone righted a tilting horseshoe of a garish bouquet festooned with a ribbon printed, "From the local children". Someone else whispered to Roman, "Father Shardar says she was famous for her special touch with children, so generous, wherever she went."

The dry-worded English rites exhaustingly endured, Marjorie suddenly squinted across the brown grass. She pointed with a childish note of discovery in her voice, "There's Mummy, buried there, under the *kikka* trees." Green mould obscured the dates and inscription, but Roman could make out the words, "Lily Westcott *née* Earnshaw." An ox bell sounded its solo reprise across the insistent chorus of the humming cicadas in the shade trees.

"And there's my father, Reginald, next to her. You see, they were together at the end. I like to think it made up for those long years apart."

Roman suddenly realized that Isabel and he would not be together "at the end". He thanked the line of pressed hands and bowing heads with a sharpening sense of absurdity. He could hardly bare to recall her plaintive suggestion that they make this trip together. There they were, Isabel and Roman in Srinagar together after all.

And there he had said goodbye. She was not here with him now, in Geneva, no matter how much longer these eulogies dragged on.

Roman would have to hear Shardar's story one more time. The chill of cathedral granite inched up his shinbones. Marjorie clasped his hand and he realized that the elderly Englishwoman was holding him steady.

" . . . in our area, as violent as it is, riven by fifteen years of insurgency and sectarian war, people have learned from bitter experience when it is dangerous to venture outside, when the curfew has fallen, where it is safe to tread and where no man, woman, or child dares venture. We all know that Doctor Hanford was not a careless, impetuous woman. She was determined to travel north for admirable reasons – to test new diagnostic tools among the embattled people of Kargil, Gurais, Sopur. We stopped at a refugee camp on the road to Dras, and found ourselves in the midst of screaming panic. A two-year-old child had wandered off the army road, past the stones marking the cleared path. There was no time to call for help, the toddler was wandering hither and thither into death's maw. Doctor Hanford was devoted to children and she did not hesitate. She was unlucky, but because her step tragically triggered a landmine, this tiny infant froze in stark terror and stood still until she could be saved . . . "

Roman's mind wandered back to a question only half-formed. He had had the impression over the last year that there was a design or pattern to his life that he had never tried to detect, an indiscernible web spun by his own unwitting hand. If only he could fly high overhead, at least as high as he stood over Spaghetti's territory, and God-like, make out the reasons – why Jonathan met his absurd end unpacking Hawaiian lava in the Michelis' city? Why Isabel kept pirouetting like a fairy-tale ballerina driven by her demonic red shoes until she dropped in a distant land? Why Mira had taken his child from the world without a word of explanation or a backward gesture?

Would the significance of everything in his life always elude him?

30

On a stifling June evening in the "City of the Olympics", a parade of concert-goers mounted the steps of the *Théâtre de Beaulieu* to join hundreds of others already milling around the airy foyer. The Geneva laser specialist and widower Dr Roman Micheli passed among them, a man of short stature and nervous mien. Deep lines etched around his mouth gave him a solemn air.

Unlike other ticket holders, he didn't search the crowd for familiar faces or rush over to join a partner chaperoning a spare drink in a discreet corner. An observer would have realized within seconds that this gentleman, expensively dressed but carelessly shaved, was attending tonight's performance alone. This music-lover belonged to no one, certainly not to one of the art students sporting "*les piercings*" and dressing up her black cotton separates with shimmery bits of Indian cotton from the import shops. Nor to a party of bankers in their light-weight suits ushering ladies with powdered shoulders away from the white squares of heat shot through the atrium ceiling by the setting sun.

In fact, he looked more than solemn; he looked angry with himself.

Roman sought the inconspicuous gloom of the bar alcove, but that too was overheated with excited strangers. He stretched up on his toes, proffering ten francs over the shoulders of two Englishmen pressing their grey-striped bellies against the bar.

"Never seen her before? She's quite something – careful

don't spill! The way she turns herself inside out on stage gives me quite a frisson. Frieda and I heard her at the Tonnehalle up in Zurich two seasons ago... Look at her web site ... Marvellous visuals. Our Quentin downloaded some video clips, mostly the ones in the low-cut gowns, well, I'm hardly likely to stop him when you see the alternatives online these – yes, here you are darling, two champagnes – oh, sorry – one more Coca Cola, please? – "

Roman vied with the genteel press of fellow customers and their curt imprecations at the bar staff for drinks and small snacks. He fought for eye contact with the younger waitress who served two white wines to her right, shot over to serve a customer on the left, took a third order and made change for everyone but Roman. His throat rasped from the pollution of a sweltering hour inching his car out of Geneva and along the expressway. The harried girl brushed a frizzled red fringe back off her perspiring forehead, took more orders and filled more glasses. Rings of sweat stained the white cotton under her arms. She repeated each order back to the customers in newly-learnt French with a heavy eastern-European accent that fought against the relaxed hubbub of the evening's throng.

"... You should listen to an interview she did for her website. It was terribly moving, about being abandoned by her birth mother, then losing her step-mother – there was something wrong with our browser, had to get Quentin's friend next door to sort that out, but it was worth it. Absolutely unaffected, but her playing! Here you are, that right? ... Quite pretty without all that stage makeup, not cheerleader pretty, if you know what I mean. Just that touch of European *sagesse*, well, you can hear it in her Brahms. She's not actually American, you know, not really..."

Roman's collar stuck to his neck. He might be better off guzzling the cold flow of tap water in the men's room before the bell rang. He'd fled Chantal's clipboard of last-minute questions and thrown off his white jacket even before the last patient had time to clamber back into her jeans.

With a sour tension in his stomach, Roman exited his clinic not even sure he could trust himself not to steer straight uphill towards the surety of solitude in his well-dusted bedroom in the Old Town. Almost to his own surprise, he'd unlocked the Saab and driven in the opposite direction, and managed the right turn across the pont du Mont-Blanc towards the route de Lausanne and the flyover heading northeast. He pointed the car kilometre by kilometre towards his designated seat – a fold-out *strapontin* at the end of the third row. Through the whole hot exodus, bumper to bumper past Nyon, Gland, Rolle, and Morges, he reassured himself he could turn back any minute. He could toss the ticket right out of the window. He could always retreat to the safety of mourning everything and risking nothing.

For the last four years, regret and recrimination had been his stalwart guardians. Why try to escape their vigil this evening? His constant desolation was, on reflection, a weirdly acceptable purgatory housing his familiar memories and self-disgust. Day by day, he lived out his half-life, realizing as the months and years after Isabel's death passed, that pain was his soul's natural state.

He hadn't reckoned on the invisible fiends of the EMI PR team stoking his latent torment. They'd plastered both banks of the Rhône with posters and billboards. For weeks these enlarged photos taunted him when he strolled through an evening drizzle to the Pizzos' shop to buy his single portion of fresh pasta. They haunted his determined solitary bicycle ride along the quai for three consecutive Sunday mornings. They gloated down at him from placards next to street lamps and record-store windows.

Eh, bien, he'd finally accepted their badgering challenge, stalked out of his clinic in suppressed rage at his own weakness and marched down the rue du Marché to the nearest Ticket-Corner to slam his credit card down on the counter. The sales girl had sworn up and down that the humble *strapontin* was the best seat left for a single purchaser – "What do you expect,

Monsieur?" – once hoards of subscription seats and charity blocks had been doled out.

Now he was amazed to find his car gliding off the express-way and mounting the steep hills of Lausanne's sun-dappled residential streets, obeying the signs pointing towards the theatre, descending into the underground parking and follow-ing the footsteps of others up into the bowels of the modern conference complex.

Regret and recrimination still accompanied him tonight after all, but they were reluctant escorts, dragging along in his wake, sullen amid the pre-concert buzz of the Beaulieu.

Recrimination growled of this evening's dangers and tried to call him back. Roman fought it off like a man escaping a cage where the door stood only slightly ajar.

Regret recalled that autumn evening years ago as a dis-interested medical professional wandered among acquaintances in the old-fashioned foyer of Victoria Hall. Roman saw himself as he once was, a serene husband at a loose end, a respected specialist mistaking the lightheadedness of flu for a passing curiosity drawing him out for the evening.

Roman bought a programme from a young woman whose trio of golden rings threaded through her pert nostril belied her conservative white shirt and black skirt. She reminded Roman of what? Of course, that good-natured Japanese with the nipple rings and the penis necklace! What was that man's name – *Shito? Shizo?* It was far easier for Roman to remember every one of the exotic tattoos, their stubborn pigments, the pulse depths and resolution speeds. And even after all that work, he'd passed out of Roman's life without a trace. So many patients came and went. They entered the clinic looking so keen, even desperate for help, relief, restoration. They regarded Roman as some kind of saviour. In the end, just like all the others, the Japanese had disappeared, leaving no more than a smear of hair oil on Chantal's disposable paper pillowcase.

Sometimes Roman wished one of them would return, just to say *merci*.

Or if not thank you, at least goodbye?

Is that why he'd dragged himself here tonight? To force a goodbye out of Mira? By now she must be in a dressing room somewhere at the end of a narrow tunnel, bathed in a halo of naked-bulbed anticipation. Roman imagined her pressing powder against those cheeks and hitching up her long skirt to slip into a pair of low-heeled pumps. Who was with her? Whose hand zipped up her gown? Who double-checked her case for the rosin and spare strings, her toilet case for the stage foundation, the rouge and hair spray, the clean, folded hand-kerchiefs and – Roman smiled to himself – no doubt, now also for the sturdy pen to sign programmes and CD cases once her performance was over?

In his breast pocket nestled his handwritten letter – drafted, redrafted and studiously copied. What a fool! He'd written the first version in French before he'd realized what he was doing – it was that long since he'd conversed with her!

His plan was to deposit this elegant note at the box office or with the stage door porter when he arrived. He'd stood in line, watching the elderly receptionist sliding envelopes and credit card receipts through her window, but when it was his turn, he baulked and turned away, red-faced and undecided.

What a retarded simpleton! What a sickened schoolboy! "Perhaps you will share a drink or dinner with me?" How pathetic! "Words do not express the confusion your silence gives me." How flat. How inadequate. Was it the English language or the poverty of his heart's vocabulary? For years absolute silence had prevailed between them, a fatal, self-perpetuating freeze congealed by his anger over what she had done. What could he say to the person who had cremated his last experience of joy and not even notified him of the burial?

Despite his resistance, the long purgatory had done its job. With the years, his outrage subsided into bleak resignation. Accepting his half-life, Roman now only wanted to bear witness to the warmth of life still radiating around Mira. He belonged among the worshipping crowd at her feet. So the neat envelope curled, undelivered, in his tightening fist.

A fussy man with a proprietary air stationed himself behind a table to set out her recordings for sale. Roman studied all the shiny plastic cases marking the passage of years – years of stunted, uninspired routine for him, a time of unstinting dedication to her blossoming career for Mira.

"May I help you, Monsieur?"

"*Ah, non, non, merci.*"

How busy she'd been! Roman read the music titles and burned with bittersweet jealousy. These were the men she caressed week after week, year after year – Bruch, Elgar, Sibelius, Mendelssohn, Schubert, Prokofiev, Brazzini, Nielsen – these were her true loves. Here was a rendition of Brahms' Sonatas for Violin and Piano – the pianist's name unrecognizable to Roman. At least, at least, there was that. The awful Anton was history.

This was agony, the sibilant voices hissed. You're not *this* strong. Let's go home. It's not too late. Yet Roman knew he must endure this, such a minor penance for such a mortal outcome. After all, unlike Isabel, unlike his child, he had at least survived. He was still here to enjoy this June evening, to inhale the soft scents of strange women through his invisible scar tissue. He expected nothing more than he deserved.

Soon enough he would be home again with only Spaghetti to witness the hanging up of the blazer, the folding of the trousers and the scrupulous flossing of the teeth.

Until then he would prove to himself he was well enough as he was, well enough alone.

"Are you alone, Doctor? May I offer you a drink?"

A tall apparition of a beautiful woman, known yet unknown, swanned up to Roman in perilous high heels, a fringed shawl of turquoise flowers draping a long flowing skirt. She carried two small glasses of red wine and smiled directly at Roman. Her shoulders were broad and her jaw a mite too thrusting.

She spoke in a husky trill. "You don't recognize me,

Doctor? Too much make-up, that's always my mistake, but it does perk a lady up, after a long day in a suit and tie, *non?*"

Of course, of course. It was that depilation case, M Courtois.

"*Enchantée, Madame.* I would be very happy to drink with you. May I compliment you on your ensemble this evening? Why, thank you very much." Roman accepted the glass and lifting it in toast, sipped the fruity non-vintage.

"*Non, non, Docteur.* It is I who must thank you, once again. I should have already written a proper thank you, from the bottom of my heart. Of course your lasering might be regarded by the surgeons as merely the finishing *touche*, but quite necessary on such a warm evening, *n'est-ce pas?*"

M Courtois lightly stroked his smooth forearms with satisfaction. Roman nodded, happy that at least this poor soul was content. He, or rather she, seemed to have come to the concert alone, too. In the end, Roman reflected, who was not alone? To think he had once believed in Mira's embracing vision of humanity, "a choir of human angels singing off-key".

"Are you well, Doctor? Working twelve hours a day as usual?"

"Perhaps one becomes addicted to the security of discipline."

"Does routine fend off boredom, however?" Courtois's sturdy frame shivered. "Is your charming assistant Chantal still with you – ?"

"Chantal – *oui*, she and her beau have finally set the date for an autumn wedding."

"I used to enjoy watching her fish circling the tank." M Courtois's manicured finger traced lazy ovals under Roman's nose. "Asking no more of life than a few plastic ferns and a toy pagoda. Wouldn't it be nice if we could all be so easily satisfied? I know I am, now that I am a very tropical, colourful fish, *ahhh . . .*"

It was not unpleasant to make small talk with the towering female while waiting for the bell. If they drew glances, Courtois seemed to relish stealing attention from the short doctor standing pale and nervous in his flamboyant shadow.

During the years hollowed-out by Isabel's absence, Roman had convinced himself that his brief winter of philandering confusion had been an uncharacteristic aberration. He'd not simply lost his bearings and his perspective, and risked his career. He'd lost his wife and his unborn child. Perhaps, looking back on his folly, he'd temporarily lost his entire mind.

Marjorie Hanford had died of one too many gins a year after Isabel, and only last summer the upright Signora Clarisse Micheli had napped in the Ticinese heat through her own death from a mercifully efficient stroke. Over the recent bleak winter, Roman had presented his bewilderment to a therapist recommended by the ever-discreet Ruedi Kessler. They filled his sessions with talk of Pygmalion syndromes and Oedipal obsessions and pursued useless lines of inquiry this way and that. The therapy occupied Roman's empty non-working hours until he realized he'd exhausted the psychologist's bag of tricks and there was nothing more to play with. He was still alone. At last, only to the trusted Kessler and no one else did Roman pose that awful question out loud – whom or what did he miss more? Mira's boundless beauty? Isabel's sensible friendship? Or the fleeting ghost of his faceless child?

For tragically, with the loss of Mira's and Isabel's tangible presences, the tantalizing wisp of a non-son had disappeared just as completely. That chimera which pulled at Roman's elbow outside the display window of a rollerblade shop or asked for help translating Latin texts, that beloved urchin had vanished on the New York streets outside Mira's brownstone. Now that Roman was theoretically free to conjure up another life, the imagined child refused to surface from the ether.

It was, Roman told Kessler one late spring afternoon spent on his brother's borrowed sailing boat, as if the embryo had somehow seeded itself in a dimension beyond his reach. No matter how hard he tried, Roman could no longer revisit his old fantasies or create new visions. The nameless figment couldn't divorce itself from the pregnancy's true fate.

The theatre bell rang at last. Roman sought out his seat with the air of a doomed man. Around him, well-dressed couples inched their way down the carpeted aisle to claim their places. Roman leaned against the side of the loge to let them pass. He tried not to stare at the curtained exit at the back of the stage. There it hung, that velvety impasse barring him and *tout le monde* from – the gifted ones. Now the curtain parted. The orchestra filtered in between their chairs, musical instruments brandished above their heads, black skirts scraping the wooden stage, practised faces tossing expert sidelong glances to check the house.

Roman unfolded his rattan seat, returned the frosty nod of the chic blonde at his left elbow and studied his programme.

Her black and white studio portrait stared out at him.

How his girl-lover had matured! Whether by sleight of lens or medical miracle, no trace of her birthmark remained. During these years of silence, he'd had only his secret set of photos to remind him – of the little girl in Beijing, those careless shots taken the first evening she turned up, vulnerable and trusting, to his clinic. Now here she was, years later, as his trained eye had envisaged her that evening in the reflection of the foyer mirror. At least she had not been cheated of that promise.

This half-smile, however, was unknown to him, more suited to an older sister. Her gaze met the camera lens with leaner cheeks and a wiser expression. One eyebrow lifted in a sardonic hint. Where was his messy, superstitious little Gypsy with the Chinese fatalism, the one who dared not ask the gods for too much happiness? Where was the schoolgirl reciting her high-school short story? His gauche Romanian-American half-woman, half-orphan who'd lettered out that childish note about "messing up their doctor-patient relationship?"

On second thoughts, who'd been the wiser?

Roman rolled the programme into a tight cylinder and tapped impatiently on his knee. And just when he was ready to despair that the evening was nothing but an endless limbo, the Finnish conductor flew forward through the velvet curtain, acknowledged the welcome applause, and called his players to attention.

Roman studied the Finn for any *signs* – of infatuation, of love, of contact with the miracle. All he saw was a straw-haired pixie of indeterminate age wearing a cross between a tuxedo and a space suit, tapping his music stand with a thin baton.

The curtain parted a third time. A woman very like Mira swept down the thin path separating the first violins from the seconds.

Roman felt awash with wonder. The girl he'd lain with, the dormant female that only he had awakened – he swore it – now stood only yards away for hundreds of strangers to covet. She stood above him, stiff ruby silk brushing her ankles topped by a tight black corset overlaid with the thinnest blouse of wine-red chiffon. Her tumultuous black hair hugged her scalp in braided coils ending in the knot of a Grecian nymph.

She stood illuminated under the spotlight, poised for her cue.

There was no handkerchief laid on the Finn's podium. There was no more need, alas, no remaining imperfection to bind her to the likes of Roman. Somewhere, after her flight to Manhattan, the first prize at the Menuhin contest, the *stage* in Moscow, the summer masterclasses in Saarbrücken and the winter tour through South America, somewhere she'd transferred the colour of her birthmark to her dress. Deep crimson was now only her standard carried into battle. What had happened to his girl, the one who feared the jealousy of the gods? Oh, how ironic that it was he who'd erased the stain that made her human and emboldened her soul to slip away. No sun melted the wax of her wings. The gods had rewarded her courage and welcomed her to their bosom.

She smiled to the first violinist and lightly flicked her fingertips across the strings of an amber violin to check its tuning. Where was her old battered mustard *copain* so familiar to him from the Saturday rehearsals? She nodded to the Finn. His baton shot up, all heads but Mira's dropped to the sheet music.

The tympanist sent out a metallic shimmer across the surface of the audience followed by a Spanish tattoo sounded on the tympanist's deepest drum. A pause. The cymbals shimmered again and the deep drum answered. The bassoons echoed the ominous beat while Mira played a lament that was overwhelmed by Benjamin Britten's insistent percussive *boom boom-ba boom-bom.*

Or was it Roman's heart? He overheard a sigh escape the lips of some afficionado sitting closer to the footlights. The music had come at last, finally, to rescue all of them, bankers and businessmen, housewives and students, Courtois back in row F, and all the empty hearts ranked and numbered, row by row. The breathing of the society lady next to Roman grew shallower as Mira launched into a frantic scherzo.

Watching her was almost unbearable. How was it possible she didn't feel his gaze pinned on her? She had closed her vision to everything but Britten's haunting opening theme. Bereft of any comfort, Roman closed his eyes with her.

Now she was bowing with the brave ferocity of a cornered innocent, fighting back in a *moto perpetuo*, an angel trapped, wings caught whirling as she tumbled with the music to meet the summoning warning of Britten's 1938 alarm of coming war. Mira clung to her elegy, defied the composer's ominous clouds with the scherzo of double-stops like a fighting bird. Roman gripped one side of his *strapontin* as she plucked out her counterpoint against the dozens of violins bathing her with insistent repeats of the flamenco theme. Winning the struggle, she gained ground and the orchestra let the girl climb alone, in ever more rapid cadenzas accompanied by determined single notes plucked – from where? how many hands, how many fingers did she have? – to carry so many thoughts in the air at once, flying over their heads, through their beings.

And as Mira's notes searched for hope among the upper ranges, she suddenly soared. The sombre horns called the string sections to follow loyally, a chant-like reminiscence that hung on a note of deep foreboding. The trombones and French horns rose and fell, but they couldn't reach Mira's elevation. The troops of violins repeated the theme beneath her wings, but in one final swell of sound and deference to her courage, they summed up all their energy in a rising scale and felt her escape from their reach.

All eyes clung to Mira now, swaying in the footlights with determination, reaching higher and higher with each fiery ascent to escape the burdensome augurs chasing her heels. She fought them back until she shook them off with barely a flute on her tail, then only a tiny piccolo struggling to follow her through the rising arcs of Britten's notes. The trumpets ordered her down from the skies, but she resisted, trilling from over their heads until at last the composer took mercy on his soloist. He released the hunted violin to flit and sail free, centre stage above the mourning and fear, to soar towards her own sweet and inhuman, inconsolable threnody.

Mira dipped down low, once or twice on the G string, to soothe the listeners over their woes yet to come, to assuage their threatened griefs. Then she danced finger by finger back to the heights where she belonged, turning back for only a few solicitous passes on the earthly range of her D string – only long enough to remind them she had once been human – before returning to the safety of the hovering E string, so high none could follow. She made only a few more swooping dives – each time becoming less reachable, less terrestrial, until her last prolonged note hung poised in the air, almost too fine for human hearing, above hundreds of mesmerized faces.

There was a frozen silence in the Beaulieu as a thousand ears clung to the tremor of her last note, longing for it, clutching at its magic echo. They heard it still, even though her bow had stopped.

The Finn turned to face the audience. The spell was broken by a tidal wave of applause breaking around Roman's ears. The conductor took Mira's hand and pulled that miracle of dexterity, still clutching its violin, high in the air. Breasts heaving, Mira hung from the Finn's supporting grasp, tossed back her head and beamed at the upper gallery. Roman heard himself shouting wordless noises of love, but his cries were drowned in the bravos ringing out from all sides.

Roman offered himself up to his anonymity with resignation, with love, with forgiveness for them all, but most importantly for himself. In the face of all this, a mystery of energy and life that he couldn't have understood if he'd been ten times older, Roman finally absolved himself. He had watched Mira winging free of regret and recrimination, those useless, life-denying, joy-sucking twins. All around him he heard the shouts for encores, the pounding, heart-stopping give-death-the-finger defiance of Britten's sombre masterpiece. He no longer felt guilty he was alive – merely amazed. Was this possibly the purest moment of his life, the clean beginning from which he could start anew?

It was at that point that Mira straightened up from her sixth bow, turned to clear her rustling skirts, and recognized Roman's haggard face staring up at her, his white knuckles clutching the edge of the seat in front of him.

31

Mira dashed down the backstage stairs to her dressing room, her hair wisps fighting free of the Grecian coils. The celestial bird sent aloft by Benjamin Britten had both feet on the ground now. She was an ordinary woman once again, perspiring and panicked.

"I should never, never have agreed to this," she burst out wild-eyed into the overlit mirror. She yanked the cumbersome skirt and tulle petticoat off her wide hips, one heel catching on the stiff netting. Cursing, she tussled with the tiny clasps running down her boned corset. With the satin armour peeled off at last, rivulets of sweat coursed down her spine.

She clutched a frayed towel to her breasts. Moist flecks of white talc drifted to the linoleum in her wake.

"Don't stare at me, Felix. Just pack up my things or we'll miss our train. Don't forget to untwist the bow."

"Don't we have to wait for Mrs Foley?"

The four-year-old locked long-lashed eyes with his mother's firm glance. She wasn't like other mothers. She certainly wasn't like other mothers he'd seen on the streets or playgrounds or even milling in their night-time finery around foyers during intermission. He watched them gossip when Uncle Charles took him to the bar for his orange juice and ham sandwich. He wondered what it was like to go home with these ordinary women who would have tucked him into bed at normal hours. Mrs Foley or Uncle Charles kept reminding him that the Sullivan entourage was a terribly special family. He had "uncles" and "aunts" far and wide whom they visited in an endless whirl of beautiful music, deafening applause, and very late dinners. He was used to falling asleep in the folds of his mother's maroon velvet cloak.

They warned him that his life would change a little once he started school. Then he would live with Great-Aunt Mary in New York. Felix didn't want anything to change. Mumma was a brightly-lit ship that steamed out into dark nights and cut through heavy waves ahead of everyone else and Felix was the secure little rowboat tied tightly to her stern by sturdy towropes of love. They rode the waves in all weathers, moving in and out of ports, always together. They watched over each other carefully across the swells and dips of the rollers and whitecaps.

Tonight Felix felt a storm brewing. She'd scolded him for eating a chocolate pastry before the curtain and she'd even forgotten their good luck kiss. She was sweating hard now, although they could hear the reward – that prolonged clapping roar – mounting without relent above their heads.

Felix gathered up her discarded evening skirt as best he could.

"Leave that, punkin. Mrs Foley'll be here in a minute. Just do the violin and bow."

Insistent pounding drummed on the dressing-room door. The boy concentrated on his task over the bellows of Uncle Charles, "Mira? Are you changing already? Mira! What about the encores? Mira?"

"I'm feeling faint! I'm not well!"

"Just the *Vocalise*!"

"I can't manage it, Charles! I'm already undressed. The heat turned my stomach."

"Then at least the flowers! Pekko is standing out there like an idiot behind a bush of red roses! The audience won't stop clapping. The orchestra's sitting waiting!"

Mira whispered in Felix's ear. "Just pack up, honey. Mumma's in a hurry."

"You're going to throw up? Do you need the wastebasket, the way you do for me?"

"Don't be silly. Do I look green?" She pulled a funny face

334

and kissed his pale brow, then pointed to her violin case. Still worried, Felix returned to his regular chores. Usually she was much happier finishing a good show. After her shower, they had a party with her backstage "best" friends. Then they had a snack somewhere outside with her "bester" friends. Everywhere they went, strangers called her "darling" and "loved her music". He preferred it when she played only for him. Or better, just sang songs to him at night while he sucked on a twisted corner of Blankie who travelled under his arm from dressing room to dressing room, city to city.

He had to tuck her violin things "into bed" the way she taught him. Robert Rosin rolled up in a scrap of blue flannel. Thomas Tube holding the spare strings, his cap shoved in tight. Shoulder-rest Sam screwed off Mr Mendelssohn's wooden tummy very carefully. Mumma said Felix was the most careful assistant in the world, reminding him that Mr Mendelssohn cost lots of money. Mumma didn't even really own Mr Mendelssohn – not yet. He belonged to a very rich Hungarian businessman in Westchester County who loved the way Mumma played dances.

Felix fastened all of these items, one by one, into their worn velvet spaces and familiar fittings. Mumma should check to see he'd done it right. Sometimes when she saw how orderly he was, how precise, she smiled strangely to herself and he felt especially loved. He shut out the pounding and the shouting outside her dressing-room door and prided himself on being very neat and careful – because Mumma often wasn't. He waited, but tonight she took no notice. For once he dared to close the sleek zipper around the green case, very slowly, no one helping.

Mira stood ready in her black slacks and summer mackintosh but had forgotten to change out of her satin shoes. Mrs Foley arrived and threw a fitted cover over the evening gown and carried it off to their car. In a second Uncle Charles had squeezed his lanky frame past the nanny's bulk and filled the interior of the car.

"You didn't have to be that abrupt. Everything's all right. The car's just outside."

"Yes, but so are they. Charles, if they –"

"They can't start a custody battle in the Green Room, even if they could find their way back here. The entire orchestra's packing up and blocking the corridor – not to mention the mess of the catering kitchen between this passage and the bar. They'd have to be heat-seeking missiles to penetrate this maze –"

"Then take Felix with you. I can manage the worst, as long as they don't see him with me."

"You're not afraid of them, are you?"

"Only his wife. I'm terrified of her innocence." Mira swept her cosmetics into the bottom of her carry-all. "I shared his love with her just long enough to know that it's wrong. It was impossible for everyone. So they'll never know. He followed me all the way to New York to persuade me to have a –" she glanced at Felix – "to change my mind. I watched him outside on the sidewalk, pounding on Mary's door. I made her turn the sound down on the answering machine for a month. My father was on his side, but I stood up to Dad then and I can dodge them now. I did what I wanted and I take the responsibility. So here we are, right, Felix?"

The bewildered child nodded, the privileged sentry in the corner guarding an instrument case almost as tall as he.

" – my decision, and I'm happy with things the way they are. I'm not sharing anyone three ways."

"Not even to know?" Her assistant pleaded.

"It's kinder that way. Ignorance is bliss." She grabbed the violin case from Felix and pulled the strap over her shoulder. "I've told you all this before, so many times. Charles, you're a dear, fussy friend and a wonderful part of the team, but don't you know when to leave well enough alone? Sometimes I actually suspect you'd rather see *certain people* living six months out of every year in Switzerland so that you'd be free to double my European bookings –"

"That's outrageous! Have I ever suggested – ?"

"Well, didn't you bully me into tonight? Isn't this exactly what I dreaded? The house was good, sure, but would have been just as full in Martigny which is twice as far from Geneva. Now just get us out of here."

Mira thrust Felix into Charles's stomach. "Go to the car with Uncle Charles, Felix!"

"Yes, Mumma."

Narrow shoulders drooping from Mira's tirade, Charles held the boy close to him, but didn't budge from the doorway. Felix felt the man's long fingers dig into the soft wool of his boyish pullover.

"That's an awful accusation, Mira. We all appreciate your fireworks once the curtain is up. And now we're just supposed to weigh anchor and sail off to Zurich. Yes, I take my little percentage with its reflected glow. You have everything you could want – everything, Mira – beauty and talent and Felix. You've worked for it. But now you toss me an appalling cliché like 'ignorance is bliss' and you claim you're doing that couple out there a favour?"

"I just don't want to cause anyone unnecessary pain."

"But you haven't asked them. More important, have you asked him?"

Their wrangling made Felix want to cry. The boy realized Uncle Charles was staring down at *him*.

Mira protested, "Charles, you have no right to talk to me like this."

"I'm suggesting you stop gambling with his happiness and start gambling with your own instead. You don't have to come if you don't want to meet her."

Mira's face turned pale underneath her caked stage make-up. "You're out of bounds, Charles. You're not family. My family's handling this in the best possible way for everyone. Including him."

Charles stiffened at her rebuke.

Anger suddenly flushed Mira's face more deeply on one side

than the other, an echo of the old days: "You invited them here, didn't you? You actually sent them tickets?"

"No. Of course not. I only saw a couple at the end of the third row and recognized him. He treated my eczema years ago."

Uncle Charles knelt down beside Felix and stroked the boy's thick black shock of curls. "Your mother says we should go outside together now, Felix, so come with me."

"No – Felix, wait! I'm not sure I can trust you, Charles."

"You said yourself, Mira. They mustn't see him with you. And you're right. They might be half-way down the stairs already."

Mira examined Charles's inscrutable expression. She had always relied on Charles, so old beyond his years. She trusted him with her earnings three years back, her bookings two years in advance and her luggage week to week. She saw a bachelor – middle-aged before his time, alone in the world – who might never live his own life, but only those of others. He needed her, and she realized, she needed him. She would have to take this risk.

She took a deep breath. "Go with Uncle Charles, Felix."

Charles grasped Felix's small hand and manoeuvred the child past a knot of viola players chatting and smoking at the end of the corridor. No one ever noticed Charles Stratford, but did that mean he wasn't man enough to risk everything, after all?

Mme Chantal Galland-Villard tumbled off the bus into a wet April morning. A tempest rising off the lake whipped open her raincoat, too skimpy now to button over her swollen belly. Tibo had offered to buy her a maternity coat once they went on sale, but there were only a few months left until summer. They'd make any economies they could while they were still only two.

Heading straight into the gale, she wrapped the morning paper around her exposed uniform, but the ink smeared into the white cotton. The Ukrainian violinist who always smiled at her broke off his rendition of "Spring" from Vivaldi's "Seasons" to point his bowtip at the spreading stains.

She laughed her thanks and threw the useless, soggy paper into the nearest bin. She tossed a two-franc coin into his instrument case, already glittering with wet coins. She'd been so busy wondering which sort of baby-minder she could afford for the coming newborn – a teenage *au pair* from the German-speaking north? or an illegal but more mature Bosnian recommended by a neighbour? – she hadn't read the paper at all.

Tant pis. Anyway, there wasn't much news: an arts feature announcing the launch of some Japanese-French crime series of *bandes dessinées* by publisher M Shino Watanatra and graphic artist Mlle Lolie Levinas.

A press conference given by the WHO leprosy officials Dr Carlos Campagna and Dr Ashok Shardar (SJ) announcing the marked reduction of leprosy around the world and a new set of targets for rehabilitation and research projects.

The opening of two new branches, in Cologny and Belle-vue, of the wildly popular Beverly Hills Spa and Laser Clinic by Dr Ferdinand-Emmanuel Bouvier, with an introductory coupon for a *Massage du Monde*, detachable along the dotted lines.

A small announcement placed by Dr and Mrs Roman Micheli (née Sullivan) of the birth of Mlle Bella Micheli, 3.5 kg, a sister for Felix, with thanks to the doctors and nurses of Genolier Clinic.

A sudden flutter rumbled up from Chantal's navel. Impatient drumming announced – her baby was kicking at last! This wonderful sensation swamped the happy young woman with animal awe and brought her to a full stop on the sidewalk to pay homage to its welcome separateness. Sheets of rainwater washed over her stomach, sheltering no longer one soul, but two. She heard St Pierre ringing from the hill overlooking the rue du Marché and she hurried on, radiant with life, to share the news with Lise.